TEPHRA RISING

THE COLONY — BOOK ONE

K. C. WESTON

Published by Lloyd Arlin Books

Copyright © 2020 by **K. C. Weston**

Tephra Rising: The Colony—Book One / By K. C. Weston

All rights reserved. No part of this publication may be reproduced, distributed or transmitted in any form or by any means, including photocopying, recording, or other electronic or mechanical methods, without the prior written permission of the publisher, except in the case of brief quotations embodied in critical reviews and certain other noncommercial uses permitted by copyright law.

Adherence to all applicable laws and regulations, including international, federal, state and local governing professional licensing, business practices, advertising, and all other aspects of doing business in the US, Canada or any other jurisdiction is the sole responsibility of the reader and consumer.

Neither the author nor the publisher assumes any responsibility or liability whatsoever on behalf of the consumer or reader of this material. Any perceived slight of any individual or organization is purely unintentional.

DEDICATIONS

To Maxine, Katherine, Kristy, Susan, and Lesley for providing shining examples of strong women who can overcome any adversity.

ONE

A NEW WAY OF LIFE

APRIL 27, 2130 — LOS ANGELES, CALIFORNIA

The alarm module mounted in Cynthia Frank's ceiling began to wail its incessant tone. 5:00 a.m. flashed across the screen of a monitor mounted to the wall opposite her bed. She slowly opened one eyelid, reached across and slammed her hand down on top of a small, white dome causing the alarm to stop.

"Ooofff, it's too early."

Pushing off the covers, Cynthia swung her legs over the bed, and lifted herself onto her feet. She stumbled toward the bathroom with her eyes mostly closed. Turning and grabbing the edge of the sink to steady herself, she gazed up into the mirror. Her hair was a mess and the bags under her eyes seemed to grow bigger during the night. Cynthia looked away, shook her head, and climbed into the shower. Waving her hand across a black square, perfectly warmed water sprang from the ceiling above.

The warm water felt good on her skin, but Cynthia was having a hard time shaking the fog from her head. Three hours of sleep was not enough. She finished showering and wrapped one towel around her body, another around her hair and ran from her bedroom to the kitchen. Cynthia grabbed a cup and placed it in the receptacle—a square in the middle of tall, wide, chrome piece of metal in the corner of her kitchen space. She waved her hand in front of the screen and the machine whirred to life. Hot water began to fill the cup, clear and steaming.

"No, no, no, that's the not morning stuff. Geez, is this thing broken again?"

Cynthia hit the side of the device with the palm of her hand. It gave out a dull thud, but kept dispensing hot water into her cup.

"Oh forget it!"

She threw the half-filled cup into the sink and made her way back to the bathroom to finish getting ready. She hurriedly fixed her hair and makeup and grabbed clothes from the closet. Scooping up a bag using the two straps hanging from one side she slipped the walking boots by the door; the same place she had flung them off a few hours earlier.

Opening the door, Cynthia stepped into the clean room—a small antechamber attached to the front of her small apartment meant to hold and sterilize her gear. The Alliance's nuclear generators built in the heart of the city weren't supposed to emit high levels of radiation but levels had steadily increased the last few months making protective gear mandatory. Even before the radiation worsened, the smog was so bad that a breathing device was practically required.

Her radiation coat was covered in thick soot. Cynthia had sterilized it the night before, but had been far too exhausted to clean it completely. She gingerly pushed her arms into the coat and lifted the hood into place. Cynthia quickly donned her breathing device and dashed out the door, hoping she left nothing behind. Were it up to her, she would have gone without the protection even if it meant she'd barely be able to breath. Cynthia hated wearing it and had only a couple blocks to go. But those caught without it were quickly rounded up. She didn't have time to deal with a detention today.

Cynthia dashed through the lobby, looking forlornly at the tall glass windows showcasing the large gym she never used. To think she planned to use the gym every day when she moved in three years ago.

The Alliance recommended indoor workouts twice per week as it was no longer possible to exercise outside, yet Cynthia hadn't set foot in the place but a handful of times. No time for that now. Must get to work. She looked down at her digital bracelet. It was flashing her location and time of arrival. She was once again running late.

Pushing the double glass doors open, Cynthia stepped outside. Turning in the direction of her office building she began her rapid march to her legal factory workplace. Another day defending the Alliance. It seemed like only yesterday she was on a U.S. Navy ship fighting the people who now employed her. Cynthia thought her side had won that war, but had they? That was seven years ago and now the Alliance had all but taken over. The treaty ending the war allowed the Alliance to stay in business because no one else could take their place, or provide the means to survive without them. The Alliance made a few concessions in the treaty so the U.S. government could save face, but it saved little else. Already a corporate monolith, after the war they also became the largest political party. Starting in the U.S. and then spreading around the world, the majority of elected officials were Alliance members. In the U.S., only Alliance members had the right to work. For everyone else it was a privilege that had to be earned, and could be taken away at any time. Either work for the Alliance, or don't work at all. Not much of a choice.

Cynthia could see the outline of her tall office building. Quickening her pace, she wrapped her arms around her chest in an attempt to fend off the harsh and piercing cold. She crossed several streets and approached the final crosswalk to her building; the light began to turn from green to yellow. Cynthia began to run, wanting to make the crossing to avoid having to wait in the cold. She suddenly lost her footing and tumbled to the ground in the middle of the crosswalk. She caught herself with the palm of her hands on the rough pavement as her bag flew out in front of her.

"Ouch!"

Cynthia looked back at her feet and saw her boots were still strapped to her feet, but the heel of the right boot was laying on the ground behind her. She stood up. Her right knee throbbed with pain, as did her left wrist. Hobbling over to retrieve her dislodged heel, Cynthia scooped up her bag and limped to the sidewalk next to her building. The dull pain from her knee and wrist were an uncomfortable reminder of her misfortune. She glanced up and down the street, seeing no one. The heavy Alliance patrols kept most people off the street. But still, it never hurt to double check. Let your guard down for a moment and a crazed, over-radiated street dweller could be all over you.

Cynthia kicked off her boots and scurried barefoot into the building. The tile floor felt cold on her feet. There was no one else in the lobby as Cynthia padded to the decontamination chamber. She entered the room and her outfit was cleared of radiation. Exiting the far side, she strode towards the empty elevator banks. Cynthia placed her eye in front of the round, red sensor to summon the lift. She glanced at the cream-colored limestone lining the walls of the lobby and gave a shudder. The lifeless tile always made her feel cold inside just looking at it. She took her breathing device off while waiting for the elevator to arrive.

The elevator doors opened, and Cynthia shuffled inside. "Thirty," she said to the auto attendant in a barely audible voice. She slouched against the elevator wall as the lift shot up to the thirtieth floor. The lift stopped, the doors slid open, and Cynthia stepped out into the lobby of the Alliance legal offices. Turning left she opened the door to the clean room. Taking off off her breathing device and coat, Cynthia hurriedly placed them in the large metal box marked with her name. Running out of the room she scurried past the empty reception desk and then down the hallway towards her assigned office.

As Cynthia walked, she glanced into the offices lining the left side of the hallway. Over half of the offices were occupied by her co-workers typing on keyboards, shuffling pages on their monitors, and looking tired but intent, just as they had the day before. She glanced to her right to look down the long row of low-slung cubicles that held the desks of the secretaries. The row of desks was empty as it was far too early for their workday to begin.

Cynthia turned into her office and the lights flicked on automatically. She threw her bag on the floor, plunked herself into her chair, and opened her bottom desk draw. She rifled around inside the large drawer until she found her spare pair of boots and quickly buckled the straps around her ankles. When she was done she sat back and gave out a sigh.

"Not another day ... not already."

Her desk had the remnants of yesterday's lunch still on it. Crinkling her nose in disgust she pushed her former meal into the trash can.

"Free lunch? Ha! Just another ploy to chain me to my desk."

Cynthia glanced around her small office looking at the bare walls painted stark white. Her eyes stopped on the only thing occupying the wall space: her law degree. She remembered hanging it up three years ago. That was a proud day. The beginning of a new life. *What went wrong?* The smile melted from Cynthia's face and turned into a slight frown. Her brow furrowed as she thought of the last three years; day and night seemed all the same from inside her stark office. Weekends and holidays passed by while she worked away inside her square box and she had never taken a day of vacation. The world around her was becoming increasingly harder to live in every year. *Will I ever get out of this prison?*

Cynthia reached over to turn on her computer. The monitor blinked to life. As the screen flashed alive she could see the same work from yesterday still occupying the display space. She sat up, pulled her keyboard closer and began typing where she had left off. She focused on the work at hand. Her small office and bleak life left her mind.

A couple hours later, she heard a voice. "Cindy, where's my documents sweetheart?" Her boss, Brad, appeared at her doorway.

Cynthia' jaw twitched. *What's with this guy?* "I put the documents on your data pad, Brad."

"Oh no you didn't! Send them again, they're not there."

Brad spun around and walked out of Cynthia's office.

She clenched her teeth and whispered under her breath, "Jerk."

Brad stopped just outside her office door and turned towards her. "What did you say?"

She looked up at Brad slowly. "Nothing ... I didn't say anything."

Brad frowned. "It had better be nothing. You seem to be getting awful mouthy lately. You had better keep your little opinions to yourself. Understand? You can't talk to an Alliance member that way."

Cynthia's eyes burned into Brad. His round, fat face made him look like a pasty ogre. She resisted the urge to punch him in the face and instead gave a quick nod of her head. *The jerk always gets away with saying crap like that.* He was a member of the Alliance and he used it to bully every non-member around him. She wasn't a member and never would be. Ex-military was not allowed to join—especially veterans of the Alliance War.

Brad shook his finger at her and stormed off. She could hear his heavy footsteps as he marched down the hallway.

Cynthia threw up her hands and pushed her chair back from her desk.

"Unbelievable!" she exclaimed.

She shot up to her feet and marched out of her office, down the hallway, and flashed her eye in front of the sensor to summon the lift. She had no idea where she was going. She just needed a break. Some time to cool off.

She stepped onto the elevator and was about to say "lobby" to the auto attendant when she said "26" instead. She remembered going to the vacant floor before to cool down from an overheated day. It was closer than the lobby and less crowded now the morning rush had begun.

The elevator stopped and the doors slid open. As Cynthia stepped off the lift she sauntered over to the nearest bank of windows. The entire twenty-sixth floor was empty and open. No walls, no hallways, no offices.

As Cynthia stared out into the smoggy world outside, she heard faint footsteps approaching her from behind. She stayed still, waiting for the footsteps to get a bit closer. She wanted to catch her predator in the act. And hopefully disarm them if necessary. Cynthia knew she could get the drop. If she moved fast. If she waited. Waited until just the right time.

"Who are you?" Cynthia spun on the heel of her boots and raised her arms in a defensive stance.

A tall woman wearing a white dress stopped in her tracks. She was only a few yards away. She held up her hands with her palms open. "Please, I mean you no harm."

"I thought this floor was vacant."

"Not today. The name is Seabreeze. Are you interested? Is that why you're here?"

"Interested? In what?"

"Our message on the free network; you saw it, yes?"

"No, I don't ... I can't ... I'm not allowed to access that sort of thing."

The free network was a way for non-members to communicate with each other. The Alliance kept close track of all electronic communications, but they couldn't monitor disposable access pods. The small rectangular devices, the size of a thumb could access the internet using a regular port on a data pad. As long as the device was disposed of within seventy-two hours after first use, it could never be traced or found. The devices were strictly illegal. And any non-member caught with one would lose everything they had. Cynthia never touched the things.

"Well you look tired, harried. Maybe you'd like to hear what we have to offer, now that you're here. A new way of life."

Seabreeze took a step closer and leaned in towards Cynthia.

She whispered, "An Alliance-free life."

Cynthia lowered her arms. She had no love for the Alliance. In fact, she wished it were gone. But an Alliance free life? That sounded impossible. Maybe even suicidal.

"What are you? A cult?"

Seabreeze smiled and shook her head. "No, of course not. Come over here, I'll show you."

She turned and walked to the far corner of the empty floor. A small group of people were huddled together. Cynthia stopped well short of the group. Seabreeze continued to join the group. She placed her hand on the shoulder of another woman dressed in white. A shorter woman. The shorter woman turned and approached Cynthia.

"What is this?" asked Cynthia.

The shorter woman scurried towards Cynthia. "Name's Ash."

"Hi ... Cynthia."

"You're a lawyer?" Ash tilted her head and flashed a knowing smile.

"Yes, how'd you know?"

"The way you're dressed ... and the bags under your eyes." Ash chuckled. "How long have you been here?"

"Three years."

"Enjoying it?"

Cynthia looked down at her feet. She wasn't sure what to say.

"Not really what I expected it to be, I guess. But the work is great."

She looked back up into Ash's face. "I am so grateful to be working with an Alliance member and—"

Ash held up her hand.

"It's ok. You can save the pre-recorded message about your work. I won't tell your boss. Or bosses." Ash gave a warm smile.

Cynthia blushed. "Yeah, it's a habit to play it safe."

Ash held up a data pad. It was eight inches wide by twelve inches long. A photo flashed across the screen. And then several more. The photos showed an idyllic world of crop fields and people working together. They were smiling. And clean—no one was wearing protective gear or breathing devices.

"Do you know what you are looking at here, Cynthia?"

"No. Some old fashioned photos of the world. The way it used to be?"

"A new life. I know how you feel. I was in your shoes myself not so long ago." Ash reached out and touched the data pad shining in her hands. "The Colony is a new way of life for people like us. We are a self-sustaining world located on the ocean floor."

"Underwater?"

"Yes, but encapsulated in a large dome. The Colony is quite large —about the size of Hawaii."

"Is it safe?"

"Oh yes. The Colony was built over a century ago. It has proven its strength over time."

"But I mean is it safe from the ... " Cynthia looked around not able to say the word.

"Alliance? Yes. We cannot be touched; we cannot even be found."

"No Alliance?" Cynthia shook her head slowly in disbelief.

"The point of the Colony is to escape the troubles on land. The Alliance way, the polluted air, the war, the pandemics. We have none of it. We are safe."

"Really? Safe?"

"Yes. But even better is the way the Colony works. It offers intellectual challenges without the nonsense. You don't fight for your life every day, you live it. You become part of something much bigger than yourself."

"Like the military?"

"Ha ... no. We are not recruiting for any army, Cynthia. We offer a new lifestyle. Take everything you are missing from your life now and start living it. Money is no object in the Colony; neither is any Alliance membership. You do your work and contribute to the greater good. We give you everything you need. That means you can do great work without worrying about being tied to the Alliance." Ash smiled and looked over at Cynthia. "How's that sound?"

"Sounds impossible."

"I know, but it's true, I joined the Colony five years ago. I was also a lawyer. The last five years have been life changing. I can't tell you how wonderful it is. Here, take this brochure, give it some thought. It's just another way of doing things. A better way."

Cynthia took the brochure and looked at it as she opened the cover. She smiled. She looked back up at the data pad in front of her. It flashed pictures of professional people doing important-looking work. She glanced back down at the colorful brochure in her hands. If felt good to hold something slick, glossy. But why paper? Why not a send a data file? Untraceable, that's probably it. The Alliance can't track down every scrap of paper. Still, she better keep it tucked away. If anyone found it on her, she'd be done. Rounded up and locked away for who knows how long.

"We have a group of new recruits heading for the Colony tomorrow," said Ash. "You're welcome to join, but you need to decide quickly. Once we leave, we won't be back for a very long time."

Suddenly, Cynthia was jolted from her thoughts by the loud ring of her digital bracelet. She grabbed for it. Held it up closer to her ear.

"Hello?"

"Cynthia, where the heck are you?" Brad's terse voice thundered through the receiver.

"I'm taking a break." She turned and took several steps away from Ash.

"We need you up here now!" The call clicked off.

She dropped her wrist to her side and turned towards Ash.

"I gotta go, bye." She turned and ran from the room.

TWO

THE CREATOR

**A Century Earlier — May 30, 2030 — Hall Enterprises
World Headquarters**

"Enough! We are going to stay on schedule." A tall man in a crisp, new suit pushed his way through a set of glass double doors.

"But sir, we can't risk the entire mission on arbitrary dates." A smaller man in a tattered sports coat ran behind him, trotting to keep up. His bald head glistened in the noon-day sun.

"Listen, what was your name again?" The tall man frowned.

"Dr. Leo Stretzel."

The tall man rolled his eyes. "Listen, Leo—are you with me on this mission? Do you really believe in it?"

"Oh yes, Mr. Hall, of course I do."

"Please, Leo, call me John." John stopped in his tracks outside the high rise building in Los Angeles with his name affixed to the top. He placed his slender, elegant hands on Leo's shoulders.

"Look we are in this thing together. Now I know that deadlines are hell. I mean, some things just don't lend themselves to deadlines, am I right?"

"Well, science can't be rushed—I suppose."

"Right, science can't be rushed. But people can, Leo. People can. And besides, I have given you extension after extension after extension. Your predecessor claimed the whole thing would be done three years ago. You meet this deadline or it's your job. Understand? I'll pull the plug on the whole darn thing! I have plenty of other scientists and engineers who would love your job. I'll clear out your whole crew and replace them with fresh, new nerds. Got it?"

Leo gulped. He looked up into the eyes of the taller man. "Yes, Mr. Hall."

"Hey, it's John, remember?" John slapped Leo on the back and gave a wink. "I believe in you Doc! Now go make this thing happen. The Colony will be your shining achievement—and all the world will know it!" John bounded down the steps in front of his building and hopped inside his waiting limousine.

"Crap!" Leo stood still as he watched John Hall's limousine pull away from the building. It all seemed so attainable a decade ago when a dozen billionaires decided to put their substantial fortunes behind John Hall's idea. And why wouldn't they? Hall made the impossible become possible. Everything he touched turned to gold. There was no industry he had not conquered, no challenge he had not tamed to his will. But an undersea civilization that could live on the bottom of the ocean indefinitely? It presented a lot of problems.

Leo turned and marched back to the building's double door. He had driven his old jalopy to the headquarters of Hall Enterprises to plead for another extension of time to get the energy generation systems working properly. *It's no different from living in space really,* thought Leo. *You might as well ask us to build a colony on Mars for heaven's sake.* He jumped inside his car and left Hall Enterprises behind.

Maybe if we used the same energy system for desalinization and oxygen generation? Is that even possible? I need to see the schematics again. What about the electrical loads? That might work. Leo parked his car in his reserved spot at Colony Engineering. He shook his head and rubbed his temples. The drive was a blur, his brain was racing with thoughts. He hustled inside the low-slung building on the edge of the Port of Los Angeles.

"So, you buy us some time?" A short, chubby man jumped in front of Leo as he entered the office. Leo shook his head and pushed past the man.

"Wait, what? We aren't even close to being ready."

Leo rolled his eyes and turned to face the chubby man. "Dammit David, not now. Have the department heads meet me in the conference room in fifteen minutes."

"Alright, alright, boss. Will do ... roger wilco ... over and out." David made a clumsy salute in mock deference to his boss.

Leo trudged back to his office and plopped into his rickety office chair. The arms of his chair were worn bare from constant use over the past decade. He spent more time in his chair than he did doing anything else—even sleeping. It all seemed so easy when he was second in charge under Dr. Erler. Erler's prestigious reputation always seemed to delight John Hall to the point of getting anything he wanted from the man. When Dr. Erler collapsed from a fatal heart attack less than a year ago, everything changed. Being in charge wasn't as easy as Dr. Erler made it look.

The Colony had taken nearly a decade to build, but was it really ready sustain life? There were so many systems that weren't quite perfected. And yet, the first set of colonists would embark on their maiden journey to their new home in just over sixty days. A vision of Mr. Hall's face flashed across Leo's thoughts.

"It's so easy to do the impossible when you're not the one doing it!" Leo picked up a glass paper weight from his desk and threw it against the wall. It hit with a thud and fell to the ground.

He rubbed his temples and shook his head. "We can do this, we can do this, we've GOT to do this." *We haven't any other options now.*

"A little stressed are we?" A middle-aged woman slid through

Leo's office door. She stood in front of his desk. Leo looked up and flashed a weak smile.

"Yeah, I guess so. Things just aren't working out like I thought they would, Cathy."

"I heard a thud and thought maybe it was your head you were slamming against the wall."

"It might as well be." Leo threw his hands in the air as he sat back in his chair. "For all the good it would do me."

"What's the problem? Mr. Hall got you down?" Cathy moved to the nearby guest chair and lowered her frame into the seat. Her brown hair was drawn back into a tight bun. She had several creases in her forehead, but Leo always thought Cathy had a youthful appearance—no matter her age. She tilted her head and formed a warm smile.

"No more extensions!" Leo shook his head. "Heck, I can't really blame him. We should have been done by now. But it all takes time. I mean we essentially are building a whole new world."

"Hey, we are closer now than we've ever been. There's light at the end of the tunnel."

"The lights not close enough. What are we supposed to do? Wave our magic wands and make it all just appear?"

"We just need to keep pushing forward."

Leo peered down at his shoes and gave out a long sigh. "I wish Dr. Erler were still here. He'd know what to do."

"I know, Leo. We all miss the venerable Dr. Erler. But you know something?" Cathy's eyes widened as she leaned forward.

Leo glanced over to her.

"You were the one getting everything done this whole time. Dr. Erler was just the face, you were the brains. We are here because of you."

Leo smiled; he felt a warm rush fill his cheeks. Cathy always seemed to know what to say. "Thanks, Cathy. That's nice of you to say. But sometimes we need a face to keep the world at bay. You know, to give us room to do our work."

"True. But we have what we have. So we will make do." Cathy stood and sauntered over to the doorway. "I'll see you in the conference room." She slipped out the door.

Leo looked up to the ceiling. *Can we do this?*

He lifted his tired frame from his chair and lumbered down the hall to the conference room. As he entered he could see the table full of weary-eyed scientists and engineers. Thirty in all. The men and women who had led the teams building the grand experiment under the sea.

"Hello, ladies and gentlemen. Thank you for meeting with me. I know you all are very busy, so I'll get right to the point. We have no more time. We must hit our current deadlines, or the project will be in jeopardy of failure." A collective gasp emanated throughout the room.

"I know, I know. You are thinking the same thing I am. We're not ready. Or we will not be ready. But now is the final push. Now is the time to finish what we started so long ago."

A woman seated to Leo's right raised her hand. "Leo, I hear what you are saying, but it can't be done. I mean it REALLY can't be done."

"We have been here before, Pat. We can do this. This is not the first time that our backs have been up against the wall. Mr. Hall himself made clear there will be no more extensions."

A man sitting halfway down the table leaned forward. "We will probably be fully operational with most life support systems in thirty days. In fact, they're already on and working as of now, we just need to finish our testing."

"Ok, good. That's good to hear," replied Leo.

"And we have the initial recruits ready to go. They have been tested and trained on their new jobs."

"Ok, also good. How many are there?"

"Nine thousand fifty-three."

"Great."

An older woman with black and grey hair cut tight and short

around her head threw up her hand. "Cloaking is working too. Not that it was crucial for inhabiting the place, but no one can find it ... except for us of course."

"Ok, that's also good. At least we'll be safe from some terrorist invasion or whatever." Leo placed his hand on the back of his neck and rubbed back and forth. He looked worn out, tired.

Pat raised her hand again. "But sir, energy generation is not complete. We need to finish our work to have the other systems remain operational indefinitely."

"Well, you have thirty days, Pat. I suggest you figure it out. Do you need more people?"

"No ... I don't know ... maybe."

"Well, let me know. As of now, the tap is still on. We have received another billion in funding."

"Really? That makes over fifty billion to date."

"Well, consider yourself lucky. When a team of billionaires want to succeed, funding becomes far easier. It's an ego thing."

A man at the far end of the conference table rose. He had a round head and dark rimmed glasses. "Leo, sir, may I take a moment to say that it may be best to allow us to finish our work ah ... on-site."

"On site?" Leo scrunched his brow. "What do you mean?"

"I mean, what if we were to move the science and engineering group—and I mean everyone—to the Colony. Take up residence there to finish our work. Not only would we have a better view of what was happening, but we could detect and react to issues much faster than we can now."

"Geez, Chuck. Are you suggesting we take a thousand people to the Colony? Has anyone even signed up to do that?"

"Yes, that is precisely what I am suggesting. I mean do we believe in our own work, in our own cause, in our own purpose, or do we not? I for one do. I would go in an instant. And we can bring our families too. The Colony needs as many people as we can muster to get it off the ground."

Leo rubbed his chin and pursed his lips. "Hmm, interesting thought. Cathy, what do you think?"

"I'd go!" Cathy shot up from her chair. "Heck, I've been begging to go. Plus, it would let us have a bit more time. I mean, not a lot more time because the dang thing has to work, but still."

Leo nodded. "Interesting."

"Look, it's real easy." Chuck left his spot and began sliding behind the row of seated scientists and engineers. "We let our people decide. If you want to finish a decade worth of work and win lasting recognition and glory, come with us to the Colony. That's our new offices, our new headquarters. Or don't. I bet you anything a majority of our people will go. I just know it."

"Well, Chuck, you seem enthusiastic about this idea. I'm game if everyone else thinks it's a good move." Leo looked around the table. He saw the faces of men and women he had shared this common goal with for the past ten years and he smiled. "I'd be honored if we all became founding colonists. How many of you would go?"

Cathy raised her hand. Chuck followed suit. Several others jutted their hands upwards. Half the room held their hands aloft. Several seconds ticked by. Those with their hands down glanced around the room. Some looked down at the table.

A man stood. "Please, you have to give us some time to think this over. Moving our whole teams, and their families? This is crazy."

Chuck walked over and placed his hand on the man's shoulder. "It just sounds crazy at first. You know because its sudden. But think about it Gene. You said yourself it takes too long to get feedback from the Colony when you make your calculation adjustments. And you heard Leo say no more extensions. Can you finish what you started from here? I don't think so."

Gene looked down and slowly nodded. "I don't know. Maybe you're right."

"Look, Gene," said Cathy, "if you don't want to go don't go. We can take over your team for you—those of us who do go."

Gene furrowed his brow and fixed his eyes on Cathy. "No! No, I will lead this team just as I have for the past ten years, thank you."

Cathy threw her hands up in front of her, palms out. "Ok, ok, I'm just giving you suggestions. Look, everyone has to decide for themselves what they want to do. Go or stay. Those are the options."

"And if we stay? Then what?" asked a woman seated across from Gene.

"Then you won't be of much help to us," replied Chuck. "But we'll do what we can without you."

Leo shook his head and sighed. "Alright, alright, everyone please sit. This is a big decision. Take some time, give it some thought, talk to your teams—to your families—and let's see how we feel about it next week."

The room fell silent. Chuck shuffled back to his chair.

"Who knows," continued Leo, "maybe our creation will be our promised land. We created a safe refuge from the chaos of this world, why not use it?"

THREE

BREAKING AWAY

APRIL 28, 2130 — LOS ANGELES, CALIFORNIA

"Day dreaming?" Christopher peaked his head around the corner of Cynthia's office door.

She startled and spun around in her chair. "Huh? Oh yeah ... I guess so." She had been gazing out through her office window. Thoughts of the Colony ran through her head. A perfect life, a purposeful life, an Alliance free life. What's not to like?

"Have you seen Brad around?"

"Ah, no. Saw him about an hour ago. I'm sure he'll be back soon."

Christopher chuckled. "Yeah, he'll be storming down the hall any time now; throwing out insults as he goes." He stepped into Cynthia's office and plunked his tall frame into her guest chair.

"What's up with you? I haven't seen you just staring out the window before. You're usually hard at work on your business deals."

"Oh I don't know." Cynthia shifted in her chair and leaned forward onto her desk. "Hey, let me ask you something. Have you ever thought about your future?"

"My future? Yeah think about it all the time." He stretched out his arms and put his hands behind his head. "I plan to retire on my own private island surrounded by models and drinking Mai Tai's all day."

"No, not fantasies!" Cynthia shook her head. "I mean there has to be more than"—she raised her hands and glanced around her small, square office—"this, right?"

"Ha! Is that what's bothering you." Christopher sat up and slapped his knee. "Being a law slave not what you thought it'd be?" He gave out a laugh.

She chuckled. "Well we're not exactly slaves."

"Well kind of. We work all hours of the day and night, work most weekends, and get yelled at constantly. Seems a bit tyrannical to me." Christopher put a finger on his chin. "But then again, non-members are just lucky to have work, right? That's what we are told."

"Ok, ok I get it."

"You thinking of leaving here?"

"Maybe. But not sure where'd I go."

"Government? I'm sure you could get a job there with your military background, right?"

Cynthia sat back. Her life as a Navy Lieutenant, in charge of weapons systems, seemed like a distant dream. Maybe she should have stayed in the Navy. But then again she wanted to tackle another challenge. She was first in her class at Annapolis, and then willed her way into Harvard Law. Being top in her class wasn't good enough, she had to be first. First in everything she did. But now, as a non-member, she couldn't go any higher. Her future would be the same as the present. There was nowhere for her to go.

"What's the point? The government has just as many Alliance members as here." Cynthia shook her head. "I don't know, maybe I'm just tired. I need to take a day to myself and clear my head."

"Yeah, we all could use that." Christopher stood and sidestepped to the office door. "Let me know if you figure out how to take a break from this rat race ... I'll follow suit." He nodded his head and strode out the door.

"Yeah ... I'll let you know." Cynthia mumbled to herself as she looked back down to her computer monitor and began typing where she had left off.

Later that night, Cynthia sat alone at her dining table eating lukewarm leftovers that the chrome device spit out when she arrived home. It was nearly midnight; another long day. The Colony brochure sat in front of her. She looked it over and thought about the conversation she had earlier with the nice lady in the white dress—Ash. The brochure seemed to be packed with wonderful promises. A great life, professional freedom, no need to worry about money. *Sure would be nice to be free of this world.*

She raised her tired body from the table and walked over to the sink to wash off her plate. She saw the empty mug still in the sink from her morning rush. *Dumb food server probably won't work tomorrow either.* She trudged off to bed and flopped flat atop the covers. Her eyes fell shut. Brad's fat, angry face flashed across her thoughts. She winced and turned over. All the yelling, all the time. Being abused by a man who's only claim to victory was being an Alliance member. She was so tired, but her mind refused to settle. Thoughts churned around and around. She sat up and ran a hand through her hair. Why did her brain torture her so? *Just give me five hours of sleep.*

She fell back down on the covers and closed her eyes tight. She pushed the thought of work out of her mind and began remembering the pictures from the Colony brochure. People, together, as a team. Not the military; that lady, Ash, made that clear. But Cynthia couldn't help but make a connection between the photos she saw and her distant memories of working aboard a Navy ship. Camaraderie, chain-of-command, order, a sense of purpose. She loved everything about it. She thought her job would be the same, but it never was. It just never was like that. She frowned. *No, no more thinking of work.*

She flipped over and imagined a life free of the Alliance. A life free of Brad. A life where she could explore her best skills. A life where she could be ... happy. A smile crept across her face. A sense of calm eased her mind. She fell fast asleep.

Morning came quickly as her alarm broke into her dreams. The morning rush started all over again. Another race to the office at 5:00 a.m. Cynthia grabbed her bag from the table as she was about to leave her apartment and the brochure caught her eye. *Impossible*, she thought. She turned to leave, but then stopped in her tracks. She reached back over to the table, grabbed the brochure, and placed it in a small hidden pocket on the inside of her bag. She tore open the door, donned her protective gear, and darted off to work.

"Dang it, Cynthia where are the documents?" Brad was yelling at Cynthia from down the hallway before she could even reach her office. It was barely past 6:00 a.m., and already he was at it again.

"Give me a sec, I'll get them to you as soon as I can." She rushed into her office, plopped down into her chair, and hit a few keys on the keyboard. The screen whirred to life. Brad came to her doorway and crossed his arms in front of his chest.

She looked up at him. His fat face, small eyes, and receding hairline made Brad look more like an aging troll than a lawyer. She noticed how the buttons of his shirt were stretched apart by the girth of his stomach. A round beach-ball gut cantilevered over his belt. His dress pants were baggy and far too long. He stood at her door scowling at her.

"Do you even understand how important this deal is, missy?"

The heat began to well up in her cheeks. She put her hands by her side and clenched her fists. She had heard this condescending tone from Brad for three solid years. Her teeth clenched and her eyes grew hard as she lowered her brow.

"Well do you? Are you going to say something or just sit there looking stupid?" Brad threw his hands up in the air and then set them on his hips. Cynthia's eyes burned into Brad.

"Where's the data pad?" asked Brad.

"What are you talking about?"

"I know you took it. Stuffed it in your bag last night as you were leaving. I saw the video feed."

"You're crazy. I didn't take anything."

"Oh really?" Brad marched over to her bag lying on the floor and scooped it up. He threw it down on her desk and ripped open the flap.

"Hey! You can't just look in there." Cynthia jumped up onto her feet.

"I saw it! I saw you put something in here last night. If not a data pad, then a pod perhaps? Something sensitive you can sell on the free network no doubt."

"I took nothing! Get your hands off my bag!" Cynthia reached for the straps of her bag and yanked the bag backwards. As the bag slid across the desk, Brad grabbed the opening and pulled it back.

"No, no, no. I am going to find it." Brad yanked the bag in his direction with a hard jerk.

Cynthia followed suit with a yank of her own. Back and forth they struggled until the straps broke loose causing Cynthia to tumble to the ground. The bag flipped over. The force of the straps coming loose caused the small hidden pocket on the inside to drop down and hang just outside the opening. Brad's eyes widened as he caught sight of the hidden object. He grabbed for it.

"No!" Yelled Cynthia.

"Ha! I thought so!" Brad yanked the square cloth from the bag and ripped open the little pocket. He fished out the Colony brochure. He unfolded the paper and frowned.

"What's this?"

"Not a data pad!" Cynthia stood and straightened her clothes.

"Are you thinking of going somewhere ... escaping?" Brad's mouth fell open as if Cynthia had committed an unspeakable crime. "You have no clearance. Why, I should call Central Enforcement right now and have you—"

"You fat pig." She said it. She couldn't believe she said it, but she said it. Not loud, not mean, not hostile, just low and firm. But loud enough for Brad to hear. It felt good to say. It felt so good to get it out at long last.

"What'd you say?"

"You fat pig." She walked around the edge of her desk as Brad dropped his hand to his sides. His mouth was agape, and his eyes were wide.

"For three years I have worked around the clock for you. I have put up with your constant abuse." Her hands came up and crossed her chest. "And now you think I'm stealing your precious secrets?" She reveled in the moment. It felt so good to finally speak her mind.

"Abuse? How dare you accuse me, of all people, of being abusive! You can't talk to an Alliance member that way and another thing—"

"No, no, you stop and listen to me for one minute. You're a terrible person and you treat everyone here like garbage. Everyone hates you, Brad. Everyone!" She shifted in her stance and placed her hands on her hips. "I'm done. Take your Alliance bull crap and shove it!" She turned to grab her bag, closing the flap and shoving it under her arm. She reached over and plucked the Colony brochure from Brad's hand.

Brad looked down and took a step backwards. His face held a look of utter shock. "You can't do that, Cynthia! You are throwing away your career. You'll never work again! You hear me?"

"Am I, Brad? Really? Well I don't want this career and I certainly don't want to work for you." She pushed past Brad and scurried out the door.

"Cynthia!" yelled Brad.

She didn't bother to look over her shoulder. She could feel her back straightening; her head was held high. She felt good for a change. Confident. More like herself than she had in a long time.

"You can't do this, Cynthia! Come back here right now!" Brad's cries had no effect on her. In a few seconds she was at the elevator bank. The doors opened. She stepped onto the lift, leaving behind the thirtieth floor for the last time.

FOUR

JOURNEY TO A NEW LIFE

Cynthia hadn't planned on leaving today, right now, but she had little choice. If Brad did call Central Enforcement, she'd be done. Every non-member agreed to it. They had to agree just to be employed, but still, it wasn't fair. No travel, no moving, no vacations, no nothing without prior approval from Central Enforcement. She didn't plan to ask for permission to join the Colony because it never would've been given. Plus, she didn't think she'd really go. But Brad forced her hand. It was rash, but it felt so good to finally speak her mind.

She flew through the door of her apartment and dashed to her bedroom closet. She pulled out two suitcases she hadn't used since she moved into the place three years ago. She grabbed several hand-fuls of clothes and threw them into a suitcase. She darted into the bathroom and grabbed her makeup and other supplies. She tossed everything into her suitcases and flipped them shut. She jerked them off the floor and trotted to the front door. She grabbed the door handle, then paused. She glanced behind her, over her shoulder. This was it. Her apartment, her life as she knew it, was over. She wondered, *should I do this?* What choice did she have? The bridge with Brad had been entirely burned. Her life here was gone. Too late to give it a second thought.

She ripped the door open and flew down the hallway. She bypassed the elevator and used the stairs to wind her way down a dozen stories. In every case she'd ever heard about, Central Enforcement usually arrived in less than fifteen minutes. She glanced down at her digital bracelet. She had spent less than five minutes in her apartment. Maybe she would make it after all.

She reached the door at the bottom of the stairs and stopped. She peeked out the doorway. Across the lobby, coming in the main entrance, she could see two men, dressed in the telltale red uniforms of Central Enforcement officers. Her digital bracelet gave out a ring. She jumped back behind the door and closed it tight. She reached down and undid the strap on the bracelet. She glanced at the face of it. It was Christopher. Wanting to get the scoop on her blowout with Brad no doubt. No time for that. She flung the bracelet as far up the stairs as she could. She wouldn't need it where she was going. She peeked back out the door. The coast was clear. The officers must have entered the elevator already.

She dashed for the side door and exited onto the sidewalk outside. She knew where to go, down by the waterfront. She just hoped she could get there in time.

"Asʜ!" Cynthia yelled out as she dashed across the cavernous hanger on the edge of the Port of Los Angeles.

"Cynthia!" Ash jumped forward and ran towards her new recruit. She stopped short and waited for Cynthia to approach her. "So happy to have you join us!"

Cynthia stopped in front of Ash and placed her suitcases on the ground next to her. She tried to catch her breath. "Thanks ... I hope I am making the right choice. I just left my job out of the blue. I hope that wasn't a huge mistake."

"I can promise you, it wasn't"

"Ok, I am trusting you, Ash."

"You know, you won't need whatever's in those suitcases when you get to the Colony."

"I won't need clothes? Well it's not all clothes anyway."

"I hope it's not makeup, you won't need that either."

Seabreeze strolled over to the pair. "Hello, Cynthia, so good to have you aboard."

"Hello ... I'm sorry, I don't remember your name."

"Seabreeze. Nice to meet you ... again."

"Hi, Seabreeze. I am so nervous. I was just telling Ash I hope I am making the right decision."

Seabreeze smiled and placed her hand on Cynthia's shoulder. "Your life is about to change for the better. You'll see. You will never look back once you are part of the Colony."

Cynthia's eyes sparkled and gleamed. Her heel bounced up and down as she stood looking at her two recruiters.

Ash turned towards Cynthia. "You'll be part of group A. Just stand over there under the sign and they will call you when ready. I have to help usher people on board the airships, so I won't see you again until we are at the Colony. Have a good trip and I'll see you on the other side." Ash jogged off towards a group of new recruits.

Cynthia walked over to the sign marked with the letter A. She put down her bags and looked around. There were signs with letters A through G stretched out in a neat row. She noticed there were far more people standing near the other letters. Her group, hovering closely to the letter A, consisted of a dozen people while the other letters seemed to have two to three times that many.

She had barely arrived at her assigned letter when a tall man in a black uniform called out from behind her. "Group A, please follow me." This was it. The group followed behind the man in black as he led them out a sliding door and onto the tarmac outside. There was a long line of hefty airships waiting on the ramp. A few dozen people, men and woman, dressed in the same black uniforms guided people from the terminal to their assigned airship. They looked to be trans-port class, the kind used to shuttle goods about the city. They were slow and bulky, but they'd work. Plus, they were so ubiquitous that no one would suspect they were being used to shuttle people to a new world.

The man in black guided Cynthia and her group to the first airship in the line. They stopped and dropped their bags.

"Leave your bags here and they will be retrieved by our ground crew." The group complied in unison. He waved his arm indicating the group should board the airship. Once inside the pilots began to wind up the engines. Everyone scurried aboard and found an open seat. The door was closed and the little A group, twelve people on two benches facing each other, said nothing.

"Hello, and good morning, this is your captain speaking." The captain's voice sprang from hidden ports in the ceiling and walls. "This will be a fairly short ride out to our transport ship. Once we land and you disembark, the ship will take you the rest of the way to your destination. Please buckle up and hold on as we get underway."

The airship rose and made an abrupt turn westward. The entire craft leaned forward and began to move quickly over the landscape below. After a few minutes the land gave way to water as the airship cruised ever faster towards the horizon.

The trip by air was a blur. Cynthia felt lifeless and bewildered. It had been less than 4 hours from when she walked out on her job, and now she was speeding across the ocean a thousand feet in the air. She felt numb inside. Sitting by the airship's door, peering out the window to the water below, it all felt unreal. Was this really happening? It felt more like a dream; she hoped it didn't turn into a nightmare.

The speeding airship started to slow and then descended onto the deck of a large ship. There were four other airships already perched on the stern. The airship touched down with a thud and the engines began to wind down. The door slid open and a new set of men dressed in the same black uniforms began to usher the occupants outside. They stood on the deck of the ship. The cool ocean air blew across the deck as the ship was already underway trawled forward. The air was crisp and much clearer than the dank, smoggy air in the city. A calm, white wake made a long line in the water behind the large boat. After the airship was emptied, the guards guided the waiting occupants below deck into a large holding area. The metal cargo hold was dimly lit and smelled oily and musty at the same time. There were people strewn about. Some were sitting on the floor others were standing or leaning on the sides of the ship. Scattered throughout the hold were large wooden crates that had been strapped to the floor with bright, yellow straps.

As Cynthia walked through the hold she looked down at the people who had claimed a spot on the floor. They did not speak. There were groups of people from all walks of life strewn throughout the space. Some of the people were huddled together. Others sat or lay on the metal surface alone. The guard guiding their group escorted them to the far side of the hold and opened a door. He stood aside as the group A people filed into a separate room.

Cynthia stepped over a large threshold on the floor. As she raised her eyes to peer around the room she saw much nicer accommodations. The room was full of chairs and tables. Several overstuffed couches were pushed up against the walls. The room was large, not as large as the cargo hold they just walked through, but still a much bigger room than she had expected. There were several dozen of people already sitting and milling about.

The guard who had escorted the group closed the hatch behind them. Cynthia began to walk towards the side of the room where a vacant couch was nestled into a corner. On her left she noticed a large table with drinks and food spread out. Most of the people who had travelled to the ship with her gathered around the table, but she didn't feel hungry. Her stomach was tight. Her muscles tensed, she just needed to sit. Still not sure this was the right move. Cynthia reached the couch and took a spot at the far end.

"Hiya, I'm Kevin." A middle-aged man sat at the middle of the couch. Cynthia looked over and shot a quick smile.

"Where are you from?" asked Kevin.

"L.A."

"Oh, nice." The man looked down at the small plate in his hand. He grabbed one of the little hors d'oeuvres and threw it in his mouth. "You an engineer?"

"Huh?"

"You part of the engineer crew?"

"I don't know." She didn't really know what she was a part of at this moment.

"Engineer. I've been an engineer all my life. I'll probably do that in the Colony."

"Oh, good, good." She could barely follow what Kevin was saying. Her mind raced as her stomach felt more upset. *What had she done? This was a dumb decision, wasn't it?*

"Electrical engineer, to be precise."

"Mmmm."

"Yup, machines, computers, you know like software mostly."

"Yeah."

"Hey, you look a little green in the gills. You ok?"

She peered over at Kevin and gave a weak smile. "Yeah, I'm ok. Just nervous, I guess. Maybe a little sea sickness."

"Oh yeah?" Kevin looked at his plate of snacks and chose his next morsel. He quickly shoved it in his mouth. "I don't ever get nervous myself." His lips smacked together as he chewed. "Don't get seasick neither. I just go for it, you know. Like yeah! Let's do this."

She smiled and nodded. *Great, that's just great.*

"Attention, please pay attention to the display monitors for an important announcement from our Supreme Principal." The voice rang out from speakers mounted throughout the large assembly room. Cynthia jumped at the voice, but then turned to find a monitor mounted on the wall to her left. The screen flicked to life as the face of an older man with salt and pepper hair appeared. She thought he looked distinguished. His white suit and clean-shaven face made him appear to be angelic.

"Hello and welcome aboard Colonial Voyager III. I am Supreme Principal Cosmotine and in just a few short hours you will arrive at your new home: the Colony. There is much to learn about our home, but before we get into all that I wanted to welcome you personally. You will soon learn that your position within the Colony comes with great benefits, but also great responsibility. You will learn all about it upon your arrival. I look forward to meeting you all in due time and watching you apply your talents to our wonderful world. Until we meet, I wish you safe travels."

The screens flicked off and all was quiet in the room for a few moments before talking resumed. Cynthia looked down at her feet. Maybe this was a good decision after all. She would have to wait to find out for sure.

The ship slowly rolled and creaked as it pushed across the ocean's surface, making for its unknown port. The hours ticked by, and weariness set in. Cynthia rested her head on the edge of the couch. The ship sailed for hours until darkness crept over the horizon and enveloped the sky. The water stretched out in every direction with no land, and no life, in sight. As the night grew darker, the ship began to slow from full steam. The water ahead of the ship began to simmer and stir until a large metal beam lurched out of the water toward the sky. As the structure rose, it revealed a massive rectangular box much larger than the ship itself. Water drained and dripped from every surface as the metal super structure rose high into the sky, far above the height of the ship.

Once the metal structure was fully aloft, the ship moved slowly forward into the middle of the large metal box. Men in matching overalls stood on either side of the box, behind guardrails ready to catch the mooring ropes from the ship. The inside of the box was a large ship berth with anchor points along each side. Once the ship was securely moored, a large metal door began to lower from the back of the berth. Once the door was fully closed, the entire metal superstructure began to descend into the ocean with the ship was safely housed inside.

From outside, once the metal structure descended underneath the waves, the water was quiet. It was as if the ship never existed. Simply vanished from sight in the middle of a dark, lifeless ocean.

Lights began to appear from the ceiling of the superstructure. The ship was carried ever lower into the sea. After nearly an hour the structure came to an abrupt halt. A guard entered the room and signaled for everyone inside to follow him into the hold. Bright lights sparked on as guards began ushering everyone to the side exits. Massive doors on the side of the ship swung open and light from outside poured into the hold from each doorway.

Cynthia was led out a large door and emerged into a large glass tube that led from the ship, across the ocean depths, and into an enormous glass dome. *The Colony?* This was the place the lady in white described back at the office. The sides of the Colony sloped up and inward as they rose from the sea floor. The sides were clear, but thick, holding back the ocean. The structure curved and spread in every direction, left and right, farther than the eye could see. The Colony structure appeared to be larger than could be comprehended. Light emanated from the within the Colony walls and lush greenery appeared to shimmer from within.

The large glass tube that flowed from the ship to the side of the Colony was equipped with moving sidewalks, ten-wide. Ten rows of people, moving without effort, streamed from the ship into the glass Colony wall and then disappeared. There was a steady stream of people in each row. As Cynthia looked left, she saw several more glass tubes ranging down the side of the large ship. Hundreds of people being carried into the colony.

At the end of the tube, the crowd entered into a massive room. There were metal benches fixed to the floor, and each row was quickly occupied by the disembarking horde. Cynthia was ushered to a row and told to move as far down the row as possible. When she could go no further down the row, she stopped and sat.

After some time, the large auditorium was full and eerily quiet. The group of people were silent. After a few minutes, the lights dimmed, and a figure walked out onto a large stage at the front of the auditorium. Massive screens were fixed to the side of the stage and more screens were fixed every fifty feet or so to the sides of the auditorium walls. As the figure appeared on stage, a corresponding image appeared on the dozens of screens ringing the auditorium. It was the man from the video announcement back on the ship.

"I am the Supreme Principal, and I want to welcome you to the Colony." His voice rang out from speakers mounted along the length of the walls. "You are now part of a great community of people who have chosen to leave the horrors of the outside world behind, and make their home here, with us." As the Supreme Principal said the word "us" a large platform behind him raised out of the floor of the stage. The platform was filled with rows of men, women, and children all dressed in white. The men wore white pants and white shirts with buttons down the front and no collars. The women wore the same. As did the children. They were all smiling; their faces beamed with warmth.

In unison they said, "we are the Colony, and this is our home." The unified voices rang throughout the auditorium and echoed as they finished their saying. "We welcome you to your new home, and we invite you to join us in changing the course of humankind." Again, all said in unison.

The Supreme Principal smiled, clearly pleased with the unified performance.

"These are colonists. Like you, they came to the Colony seeking something new. And together they not only found something new, they built it to be better. They made the Colony their own."

The lights dimmed and a pre-recorded video began to play. A deep voice sounded throughout the auditorium speakers, as the video began to show images of the Colony.

"The Colony is a self-supported living environment placed at the bottom of the Pacific Ocean. It allows its inhabitants to live peaceably away from the harmful effects of global warming, pandemics, and threat of war.

"The Colony consists of ten levels. The top level is One, and the bottom level is Ten. Most new arrivals to the Colony begin at Seven—the largest level. Seven sits on the sea floor and encompasses an area the size of Hawaii's big island. Seven is where all food is grown, drinks made (except for water purification), and nearly all materials required to run the Colony are manufactured."

Images of fields full of crops flashed on the screen as the faceless voice spoke. Cynthia looked in amazement at the sheer size of the crop fields. They seemed to stretch on for miles. When sweeping views of Seven where shown, a collective gasp emanated from the crowd.

"There are three levels below Seven, and below ground. Eight houses the water purification system, and the desalinization plant. Nine houses all mechanical systems required to run the Colony's life support systems. Ten is where mineral deposits are mined and processed.

"Above Seven are levels One through Six. One is where the Supreme Principal and his executive team live and work. Levels Two, Three, and Four contain all the professionals required to run the Colony. Engineers of all types, doctors, dentists, biologists, educators, geologists, botanists, oceanographers, architects, designers, manufacturing experts, just to name a few. This is also where a new generation of experts are taught through extensive apprenticeships. Some of you will join the apprenticeship ranks to learn how to run and grow a better Colony."

"Hey, that'll probably be my floor!" exclaimed Kevin as he bounced his eyebrows up and down and looked over at Cynthia to give her a wink. Cynthia gave a little smile in an attempt not to engage too much with Kevin.

"Five is home to the Colony guards. The Colony guards provide protection from international threats and police the Colony. Although, policing is hardly required because all colonists live in peace and harmony. And finally, Six is where clothes, linens, and other textiles are processed into usable goods.

"The Colony is governed by the Masters Twelve. Each Master has reached the Master rank through the skills, knowledge, and expertise required to lead the level they represent. There is one Master for each level, except Seven and Five, which have two Masters each. The Masters make all important decisions for the Colony and appoint the executive leader known as the Supreme Principal.

"Each of the levels above Seven are less than half the size of Seven. As the Colony angles to a point at top, the levels become smaller—rather like a beehive. The Masters Twelve occupy the smallest level, located above One and referred to as the Masters Level. No one is allowed to see the face of a Master. This practice allows the Masters to speak as one. No one Master is above the others, they are unified in their actions and in their voice. The Masters choose their own replacements, and their decrees are law in the Colony.

The narrated voice was interrupted by the image of an older woman, dressed in a white dress that flowed down to her feet. "For over one hundred years," said the woman, "our grand experiment has grown and flourished into the Colony you see before you today." The text below the woman's face identified her as River, an "Equal from level One." The woman continued, "It has exceeded every measure of success and now thrives." The pre-recorded image stopped, and the screens showed the same woman, River, walking out onto the stage.

River came to a stop to stand next to the man in white, her enthusiasm was fresh and on full display. Her clean face shined on the screens, while her white robes draped down her slight figure and pooled on the floor at her feet. Behind her a wall mural depicting the Masters Twelve rose from the floor. Each Master was larger than life —quite literally. The Masters were depicted in the mural at twice their actual size. However, none of their faces were recognizable.

Instead of a face, the murals had a simple humanistic form, slender black oblong circles for eyes, and sleek shining noses, with squared check bones. They all had the same nondescript faces.

The narrator's voice came over the loud speakers again, "Over a century ago, the colony was envisioned as a place to escape global warming, wars, pandemics, and continual economic melt-down cycles. A place where people can work towards a common good. You have entered a world quite different from your own. It will forever change you and your families. You will learn new skills, live among friends, and grow the Colony together. Welcome home!"

The presentation ended. A different, more nasally, voice came over the loud speaker instructing everyone to stand and exit the auditorium to the right. Cynthia stood. She still was confused where she would be going. She began shuffling to her right. She couldn't believe the size of the Colony. Nothing in the glossy brochure had prepared her for this.

FIVE

IT'S SCIENCE

**A Century Earlier — June 5, 2030 — Colony
Engineering Offices**

"We've been through this a thousand times; we need a scientifically sound system." Leo's eyes widened as he spoke. "Darn it Sal, we're on the verge of moving to the Colony. The system has to be completed."

"Yes, I know and that's what we have here—science. It works just like we all agreed it should."

Sal stood opposite Leo's desk. He pointed at various papers arrayed before him. "Personality is gauged, aptitude, intelligence."

"So what is that, a full psychological test?"

"Not really. I mean we managed to get it streamlined into a single testing sequence. We can prove where people belong. Where they will do the most good."

"Ah a *probatum*. A thing proved."

"Yes, if you want to give it a more formal name, I suppose. It's a placement tool. During the test—"

"*Probatum*." Leo smiled at his own clever use of Latin. It never hurt to give something mundane a little dressing up.

"Fine, *probatum*. During the *probatum*, the subsequent questions change as the prior questions are answered—kind of steers the person in the right direction."

"A tool? That makes it sound like it's part of a larger process."

"Yes, we will give the leaders a say in how to use the results so that ...."

"No! That's what I am talking about. That's what we don't want. Don't you see the problem with that?"

Sal sighed and ran his hand through his hair. "No, Leo. I don't follow."

Leo stood and grabbed one of the organization charts sitting on his desk. "Ok, what if I do a *probatum* and the results say I should be an engineer—that'd be level Four right?"

"Yes, correct."

"Ok, but then the colonists, the leaders, whomever, they decide I shouldn't be an engineer. Instead, they put me somewhere else."

"Where *else* would they put you?"

"I don't know, let's say they put me as a miner on Ten, or a guard on Five."

"Why would they do that?"

"Politics, plain and simple. If we leave any wiggle room at all for anyone to vary the placement dictated by the *probatum*, then we open up the entire system to the nasty side of human nature."

"Really, Leo?" Sal put his hand on his chin. "You think that poorly of people that they would put a perfectly good engineer in the mines? Do you think the leaders of the Colony would be so capricious?"

Leo smirked. "It's not just me. We all talked about this very thing. We want the process to be vetted, scientific ... fair."

He shook his head and tapped a finger on his desk. "Let me ask you, you think Dr. Erler got this job because he was a great scientist?"

"Well, Leo, he was a world-renowned physicist. I mean he had the whole package. Scientific family, Ivy League education ...."

"Look, I loved Dr. Erler like a brother, and I'm still mourning his loss." Leo put his hands on his hips. "But let's be honest, he did no work here. He discovered nothing. As you said, he came from a famous scientific family, and he rode that wave to the top. It was a popularity contest. We must avoid that sort of thing at all costs."

"Jaded, Leo. That's a very jaded view." Sal took a step backwards and sat in a chair opposite Leo's desk. He shook his head and sighed. "Is our new world going to be so jaded too?"

"No. It won't be because in order to protect it, in order to ensure maximum efficiency, we will use your test—your *probatum*—as the only indicator of placement in the Colony. Everyone sees the results of their *probatum* as soon as it's complete so there can be no funny business. The results will be law." Leo smiled. The solution was perfect. Decisions based solely on results—free of human meddling.

Sal pursed his lips. "Hmmm."

"Think about it, Sal. You have already devised the perfect system. Once we discover the personality traits and skills of a person, we can determine how best to use their strengths for the good of the Colony. That's what the Colony is all about."

"Yeah, I guess so."

"And people will be happiest when they have a job that uses their strengths."

"Not always."

Leo frowned. "What do you mean not always?"

"Sometimes people want to do something they aren't so good at."

"Like what?"

Sal shrugged. "I want to be a starting pitcher for the Dodgers, but I'm not on the field. Can't throw fast enough."

Leo rolled his eyes. "Well the Colony won't have the Dodgers. Besides, the Colony can only survive with efficiency."

"Hey, Leo—" David scurried into Leo's office. He was panting. "Leo, your speech, you need to have it ready in one hour."

Leo plopped into his chair and let out a long sigh. "I know, I know."

Sal glanced over his shoulder at David. "Speech?"

David nodded. "Yes, Leo has to give a big speech to the whole team. He's trying to convince them to join us in the Colony."

Sal shook his head. "Don't envy him that." He turned to face Leo. "What do you plan to say?"

Leo shrugged. "I don't know. Speeches aren't really my thing. But I need to get through to everyone how vital it is that we finish our work in the Colony. We can do this if we stick together."

Sal smiled. "That sounds good. Maybe just say that."

"Thanks, Sal. But I think it's going to take more than that to get through to everyone."

"You might be surprised, boss." Sal leaned forward in his chair. "People want to follow you more than you know. Try not to be so jaded all of the time." Sal stood and collected the papers spread out on Leo's desk. He stacked them neatly and walked to the door. David stepped aside to give him room to pass. "Maybe your speech is the first *probatum*. We'll see if you are placed as our new leader in the Colony."

Leo frowned. "Oh please, I don't need that pressure."

"It's not pressure—it's science."

SIX

PROBATUM

April 30, 2130 — The Colony — Level Seven, New Recruit Processing

"Please line up in a row." Cynthia entered the room to the right of the auditorium. She shuffled in a few steps and then stopped. Glancing around, she saw rows of people lined up neatly in front of doors. The rows stretched down the length of the room. Attendants flittered about directing people where to stand. Other new recruits filtered around her as she stood still gawking.

An attendant rushed over to Cynthia and held his hand out to direct her forward. "Please follow me."

"Huh?" Cynthia jumped. She hadn't noticed the man approaching her. "Oh, ok."

"You will line up here for your *probatum.*"

"What? *Probatum?*" The word sounded ominous, but what the heck was it?

"Yes. You were told of it upon recruitment, correct?"

"No, I don't know what you are talking about."

The man rolled his eyes and gave out a sigh. "Recruiters," he mumbled. The man glanced around at the people standing close by. "Has everyone here been told of the *probatum?*"

Two or three people nodded, the rest stared back with blank looks, some shook their heads.

"Alright, listen please." The man cleared his throat and raised his chin. "You all are about to take your first *probatum*. It is a test. A placement test. The *probatum* will determine where you begin your work in the Colony."

The man looked around locking eyes with some of the people. He turned his body slowly in a circle as he spoke. "Those of us born here take our first *probatum* at age twelve. Every two years you sit for another *probatum* to ensure you are still placed in your most efficient role. You can also request to take a *probatum* every other month if you wish to be placed in a different role. However, no one"—the man spun around as he frowned—"is allowed to be placed on a particular level or in a particular job for which he or she did not test into." The man came to a stop and peered around. "Understood?"

The group of people nodded their heads. "Excuse me." Cynthia half raised her hand.

"Yes, what is it?" The man placed his hands on his hips and tapped his foot.

"How do we know what job we get?"

"You will see your results immediately after your *probatum*." The man turned and began herding people along. "Please get back in line. Inside each room is a computer where the *probatum* will take place. It takes several minutes. Your results will be given to you immediately and then we will take you to your new placement. Thank you. No more questions, please line up." The man waved his arms and pointed towards the lines. People shuffled into neat rows.

Cynthia stood in a line ten people deep. Each row of new recruits stood in front of matching white doors spread equally across the wall of the room. An attendant stood next to each door. Every ten to fifteen minutes, the door opened, and a new recruit was ushered inside. She shuffled forward as the line progressed and glanced around. Everyone was silent. Nervous perhaps? She bit her lip and curled her long, brown hair around her finger. She was good at tests. Really good at tests, but was this really a test? She hadn't anything to study. *Please let me get a good job here.*

After waiting for what seemed like hours, she was at the front of the line. The door in front of her slid open and she took a breath. The attendant waved her into the room. She stepped forward. Once inside the door slid closed behind her. There was a single monitor and keyboard sitting on a raised table at the center of the small room. She stepped up to the monitor and looked down. The monitor screen flicked on.

"Welcome, Cynthia." A voice floated through the room.

Cynthia glanced over her shoulder, but saw nothing.

"This is your *probatum.* Please place both hands on the keyboard in front of you."

As Cynthia placed her hands onto the keyboard she noticed it was not a normal keyboard. There were no keys, but ten slight indentions. Each indention lined up with a finger on each hand. She placed her hand on the keyboard and slid her fingers into the indentions. Once all her fingers were in place, the screen changed color. Red, blue, green. Then a series of images flashed before her.

"Please keep your focus on the screen in front of you," said the voice.

Cynthia stared at the screen. After several seconds of flashing images, the screen turned white and a series of written questions flashed before her. She was instructed to answer by putting pressure on a certain finger. Each finger represented a different answer. As she answered the questions, she noticed some questions were about her, others were a test of what she knew, and still others seemed to make no sense at all.

"Who was the first U.S. President." *Hmm, they must be starting off with an easy one.* Cynthia pressed her right index finger down. The screen flashed green and the next question appeared.

"Is it better to be feared or loved?" She shook her head and smirked. Right into the tough ones. *Can't I answer 'neither'?* Seeing only two choices, she picked one. *Shoot, I meant to choose loved, not feared.* The screen flashed white and the next question appeared.

"Do you enjoy vibrant social events with lots of people?" Cynthia paused for a moment. Was this a trick question? She quickly answered yes, and the screen flashed white.

"Who was Dr. Herbert Erler?" Oh yes, the founder of course. Cynthia remembered seeing that name plastered throughout the Colony brochure.

"It is sometimes acceptable to hurt a person for the good of many people, true or false?"

Cynthia paused. She hated such questions with no right answers. She punched in true and waited the next query.

"Do you enjoy discussing different theories on how the world might look like in the future?"

Yes.

"Do you focus on present realities or future possibilities?"

Future possibilities of course. She rolled her eyes and sighed. The questions continued. She answered each one quicker than the next— just wanting to be done with the empty exercise.

After several more minutes a voice rang out, "Complete." The screen turned white. A single word flashed before her. "Results ... Results ... Results."

Cynthia removed her hands from the keyboard and took a half step backwards. Before her results appeared, the screen went black. A door behind the computer monitor slid open and a woman stepped inside.

Cynthia startled. She glanced around the monitor. "Please, follow me." The woman held out her hand, guiding Cynthia from the room.

"Oh ... ok." Cynthia exited the room. She was guided down a long hallway to a door simply marked "reserved." The attendant opened the door, moved her hand forward to indicate she should enter. As she was about to step into the room, she heard a loud voice from the hallway to her left.

"No, no, no, that has to be wrong!"

Cynthia glanced left and saw Kevin, the guy from her voyage to the Colony.

"I'm an engineer, I don't dig holes ... I'm not a miner!" Kevin was waving his arms and his face glowed red.

Cynthia frowned. She turned towards the yelling and was about to step towards Kevin when the attendant placed a hand on her shoulder.

"Please ... enter."

Cynthia froze. Two men grabbed Kevin by the arms and ushered him quickly through a door. The door slid closed and all was quiet. Cynthia gasped. Why the use of force? She looked over her shoulder at the woman still standing behind her.

"Please ... enter." The attendant arched her eyebrows and pointed to the room beyond the door with her head.

Cynthia turned to face the room. She took a breath and stepped over the threshold. The door slid closed behind her.

Inside the room, a half dozen people dressed in white were working behind a counter. There were a dozen or more other new recruits being assisted by the people dressed in white. As Cynthia entered, one of the attendants came out from behind her desk and approached her.

"Welcome, Cynthia, so good to see you." Cynthia was taken aback. *How does this stranger know my name?*

"Don't worry, we know everyone's name here. I'm Raindrop, please have a seat."

"Hi." Cynthia sat in the chair opposite Raindrop's desk. She raised her finger and leaned forward. "I didn't get my results ... from the test ... I mean the *probatum*."

"Don't worry about that, you were chosen for One."

"Chosen for One? How do you know?"

"Oh, we know. That's our job to know."

"But what will be my job when I get there? What will I do?" Cynthia sat back in her chair and placed her hand on her leg.

"It is quite an honor!" said the woman seated next to Raindrop. "Hi, I'm Glacier. It really is an honor to be in this room, I am so excited for you," Glacier continued with a beaming smile on her face.

"Raindrop, Glacier?" asked Cynthia with a puzzled look on her face. Not their birth-names, Cynthia surmised.

"You'll see," said Raindrop. "Once we have processed you into the Colony, you'll be assigned a name that depicts the natural elements of our world: earth, water, fire, or air. Our names come from the elements in one form or another. Names are assigned at processing, except in your case. Special guests are sent to One and receive their names directly from the Supreme Principal!"

"Can you just imagine it!" exclaimed Glacier. "Getting your name from the Supreme Principal!" .

Cynthia nodded, not knowing quite what to say. She hadn't anticipated a new name—that wasn't in the brochure. But these two certainly seemed excited about it.

Raindrop continued, "As you just heard in the orientation, most new recruits start on Seven, the largest level. You, however, have been chosen for One. There are rules to follow on One. Failure to follow those rules will result in you being reassigned."

"I'm sorry, I don't mean to interrupt, but what exactly will be my job on One?" Cynthia leaned forward and tried her question again.

"Only the Supreme Principal knows the answer to that question," said Raindrop.

"But I bet you'll know soon enough!" Glacier beamed with excitement.

"The reason behind these decisions are not known to us, nor do we care to know them," explained Raindrop. "We are honored to work for the Colony in helping those chosen to be a guest of One to transition onto that level. You should know that few new colonists are ever placed there. And fewer still of our existing colonists ever see One. In fact, neither Glacier nor I have ever seen that level. But we know it's perfect. It's where the Supreme Principal lives so it deserves the best."

Cynthia nodded. "Sounds ... great."

Raindrop and Glacier looked quizzically at Cynthia. She sat in her chair looking back at them.

"I mean, I'm really excited!" she sat up straight as she spoke in an attempt to sell her statement. The two attendants relaxed and smiled.

"You'll see. Once you are on One you will see how perfect it is." Raindrop beamed, smiled wide, and tilted her head sideways.

"Hey, can I ask you something?"

"Of course!"

"How does someone leave the Colony?"

"Leave the Colony? Whatever for?"

"I just mean, for those who choose to leave, how does that work?"

Raindrop turned her head slowly to look at Glacier. The two frowned and shook their heads in unison. "No one leaves the Colony. No one wants to."

SEVEN

THE EQUALS OF ONE

Cynthia took a cautious step forward. She kept one foot behind her and one in front as she peered ahead. The glass wall of the elevator was nearly within reach. She wasn't afraid of heights, but watching the terrain of Seven become ever smaller around her didn't feel quite natural. The elevator shot up with electric-smooth speed. She gazed back and forth taking in as much as she could. The vast expanse of the Colony's main level was impossible to comprehend. It was enormous. Cynthia noticed that the terrain was light and bright as if the sun was shining down without being hindered by the water outside. *There must be some artificial light source,* she thought. *But it sure looks like sunlight.*

Cynthia flinched as the elevator plunged into darkness. It had reached the top of Seven and moved into a dark shaft that passed in between the upper levels. The lights flicked on from above. The solid elevator shaft rushed by outside as Cynthia stepped back and leaned against the lift's hand rail. After several more minutes of speeding upwards, the lift stopped and the doors slid smoothly open. Outside was a room of all white, lit from above with glowing light. She could hear no sounds and see no people. She took a small, tentative step forward to peer out of the elevator. As she peered right, a voice came from her left.

"Welcome," said the voice. Cynthia startled and looked to her left.

"Please follow me," said a woman dressed in a long, flowing white dress. The woman motioned with her hand for her to follow. She complied.

The pair began walking down a long white corridor. Cynthia looked at the walls, ceiling and floor, nothing but clean, bright white shone back at her. It looked modern. Cynthia liked the clean look. She always preferred simple elegance. As the pair walked through a set of glass double doors, Cynthia gasped at the enormity of the space. She walked towards a curving glass wall to her right. The vast farmlands of Seven could be seen stretching out far below. She marveled at the sights of vehicles and people moving about in every direction.

"Please, come along." The woman gently instructed. Cynthia turned and followed behind. She looked up and saw the tall walls arching upwards towards a point in the ceiling far above. The pair walked into a broad corridor. There were doors on either side, but the ceiling was open, and she could still see the arched walls above.

"Welcome to One," said the woman in front of her. The woman spoke without looking back at Cynthia. "You have seen Seven below, but you might not have noticed levels Two through Six just below us. Each level below is slightly larger than this one, and they each house a different segment of the Colony as you learned in your orientation." Cynthia nodded her acknowledgment even though the woman didn't look back at her.

"Now that you are here, you must know that you are expected to act your part. Everyone on One is considered an equal." With that statement the woman made a sharp left and stopped at the entrance of a door. With a wave of her hand over a sensor next to the door the door slid open revealing a room beyond. Cynthia followed the woman inside, and saw they were in what appeared to be a one-bedroom apartment. It was furnished with simple, modern furniture. All smooth and white. Cynthia smiled and slid into the room. It felt like it fit her just fine. She glanced at the opposite wall where a line of round portholes gave sight to the sea beyond. The dark sea against the bright white walls made for a pleasing contrast.

"Please sit," said the woman as she took her place in a seat across from Cynthia. "Cynthia, I am Ember. Your life has changed, and you need to understand what that means for you." Cynthia shifted in her chair. She leaned forward. A rush of excitement shot through her gut. This is it, what she had been waiting for ever since she walked out on Brad. Her new life, her new purpose, about to be revealed.

"Why am I here ... on One?" asked Cynthia.

"Your *probatum* placed you here, I would presume. But then remaining here is never guaranteed. While you have been identified as an equal, the true test comes from your performance." Ember shifted in her seat. She looked Cynthia over from head to toe and then tilted her head slightly. "We shall see if you pass that test ... or not."

"Our colonists are dedicated to improving our lives through reason and science rather than destroying each other through wars." As Ember said the word "wars" a look of disgust came across her face in the first sign of anger she had shown; the first sign of any emotion really.

"Ok, but I am no scientist. I am a lawyer. What executive role do you expect me to fill? Why am I really here?"

"I'm told you are intelligent, competitive, and a former Navy officer. Sounds promising. I'm told you walked out on your job to join us. Seems bold." Ember shifted in her chair again and raised her chin. "Or maybe just rash. Who knows? But time will tell. Time tests all who stand before it. The worthy survive One and those not suited go elsewhere."

Cynthia sat up a bit straighter. "That sounds ominous."

"No, no, just true. You will either earn your spot among the equals of One, or you will be reassigned to a level more befitted your skills. It's just that simple. Nothing personal mind you, just effi-ciency. It applies to everyone in the Colony. Skills are measured and tested—regularly. The *probatum* determines your placement within the Colony. When your talent and skills match your work, you achieve happiness."

"I see."

"You can change your skills, of course, and thereby undergo another *probatum* to change your role in the Colony. But few do so. In order for the Colony to survive, for everyone to have a happy life, we must all play our part using the skills and talent we have. You understand?"

"I think so."

"And since you do not want for money, you can explore your best skills—and we can change your role—without you fearing a loss. You will eat, you will be cared for, no matter your role."

"Right. That sounds ... good." Cynthia rubbed her hands together. She was anxious to prove herself. Show that she had the necessary talent to be someone special in this new home even though she had no idea what she was supposed to do.

Ember flashed a smile. "You have a chance to accomplish great things as a member of the Colony. Far greater than in your past life. As you progress in your learning here with us, you will be able to answer your own question as to why you are here. The only answer I can give you now is that you are here to make use of a rare opportu-nity. You will begin by learning. From there you will find your place among us."

"However, there are a few guidelines by which you must conduct yourself in the Colony. To survive, the Colony has a hierarchy that must be obeyed. Failure to obey could lead to a breakdown of order. Within our self-sustaining environment, we need order to survive. We have everything here in the Colony that we need to live indefi-nitely so long as every colonist does their part as expected."

Cynthia nodded. It seemed to make sense, but then again she still didn't understand what she would do—really do—now that she was here. Cynthia's stomach growled with hunger. She grabbed her waist and blushed.

"So, when do we eat?" asked Cynthia.

"All meals are served on demand here, in your room. Dinner is the only exception. Most nights you will be expected to join a pre-assigned table in the Hall of Equals. If you do not receive a table assignment, then you are expected to eat here in your room."

"How about a drink, you have wine in this place?" asked Cynthia. She was trying to needle Ember a bit, but also desperately needed some wine.

"Yes, the Colony produces a wonderful abundance of wine," answered Ember with a proud smile. "But you are not allowed to drink alcohol in your room. Alcohol is strictly regulated to ensure no one over indulges. You also cannot drink outside your room with the exception of wine served during dinner in the Hall of Equals."

Can we please go to dinner in this hall place then? Thought Cynthia. She desperately wanted to tell this robotic woman to shut up and find some wine, but she held her words. Clearly, spouting off was a zero-sum game with Ember.

"In the closet is your new wardrobe." Ember stood. Cynthia remained seated on the sleek, white couch. "Your dinner assignment, should you receive one, will appear on your monitor," continued Ember. "And finally, at dinner in the Hall of Equals you will be assigned a new name." Ember quickly turned and walked briskly out the door.

For the first time, Cynthia was alone. She was tired, hungry, and needed a drink. She walked over to the bed and fell flat. Sleep came fast as the blur of the past few days faded away.

EIGHT

FLINT FROM THE FIELD

"Flint go get the last bushel of wheat and meet me down at the ware-house," yelled Misty with a hand cupped around her mouth. Her black hair was cut short; strands of grey raced through it. Her field-worn features were a mixture of tough and tired.

"Yes, Ma'am," Flint responded. Flint used to enjoy the physical work on the farm. He didn't care for reading and writing, and he was never taught to do much of either anyway. Instead, he could spend hours tending the crops, hauling things around, and taking orders barked at him from Misty on a regular basis. He liked Misty because she was straightforward. She'd yell at him one minute, and then share a joke the next. Fine with Flint. "Just tell me what to do and I'll do it," he'd say. But that changed a few days ago when his grandpa handed him a photo of stars. He started thinking. Maybe the Colony wasn't the only way.

He folded his tall, muscular frame into his truck and drove over to the edge of the wheat fields. The truck's electric motor gave off a high-pitched whine as he sped along the paved road. The truck was riddled with dents. The seats inside were worn. It had been around as long as he could remember. Most of their farming equipment was

53

from the inception of the Colony. Patched up and repaired, the century old machines kept plugging along. Every now and again some new technology would be bolted on. The truck's electric motor, upgraded a few years back, moved it fast as heck across the ground. Too fast it turned out. The motor was dialed down and now it ran about the same as it ever did—slow and steady, but far more efficient. Halfway to his destination, in the middle of a deserted field, Flint stopped the truck. He looked around slowly to see if anyone was around, and then he pulled out the photo of the night sky his grandpa had given him. "What are they? Why are they there?" he asked softly to himself. "And why am I here?"

<hr>

"Wᴏᴀᴛ ɪᴀ ɪᴛ, ɢʀᴀɴᴅᴘᴀ?"

"The night sky, Flint."

"Where?"

"On land, my boy, on land."

"What are the dots, the round ... dots?" Flint held the photograph up to his face. His mouth dropped open as his eyes grew wide.

"Stars."

"What are stars?"

"A billion suns. Probably a billion planets too."

"But how? I've never seen anything like this before."

"I know, Flint. You were never on land. I realize now that there are so many things you missed out on. I didn't mean for that to happen."

Flint glanced over to his grandfather. The old man had deep lines running across his forehead. A life spent working in the fields had taken its toll. His eyes looked watery.

"Did you like land, grandpa?"

"No!" Grandpa turned his back to Flint. He raised a cloth up to his face and blew his nose. "No, no, too violent. Much too chaotic."

Grandpa turned and placed his hand on Flint's arm. "That's why I brought my family here. Your father was just a boy then."

Flint nodded his head. He glanced back down at the photo and then back up to his grandfather. "Why did you show me this?"

"You need to know, Flint, that you have a choice. I know you've been taking *probatums* every couple of months in hopes of being placed as a Colony guard. And I know you keep getting placed right back here on Seven. But that's not the only choice you have. There's a big world up on land. While I don't care for it—in fact I'll never go back—you need to know there's more to this life than the Colony ... if that's what you really want."

Flint looked down at the ground and nodded his head. The thought had never occurred to him. *Return to land? Was that even possible?*

He shoved the photo back into his pocket and took off quickly in his truck. He needed to finish his chores before his absence seemed too long. That would raise suspicion. And lately people who raised suspicion didn't continue living on Seven. They were taken to Ten where the work was hard, living conditions were sparse, and the meals were meager, so he had been told.

He began driving again to the edge of the field, but he travelled slower now. Stars were on his mind and he couldn't stop thinking about the world beyond the sea. The confines of the Colony's glass walls felt small to Flint at the moment. He glanced to his right and looked at the dark waters beyond the glass barriers. There was nowhere to go, no world to see inside the glass dome. But land ... it sounded like a place where someone could do something different.

His truck pulled up at the edge of the field before he even realized he had arrived. He was driving in such a thoughtful haze he didn't recall the last several miles. He stepped out, grabbed the last bushel of wheat and threw it in the back of his truck. He made a hard turn right and headed for the warehouse. When he arrived Misty was waiting, looking agitated.

"What the heck took you so long, boy? You know we've been out here all day and I'd like to go home eventually!"

"I know, I'm sorry, just took longer than I thought it would. The roads are getting torn up and I had to slow down to miss the potholes," Flint lamely responded with his standard excuse.

"Well that's funny because I don't see you slowing down for anything when I'm in the truck with you."

He hauled the wheat out of the back of the truck and lumbered into the warehouse. The warehouse was a large facility that held a majority of the crops from Misty's sector. Seven was divided in multiple sectors. Each sector had a warehouse, and each warehouse was the size of three football fields. From here the crops would be processed into different types of food. The place buzzed with activity and machine noises.

He threw the wheat down and began to walk off, when Misty grabbed his arm. "Listen, Flint, I don't know what is going through your head, but something is off with you." Flint looked down not wanting to make eye contact with Misty. "Yeah, see there, you looking down tells me a lot. What's bothering you, Flint?"

"Misty when am I going to get my chance to be a crop supervisor ... or a guard? I'd be a real good guard, you know that."

"Flint we've had this conversation before. Your *probatum* didn't place you as a guard ... or a crop supervisor. Your skills placed you right where you should be."

"Aw shoot Misty that's just bull. You know I don't test so good. I have a hard time with the reading. And sometimes there's a math problem that don't make no sense. I do fine with identifying pictures, but I need help. With your help I can get there."

"Flint I helped you all I can. You were meant to be a field hand. And you are a good one. You're the best field hand I got. Look the colonial *probatum* doesn't lie. It makes the right choice for you."

"It don't feel like this is the right choice for me."

"Everything was fine with you until a few weeks ago. You enjoyed being here. You always felt it was the right choice. What's gotten into your head?"

"Nothing ... I don't know." Flint ran his hand through his hair as he let out a low sigh. "I've been through the *probatum* a few too many times. I guess the last one was a bit too much. Every time I end up right back here where I started. I know I can do more, Misty, I just know it. Why don't my *probatum* prove that?"

Misty flashed a smile and placed her hand on Flint's arm. "The *probatum* has its purpose Flint. Try not to worry about it. You're doing fine. Just enjoy your job and keep your nose clean. Besides you wouldn't like being a guard. That's why you ain't been placed on Five. It's science. You can't be something you aren't, honey."

He knew that Misty cared for him, but he didn't want to worry her and cause problems. After a long pause, Flint looked up at Misty and said, "You're right. I'll be fine, Misty, just a bit tired. Harvest season takes it out of a guy, you know that." Flint shook loose of Misty's grip on his arm and walked off. His shift was over, and he wanted to go home.

As we walked off, Misty called after him, "Don't dream of land tonight, Flint. And don't dream of stars. Those dreams turn into nightmares around here these days."

Flint heard the words and slumped a bit lower in the shoulders as he continued to walk away. *Why did Misty mention stars? Did she know?*

NINE

THE SUPREME'S NEW RECRUITS

"Supreme Principal Cosmotine, your new recruits await your instructions." Ember gave a slight bow as she entered the Supreme Principal's business office to give her update.

"Excellent, Ember. I have a good feeling about this group of recruits. Hopefully we found some people who can replace some recent vacancies on One. How many are there in all?"

"We have several hundred in all. Forty have been placed on Three and Four as new engineers. Twenty-five have been placed on One."

"Excellent news, Ember. You see our recent scouting trip was worth the effort after all. Now, when will the new recruits for One be ready?"

"Some today, the rest over the next few days."

Cosmotine rose from his chair, turned, and took a step towards the thick glass wall holding the crushing ocean at bay. "You know, the Colony is hurting right now." He turned to look into Ember's face as he approached her. "After that unfortunate plot, it was hard to determine who all was involved."

"I never understood the nature of the plot, what was it about?"

"Don't concern yourself about it, Ember. The Commodore made a thorough sweep of each level affected, except for One. I thought everyone on One was with me. Loyal. Dedicated."

"I would think the same, Supreme."

"Yes, we would all think the same, but I have reason to believe there are people on One who do not belong here any longer. Disillusioned people. Those who have lost faith in the Colony."

"I certainly hope not! I know of no such people, Supreme!"

"We have intercepted communications. They want me gone, Ember. They seek to destroy the Supreme Principal ... probably destroy the Colony itself."

"Why would they be so foolish?"

"Change can breed resentment."

"What change?"

"You know that I have made changes to improve the efficiency of the Colony. But perhaps you do not know the full extent of those changes."

"I think I know, Supreme. You have made those on One equals in name as they were previously in action and you asked for everyone to be silent at dinner to allow them to reflect on how they can continue to improve themselves and to show gratitude for the ways the Colony has improved their life."

"And I have breathed new life in how equals are chosen, and ultimately chosen to leave."

"All through the *probatum* as they always have been, I presume."

"The *probatum* has its limitations, Ember. It is flawed. The *probatum* cannot capture what matters most to me."

Ember looked down at her feet and wrinkled her brow. She glanced back up to Cosmotine. "But Supreme, the *probatum* provides guidance, order, efficiency. Without it we are no better than surface dwellers."

Cosmotine smiled, turned around and sauntered back to the chair behind his desk. "Strong words from one who so handsomely profited from bypassing a few *probata*."

"What? Are you suggesting I am here without placement by my *probatum?*"

"Don't look so surprised. Surely, you must have known." Cosmotine sat at his chair, leaned backwards and folded his hands in his lap. "You didn't think that someone so young could ascend to One? Your skills are excellent, don't get me wrong, but your *probatum* would have kept you on Four—crunching numbers and doing menial engineering tasks. I needed a loyal lieutenant. And I found one in you."

"Yes, Supreme." Ember reached up to rub her temple. "How does this apply to others? Has this applied to others?" Ember grabbed her stomach at the thought of other people having sidestepped a proper *probatum.*

"A few, but not many. I have full control of those who ascend in spite of their *probatum*. I have a plan, Ember. And I can evaluate the people I need around me better than any *probatum* ever could."

"Yes, Supreme." Ember looked down at her feet again. Her fingers touched her parted lips as she pondered the Supreme Principal's words.

"We must focus back on the task at hand. We must destroy those who would try to hurt our Colony, Ember. Don't you agree?"

Ember glanced up. "Yes! Of course I agree. This is mutiny. It cannot stand."

"Good, I'm glad we agree, Ember." Cosmotine rose from his seat and began to slide around his desk. As he approached Ember, he held out his hand and gently placed it on her shoulder. "The new recruits are not yet fully indoctrinated into the colony," said Cosmotine as he looked into Ember's eyes. "The rebels will view them as easy targets."

He lowered his arm and turned to walk away from Ember, moving towards the thick glass wall that rimmed the outside of his office. Cosmotine peered into the dark ocean outside as he spoke.

"You watch the new recruits closely. Have them mingle with the others. Put them at different tables for dinner in the Hall of Equals. We will see who takes the bait."

"Yes, Supreme Principal," replied Ember. "I will do as you ask. Let me go now to prepare for dinner."

"Good, and let's not bring all the recruits out at once, let's use a few at a time. Each night we can bring out a new crop. Let the recruits we don't need wait in their quarters until we need them." The Supreme Principal smiled, seemingly pleased with his own plan.

"Yes, Supreme Principal, I will arrange it now." Ember turned and left Cosmotine standing in his office, staring out the window into the dark abyss.

TEN

THE SPEECH

A Century Earlier — June 5, 2030 — Colony Engineering Offices

"Over a decade ago ... um ... we embarked on creating the grand experiment under the sea—the Colony. Creating a new world ... ah ... a self-sustaining world, under the ocean has been a ... um ... monumental challenge requiring dedicated effort from ... um ... our teams of scientists and engineers." Leo glanced around the large warehouse. He had rarely seen the entire team assembled together; and never imagined he would be addressing them all. A sea of faces looked back at him. His heart fluttered. A bead of sweat formed on his upper lip. He gulped and looked down at his notes. His hands were shaking. He put his left hand in his pocket to hide the tremors. He laid his right hand flat on the podium.

"At this time ... um ... I have asked you all to assemble to ...." Leo gulped. He glanced down and felt a sudden rush of panic. He had lost his place. He squinted at his notes trying to focus on where he left off. "I'm sorry ... I lost my place here ...." The speakers let out a loud screech as feedback from the microphone reverberated through the warehouse. He clenched his teeth as he tried to find his place. Seconds ticked by. Each second felt like an hour of silence. He shook his head and looked up.

"Look ... I'm not real great at giving speeches." He turned his notes over and stood up straight. Taking a deep breath, he grabbed the podium before him with both hands.

"So let me just say this: This is it, folks. I mean, this really is it." He gained his composure and looked around the room. "We have come this far, and we are on the verge of completing our new world, but there's only one way this thing is going to get done. We all have to join together and make the journey."

He smiled and tilted his head. "Mr. Hall and the other backers have ran out of patience. Who can blame them? A decade of work and nearly fifty billion dollars have been invested in the Colony. But it's not been a waste. You all know this better than I do. Your work, your hard work, has produced a place that is almost ready to inhabit. Think about it. It's no different from having a habitable ecosystem on Mars. Self-sustaining life for the rest of time. A world where science determines how we live, how we work. No more money troubles, no more wasteful wars. It will be perfect."

He shifted in his stance. "But it won't even get started if we don't finish our work. And now, with the mandate we have been given, we may never finish our work. I mean, what if they bring in all new people? They've threatened me with that, you know. Or what if they pull the plug altogether? They've told me that too."

He raised his hand and pointed upwards. "Once we are there, in the Colony, living there, working there, we can finish what we started. We will have all the equipment, tools, people, minerals, whatever we need to finish our work. And better yet, we will have no one to answer to but ourselves. The Colony is us. We are the Colony. You see, we can start this journey—all of you—together."

He placed his hands on the podium and scrunched his forehead. He took a large breath. "I know this is scary, to leave this world we know, here on land. But isn't it exciting to go to our new world? A world we created, there under the sea. You are all invited to join in this journey. And your families too. We need as many people as we can get. It's sudden, I know it's sudden. Not how we usually do things around here, but it gives us our only hope of finishing what we started."

He sighed and shook his head. "Unfortunately, there will be no work, no place left, for those who stay behind. I hate to say that, but once we leave, there is no turning back. You don't have to go to the Colony, but Colony Engineering, this place we have worked at around the clock for so long will cease to exist. It will be effectively shut down because ... well I don't know. I hope most—I mean a majority—of you will join up. Here and now.

"I know that I'm no Dr. Erler. He would've done a much better job of talking to you all. He was great at speeches and I'm not so ... good. I've done the best I can with what skills I have, but I would be honored if you—and I mean all of you—would join me in going to the Colony to finish our work and start a new life. We leave three weeks from now. Please think it over."

He looked down and stepped back from the podium. The warehouse, packed with the entire staff of Colony engineering, was quiet. Leo glanced up and then back down. He rubbed the back of his neck. He blew it. The silence was crushing. He could hear a ringing in his ears. A silent rebuke to his last plea for help. If only he could speak better, maybe this wouldn't have happened. *Shoot, I wish I was better at this.*

David, who was standing with the department heads behind Leo, trudged up to the podium. He grabbed the microphone and craned it lower to reach closer to his lips. He took a large breath and then leaned in to the mic. "You heard the man, are you joining him or not? Let's hear it, who's in?" His voice rang through the speakers and filled the open space. A second ticked by and then the entire warehouse erupted in applause. The audience jumped onto their feet and began clapping and hollering.

Leo looked up. He swiveled his head from side to side. All the people, his entire team, were cheering wildly for his idea. To join him in their own creation. A smile crept over his face as his eyes welled with tears. Could this be real? The noise was deafening, but it sounded so sweet.

"Well I'll be damned," he mumbled.

David turned around with a broad smile on his face. "They're behind you, Leo. They always were—I mean we always were." He patted Leo on the shoulder. The other department heads surrounded their leader, taking turns patting him on the back.

"Looks like you have your answer, Leo," said Chuck. "We're all in!"

ELEVEN

EXPLORATION

May 1, 2130 — The Colony — Level One

Cynthia jolted awake. Her room was dark and her monitor was giving off a beeping noise as the screen flashed the word "message." She had no idea where she was. It felt like she was waking up in her room back home on land. Another early morning, rushing to get ready, trying to get the auto food server to work, and running to the office. As she sat up, the lights in her quarters came on automatically revealing an all-white room. Her heart sank as she suddenly remembered she was in a strange new room at the bottom of the ocean. Was this really a new beginning? It felt good not to rush off to a job she hated, but she still felt unsettled, uneasy, not knowing why she was here or what she was to do.

She sat up slowly and made her way to a nearby chair to sit down and gain her bearings. *What is happening? Why is it happening? How do I go home?* The questions swirled in her mind without any conscious effort to answer them. After a minute or two of waking up, she raised her head and pushed a button next to the monitor to reveal its seemingly urgent message. The monitor came to life and began playing a video.

"Hello Cynthia, and welcome to the Colony," said a woman with short blond hair wearing a white dress on the television monitor. Cynthia rolled her eyes; *I wish people would stop welcoming me to this place and just tell me what I am doing on One.*

"Tonight, you will dine in the Hall of Equals with the Supreme Principal and his loyal guests. You must wear the dinner dress, which can be found in your closet ready for you to wear. You will leave your quarters at 18:15 precisely and proceed to the hall using the directions contained on the map next to this monitor. Your attendance at dinner is mandatory. We look forward to seeing you." The woman in the video gave a wide, fake smile, and the video turned off automatically.

"Perhaps," mumbled Cynthia, "I can get some answers at dinner." She stood up and looked around. Her bags had not been delivered to her room. She had none of the things she had so carefully packed before leaving her apartment behind. She walked over to the bathroom mirror. As she looked up, she was a bit horrified. Her hair was matted to one side of her head, her makeup was smeared and running, and she looked tired, with large bags under her brown eyes. Perhaps a shower and fresh makeup was in order. She grabbed for one of the drawers and found a small card that read "makeup is not provided, nor required. We request that you provide the Colony with your natural beauty."

"Wonderful!" *that's just great.*

She peered into the shower and saw it was fully stocked with soap, shampoo, conditioner, and various body lotions.

"At least they don't mind a clean body," she said as she slipped out of her clothes and entered the shower.

The hot water felt soothing on her body. Cleaning away the craziest days of her life felt refreshing. As she stepped out of the shower, a small bench and a towel bar automatically came jutting out of the wall towards her. *Fancy*. She dried herself off and went to the closet to find her dinner outfit.

When she pushed open the closet door she saw a single white dress hanging in the center of the closet. There were no other clothes. On the floor of the closet were a pair of white flats.

"One outfit makes choosing what to wear a lot easier at least."

She grabbed the dress and put it on. It fit perfectly. It was a simple white dress with a high neckline and a hem that stopped at her calves. She slipped on the white shoes and looked in the mirror. White had never been her favorite dress color, but it looked elegant and clean. Not bad for being so far from home.

As she admired herself in the mirror, her monitor beeped a reminder message. It was time to go. Cynthia walked towards the door, which automatically opened for her. She stepped out into the hallway and had a sudden feeling that she would never be back to this room again. She looked back into the room as the door slowly slid closed. She saw her clothes, the ones she had worn for the last several days, the ones she had picked out and put on at home several mornings ago, in a mound on the bed. Her last connection to her old life laying in a pile. The door closed. Cynthia hesitated. She felt an urge to run back into the room. To cling to those clothes as if they could take her back home. And yet, they were just clothes. Just a pile of cloth sitting on a bed. They could provide her no help.

Cynthia dismissed the thought and turned in the direction of the Hall of Equals. It was time to go find out what this was all about.

Cynthia glanced around as she traipsed down the wide corridor. There were people leaving their rooms and walking in the same direction as she. They said nothing to her or to each other. After several yards, she noticed a smaller hallway crossing paths with the wide corridor. People flowed from the hallway and turned down the corridor in the same direction as everyone else. She stopped. The people continued filtering around her, walking past, in total silence.

Are they zombies, or robots? She reached her hand to her temple, and gently rubbed her fingers against her forehead. Seems a bit strange. She looked to her right. The flow out of the adjoining hallway had stopped momentarily. She slipped across the corridor and stood at the mouth of the smaller hallway. She looked over her shoulder. People were coming, but none seemed to notice her. They all had their eyes fixed dead ahead. She turned and scampered up the hallway.

She had no idea what she was looking for, but a little look around couldn't hurt. Her body was close to the wall as she walked, her arm brushed lightly against the side. The hallway curved around for several yards, and then met up with adjoining passages. Cynthia stood at the intersection of the hallway and another passage. She peered left and then right. Both directions looked the same. Long, white halls devoid of people. She turned left and scurried a bit faster. She didn't know if what she was doing was allowed. Maybe it was a violation of the rules. Too late. She shook the thought from her head and continued on.

She came upon an open door. She stopped short and pressed her back up against the wall. She strained her ears trying to pick up any sound coming from the room beyond the open door. All seemed quiet. She sidestepped over to the opening and peeked around the door jamb. She saw a large office. A big glass desk perched in the center of a sweeping glass wall holding back the ocean outside. A large conference table to one side, a seating area to the other. *Fancy place. Must be someone important who sits in here.*

She slid her foot inside the room and then scooted along the outer wall of the office. The desk was clean with nothing on it. As she slid along the wall her wrist bumped into a hard metal object. "Ouch." She grabbed her wrist with her other hand and looked down. A handle, painted white, protruded from the wall. As Cynthia took a step back she could barely make out the outline of a doorway. It was hidden in the wall. She was in the far corner of the office. Well away from the door she had used to enter.

What am I doing here? She shook her head and sighed. Suddenly her exploration trip seemed silly. She turned to return to the entrance door when she heard loud footsteps approaching. She glanced around, right and then left looking for a place to hide. She lunged forward, grabbed the white handle, and tore the hidden door open. She threw herself through the doorway and shut the door swiftly behind her. She breathed in as her eyes grew wide. Her pulse quickened.

The room inside was dark. She pressed her ear up against the door; her hand grabbed the inside door handle. The footsteps continued their approach. She could hear someone entering the office. They gained in volume as the steps neared the door behind where she was perched. She held her breath. She let go of the handle and stood forward on her toes.

The door swung open as light poured in from around it. A tall figure in a black uniform stood at the doorway. His wide shoulders filled the doorframe. He took a step into the room and the lights flicked on from above. She peered at him through the cracks of two file cabinets. She leapt behind the cabinets as the door was swung open. *Did he notice?*

The man entered, turned his back to her, and walked to the other side of the room. With the lights now on, she could see that the room was larger than she thought. At least twenty feet wide and fifteen feet deep. Computers and monitors filled the space. The man stepped up to a counter and began working a keyboard below a monitor. Schematics appeared on the screen. She could see what appeared to be blueprints. She looked back towards the little entrance door. The man had left the door open. He seemed to be intently looking at information on the computer screen.

She shifted her weight to the right and shuffled to the opposite side of the filing cabinets. She glanced at the man to see if he was still occupied.

"Commodore," a voice crackled from the man's radio. She could see him grab for the receiver on his shoulder.

"Yes, what is it?"

She moved around the back side of the cabinets. She lined herself up, ready to make a dash for the doorway.

"We have a data breach, engineering, top secret information." The man turned. She froze. Blood rushed to her cheeks as she crouched herself into an ever-tighter ball.

"On my way." The man jumped forward and raced out of the little room. He slammed the door shut. She could hear his heavy footsteps racing out of the office outside. She peered up, jumped for the door and pushed it open. She poked her head out; all was clear. She turned back towards the room and jogged over to the computer monitor. A small cartridge, no bigger than her thumb, sat on the desk. She scooped it in to the palm of her hand, and then raced out of the room. She made a mad dash for the office door and stopped in her tracks. She poked her head out. No sign of the man or anyone. She leapt into the hallway and retraced her steps back to the main corridor.

TWELVE

FLUNKED

One Year Earlier — June 7, 2129 — The Colony, Level Seven

"Do you enjoy vibrant social events with lots of people?" Flint paused. *I don't even know what that means.* He rolled his eyes and punched yes.

"It is sometimes acceptable to hurt a person for the good of many people, true or false?" *Good lord, no.* Flint shook his head. *What does any of this have to do with being a guard?*

"Complete the following math problems ...." A series of multiplication problems flashed on the screen. Flint frowned and let out a loud sigh. *Not math!* He did the best he could, but guessed at most of the answers. Five times nine. *Fifty-nine sounded right. I don't know!*

"Do you enjoy discussing different theories on how the world might look like in the future?" *No.*

"How long does it take for wheat to be ready to harvest?" Flint rolled his eyes. *Four months of course.*

A series of questions popped up about crops. Time to ripen, time to harvest, uses. Flint shook his head. He knew the answers but feared the questions were likely to give him another result he didn't want. Maybe he should lie, get some of these wrong. He just couldn't do it.

The test ground on and Flint answered as best he could. The screen flashed white and the familiar voice sounded out "complete, complete." Here was the moment of truth.

"Come on now, give me something good." Flint squinted and held his breath. *Guard, guard, guard.* "Field Hand—level Seven" flashed on the screen. "Dammit!" Flint hit the control panel with his fist. Same as always.

The door to the *probatum* room slid open. He trudged out the passageway and down the corridor. Why did he keep torturing himself like this? He must know by now that his life—his placement —wasn't going to change. Not now and probably not ever.

Every two months for the past year he made the trek to the *probatum* room. The attendant had taken to asking him the same question every time he appeared, "Again?"

At first, he thought he just needed to study more. Learn some math or something like that. He worked with Misty and some of his friends, but that didn't seem to be working. He never was any good at math anyway. Not that he learned much of it. He liked working with his hands and hauling things around. Being a field hand was fine. Just fine. But forever? Like, for the rest of his life?

He saw how the guards, in their sharp black uniforms, seemed to move through the Colony as they pleased. And they had something he didn't, respect. People seemed to respect the guards. Give them compliments, look up to them. Not that they were around much. Or at least they didn't used to be. All growing up he would rarely see a guard on Seven. Probably why they were viewed as being special.

Lately, the guards were around more. In fact, some of his friends —field hands—were being taken up to Five. Guess they must have done well on their *probatum*, though he didn't remember half of them taking *probata*. If they did, they didn't tell him about it. No matter, if they could do it, so could he. So he figured. But it didn't turn out that way.

Flint slumped his shoulders and trudged back to his apartment building. He lived on the second floor. He climbed the steps and turned towards his door. The hallway to his left was open to the outside. The weather was always the same. Seventy-six and "sunny."

"Hey, Flint!"

Flint glanced to his left and shuffled over to the railing. He glanced below and caught sight of his grandfather.

"Hey, granddad."

"How'd you do?"

"Not great. Still a field hand ... on Seven."

"Good for you!" His grandpa held out a thumbs up. "Our whole family is field hands. Nothing wrong with that."

Flint flashed a quick smile and then looked down at the railing. "Yeah, thanks ... granddad. I'm tired. I'm gonna go take a nap or somethin'."

"Alright, well don't be down, boy. Field work is noble work—for the good of the Colony!" His grandpa shuffled off down the walkway. Flint nodded his head.

"Yeah ... noble work. Right." Flint turned and made for his apartment door. He didn't feel like he was doing noble work. Not when his friends were finding new roles up on Five.

THIRTEEN

THE INVITATION

May 1, 2130 — The Colony — Level One

A pair of large, white arched doors marked the entrance to the Hall of
Equals. People were streaming in from all directions. There was no
talking, and most of the dinner guests seemed to look down as they
walked. It felt to Cynthia more like a church than a dinner. She
entered the hall and peered around.

Inside the grand, white doors, the hall was enormous. The walls
arched upwards on all sides. The hall itself appeared to be roughly
circular and the walls arched into the ceiling, which came to a point
at the center. There were larger than life portraits hung on the walls
encircling the entire room. Each portrait had a single person, dressed
in all white, and looking regal, or trying to look regal in any event.
Some pulled it off better than others. The portraits were a mix of men
and women of various ethnicities.

Everyone streaming into the hall was dressed in white, just like
Cynthia. Women wore the same simple white dress and the men
wore white pants with a collarless, white buttoned-down shirt. They
all seemed to know exactly where they were going as they walked

into the hall and made directly for their seat, where they promptly sat down. There was no mingling or small talk. Just walk in and sit.

"Look around the hall and you will see the faces of our past Supreme Principals," said Ember as she approached Cynthia from behind. Cynthia jumped slightly; she was surprised to hear Ember's voice. Cynthia glanced at the large portraits again but was no more impressed than the last time she looked at them several seconds before.

"You are assigned to table thirteen." Ember held out her arm to help usher Cynthia in the right direction.

"Great, thirteen is my lucky number," said Cynthia with a smile. Ember starred back at Cynthia, looking her directly in the eyes, without responding. Cynthia blinked. *No sense of humor here.*

Finally, Ember said, "Please follow me," and brushed past Cynthia. Cynthia turned sheepishly and followed along behind. Apparently, this new world under the sea came without the usual social interactions she was used to back on land. *Who the hell died that everyone is acting so somber?* This was just a dinner party after all, no need to treat it like a wake.

Ember seemed to glide as she walked in her long white dress. Unlike Cynthia, Ember's dress went all the way to the ground, with a small piece that trailed behind her. The dress hid her feet and shoes. Ember's slender figure made her look tall and angelic. Although her stern face and curt words, made her seem decidedly otherwise.

"Here's your table," said Ember as she pointed. "Since you are new, you are required to sit at seat ten." *Geez, are you serious?* Of course, she now knew not to share her thoughts with Ember.

Cynthia responded, "Yes, thank you." She flashed a fake smile at Ember and quickly found her prescribed chair. She sat and looked around her.

"I will be on the dais with the Supreme Principal, we will meet after dinner," said Ember. Cynthia nodded, not knowing what Ember was talking about really. Ember twirled around and glided off towards the center of the room.

People flocked into the great hall and dutifully found their assigned seats. Cynthia's table filled with people in white outfits, none of whom said a word to those around them, or to her. She attempted to make eye contact and smile at her table mates, but to no avail. All eyes were pointed either down at the table or up at the large screens positioned around the center of the room. The room was silent except for the sounds of soft-soled shoes on the floor as people shuffled in and found their places.

A woman approached Cynthia and tapped her on the shoulder. Cynthia looked up with a smile. The woman smiled back and leaned down to speak with her quietly. "Remember me?"

"Ash!" Cynthia jumped up and embraced Ash with both arms. A warm flush raced across her cheeks. She smiled wide and took a half-step backwards. "It's so good to see you." She clasped both her hands on Ash's forearm. "I was worried we wouldn't find each other once I finally got here."

Ash put a finger up to her mouth, "Shhh." She looked around as she and Cynthia sat down. "We aren't supposed to talk, but you look like you needed a little support." Cynthia took her assigned chair number ten; Ash occupied the chair next to her.

"Yes, and makeup ... and some wine," replied Cynthia with a smile.

A man approached the pair and stopped next to Ash. He looked at her expectantly, his eyes darting down and then back up towards the wall. Cynthia smirked and motioned to the man with her chin causing Ash to swing her head back and peer up at him.

"Go to table 18, seat 5," instructed Ash. The man stood starring at Ash for a moment and then turned and followed her instructions without ever uttering a word. Ash turned her attention back to Cynthia.

"Oh ... um ... people get confused where to sit sometimes," Ash rubbed the back of her neck as she bit her lip. She looked over her shoulder and watched the man walk away for a moment before returning her gaze to Cynthia.

Cynthia leaned in a bit closer and said in a hushed tone, "Is it just me, or are people here a bit—"

"Weird," said Ash finishing Cynthia's sentence.

"Yeah, weird. I mean when I talk to Ember she seems to have no sense of humor at all."

"Oh yes, Cosmotine's robot," said Ash with a smile and a laugh. She lowered her head and raised her hand to cover her mouth.

"Why can't people talk here?" asked Cynthia.

Ash looked around and then leaned in close to Cynthia, "New orders of the Supreme Principal. He started this routine almost a year ago. He says it's so we have time to reflect, but really he's deathly afraid of people working against him, speaking negatively about him behind his back." Ash sat back in her chair. Cynthia nodded slowly.

"But we can talk, you and I," continued Ash. "They can't be everywhere at once."

"Who's they?"

"The guards. The people dressed in black. They enforce Cosmotine's rules. They are vigilant here on One, but they can't be everywhere."

Cynthia nodded her head as she slowly looked around the room to spot the people dressed in black. She noticed a couple of them around the main entry doors.

"There are places they cannot find here on One. Places where people can meet and discuss the state of the Colony whether Cosmotine likes it or not." Ash raised an eyebrow as she spoke. Cynthia was not sure why Ash was telling her this, but she gave a knowing nod all the same as if to agree with Ash.

"Listen, I would like you to join me tonight, room 795. A group of us are getting together. Drinks and some jokes. Nothing serious. Meet us there immediately after dinner, ok?"

Cynthia nodded.

"Don't go with Ember. She will try to get you to go to some ... boring thing for new recruits. Just say you don't feel well and come to 795. Got it?"

Cynthia nodded again. "Yes, yes, 795. I'll meet you there." She sat back, alert in her chair.

The lights dimmed slightly throughout the hall, and all eyes turned towards the large screens. A loud, booming voice shot out of the speakers and made its way around the room. "Equals of One, please rise to greet our Supreme Principal." Everyone through the great hall rose to their feet in unison and stood quietly. The Supreme Principal entered from the far side of the room, flanked by a half dozen men in black uniforms. Supreme Principal Cosmotine was smiling broadly and gave a shallow nod of his head to either side of the room as he walked towards the center dais. No one clapped. No one said a word. The room was deathly quiet. As Cosmotine reached the first step onto the dais, a loud gong sound washed over the room. Three gongs in all with a long pause in between each. Cosmotine reached the stage and walked to a single microphone at the center.

"My equals," said Cosmotine as he flashed a broad smile, "I welcome you to tonight's dinner. In this room, on this floor, we are one. Singular in purpose. Our fellow colonists below work for the good of all, but they do not have the vision, the strength, to lead our Colony. For that, we have chosen those among us that have the strength of character, the intelligence, the loyalty, the desire to see our Colony survive and thrive for the next century and beyond. Without our collective fortitude this grand experiment, first in the history of humankind, our beloved home of peace, cannot continue.

"And yet, for all our accomplishments, there are those among us who would seek to end our prosperity." A murmur of disapproval rose around the hall after Cosmotine finished this sentence. From somewhere in the crowd, someone yelled "impossible!"

"No, no, I understand the disbelief you must feel. I too thought it impossible. Why would someone want to end our prosperity, our peaceful lifestyle, our very existence? Where have we gone wrong if there are rebels among us who seek to return to land? Or worse yet, seek to bring the curses of land here, to our Colony?"

"We need to speak with the Masters Twelve!" someone shouted

from the sea of white clothes. Cosmotine looked in the direction of the voice. A tall woman stood up and continued "No one has seen the Masters for over two years, we need their wisdom, their guidance, their vision, why can no one see them?"

Cosmotine squinted slightly. "Seabreeze, thank you for your input," he replied tersely.

"The Masters Twelve have been working hard to manage the Colony," explained Cosmotine. "I do not know why they have not made an appearance among us in such a long time as that is their prerogative. Perhaps they think we need to help ourselves more often and not rely on them with every crisis. However, I do have a message from the Master's now."

The screens switched to a recording of a masked person. The mask was ornately decorated with sea creatures.

The masked figure was seated at a desk, with a dozen other masked people seated around a long oblong table behind. "Thank you, equals, for taking the time to come together in a meal of unity. Unity is the core value of the Colony. Unity of purposes, unity of vision, unity of life. As you know, the Masters Twelve have been working around the clock to help protect and preserve the Colony. There are threats that you need not know about from the outside world. We have successfully kept those threats at bay, but it will not last without our vigilant efforts."

Cynthia noticed that the voice sounded off. It had been digitally modulated and had a slightly mechanical sound to it.

"Our absence from your daily lives, however, is an added blessing to you. You must learn how to survive. You must rise up to be the leaders the Colony needs you to be. You are members of One; our best and our brightest. Supreme Principal Cosmotine needs your support now more than ever. We ask you to join the Supreme Principal to make our Colony safe, and prosperous, for the years ahead."

The screen faded to black and then the view of Cosmotine at the microphone returned. "You see," Cosmotine continued. "The

Masters are working hard for you. I do not know why they choose to work undisturbed."

Seabreeze stood again, this time a more defiant look on her face. "Cosmotine, we will go to see the Masters tonight, we can wait no longer!"

Cosmotine smiled. He looked over to one of the uniformed guards and nodded his head. The guard marched over to Seabreeze. Cosmotine replied, "Of course, Seabreeze, we will take you there immediately so you can see the Masters for yourself." Seabreeze paused and tensed for a moment. Finally, she turned and strode to the nearest door, holding her head high. The guard followed closely behind. They exited the room, and all was quiet.

After the door shut completely, Cosmotine spoke again. "Please sit, eat, and drink to your heart's content. We will worry no more as the Colony will provide for us as it has for so many others for so many years. We will persevere." The crowd gave a hushed, short applause and then everyone sat.

As Cynthia began to sit down, Ash took off towards the nearest exit. She wanted to ask Ash where she was going, but there was no chance. Ash disappeared from the room before Cynthia knew what happened. So she sat by herself, alone again.

She looked down and stared at her plate. She felt no hunger. *Was Seabreeze alone in her convictions? Why was she so defiant?*

FOURTEEN

A HEAD FULL OF STARS

Flint lifted his head as he woke. He felt groggy and confused as to where he was. He looked down and saw his dinner table. He had fallen asleep in his chair after dinner. Lifting his hand to rub his eyes, he saw the photo of the night stars still in his grip. His daydreaming of stars had turned into sleep, where he dreamed not at all.

Flint rose from the table slowly. He was still dressed in his work clothes. Outside, all was quiet and dark, except for the slight blue hue barely glowing from up high. Flint trudged to the bathroom and emptied his bladder. He then turned towards his bed, but he didn't feel like sleeping. He was awake, and now a bit disturbed. The thoughts of stars, land, and life outside the Colony had weighed on him heavily this day. He needed to walk, clear his head. Flint ambled to the door of his apartment and stepped outside.

As he walked down the hallway, he tried to step quietly so as not to disturb his neighbors. He drifted down the stairs and out into the yard. Normally, Flint would walk in the center common area where there were paved paths and benches. But he needed different scenery at the moment, so instead he turned in the direction of the fields across the road and traipsed towards it.

At the back of his apartment complex was a single-lane road, with a shallow field on the other side. He walked down the lane and stopped just before the tube that he had been told many times was one of many elevator shafts that went from One to Ten. Besides the main elevator complex at the center of Seven, where many elevator shafts were amassed around the main freight elevator, there were single elevator shafts throughout the Colony; mostly around the circumference of the structure. There was a small, cement block building built around the base of the tube as it approached the ground. Perhaps there was a door inside to enter and exit the elevator? He didn't know for sure because the door to the cement block room was locked. He had never seen anyone enter or exit the room. But now he wanted to know.

As Flint approached the building, a flash of white light emanated from above. He looked up. He had always thought the tube was solid, but it must have been opaque. He could see a light from up high on the tube. The light was descending. As the light moved closer to the ground, it appeared to grow in size. His eyes followed the light's path downward until it disappeared at the top of the building. *Was that the elevator?*

Before now, Flint had never noticed any light emanating from the tube. He had never seen any light descend from up high. But then again, he had never paid much attention to the tube at all.

He wandered to the cement building and leaned against it. The cement block was cold to the touch and all was quiet. The light was gone, and he couldn't hear anything coming from inside. He bent his knees, slid is back down the block wall and sat in the dirt and waited. There must be some clue, something he could learn if he waited, or observed.

Flint's head became heavy after a while and he began to nod off. His head would dip down and he would wake up fast. Open his eyes, and then close them again. He repeated this sequence several times before finally succumbing to the sleep washing over him.

He was jolted awake by the sound of machinery coming from

inside the cement block building. He looked up quickly and then got to his feet. He could hear the sound of metal hinges creaking open. He slid to the corner of the building and peaked around. The large, locked metal door was around the corner. He watched and waited. He saw the doorknob on the door move to the left, and then the door swung open. Two men dressed in all black emerged from the opening. One of the men grabbed a large rock and placed it at the foot of the door to keep it from closing.

"What the heck is this?" said one of the men in black. "I thought we were near the tavern."

"No, we used the back elevator, remember," replied the other man. "We are in the middle of the harvest fields. I'm just stepping out to take a smoke." With that, one of the men sat down, produced a cigarette from his pocket and lit it.

"You know, you're not supposed to smoke in the Colony, Granite."

"Yeah, I know smart acre, but I have to work with you, Basalt, and you're a pain in everyone's rear."

Basalt gave a shrug of his shoulders as if to say "whatever." He remained standing and surveyed the dark field by looking around slowly. He failed to notice Flint peaking at them from the corner of the building. "You know now that I take a better look at it Seven isn't so bad. I kinda like this idyllic, rural lifestyle." Basalt put his hands on his hips.

"Well they would love to have you working behind a plow, dummy. If you talk to the boss, I'm sure he could arrange a transfer. Personally, I think Seven is a bunch of manure and hicks, but we need 'em right?"

"Whatever, I'm just saying Seven isn't so bad." Basalt lowered his hands from his hips and turned to look down at Granite sitting on the ground. "Sure beats Ten. I haven't taken someone to Ten in a while, and I never enjoy seeing that place. So, depressing down there."

"Yeah, well I have a feeling we're going to be taking more and more of those white-robbed jerks from One down to Ten for the foreseeable future. Old Cosmotine has his panties in a bunch and wants to purge half of them … maybe more." He took a long drag of his cigarette and then flicked the ashes off in the dirt.

"You think the group we brought down tonight were really rebels?" asked Basalt.

"Doubt it. They looked like scarred little rabbits. They couldn't rebel against their own togas if they wanted to," answered Granite.

"You done with that cigarette, man? We need to get back upstairs, or someone is going to send you to Ten."

Granite stood and flicked what was left of his cigarette out into the dirt. He spun around and looked at Basalt. With the wave of his hand he said, "After you, your majesty" with mock deference. The two disappeared into the building. Granite kicked the rock away and slammed the metal door shut with a loud clang. The machinery inside whirred into life again, and the light from the tube rose from the block building and made its way back up into the night sky.

That's definitely the elevator, thought Flint. *And I need to be on it.* Flint was now more determined than ever to find a way into the elevator shaft and ride that white light to freedom.

FIFTEEN

LIEUTENANT FRANK

Seven Years Earlier — June 5, 2123 — Pacific Theatre, Alliance War

Cynthia picked herself up off the cold metal of the ship's deck and stumbled to the nearest bulkhead. She glanced around and eyed an open hatch. Metal beams and debris littered the room. She couldn't walk straight to the hatch, but if she squeezed through a fallen bulkhead, she could see a way to the door.

She took several steps towards her escape route and the ship lurched hard to starboard, nearly knocking her down. She threw both arms around a metal support beam and waited until the ship settled. Her head was in a fog. She reached up to touch her forehead. It was covered in slick, wet blood emanating from the top of her head. She knew she had to move if she were to survive. She could smell the smoke getting nearer ... thicker.

"Lieutenant Frank!" A man's voice wafted across the room. She glanced to her right and saw a young man lying on the floor. The floor was slanted to starboard making it difficult to walk. Cynthia edged her way along the hull and then used the support beams to steady her advance towards the young man.

"Sailor, are you able to walk?"

The young man glanced down at his legs. A large gash ran down his left thigh. He placed his hands on the floor and began hoisting himself up. He groaned and fell back down. Cynthia reached under his arm and leaned backwards.

"Lean on me and push up with your right leg," she ordered. The young sailor did as instructed. He hopped on his right leg and flung his arm around Cynthia's shoulder.

"Alright, let's move together. We need to get outside." As they neared the hatch, Cynthia could hear voices outside. Men and women scurried about following orders barked by an unseen voice.

"Damn," mumbled the young solider. "What happened Lieutenant?"

"We were hit. Alliance ship. They couldn't wait to tear us apart." Cynthia struggled under the weight of the young man. Her head began to throb as blood trickled into her left eye. She stopped to wipe her eyes. "Hold on. Give me a sec."

"We didn't even have a chance to fire." The young sailor's breath was getting heavier. She figured he must be losing blood pretty fast. Must keep him moving to get help if there was any help out there to find.

Cynthia repositioned the sailor's arm over her shoulder and stepped forward. *I should have ordered the crew to fire sooner. I know better than that.* The battle simulations had been so much easier. The assignment was known. The pace of the battle was slower. The enemy ships were clearly defined. In a real battle everything was chaos. She wasn't sure it was an enemy ship. Her gut said yes, her mind wavered. She was just about to order the crew to fire their stock of laser missiles when they were hit and her world went dark. Now all they could do was try to survive.

Cynthia glanced around the room as they neared the exit hatch.

Some of her subordinates lay lifeless at their battle stations. Many had already escaped through the hatch. She wondered what the rest of the destroyer looked like. She guided the young sailor through the hatch and out a series of passageways until they were on the open deck. Another explosion rocked the stern of the destroyer throwing both of them against the side railing. They slid down and sat on the deck of the ship. Sailors making up the damage control crew ran in every direction trying to contain the fires. Cynthia reached up and placed her hand over the top of her head. She winced in pain. She could feel a large gash at the top of her skull and her hair was matted with blood.

"We need to get you two on the life hover boats." A petty officer ran up and stood beside the wounded pair. He motioned with his hands; calling over a group of sailors. "Grab these two and take them to boat three. Get them off quickly, we got more wounded around the corner."

The sailors reached down and lifted the pair to their feet. They scurried over to the side of the ship and lowered them into a boat that was perched over the railing. A couple dozen sailors were already aboard. A dozen more were added to the small craft and then it was lowered into the sea by the wire cables attached to each end.

As the hover boat descended, Cynthia grabbed the top of her shirt sleeve and ripped it off. She removed it from her arm and tied it tight around the sailor's upper thigh creating a tourniquet for his wounded leg. Then she ripped off her other sleeve and wrapped it around the top of her head and under her chin. Cynthia glanced around and realized she was the ranking officer on the boat. She clambered to the back of the boat and grabbed for the engine starter. The hover motors whirred to life as the boat glided just above the waves. Once the craft was stable over the water, she ordered her newly assembled crew to remove the cables. She grabbed the controls and steered it hard to port moving away from the damaged destroyer. She knew she had to get as much distance between them and the destroyer as possible. If it went down, the wake could take them with it.

Cynthia glanced up into the night sky. The stars were clear. She got her bearings and guided the craft due North. She glanced back down to take stock of the crew she had on board. Three dozen sailors, most of whom were wounded. Most were enlisted men and women. She looked to see if a petty officer was aboard. They weren't out of danger yet and she needed help.

"Hey, petty officer, what's your name?"

"Stevens, Ma'am." A younger man near the front of the boat turned to address Cynthia. "Alright Stevens, keep watch ahead. And then place a sailor on lookout port and starboard. The Alliance ships could be anywhere, and we don't want to run into one if we can avoid it."

"Aye, aye, Ma'am." Stevens moved around the boat and positioned his lookouts. The moon was full. The surrounding swells shimmered from the bright moonlight. Cynthia swiveled her head back and forth. She glanced aft making sure there were no enemy ships near. The Alliance wasn't supposed to be an enemy. A private Navy built to protect the oil platforms of Hall Enterprises. It had been formed a hundred years ago to defend against pirates but recently its mission had changed. In the past decade, oil had become scarce, but demand remained high. The U.S. decided no oil could be sold to foreign governments. Hall Enterprises disagreed—their allies around the world joined them. The Alliance was born. Cynthia hadn't bargained on being at war when she joined the Navy. But then who does?

"Stevens, you see any weapons aboard this boat?" Cynthia figured it was only a matter of time before they ran into trouble.

"Aye, ma'am, we have a dozen assault rifles."

"Power them up. We won't be alone for long." She heard the stories. "Prisoners of War" had a way of becoming "Killed in Action" when the Alliance captured them. The life boat's engine strained under the weight of the boat and its crew. The hover boat could only float a foot above the surface. The swells rose around them, lifting the boat up and down in rhythmic fashion. Cynthia worked the controls, keeping the boat on course as best she could. Every now and again she had to steer off course to take a swell head-on rather than let it hit athwart the hull. Once the swell passed, she corrected course.

"Ma'am, ship to starboard!" a soldier called out. Cynthia glanced to her right. She could see the faint outline of a destroyer five knots off the starboard side. She killed the engine. The hover boat settled into the water, rocking slowly back and forth in the sea.

"Kill the lights and keep down." The crew complied and everyone lowered themselves below the railing.

"Is it Alliance?" asked Stevens.

"Don't know. They look the same from here. Just keep quiet, we'll know soon enough." Cynthia kept her eyes trained on the distant ship. It looked to be steaming ahead at full speed.

"If it's friendly, we should shoot a marker beacon," said Stevens. "We need to get their attention to pick us up."

"And if it's Alliance? You still want to shoot a beacon for the whole dang ocean to see?" Cynthia spoke in a hushed tone. Shooting beacons at unknown ships wasn't a great idea, in her opinion. "Just stay put. We need to be certain." She wasn't about to risk the lives of three dozen wounded sailors without knowing for sure.

Stevens picked his way through the sailors to crouch next to Cynthia. "But ma'am," he whispered. "Some of these sailors, their wounds are severe. They won't make it if we don't get them help soon."

Cynthia glanced to her left and surveyed her wounded crew. Stevens was right. There were some people badly hurt. They needed help. She glanced back at the distant destroyer. She was taught at Annapolis how to spot a friendly ship versus an Alliance ship. The silhouette was different. Not by a lot, but enough. She lifted her head above the railing. She steadied herself as best she could and studied the dark outline against the moonlight.

"Can you tell?" asked Stevens.

Cynthia strained her eyes. Her head was still throbbing. She had to choose. Was it friendly or was it not? She studied the dark silhouette of the ship a bit longer. She knew the answer in her gut, but her mind wavered. Was it really? Could it be?

She reached back to the helm and opened a door below the control panel. She grabbed the marker beacon, positioned it in her palm and touched the sides with her thumb and fore finger. The beacon leapt into the air. It propelled itself high above and flashed a bright red light along with a piercing siren. Cynthia kept her eyes on the distant ship. It slowly turned towards them. Bright searchlights flicked on. Their run was over. They were about to be saved ... or be slaughtered. In several short minutes, they would have their answer for sure.

SIXTEEN

A CHANGE OF COURSE

**May 1, 2130 — The Colony — Level One,
Hall of Equals**

"Now that you all have enjoyed the bountiful harvest of our Colony, I would like to introduce our newest recruits." Supreme Principal Cosmotine rose and smiled as he spoke. A man Cynthia did not recognize approached her and signaled her to follow. A half dozen other people stood at this moment and meandered to the front of the room. Some of them seemed eager, with large smiles on their faces. Others appeared more timid and looked around with worried glances. Cynthia stood giving off no emotion at all. She walked deliberately towards the middle of the room. The recruits were ushered to a set of stairs leading onto the main stage. They spread out behind Cosmotine.

"These recruits will join One," stated Cosmotine, "to help the colony continue to operate peacefully, and efficiently. But as with all new recruits, they must first receive their new names. You new recruits have not just elected a new life you also have the opportunity for a new beginning. Your new name signifies your first step on the road of your new life."

Cosmotine looked back at the recruits with a large smile as if he had just bestowed a gift on each of them. The recruits starred back with blank looks on their faces.

"Every name in the Colony takes it origin from nature," continued Cosmotine. "Earth, water, fire, and air provide the inspiration for our names. The Colony is an assemblage of these elements, and our names reflect this fact."

"Cynthia, please approach." Cosmotine spoke while looking directly at Cynthia and waving his hand. It was as if he could read her thoughts and knew he needed to start with her.

"You have come to the Colony and we are delighted to have you here. We now give you your new name," said Cosmotine.

There was a pause and then a name flashed on the screens above, "Tephra!"

"Tephra, I welcome you to the Colony!" Cosmotine said with uncharacteristic enthusiasm. The entire hall erupted in wild applause. Suddenly, the subdued nature of the place vanished, and the crowd cheered enthusiastically. Cynthia's hand flew to her chest. *What is happening with the crowd? What is a Tephra?* Her eyes grew wide and she peered around.

After several seconds, she shook the shock from her head and advanced forward to shake Cosmotine's hand. Cosmotine grasped her hand firmly and smiled. He leaned forward and whispered in her ear, "Mind who you interact with, Tephra, the Colony can be a dangerous place for new comers." He moved away and continued "now, please hold your applause, let's continue to our next, new recruit."

Tephra felt a hand pull on her arm. She turned and was guided off the stage. She was taken to the nearest door and ushered into a small waiting room. The room had white chairs positioned against the walls. "Please take a seat, Tephra. We will be with you shortly," the person guiding her said quietly before disappearing back out the door.

She took a few steps towards a chair when her feet stopped. She looked straight ahead as her hand rose to touch the base of her neck. *What just happened?* The name, the sudden exploding applause. *Was it real?* She turned and looked back at the door. She could hear the faint bass from the speakers filling the hall just outside with the deep voice of Cosmotine. *What am I waiting here for?*

Everything had happened so fast. Where would Ember take her after the naming ceremony was over? Ash mentioned something about that. And what did Ash want with her? Questions swirled around in her head. She wasn't going to get any answers sitting here in this room by herself. *I need to see what Ash wants. Maybe find a few more answers.*

She glanced at a set of double doors on the wall opposite the door she used to enter the room. She trotted to the double doors and pushed her way through. She looked quickly to her right and then left. A long stretch of hallway looked identical in either direction. She turned right and jogged as fast as her short stride would take her down the hallway.

She made several random turns down various hallways until she picked up room numbers close to 795. 750, 760, 789, she was close. She came to the designed door and stopped short. *Was this the right thing to do?* She shook the thought out of her head and reached out to knock on the door. Before her hand could make contact, the door slid open automatically. Ash stood looking at her on the other side.

"Oh my ... Tephra ... hello." Ash smiled. "I was just about to go out looking for you. Don't want you getting lost."

Tephra wrinkled her brow. "Tephra? You know my new name?"

Ash giggled and reached out for Tephra's hand. "Of course, we all know. It's not a secret. See, we have it on the monitor." Ash guided Tephra into the room with one hand while she pointed to a large monitor mounted on the wall with her free hand. The screen showed what looked like a live feed from the Hall of Equals. Tephra nodded her acknowledgement.

Tephra looked around the large room. She was surprised to see a few dozen people standing, milling about, talking.

"There's refreshments over there," said Ash with a wave of her hand. "Why don't you grab something ... wine probably for you ... and I'll meet up with you in a bit." Tephra nodded as Ash turned and disappeared through a group of people.

Tephra pushed through the crowd, poured herself a small glass of wine and turned to survey the room. A group of six stood to her right talking among themselves.

"Are you all equals? All got recruited to One?" Tephra asked.

"We weren't called equals before Cosmotine, you know," a man in the small group was looking directly at Tephra. Her eyes locked on his and she gave a quick smile. "That was his idea. His convention." She nodded, not sure what to say in response.

"And yet we seem to be less equal than before, aren't we Gypsum?" added a woman standing in the group. Tephra took a small step forward to join the circle of discussion. The others moved slightly back to make room for her.

"True, when we were merely part of the executive class we were far more equal than we are now. Funny how things can change in a year or two." Gypsum's green eyes shot away from the woman asking her question and locked back on Tephra. She glanced down.

"Perhaps a new name, a new routine, provides cover for something else." Each person in the circle took turns adding their thoughts to the growing conversation. Tephra sipped her wine while her eyes darted from one person speaking to another.

"A misnomer, is that what you are implying?"

"Indeed. Call us equals when we are not. You can call a ferocious bear a friendly dog, but the animal remains the same."

Tephra twisted her lips. "I don't understand any of this. I thought this was a great place where skills were tested, and people put in their optimum job and everyone worked toward the greater good without the greed of money getting in the way."

"Yes, that correctly describes the Colony," said Gypsum. "It does not correctly describe Cosmotine, unfortunately."

"So why is he still in charge?"

"We don't know for sure. In the past the Masters Twelve would resolve such dilemmas for us. Supreme Principals who went off their approved paths would either be counseled or removed."

"And the Supreme Principal was not allowed to bring guards up here to One," added a woman.

"There was never a guard who stepped foot on One for nearly fifty years before Cosmotine. Except for their leader, the Commodore, of course. But he would come alone to confer with the Masters, the Supreme, and other executive class people."

"Wait," said Tephra, "you mean the guards in black uniforms? Weren't they escorting Cosmotine into the hall tonight at dinner?"

"Yes, those are the guards. And yes they were indeed 'escorting' Cosmotine. My point exactly."

"The Masters Twelve are supposed to protect us," said another man who had been silent up until now. "The Supreme has absolute authority, he answers only to the Masters. They protect the Colony way."

"So why have they not done so?" asked Tephra.

"We do not know."

"No one has seen a Master in over two years!" The group of people began adding their thoughts at random once more.

"Cosmotine took over as Supreme Principal nearly five years ago."

"I think he has done something to them." Tephra's eyes darted around the group as they spoke in turn.

"Wrapped them around his finger, at a minimum. Hopefully nothing worse than that."

"If only we could see them, talk to them."

"That's why we are here after all, to help them."

The group paused as each person seemed to ponder their conversation. A woman turned and walked towards a different group of people. She said nothing as she left.

Tephra glanced at the others still standing in the little group. They all seemed so down. As if there was nothing that could be done about the situation they were in. All resigned to their fate. *This can't be right.* "So why stand here talking about it? Why not do something, like confront Cosmotine?"

"Not so easy, my dear," replied Gypsum. "Challenging the Supreme is tantamount to challenging the Masters, which is the same as challenging the Colony itself. The Supreme speaks for the Masters, he is their representative."

"Besides," added a man to Tephra's left, "the changes have been made slowly over time. Being called equals sounded good at first. No one fully realized the dilemma until much had changed. Even the guards have been brought onto One in a clever fashion, I think."

"Under the guise of training," added Gypsum. "As if an entire platoon could learn from the executive level."

"We didn't know it was an entire platoon though, did we?"

The man shook his head. "No, we didn't."

"And what of Seabreeze?" asked the man. "She made a foolish move tonight, I think."

"Yes, it was rash," said Gypsum. "She was fed up, no doubt, but it was a mistake to challenge Cosmotine so openly. I tried to warn her, but—"

"Maybe you need to be cleverer than he is." Tephra answered. "He's just a man after all, right?" Gypsum smiled and nodded his head. He took a slow drink from his glass and then tiled his head sideways.

"You took your *probatum* right, Tephra. Did you see your results?"

"No. I was just told I had been chosen for One."

A woman on Tephra's right scoffed. "No one should be chosen for One; they should be placed on One because of their *probatum.*"

"Wait, did you all see your results?"

"Yes." Gypsum took Tephra's hand. "Our results showed us One. We see the results so we know where our skills have placed us. No surprises, no accidents. Your results might have also been One, but it is odd you weren't allowed to see them, and you were told you were chosen, not placed."

"So, do I not belong on One then?"

Gypsum reached his hand to his jaw. He slowly rubbed the stubble on his chin. "That's the question, isn't it? That's the question we must answer."

SEVENTEEN

THE REBEL LIST

"Run, Ember, run!" She heard the voice but couldn't turn to look. Fear filled her mind. Her body coursed with adrenaline. She gripped her rail gun in her hands and raced from behind the door. She ran as fast as her legs could carry her leaving the little shack behind. The large field filled with waist-high wheat stretched on for what seemed like miles. A row of trees rimmed the edge of the field. Ember fixed her gaze on the trees looking for traces of small-arms fire. She moved her finger onto the trigger; ready to raise her weapon and fire. Her legs burned with pain from sprinting. As she neared the tree line a deafening explosion rang out all around her. She flew into the air and landed with a thud on top of a low growing bush. Pain shot through her arm and shoulder. Ember glanced into the air. Dirt and rocks showered down on top of her. The rocks turned red as body parts began to fill the air around her. Arms and legs rained down instead of dirt and rocks. Her eyes went wide. She opened her mouth and screamed using all the air in her lungs. Everything turned pitch black.

Ember sat up. Her forehead was filled with sweat; hair matted to her head. Her heart was racing. She grabbed her arm and looked at it.

All was fine. Another nightmare. She pushed the covers off her legs and swung them to the ground. Her small bed was low to the floor. She placed both hands on her temples and slowed her breathing. When would they stop? Memories of her past life: fighting, running, surviving ... barely.

Ember shook her head and stood. She clambered over to the bathroom and grabbed a glass sitting by the sink. She filled it and took a sip of cool water. She glanced up and caught sight of her face in the mirror. She had aged considerably over the past several years. But she could still see the frightened child in her face. The terror of living day-to-day with no hope of survival.

She sniffed and put her glass down on the counter. The nightmares came and went from time to time. But why had they come back so regularly now? Nearly every night. Waking up in a cold sweat. What was she afraid of? She had come so far.

She turned and slipped into the living room. The lights flicked on as she walked in. She sat on the couch and rubbed her right temple with the palm of her hand. Her head throbbed. She felt exhausted. Another tiring day trying to ensure order in a world built to prevent war. Yet, chaos seemed ready to grip her and her new world at any moment.

Cosmotine's voice echoed through her head. "Find out who is friendly with Seabreeze," he commanded before she left the Hall that night. Ember had a feeling that Seabreeze was dangerous. She clearly had no qualms about directly challenging the Supreme Principal in public. "What has this Colony come to when the Supreme Principal is challenged so openly," said Ember to herself.

Two decades before her parents escaped certain death by joining the Colony. A recruiter came to their small village perched on a hill in the middle of the Balkans. They had been fighting a war that they don't remember starting. Trying to survive with little hope of a peaceful future. The promise of a peaceful life, built on science and reason, was too good to pass up. The Colony did not disappoint. Her family had thrived here. She had taken to farming on Seven until her first *probatum* placed her as an engineering apprentice on Four. She took her studies seriously, wanting to help keep her new home safe—and more importantly peaceful. She loved the Colony's peace, efficiency, and most of all, its order. Things were predictable in the Colony because its laws and rules were precise.

After a chance encounter with a young man placed on One, she was whisked away to become his apprentice. Cosmotine was his name. He had grand ideas, and charismatic energy. She was swept up in his vision of a future that had no bounds. On One she was taught far more complex subjects than were offered on Four. She was too young to be a member of One, equals were supposed to be at least thirty-two, but as Cosmotine's apprentice, she could live and learn there temporarily. When her apprenticeship ended she returned to Four and continued her studies. She developed her skills quickly. Cosmotine took notice.

After working for several years as a full-fledged engineer on Four, she sat for a *probatum*. She was placed on One at the age of twenty-seven; five years below the traditional age requirement. How had it happened? She had never seen her results. Was it a violation of the order she loved so much in the Colony? And was it that Cosmotine had suggested; that it wasn't her *probatum* that placed her here?

No. Her placement on One felt right. Her *probatum* placed her here. She shook her head and walked over to her small kitchen; she had a job to do. She opened a small fridge and took out a container of clear liquid. She poured a small glass and put the container to her mouth. She threw her head back and emptied the glass. She let out a breath. "To peace and order," she mumbled to herself. She poured another small glass of the clear liquid and gulped it down.

Ember sauntered over to a desk in her living room and lowered herself into a slender white chair. She punched several buttons on a keyboard in front of her. A large computer monitor flicked to life. She began searching through various computer files.

Two years ago, Cosmotine had begun a policy of weeding out dissenters and detractors from One. Ember searched through a list of files. Each file was titled with the name of a different equal. She found the file for Seabreeze and opened it. A list of subfolders sprang onto the screen. Actions, conversations, viewpoints, and connections were the titles of the various subfolders.

Cosmotine had started slowly, ridding One of a few equals over several months. But in the last twelve months he had quickened his pace, ridding One of over three dozen equals. Ember was delighted. Dissenters caused chaos. There was no room for chaos in her Colony.

Ember opened the contacts subfolder and a long list of names appeared before her. Apparently, Seabreeze had made quite a few friends among the equals of One. *Not good*, thought Ember. *Not good at all.*

Ember downloaded the list of connections onto her data pad. She sat back and tilted her head up. What has this Colony come to when so many equals seem content to challenge their leader? No matter. She would go see Commodore Topaz first thing in the morning. Time was running short. Dissenters must be caught and rehabilitated. There was no other way to ensure order. Of that, she was certain.

EIGHTEEN

THE RECRUITER

Flint woke up next to the metal door on the block building. He had tried to open the door after the guards left, but it wouldn't budge. He knew he had to keep trying, but now was not the time. It was morning and Misty would be expecting him at the warehouse soon. If he didn't show up, there'd be trouble.

Flint lifted himself up, dusted himself off, and sprinted back to his apartment. He had to shower and change quickly. He was expected at the warehouse in twenty minutes, he had little time to spare.

Flint rushed into the warehouse.

"Sorry Misty, I got caught up at the complex and I made my way over here as quickly .... " Flint stopped in his tracks when he spotted the stoic look on Misty's face, a look Flint had never seen before. He glanced left and saw a guard. The man wore a black uniform with gold stripes on his shoulder. There were six more guards lined up behind him, but their outfits had no gold stripes. Flint slowly turned his broad shoulders to square off in front of the guard.

At six foot, seven inches, Flint made a sizable impression. Far taller and more muscular than any of his co-workers. The guard with the gold stripes on his shoulder smiled.

Misty gave a sideways glance at Flint and whispered out the side of her mouth, "You should've stayed home today."

"What do we have here?" The guard walked closer to Flint and craned his neck back to look into Flint's eyes. "I am Captain Rotifer of the Colony Guards. Give me your name, field worker."

"Flint, sir."

"Flint, I think you might make an excellent guard. We need good, strong men who can follow orders. Does that sound like you, Flint?" He smiled as he ended his sentence and looked closely at Flint's eyes awaiting a response.

"You bet that's me. Why just ask Misty here, I follow orders all the time, don't I Misty?" Flint turned his head towards Misty with a big smile on his face. Misty looked up at Flint with a stern look, and squinted eyes, as if to say, "shut up you moron."

Flint knew the "shut up you moron" look because he saw it several times per week. Flint didn't care this time. Sure Misty was concerned for him, but he knew what he wanted. He would be a great guard. Maybe the higher-ups had finally seen the promise in Flint too. Plus, he saw the men dressed all in black at the cement block building. They were able to come and go as they pleased. They were able to ride that beautiful, glowing white elevator into the sky. That black uniform clearly meant something important that allowed them to go where Flint could not. He wanted that uniform. He didn't care so much about the guards anymore, about Captain what's his name, nor about why they wanted Flint to join. He just wanted the keys to the Colony—that looked like freedom for sure.

"Do I get to wear one of those black uniforms your men have on back there?" Flint had an expectant look on his face like a child about to receive a new toy.

Captain Rotifer smirked. "Yes, if chosen you will be given the Colony guard uniform, the same as the rest."

"Flint stand over there, by the guards in their black uniforms," said Captain Rotifer.

Flint jumped forward and sprinted over to the guards. He stood at the end of their row and straightened his shoulders. He put his chest out slightly. He wanted to look the part even though he was wearing an old t-shirt and dirty overalls.

"Captain, please reconsider," pleaded Misty. "Flint looks big and muscular, but he is not fit to serve as one of your guards. You need people who can think for themselves, self-motivated types. That's not Flint. Not by a long shot. Besides he took the *probatum* half a dozen times ... been placed back here on Seven each time."

"You are a crop supervisor, correct?" asked Captain Rotifer. Misty nodded her head in agreement. "And I am a captain of the Colony Guards. Let me decide who is, and who is not, fit for service in the guards, and I will let you decide who is fit for service as your field hands. He will take a *probatum*, to be sure, but I know a good candidate when I see one." Captain Rotifer flashed a quick, fake smile at Misty and then brushed past her. He walked down the line of field hands looking them over from head to toe.

Captain Rotifer walked up and down the line of men and selected five more recruits. He marched back to Misty and curtly said, "That will do, good day."

The six new recruits were ushered by the six colony guards into a large van. The Captain hoped into the passenger's seat. Flint looked out the window and saw Misty welling up with tears. For a moment, he wondered if he had made the right choice, but then he remembered the tube and the freedom, and he turned around and didn't glance back again.

NINETEEN
COMMODORE'S PURSUIT

"We had an incident at the hall of equals last night." Ember entered Commodore Topaz' office on Five and sat in a chair opposite his desk. Topaz was head of the Colony guards.

"Yes, I am aware." Topaz was glancing at his data pad, scrolling through pages. He shifted his gaze towards Ember, put down his data pad, and placed both hands on the desk in front of him.

"We need to find her cohorts," continued Ember.

"Hmmm." Topaz leaned back in his chair and folded his hands in his lap. "Do we know who they are?"

"Yes, well most of them anyway. I've compiled a list."

Topaz nodded. "All equals?"

"Yes."

"Still on One?"

"Yes."

Topaz sighed. He sat straight up in his chair and reached for the comm link on his desk. He entered a sequence of numbers and held the comm link to his ear. "Meet me at the guard station on One. Bring your scout team. What? No just the scout team. Let's keep this controlled." Topaz slammed the comm link down in its cradle.

"You will exercise discretion, yes?"

"Of course!" Topaz' eyes widened. "I know the drill to root out an equal—using *discretion.*"

"Good." Ember stood and crossed her arms. She leered down at Topaz. "This is the biggest group we have asked you to detain so far. You need to be more careful than usual. We don't want it causing a panic ... or worse yet, an all-out riot. Understand?"

Topaz' eyes narrowed. "Yes, I understand perfectly. Why don't you accompany me up to One? You can see for yourself." Topaz rose and grabbed a long baton from his desk. He placed the baton on his holster and pushed past Ember as he left his office. Ember smiled and turned to follow behind. She always enjoyed getting under Topaz's skin.

The pair marched down the hallway and entered the elevator lobby of Five. Topaz mashed the call button and stepped back from the lift door. A garbled voice rang out from the radio receiver strapped to Topaz' shoulder. He grabbed for the receiver. "Lock down sector four." His eyes flashed over to Ember who looked back at him with a stern look set on her face. "And use discretion. Only those who are on the list should be detained. Take them to the primary conference chamber as soon as you find one. No delay."

"Yes, sir," the garbled voice called out from the receiver.

The lift arrived and the elevator doors slid open. Topaz hopped aboard and Ember glided onto the lift behind him. The doors shut and the elevator began its ascent to One.

"Where will these equals be sent?" asked Topaz.

"To Ten for rehabilitation, of course."

"Geez, that will make close to thirty in just over four months."

"Would you like to take up that issue with Supreme Principal Cosmotine?"

Topaz frowned and looked over towards Ember. She held her gaze on the elevator door. "No, if those are his orders, then I will comply."

Ember smirked. She knew Topaz wouldn't dare confront Cosmotine. She turned her head and set her gaze on Topaz. "The primary target is an equal by the name of Ash. We believe she was Seabreeze's second-in-command."

Topaz nodded. "Fine. We'll start there."

As soon as the elevator stopped and the doors were open, Topaz leapt from the lift. "I'll meet you in the primary conference chamber after we have our captives." He turned and raced up the corridor. Ember stepped off the elevator and watched the Commodore. She scoffed. *Such a fool, but so far you've played your part well.* She turned and glided up the hallway towards her office.

As Ember neared her office Supreme Principal Cosmotine emerged from a nearby corridor. He strode by her, flanked by a crew of six Colony guards.

"What has come of my request, Ember?" asked Cosmotine with a stern tone in his voice. He spoke without stopping. Ember jump forward and rushed along beside him to keep up.

"Supreme, we have compiled a list of rebels with contacts to Seabreeze, fifteen in all. Commodore Topaz has been given the list and has ordered a complete lockdown of sector four. He is personally leading the search for the rebels. We will have them soon."

Cosmotine's stern look softened. "Good, good," he said as he continued striding down the hallway. "I want regular updates from Topaz, let him know to notify me immediately once anyone is found. Hold all rebels on One until I have a chance to personally interrogate them." Ember nodded.

"Supreme, there is one more issue, a new recruit is missing, she did not return to her room last night and—"

"Which new recruit?" Cosmotine asked as his face hardened and his brow furrowed, his teeth noticeable clenching under his lips.

"Tephra."

"You see, I told you the new recruits would bring the rebels out of hiding. Seabreeze and her dissenters will pay dearly for taking my new recruit. We may have to implement a new punishment, Ember. I have devised a little surprise for the rebels. We will test it out on the first person Topaz captures," sneered Cosmotine.

"Yes, Supreme." Ember was not aware of any new method of punishment. *What was it? What could be worse than being sent to Ten?* She wondered.

"You will soon see, Ember, that the equals of One will learn to respect their Supreme Principal or they will be destroyed. Now we have them where we want them." Cosmotine was looking out into the distance as he spoke. Ember could almost see him thinking, but she sensed that there were many plans to which she was not privy.

"I will be in my chambers. I want you to oversee this search with Topaz. Do not let the guards make any foolish mistakes." He marched off with this half dozen personal bodyguards marching behind, leaving Ember standing alone.

Ember watched as Cosmotine left. She was confused. This was the largest group of equals to be rounded up, that was one thing. But a new punishment? Something had changed. Cosmotine had hardened. Hopefully, the new punishment would end the dissent. She couldn't fathom why anyone would disobey a command from the Supreme Principal, unless it violated an order from the Masters Twelve.

Ember shook off the heavy thoughts and rushed to find Topaz. For now, she needed to oversee the hunt for the rebels. She wanted to see them for herself. Hear what they had to say. And most importantly, find Tephra.

TWENTY

THE BIG RETREAT

A Century Earlier — June 29, 2030 — Colony Engineering Offices

"That's right, Mr. Hall, the entire engineering and scientific staff—several thousands in all if you count their family members. Can you believe it?" Leo spoke into his mobile phone after picking up a call from John Hall. It was only a month ago that the decision had been made to move the entire engineering and scientific team to the Colony. Leo hadn't bothered to mention it to John Hall. Why bother? His directive was clear. Hit the deadline or else.

"No, Leo, I can't believe it because you are all out of your frickin' minds!" Leo's heart skipped a beat. *Why the anger?* "You can't go, Leo, for one. And your department heads need to stay too."

"Whatever for? You want us to meet the deadline. What better way than to work on-site, right in the Colony? The life support systems are up and running—for the most part."

"And what about the other colonists—the starting class?"

"Yes, they are at the Colony now along with most of our team who—"

"You idiot! What the heck are you thinking?"

"Well we are meeting our mandate as you required us to. Why is this a problem?"

"Publicity! You understand that concept, you scientific moron!" Leo held the phone back from his ear.

"I ... I ... I don't understand."

"No, you don't understand because now I won't be able to take you and your other nerds on a world-wide trip to spread the good news of MY most important accomplishment! You get it?"

Leo bit his lip and looked down at his worn shoes.

"And another thing, Leo, I was supposed to lead the initial colonists to the Colony. Me!"

"I had no idea you intended to live in the Colony, sir."

"Not live there forever, just to lead them there. Stay a while, get the photos out of the way and then head back. You know, show everyone that I am leading the way!"

"But sir, that's not so easy to do because of the—"

"Look Leo, you either drop this stupid idea or there will be consequences! You understand me? I won't let you ruin my crowning achievement. I'm considered a saint to humanity because of this project!"

"Well ... sir ... I ... "

"Stop stammering Doc, just put a stop to this now!" The line went dead, and Leo glanced at his phone. He stared out the window of his little office. *Now what?*

"David—David!" Leo stormed out of his office and nearly ran headlong into his chief engineer.

"Leo, what? What is it?" The short chubby man was panting from having run a few short steps to reach Leo' office.

"We have to leave now!"

"What? What do you mean leave now?"

"Mr. Hall was upset. He was very upset."

"What? Why?"

"He was very cross at the idea of us moving to the Colony."

"Why? I thought it was a great idea."

"Yes, well he didn't seem to agree with our assessment. How many of our people have already left for the Colony?"

"Everyone. You, me, and our direct staff is all that's left."

"When can we leave?"

"Ah ... I don't know. Let's see." David rubbed his temple with his hand. "We should be ready to leave by tonight. Tomorrow morning at the latest."

Leo wrung his hands as he nodded his head. "Ok, good, good. Well, let's get a move on. We need to set sail immediately."

"Ok, ok. I'll finish our preparations. Guess you better pack your toothbrush. We won't be coming back."

"Yes, yes, I know."

David turned and scurried down the hall. Leo stared off into the distance. He frowned and glanced over to David. "Oh, David."

David stopped and spun around. "Yeah? What?"

"Do be sure not to tell anyone you and I are leaving tonight. We can't let this get out."

David nodded. "Yeah, yeah, ok. I'll keep it quiet." He drew his hands across his lips as if zipping a zipper. He spun on his heals and scurried away.

"Yes, this is good. We must do this." Leo turned and walked back to his desk. He stared out his window. He never meant to anger his boss. But his life's work must not fail. He had to be sure it would work. And what better way to ensure the Colony's survival than to be a founding member. Having to live in his own creation would surely help ensure it operated as best it could. Yes, this was the only answer now.

TWENTY-ONE

THE BIG NEW PROJECT

May 2, 2130 — The Colony — Level One

"Tea?" Ash stood above Tephra, who was lying on the couch. She held up a white mug and smiled down at her.

Tephra startled awake. She raised her head and looked around. She didn't remember falling asleep on the couch. But then again, she didn't remember half of what happened the night before. She moved her feet to the floor, sat upright on the couch, and cradled the mug in her hands. "Thank you."

"Sound sleeper." Ash took a seat in a chair opposite the couch.

"Yeah, well ... I guess so." Tephra smiled. She looked down at the opaque brown liquid in the white cup. Steam rose to warm her face. She dipped her head down and took a small sip. It tasted strong, and felt warm, comforting. "Why am I still here?"

"The main reason: wine." Ash smiled. She took a quick sip of tea and sat back in her chair.

"Oh, right." Tephra smiled. She could feel her cheeks turn flush as she looked back down at her mug. She didn't mean to pass out in front of her friend. "Sorry about that."

"No, no, you're fine. In fact, I'm glad you're here this morning. I thought maybe you and I could talk a bit more."

"Oh, great. Well then let's say I drank too much wine on purpose."

"It was no accident." Ash reached over and put her mug on the low-slung table in front of her. There was a mess of data pads displaying charts spread out on the table. Each data pad looked like a thin piece of glass, eight inches by ten inches. "Hungry? I made some breakfast."

"No, not really. I just ... this tea is all I need."

Ash didn't seem to hear her as she was already walking toward the kitchen. Tephra placed her mug on the table as well. A colorful chart laying to one side caught her eye. She titled her head and moved the data pads so she could see them better. They looked like organizational charts. Names, titles, dates in each little box. Lines between the boxes. The other charts had rows of various data. Numbers mainly. The title on each sheet identified its apparent data set. Different types of crops, minerals, production levels apparently.

"You want some toast?" Ash yelled out from the kitchen door that was across the room from where Tephra sat on the couch.

"No, no thank you." Tephra turned her head to respond but kept her eyes glued on the charts. She moved the sheets around with a flick of her finger across the front of each data pad, looking at each in turn. She furrowed her brow as she organized the data pads to her liking.

"See anything interesting there?" Ash returned from the kitchen carrying two plates. She sat one down on the low table next to Tephra and flopped into her chair cradling the other plate of food in her lap. "You brought us some interesting stuff."

"Me? What are you talking about?"

"The data pod. We found it next to you on the couch after you ... uh ... fell asleep shall we say?" Ash smiled. Tephra blushed again at the thought. Ash grabbed a piece of toast and took a bite.

"Oh, right, that."

"Where'd you get it?"

"A little sight-seeing before dinner. Some big office with a huge glass desk. It had a smaller office attached to it."

"Really?" Ash arched her eyebrows upwards as she peered at Tephra. "You walked yourself into Cosmotine's office? Unannounced?"

Tephra flashed a smile and shrugged. "I guess so. I had no idea what it was."

"Why'd you take it? Did you know what it contained?"

Tephra shook her head. "No, no, I don't know. Just thought I could learn something, I guess. The information on the screen looked important to me."

"So what do you make of this info?"

"Well I don't know what I'm looking at really, but look at the mineral production. It has gone up in line with these other productions figures going down. See, month by month you can see the change. Corn down, minerals up, wheat down, minerals up. Seems to have happened consistently over twelve months at least."

"Yeah, that's what we think too."

"And what about the construction materials?"

"What? What construction materials?"

"Right here, the footnote on the iron production chart. It has information about new construction manufacturing levels."

"Let me see that." Ash reached across and took the data pad from Tephra's hand. "Dang, you're right."

"Any big new projects you know of?" Tephra grabbed a piece of toast and took a small bite.

"No. Nothing new."

"Maybe you just don't know."

"No, we would know of something this size. There's no way we wouldn't know. We have people at every level who talk to us about …."

"About what?"

"Things."

"Hmmm." Tephra nodded. She looked at Ash while Ash scoured the report. *What was Ash thinking?* There was something she wasn't saying, it seemed.

Ash's eyes grew wide as she slowly raised the data pad to her face. "Only the Masters Twelve could authorize something of this size. We've heard nothing from them."

Tephra took a sip of her tea and then sat up straight on the couch. She had a sick feeling in her stomach. Everything seemed off. So far, nothing here was as it seemed—and certainly not as promised by Ash and her slick brochure. Had she been lied to? Was this all a scam of some sort?

She raised her eyebrow. "What's going on here, Ash? You recruited me to come to this place, but now it seems something isn't right."

"Recruitment is part of my job. I had no choice."

"Really? Why bring me here? Why didn't you just escape on land when you had the chance?"

Ash placed the data pad back on the table. She sat up in her chair, but kept her eyes on the low table in front of her. "The thing is ... when we ... look...." Ash raised her eyes slowly to meet Tephra's gaze. "We need help. We need smart people. Outsiders. People who aren't yet trained to follow a Supreme Principal without question. We want things to be the way they were ... before Cosmotine rose to power."

"And you didn't bother to tell me this before?"

"You wouldn't have come!" Ash jumped from her chair. She put her plate down on the table with a bang. She turned around and put her back to Tephra. "I know you; I know your type because I was the same. I am the same. You wouldn't have come had I told you the truth."

"Now what?"

Ash spun around and fixed her eyes on Tephra. "You need to choose, Tephra. The Colony is a place worth fighting for, but most of the colonists have no idea how much trouble they're in with Cosmotine in charge. I don't even fully know. I just know it's bad."

"Maybe I just need to leave."

"That is not an option for you. NO one leaves the Colony now. Not by choice. Besides what have you got to go back to? Land is in terrible condition and you burned your bridge with an Alliance member. Will you ever work there again? No!"

"That sounds like an ultimatum. Join or die."

"Tephra ... listen to me. You have a chance to make a big difference here. If you help us restore the colony to what it truly is—to what it should be—you will be a big deal here. You understand?"

"Ah, yeah I understand you are going to get me in big trouble, probably."

"I'm not the only one. There are others, you know that. You met them last night. We are working together to restore the Colony."

"I'm no puppet. I don't work for you and I don't work for ... wait who do I work for now?"

"You have to decide that for yourself, Tephra. This is a dangerous time for the Colony."

Ash spun around as the door to her room flew open. A man rushed in and stopped short of Ash. "They're coming!" Tephra recognized the man as Gypsum—the guy she talked to the night before.

"Shoot, we gotta go." Ash reached around the couch and grabbed Tephra's wrist. She yanked her off the couch as the two ran to the bedroom.

"Wait, what? Who's coming?" Tephra's free hand flew to her chest as she craned her head around to look back at Gypsum.

"Come on, come on. There's no time!" Gypsum placed his hand on Tephra's back and pushed her forward. "They already shut down sector four."

Ash reached her closet door and ripped it open. She kneeled down to crouch under the row of dresses hanging from the bar above them.

"Are we hiding in the closet?" asked Tephra.

Ash used her foot to kick the wall at the back of the closet. A small door flew open and she raced through pulling on Tephra's arm while Gypsum pushed at her back. They emerged into a small corridor, barely three feet wide. It was dark. There was enough room for them to stand, which they did. Gypsum slammed the trap door shut and the corridor feel into complete darkness.

Tephra could hear footsteps in the room they just vacated. A deep, male voice barked out orders as the sound of multiple pairs of heavy boots clomped around the space.

"Try to be quiet," admonished Ash in a hushed tone. She picked her way down the corridor in the darkness keeping her hand fixed around Tephra's wrist as she followed behind. The three padded down the narrow passage. They squeezed around corners making several twists and turns. Tephra shuffled quickly behind Ash wondering where they were going. After walking for what seemed like ages, they stopped.

Tephra could hear Ash feeling around on the wall to her side. She let go of Tephra's wrist. Light began to stream in from the cracks of a small doorway. The door swung open, the light momentarily blinded Tephra, but she could make out Ash's silhouette as she knelt down and crawled through the door. She felt a gentle push on her back. She knelt down and followed behind Ash emerging into a small room.

Ash held her finger in front of her mouth. She turned and slipped to the door of the room. She used her hand to move the door open enough to pop her head out. She looked back over her shoulder and waved the other two over to her.

She slid the door the rest of the way open and stepped out into the hallway. "Gypsum, go tell the others. Tephra and I have some homework to do." Gypsum nodded, turned, and ran off down the hallway.

Ash jogged in the opposite direction. Tephra stood not sure which way to go. She watched Gypsum disappear down the corridor and around a corner. Then she turned and ran to catch up with Ash.

TWENTY-TWO

THE MASTERS TRIBUNAL

**Five Years Earlier — May 1, 2125 — The Colony,
Masters Level**

"No, no, no, I cannot accept that." An older woman in a long white dress stood beside a taller man. She wrung her hands and shook her head. "We've come too far and accomplished too much. I refuse to allow the Colony to be placed in reckless hands. You must see that, Gypsum."

"But Supreme Principal Flora, you are pursuing serious charges. You must be certain you will prevail. There is too much at stake if you lose."

"You are talking about someone who intentionally violated the rules of the *probatum*."

"But did he?"

"Yes! I know he did. I just know it." She looked down at her feet and let out a sigh. She glanced over her shoulder. At the other end of the small chamber stood a tall, slender woman. Flora glanced back towards Gypsum and lowered her voice. "Ember ... you remember her ascent to One?"

Gypsum's eyes darted to Ember standing in the corner. He turned his shoulder away from her and spoke in a hushed tone. "No ... it was never proven."

The elevator doors slid open and two men stepped off the lift. Flora and Gypsum turned to face them.

One of the men flashed a broad smile. "Ah ... Supreme Principal Flora, Gypsum. So good to see you."

Ember's face lit up as she stepped over to Cosmotine's side. She nodded her head in greeting to Commodore Mercury—the man who accompanied Cosmotine in the elevator.

"Cosmotine," Flora set her jaw and squared her shoulders. Her cheeks flushed red. "Are you sure you want to proceed?"

"Yes, of course I do." Cosmotine stiffened. "These are serious charges after all; and I am anxious to clear my good name."

"What if you don't clear your name?"

Cosmotine took two swift steps towards Flora. His eyes narrowed. He held his mouth in a snarl, bearing his teeth as he leaned in closer to his prey. "And what if you don't clear yours? Your Supreme Principalship is on the line here, Flora. You are playing a dangerous game."

Flora swallowed hard; she kept her eyes locked on Cosmotine's steely blue eyes. "I will do what I must for the good of the Colony. I would hope the same is true of you."

A thin smile traced across Cosmotine's face. "Yes, I too will act for the good of the Colony."

Flora scowled as she twisted her lips downward. She opened her mouth to respond when the double doors flew open and an attendant dressed in a purple uniform appeared. "The Masters Twelve will see you now."

Cosmotine waved his hand and bowed his head indicating to Flora that she should enter first. Flora and Gypsum nodded in turn and entered the room. Commodore Mercury followed behind.

Ember stepped up next to Cosmotine. "Are you sure about this?"

Ember's eyes widened as she whispered to Cosmotine. "It could be a trap."

Cosmotine kept his eyes fixed on the room in front of him. "I'm sure. Do your part well. I have taken certain precautions. We will prevail." He took a step forward and walked into the conference chamber of the Masters Twelve with Ember in tow.

Ember glanced up at the dome shaped room. The walls of thick glass held the ocean at bay. Thick pillars rose from the floor and met at a single point in the center of the room. Each pillar was carved with ornate figures of sea creatures. In the center of the room was an oblong conference table that stretched across the length of the chamber. Soft white light emanated from an unseen panel high above, and from behind the pillars.

The group shuffled to the end of the long conference table and took their designated seats. Each person had their name on a placard placed on the table opposite their assigned chair. Supreme Principal Flora and her designated representative, Gypsum, sat to the left. The others sat to the right of the table's center line.

Ember took her assigned seat and eyed the Masters Twelve who sat around the table dressed in their purple robes. Each wore a mask inscribed with ornate sea creatures. A Master at the far end of the table stood. "We are gathered in tribunal session to hear the charges brought by Supreme Principal Flora against Cosmotine of One. Supreme Principal, please rise. Colonist Cosmotine of One, please rise." The two rose in unison from their chairs as the rest of the group remained seated.

"Colonist Cosmotine you are accused of altering *probatum* results. In addition, you are accused of placing colonists on One in spite of *probatum* results that would have placed them elsewhere. Do you understand the charges made against you?"

Cosmotine bowed his head. "I do."

"Supreme Principal Flora, you are the accuser. Your burden is to prove your accusations as true to the satisfaction of a majority of the Masters Twelve. Do you understand your burden?"

Flora swallowed and peered down at the table. "Yes. I do."

"These charges are class one violations. If proven true, the punishment is rehabilitation on Ten for an indefinite period. At this time, should you wish to admit wrongdoing, the Masters Twelve have the option to consider and implement a less severe punishment. Colonist Cosmotine, do you understand the punishment you will face if the accusations are proven true? And do you wish to admit to wrongdoing at this time?"

Cosmotine shifted in his stance. His chin pushed out as he straightened his back, "I admit of no wrongdoing; and I fully understand the punishment afforded these serious accusations, of which I am innocent."

The Master presiding over the tribunal nodded his masked head in response. "Supreme Principal Flora, as the accuser of a class one violation, you too face punishment if you do not prevail in proving your accusations. Should Colonist Cosmotine prevail, you will be stripped of your title and rank as Supreme Principal, and you will be sent for rehabilitation on Ten for an indefinite period. You have the option of withdrawing your charges and requesting adjournment of this tribunal hearing at this time. Do you understand the punishment you will face if you do not prevail? And do you wish to withdraw your accusations at this time?"

Flora rubbed her hands together. She glanced over to Cosmotine and then back to the Masters Twelve arrayed before her. She slowly nodded her head. "Yes, I understand."

The presiding Master titled his head. "And do you wish to withdraw your accusations?"

Flora stared at the glossy black conference table in front of her. All was quiet. Ember glanced over to the Supreme Principal. What was she thinking? *She has doubts. Wait, is she going to withdraw her—*

"No!" Flora looked up. She took a large breath and straightened her stance. "No, my accusations stand. I will not withdraw them."

"Very well. Each of you have named your representative for this tribunal hearing. The representatives are immune from punishment for anything they say during this tribunal. They may speak freely during this process. The proceedings may now commence. Gypsum, you have the floor to present your evidence and argument in favor of Supreme Principal Flora's accusations."

Flora and Cosmotine both took their seats as Gypsum rose from his chair.

"Thank you, Master." Gypsum cleared his throat. "We have reason to believe that several members of the executive class on One have been placed there in violation of their *probatum* results."

Gypsum took several steps away from the conference table. He stopped and turned to face the seated Masters. His face held an intense stare. "For nearly a century, the Colony has thrived thanks to the rules by which we live. The *probatum*, perhaps our most important tool to measure and enforce efficiency, is at the heart of the Colony's success."

Gypsum put his hand on his chin. "And yet—for what is undoubtably the first time in our history, the sacred rules of the *probatum* have been violated." He walked back to his chair and placed his hands on the back of it. "We first became aware of this transgression six months ago when something peculiar occurred. Half a dozen people joined One in a three-month period. Six new colonists were made members of the executive class. And to further fuel suspicion, these colonists were pre-existing on other levels—they were not new recruits from land. In other words, these were colonists for whom a *probatum* had been given many times before without a single one of them being placed on One prior to now."

"Now hold on!" Ember jumped from her chair and placed her hands on the conference table. "Colonists have the right to learn new skills, to take a new *probatum*, to find new placements when their skills allow for it. Happens all the time."

"Order, order." The presiding Master raised his hand. "Ember, you will have your chance to respond. Please ... sit."

Ember frowned. She slowly lowered herself into her chair and crossed her arms.

"Yes, colonists can take new *probata*." Gypsum sauntered back to the long conference table. "Ember is correct. But never in our history have six new colonists been placed on One in a three-month period. In fact, only two to three new colonists are placed on One over the course of two years. The chances of six new colonists being placed in a three-month period are astronomical. No, the circumstances point to something far more sinister than chance."

"What's more, all six new colonists have shown decided loyalty to colonist Cosmotine."

"Seriously!" Ember jumped from her chair again. "Loyalty? How can that even be measured? Besides, Cosmotine is an inspiring colonist of One. Naturally, a shining light will gather many admirers."

"Order, order. Colonist Ember, please wait your turn." The Master raised his hand again.

Ember took her seat and smirked. She knew the rules of the tribunal of course. But throwing Gypsum off his game every now and then wasn't such a bad thing.

Gypsum turned to face Ember. "Isn't it fitting that Cosmotine's most egregious violation is here with us today." Gypsum pointed a finger at Ember. "Colonist Ember is our primary example of *probatum* manipulation."

"How dare you!" Ember jumped up and turned to face Gypsum with a scowl. "I am not on trial here! Produce your evidence or sit down!"

The presiding Master stood and put both his hands out in front of him. "Order, order! Colonist Ember this is your final warning. Sit down and await your turn."

Ember turned to face the Master at the end of the table and clenched her teeth. "Yes, Master."

Gypsum continued, "Let me explain. Three years ago, at age twenty-seven, Ember ascended to the executive class—Level One. Previously, an engineer apprentice and then junior engineer on Four. Placed there by her *probatum*." Gypsum took several steps to his left, raising his hand to his chin as he moved. "Out of the blue, she is placed on One after a *probatum* for which we have no results recorded. Five years too young."

"Excuse me, colonists Gypsum, but isn't the minimum age more of a guideline as opposed to a hard rule?" The Master closest to the end of the table titled her head as the question emanated from underneath her ornate mask.

"Yes, but it has never been violated in nearly a century." Gypsum turned and placed his hand on his hip. "And Ember's *probatum* results were never published ... no record, no detail remains."

"Are you suggesting," said a Master, "that her results did not place her on One?"

"I am suggesting," replied Gypsum, "that her results cannot be found. We know not what her proper placement would be. And yet, here she is. A former apprentice of Cosmotine now a member of One . There could be no explanation for her ascendency except that she was allowed to join One without proper *probatum* results."

"How would she have been placed on One without her *probatum* results being recorded?"

"The placement order was generated, same as always. Only now, when we go back in the records to review her results, have we found them missing."

"Have there been other instances of *probatum* results not being published or recorded?" asked a Master.

"Yes!" Ember stood. She grabbed a data pad from in front of her and brought up a record. "The Colony records indicate several dozen instances when *probatum* results were not published or recorded. Errors can occur—at times."

"At times, she says." Gypsum strolled back to the conference table, then turned to face the Masters. "There have been only two dozen unrecorded *probatum* results over nearly a hundred years. And those errors placed colonists on various levels throughout the Colony. Errors can occur." He turned his head and smiled at Ember and Cosmotine. "But can they explain a half dozen that all occurred within three months—and all elevating certain colonists to a single level: One." He lifted his finger into the air. "Errors tend not to be so convenient most of the time."

"Have you any documentary proof other than your arguments before us now?" asked a Master.

"Yes, Master. We have the *probatum* records demonstrating missing results for six colonists over three months. We also have logic. It simply stands to reason that no set of circumstances could lead to these results in a three-month period."

"But what of Colonist Cosmotine's involvement? Have you documentary evidence that implicates him?"

"Here again, reason would dictate that no one else on One benefitted from these actions to the degree that Cosmotine has."

"Very well." The presiding Master stood. "The Masters Twelve will now hear the rebuttal from colonist Cosmotine's representative."

"But Master, I am not finished with my presentation." Gypsum leapt to the table and placed both hands on it. "I have more to describe."

"Without documentary proof implicating Cosmotine, your statements are mere conjecture, Colonist Gypsum. Besides, we decide the length of your presentation, not you. Please ... sit."

"I object!" Supreme Principal Flora rose from her chair. "Gypsum has only begun our case-in-chief. He has more proof. You must let him finish!"

"You will have your chance at your rebuttal. The Masters have spoken. Please, sit."

Flora glanced at Gypsum. He shrugged his shoulders. They both slowly sat in their chairs.

"Colonist Ember, please proceed," said the presiding Master.

"Masters Twelve, thank you for your time and attention to these serious accusations." Ember stood and cleared her throat. "Being targeted personally by my adversary, I feel an even greater sense of duty to explain why we are here."

"Let me begin by saying that I take the Colony rules very seriously. The rules provide guidance, efficiency, and order. Without these traits, there would be chaos. And chaos would kill our very existence. Cosmotine understands these rules and believes in them just as I do—as we all do. And yet, Supreme Principal Flora believes he is guilty even though she has no proof, no evidence, to support her accusations."

Ember took several steps to stand directly behind Cosmotine. "In essence, this man's character is on trial. Either the Masters believe him to be so corrupt as to violate one of our most sacred colonial rules, or you believe that a man of his character, of his accomplishments, of his contributions towards the good of the Colony could not possibly be guilty of these charges."

Ember strode back to her spot at the conference table and nodded her head to the attendant standing at the side of the room. The attendant hurried to the far end of the conference table and began working a keyboard. As she did so, a screen rose from the end of the table and images began to appear on the screen.

"Cosmotine, as a member of the executive class, was tasked with increasing the efficiency of the mining production on Ten." A chart detailing mining productions flashed on the display screen. The Masters turned their heads in unison to study the screen. "In just over twelve months he increased production by forty-five percent." Several of the Masters nodded their heads in agreement.

"Cosmotine was asked to help Commodore Mercury reorganize the Colony guards and increase their efficiency, which he did successfully." A series of photos showing Cosmotine among the guards on Five flashed on the screen. Ember turned to face Commodore Mercury who was seated on the other side of Cosmotine. "Commodore Mercury, don't you agree that Cosmotine assisted in increasing efficiency in the Colony guards?"

Commodore Mercury rose from his seat. "I do not wish to testify in these proceedings. As head of the Colony guards, I am here to maintain the peaceful and civilized nature of these proceedings. I feel it is my duty to remain neutral and therefore I will not testify."

Ember scowled at Mercury. *The fool. How could he refuse to testify now when he seemed all too eager to talk before?* She glanced down at Cosmotine. She thought she noticed a flicker of rage flash across his face. But it was gone in an instant. He stared ahead with no emotion at all.

"The fact remains," continued Ember, "that the Colony guards have been organized into a more efficient force to help protect the Colony from within and without. And Cosmotine was also tasked with helping colonists who wished to change their skills, improve their ability to help the Colony, for the good of all. He did so successfully. So successfully, in fact, that an unprecedented number of colonists joined the executive class on One over a three-month period."

Ember turned to face Flora. "The Supreme Principal could have brought her concerns to Cosmotine directly and avoided this proceeding altogether. However, for reasons seemingly known only to her, she failed to do so." Ember glanced towards the Masters. "Instead, choosing to bring the most serious of charges before this tribunal."

"I object!" Flora shot up from her chair. Her face turned bright red and she thrust her fists onto the table in front of her. "It was Cosmotine that demanded this tribunal, not me!"

"Please ... Supreme ... take your seat," the presiding Master spoke without moving.

"But you haven't given me a chance to finish stating my case!"

"Please, sit."

Gypsum raised his hand to Flora's arm and gently pulled her back down into her chair. The Supreme Principal glowered at Ember. Ember glanced at her and then fixed her eyes on the Masters. *What was Flora thinking? Why did she agree to this in the first place?* Ember glanced at Cosmotine. He sat with his hands folded in his lap. He looked calm, almost serene. *I thought Flora demanded this. Perhaps she was forced.*

"Colonist Ember ... you may proceed." The presiding Master waved a hand towards Ember.

Ember shook the thoughts from her head and peered up at the Masters. "Yes, where was I? Allow me to conclude by saying that were it not for the contributions of colonists like Cosmotine, our way of life would be far worse than it is now. We need leaders on One with vision and the ability to get results. Cosmotine has proven himself worthy of our praise. The accusations should be dismissed."

Ember sat in her chair. She glanced at Cosmotine thinking perhaps he would give her some feedback on her performance. He didn't move. He kept his gaze locked on the Masters.

Gypsum rose from his chair. He tapped the table in front of him with his finger. "Masters, we have one more piece of evidence for your consideration." Gypsum glanced at the attendant still standing next to the keyboard at the end of the conference table. The attendant punched several buttons on the keyboard. An image took shape on the display screen. Ember squinted and leaned forward. The image was dark and grainy. She titled her head and tried to make sense of what she was seeing.

"Cosmotine," continued Gypsum, "here in this image, working at a computer terminal on Four—the engineering level. The only level where *probatum* results are processed and recorded." Gypsum turned towards Ember. "The only level where *probatum* results could be accessed and manipulated."

"Computer terminals are spread throughout Four, are they not colonist Gypsum?" A Master at the center of the table raised a hand as he spoke. "How can we tell that this image is from the *probatum* computers?"

"There's more." Gypsum placed both hands on the table and leaned forward. "We have the results of this computer access." His eyes jumped to the attendant as he gave a nod. She punched the keyboard. The display screen flashed white and then went black.

"Please, the next slide," said Gypsum. The attendant glanced up and then began hitting keys on the keyboard again.

"Do you have it?" Gypsum stood up straight. His mouth opened and his eyes widened. Ember furrowed her brow. She glanced up at Gypsum. A bead of sweat formed on his forehead. She noticed his hand begin to shake.

"I ... I don't know ... something is ... wrong." The attendant glanced up to the display screen and back down to her keyboard. The screen remained black. The attendant lifted her head and shook it slowly.

"What?! What have you done with the next slide?" Gypsum jumped around his chair and scrambled towards the attendant. Commodore Mercury shot up and ran behind him. He hustled in front of Gypsum and threw up his hand. Gypsum stopped.

"Colonist Gypsum," said the presiding Master, "please take your seat."

"But Master, my slide, my evidence, it was there before we started." Gypsum waved his hands in front of him as he spoke. "I need to see what happened."

"You need to take your seat," said Mercury.

The presiding Master stood slowly from his chair. Gypsum glanced back at Flora and then looked at Mercury. The Commodore stood his ground.

"Fine," said Gypsum, "I will do as you ask." He turned and plodded back to his chair with Mercury marching behind.

"I must protest, Masters, as it seems someone has interfered with my evidence." Gypsum crossed his arms and set his jaw.

"I see no proof of that, colonist Gypsum." The presiding Master looked at the attendant. "Are you able to access the slide?" The attendant shook her head no. "Have you or anyone else tampered with the file?" The attendant shook her head no again. "Colonist Gypsum, please sit. Your time has expired."

Gypsum eye's narrowed. Ember studied Gypsum's face. For the first time in the proceedings his cheeks turned red. His jaw worked back and forth. She wondered if he might lash out across the table, but instead he sat. He folded his hands in his lap and looked down at his feet. So defeated in so a short amount of time, it would seem.

"The Masters Twelve shall convene in private to consider the information presented and to render our verdict. You are excused." The presiding Master sat. The litigants and their representatives stood. They turned and left the room.

Outside in the small foyer, the others boarded the elevator to travel down to One. Cosmotine and Ember held back, waiting for the next lift. Cosmotine glanced towards Ember and shot her a quick smile. "Good work, Ember. Glad you were able to explain how I managed to select so many good colonists to join our cause."

"Select? Are you suggesting you brought them here, in violation of their *probatum* results?"

"No, no, I meant helped them to be placed. Don't be foolish, Ember. You did good work today. You stood up for me and I will long remember it."

"Thank you. I think you will prevail."

"Yes, of that I am certain." Cosmotine's mouth curved into a devilish smile. "And once I do, I am also certain that I will be named as the next Supreme Principal."

"I would welcome that change. The Colony could only benefit from your leadership."

"Thank you, Ember. Kind words indeed."

"And what of Commodore Mercury? Will he continue under your leadership?"

Cosmotine's face hardened as he set his jaw. "The Commodore is a fool. He will rot on Ten along with Flora. I need loyal lieutenants, Ember. People like you who believe in my leadership."

Ember nodded. *The traitor will get his punishment.*

TWENTY-THREE

FRESH CADETS

The large van came to a hard stop outside the main elevator complex. Flint filed out the back of the van and glanced up at the huge elevator shafts rising from the ground. They were in the middle of Seven where supplies and large cargo were hauled up and down throughout the Colony. Flint squinted as he looked up at the bright elevator shafts. The entire complex was teaming with activity as people and cargo were hauled in an out.

Capital Rotifer exited the van and approached the men. The guards, in their black uniforms were lined up neatly to one side. The newly recruited field hands were milling about and looking in every direction. Rotifer rolled his eyes and sighed. "Recruits!" He spat out the word with an exasperated yell. "You are to stand in a line each one of you directly opposite a guard."

The field hands turned and ran into each other trying in vain to line up with the guards on the opposite side. Rotifer rubbed the back of his neck and shook his head. He stiffened his posture and pointed his index finger. "You! What's your name?"

"Flint, sir." Flint spoke with enthusiasm. He had a smile on his face. He didn't mind being hollered at. Misty had trained him well for that. He was just happy to be here, with them, on the verge of becoming a guard.

"Flint, stand here." Rotifer pointed to a spot on the ground. Flint complied with the order and stood in his designated spot. He stuck his chest out and rotated his shoulders back to look the part. Rotifer walked down the line of field hands, shouting and pointing at different spots on the ground. After several minutes he had his new recruits lined up in a neat row opposite his well-trained guards.

"You are all now cadets in the Colony Guards." Rotifer began a slow pace in front of his line of new recruits. "You will start your training here by partnering up with the guard across from you. You will follow that guard in everything he does. You will learn from him, and you will also attend training sessions ." When Rotifer reached the end of the line, he turned on his heels and walked back again.

A field hand in the middle of the line leaned his head out as he put his hand in the air to ask a question. "But pardon me, Mister Rotifer, sir—"

"Captain Rotifer!" Rotifer took two quick steps to stand opposite the field hand.

"Oh yeah sorry, Captain Rotifer, sir, we ain't taken a new *probatum* and you said we was guards, but I thought that—"

"Stop thinking!" Rotifer leaned forward. He glared at the field hand. Flint couldn't help but to let out a chuckle. This was great. He didn't care how he became a guard. *Probatum* or not.

"If I tell you that you are now cadets in the Colony guards, then your job is to shut up and be a cadet. Understand?"

"Yes ... yes, sir." The field hand looked down at his feet. Rotifer turned and marched back to Flint.

"Granite, you are assigned Flint. Get your cadet suited up and start your training."

Granite smirked at Flint. "Yes, sir." Flint sensed a lack of enthusiasm in Granite's voice.

Granite took three steps and was standing nearly toe-to-toe with Flint. Flint towered over him. "Cadet Flint ... " Granite turned his head towards Captain Rotifer. He waited for Rotifer to take several more paces and then turned his head back to Flint. "Cadets are a pain in the rear. You will do what you're told, when you're told to do it, and keep your mouth shut, you got that?"

"Yes, sir!" exclaimed Flint.

"You can drop the 'sir' crap too. It's Sergeant, you got that? Sergeant."

"Yes, Sergeant!"

"Now turn around and go get outfitted with your uniform in the barracks behind you. And get your hair cut to standard Guard length ... and take a shower! You're a guard now, not a dirt-kicker."

"Yes, Sergeant!" Flint stood looking down at Sergeant Granite and smiled.

"Well get going now cadet! Now! Go, go go!" ordered Granite.

Flint spun on his heels and took off for the guard barracks. He filed into line with the other recruits. His stomach fluttered with excitement. This is it. What he had been waiting for, and working so hard to reach. So many *probata* he had taken. And to think, he made it here without a new *probatum* at all. What luck! Things were changing for the better as far as Flint was concerned.

TWENTY-FOUR

MINERALS

"Where are we going?" Tephra hustled to catch up to Ash.

"We need to find a computer ...." Ash stopped at an adjoining hallway and poked her head around the corner. "All clear, let's go!"

The two flew up the hallway. Ash made several turns until she reached a door and stopped. She looked back down the corridor they had just traversed as Tephra pulled up beside her. "Give me your hand." Ash grabbed Tephra's wrist and placed her hand on a black square next to the door. The door slid open and Ash pulled Tephra inside.

"What was that?"

"I can't get in the door with my imprint, they'd find us in a second."

Tephra looked around the room. It was a sparsely furnished office with a white desk and two chairs. Ash walked around the desk and began punching buttons on a keyboard that lay on a counter behind the desk. A panel on the wall slid upwards revealing a computer monitor.

"We need to find those plans." Ash looked up at the monitor and then back down to the keyboard.

"What plans?"

"The construction you pointed out; we need to know more about it."

Tephra pulled a chair around the desk and sat down. Ash grabbed the chair nearest her and did the same.

"You think you can find something like that?" asked Tephra.

"I don't know. We need help from our friends on Four—the engineers."

***

"Where the hell is the main target?" Topaz slammed his fist down on the table in front of him. Ember sat to his side. Her arms crossed, starring up at the guard across the table.

"We will find her, sir. We have rounded up the rest of the group already."

"Yes, yes, I know, but the Supreme Principal wants Ash. How could you not find her by now?"

"She wasn't in her quarters. Someone must have tipped her off."

"Well get out there and find her. She has to record an imprint eventually. She can't just hide in the hallways forever." Topaz walked around the table and sneered at the guard standing before him. "You either find that rebel or I'll send you to Ten! Understand!"

"Yes, sir!" The guard spun on his heels and darted out of the room.

"You sure you're up to the task, Commodore?" asked Ember. A wry smile formed on her face.

"How dare you?" Topaz turned and fixed his eyes on Ember. "We will find our prey. We always do." Topaz sneered. "They can't hide forever."

"Perhaps you need to try a different tactic."

"What do you suggest, Ember? You think you're better at this than I am? By all means, enlighten me."

"Do you honestly think Ash would use her own imprint to enter a room? Surely, she is not that stupid."

"Well she has to eventually. We will find her all too quickly in the hallways."

Ember stood. She sauntered to the end of the table and crossed her arms. "Just like you found her all too quickly in her quarters?"

"She had been tipped off!" Topaz scratched his head. "At least I think."

"Try searching for a different imprint." Ember shifted in her stance.

"Whose imprint?"

"Ash, are we safe here?" asked Tephra. She touched her lips and peered over at the closed door they had used to enter just moments ago. Several hours had ticked by since they made their escape from Ash's room.

"For now." Ash spoke while keeping her eyes fixed on the screen. "Increased mineral production could only be coming from Ten. Maybe that's where the construction is taking place."

"What about Eight and Nine?" asked Tephra as she looked up at the computer screen.

"Those levels are largely unmanned. They house the desalination plant, power plant, that sort of thing."

"And Ten is mining?"

"Primarily, yes." Ash worked the keyboard to scroll through documents displayed on the screen.

"What's Ten like?"

"I don't know, I've never been down there."

"What type of people work there?"

Ash paused and turned her head towards Tephra. "You know I've never met anyone from Ten before. Funny seeing as how I've met colonists from every other level. Never really thought much of it I guess."

Ash turned her eyes back to the computer screen and raised her right eyebrow. "Just got another file from my friend on Four. Engineering diagrams. Whoa there's a lot here. Not sure what I'm even looking at."

Tephra squinted at the screen and then sat back in her chair. "Schematics. Reminds me of the patents I used to review as part of our large corporate mergers."

"How is this like a patent?"

"Well patents have schematics showing how the device being patented works, generally. I have a degree in mechanical engineering, so I was the patent review associate. They sent me nearly all of them because most of the other lawyers had no idea what they were looking at."

"Any idea what you're looking at here?"

Tephra squinted at the screen and tilted her head one way and then another. "Not really ... but look at that sign."

"What? Where?"

"The symbol at the bottom, you know what that is don't you?"

"No."

"Chemical symbol for uranium."

"Uranium?"

TWENTY-FIVE

A FREE FUTURE

A Century Earlier — July 1, 2030 — Pacific Ocean, 40 Miles Off the Coast of Los Angeles

Leo's cell phone rang. He grabbed it from his pocket and looked at the screen. John Hall again. He declined the call. He glanced back to the shore from where his transport ship had set sail half an hour ago. A smile creeped across his face. For the first time in quite a while he felt relieved. In his new home, there would be no boss. Science would be the only guide.

"You making phone calls up here?" David waddled across the deck to stand by Leo's side. Leo shook his head. "No, just declining calls from Mr. hall."

"Oh yeah? I bet he's hopping mad by now."

"I suppose." Leo looked down at the water passing by the hull of their ship. "Do you think we made the right choice?"

"What? Going to the Colony? Of course we did. It's our baby. It's where we belong after so many years of hard work. Once we get there, there's nothing we can't do. We have all the tools, the equipment, and the minerals to mine. We'll be set." David slapped Leo on the back. "You did a hell of a job Leo. You really did."

Leo smiled and glanced up at the full moon illuminating the sky. "Thanks, David. You too."

"Besides, no one can find us once we get there. We have all our team, the charts, the way points. And the cloaking is working to hide the Colony from the outside world. We have a whole template for how our new world will work. It's a whole new civilization."

"Yeah, I guess you're right."

Leo's cell phone began to ring again. He glanced down to see Mr. Hall's name light up the display. He shook his head and smirked. "This guy just can't leave us alone."

"Mr. Hall, the king of all creation—so he thinks."

"Well the richest man in the world probably is king of all creation."

"Only on land, Leo. Only on land. Under the waves, you will be the new king."

Leo scoffed. "Oh Gosh, I hope not. I don't want to be anyone's king."

"Well you are our leader, Leo. We trust you implicitly."

Leo turned and looked into David's eyes. "Well I prefer to consider us equals."

"Ok, then you are first among equals. The principal."

Leo smiled and shook his head. He leaned on the ships railing and watched the water roll by. He never thought his work would end with what felt like a swift retreat. But then again, something about this move felt right. His cell phone lit up. He looked down. "Mr. Hall ... again."

"Hey, why don't you get rid of that thing," said David. "I already threw mine overboard."

"You did what?"

"I chucked it in the sea. What the heck am I going to do with it in the Colony?"

Leo looked down at his cell phone and then glanced across the water stretching out before him. He nodded. "Yeah, maybe you're right." He pulled his arm back and swung it forward releasing his cell phone in midair. It spun out of his hand and shot nearly straight up. It fell back down, bounced on the handrail in front of the two men and then scattered down the hull of the boat and into the sea.

"I've never been good at throwing," said Leo.

"Well, it got the job done! You're a free scientist now. Only our science and reason will guide us from here forward."

"Yes, your hypothesis will undoubtedly prove true." Leo stretched out his hand and gently patted David on the shoulder. "Let's go inside. It's getting cold. We will rendezvous with our submarine soon. Might as well prepare for the next leg of our journey."

"Sounds good, Leo. Lead the way." David gave a weak salute in mock deference to his boss. Leo gave a shallow bow and marched towards the cabin door. They both chuckled as they scurried inside. Leo paused and glanced back at the full moon.

"Finally, a perfect world free of nonsense," said Leo to himself. "The future never felt so free."

As the two scientists traipsed to their quarters, an older man in a white uniform came bounding towards them. "Doc! Doc!"

Leo glanced around David, who was in front of him. "Captain?"

"Doc, we got trouble. You better come with me to the bridge."

"Trouble? What is it?"

"Come see for yourself." The captain turned and hustled back up the ship's narrow corridor. Leo and David followed behind. They climbed several staircases and came into the ship's bridge.

"Right there, off our Starboard bow, a ship." The captain pointed in the direction of the oncoming vessel.

"Ok, so?"

"No, it's a destroyer, Doc. It has hailed us three times already. It wants to board."

"Board us?"

"Yes, I fear it spells trouble for you and your pal here."

"Why would a Navy destroyer want to board our ship?" asked Leo. He scratched his head and shot the captain a quizzical look.

"It's not Navy, Doc. It's Hall Shipping Defense."

"What?"

"Hall Enterprises has their own fleet of destroyers to defend their off-shore drilling rigs. This is one of them."

"Oh crap!" exclaimed David. "They're coming after US!"

"Alright, alright, just calm down." Leo paced back and forth across the bridge. "We can't stop for them, captain. We must keep going."

"We can keep going if you want, but that destroyer is armed. They can take us down in no time. We have two dozen of your people aboard. They could get hurt ... or worse."

"Can you outrun them?"

The captain sighed and rubbed his forehead. "Not likely. I mean we could try, but outrunning a destroyer is not so easy."

"Turn hard to port and give it full power!" Leo's eyes widened as he locked his eyes on the distant destroyer. "They wouldn't dare fire at us."

"Aye, aye. You heard the man, hard port and full steam ahead." The Captain shook his head. "This is risky, Doc. Very risky."

The ship shifted as it turned to the left and picked up speed as it changed course. The captain stepped to the front window and held binoculars up to his eyes. A voice cracked over the radio speakers on the bridge.

"S.S. Colony Voyager, this is H.S.S. Destroyer League Twenty. You are instructed to stop and allow boarding. This is your final warning. Failure to comply within the next two minutes will result in use of force."

"That doesn't sound good, Leo." David slid next to Leo and put his hand on Leo's arm. "Maybe we should stop. See what they want."

"I already know what they want, David. They want us. We aren't going anywhere if we stop. Is that what you want?"

"Well no, but I also don't want to be torpedoed out of the water. I mean imagine if—"

The speakers crackled above their heads. "Listen here, S.S. Colony whatever." The voice rang throughout the bridge. "This is John T. Hall. If Dr. Leo what's-his-name can hear me, and I think he can, then he had better stop that ship and let us board it … now!"

"Leo, I don't think he's joking." David gulped.

Leo stared out the bridge windows at the distant destroyer gaining on them. He glanced at the captain, who shrugged in response. Leo glanced at David. He could see sweat pouring down David's forehead. He was breathing hard; his eyes wide with terror.

Leo slowly shook his head. "No."

"What? Leo, you're crazy!" David spun around and placed both hands on his head. "They'll kill us, he's not messing around … you're crazy!"

"No, he wouldn't dare."

The speakers crackled to life. "Come in Colony Ship. This is your last warning. This is John T. Hall and I want that doctor and I want him now. You stop or we will sink you. The clock is ticking!"

"Captain, can you increase our speed?" Leo shot the captain a stern look.

"No, doc. We're at full speed already and that destroyer is gaining. It's stop or sink now."

Leo rubbed his chin and looked down at the floor. They would be meeting their transport submarine shortly. Surely, they could hold on long enough to escape under the waves. They just needed to—

"Incoming! Hit the deck!" The captain grabbed Leo around the middle and shoved him to the floor. Leo landed with a thud. The air left his lungs as he rolled onto his back. Through the large windows on the bridge he could see a bright light streaking across the sky. His eyes went wide as he held his hands up over his face.

A thunderous explosion ripped across the ship. The vessel rocked hard to port and then shifted back to starboard. The lights of the ship went dark. Shrapnel littered the water around the ship. After several more minutes of rocking, all was quiet.

Leo peeked out between his fingers. His ears were ringing from the blast. He sat up and looked around. The lights in the bridge flashed back on and the crew began picking themselves up off the floor.

"Were we hit?" asked David as he rolled onto his backside and grabbed the hands of a crew member standing above him.

"We were warned!" The captain stood and grabbed the radio mic. He paused and looked down at Leo. "Get up here doc. I think our run is over. Next time the shell won't be set to explode above us."

Leo grabbed the edge of the control panel and lifted himself upright. "Crap!" He turned and looked at David. David stumbled backwards and plopped into a chair.

"Leo, please, we have to stop," pleaded David. "Please stop ... "

TWENTY-SIX

THE NEW PUNISHMENT

May 3, 2130 — The Colony — Level One, Primary Conference Chamber

"Commodore." A guard entered the primary conference chamber where Topaz and Ember were awaiting news of the search for Ash and Tephra. He stopped short of the long conference table and locked eyes with Topaz. "We have an imprint." Ember turned in her chair and fixed her gaze on the guard.

"Where was the imprint?" asked Ember.

"Sector six."

Topaz stood and pointed his finger at the guard. "Lock down sector six and shift all guards to that area. I want every nook and cranny searched until we find them!"

Topaz looked down at Ember as she looked up at him and smirked.

Tephra had a pit in her stomach. They had been in the little office far too long. Something didn't feel right. She glanced at the door and then back to Ash. "Ash, I think we should leave. We need to keep moving, don't we?"

"Just a few more minutes. I'm almost done with—"

The door to the office was ripped open and six guards quickly flooded the room. Tephra gasped and jumped from her chair while Ash punched several buttons on the keyboard causing the monitor to shut down. The guards grabbed Tephra by the arm and tore Ash from her chair.

"Well, what have we here? The rebel and the new recruit." A guard sneered at Ash.

Another guard grabbed for the radio received on his shoulder. "Sir, we have the rebels."

"Bring them to the primary conference chamber immediately." A voice rang out from the receiver.

The Guards guided their captives down the winding corridors until they reached the entrance to the primary conference chamber.

"Well hello, Ash. You certainly made yourself scarce for a while."

"Topaz! Why are you doing this to the Colony?" asked Ash.

Commodore Topaz rose from his chair and flashed a smile. "Following orders of the Supreme Principal, Ash. As we all must do."

"No, not now, not when the Supreme Principal is stepping so far beyond his rights. Topaz, he is using you and your guards. You know something isn't right. There is something wrong with Cosmotine!"

Ember stayed seated with her hands flat on the conference table. She locked eyes on Tephra. A door at the far end of the room slid open. Cosmotine, along with his bodyguards, entered the room. Tephra heard Ash's sigh.

"We have the rebel and the new recruit, Supreme Principal," Topaz jogged over to Cosmotine; looking all too eager to please his master.

"Excellent. And what of the others?" asked Cosmotine.

"We have detained ten rebels in sector four and five more in sector three. They are being held in the interrogation rooms and await disposition on your orders."

"Good work, Commodore."

Cosmotine continued sauntering across the room until he came to a stop in front of Ash. "You see you rebels aren't so hard to find after all." Ember moved quickly to Cosmotine's side.

"We believe Ash is second in command under Seabreeze," said Ember. "And, of course, our new recruit, Tephra."

Ash rolled her eyes. "There is no chain of command, Ember. We just want the Supreme Principal to act according to our laws ... Colony laws."

"I AM Colony law," barked Cosmotine. "Why do you and your rebels not see that?"

"We demand to see the Masters Twelve, where are they?"

Cosmotine stepped closer to Ash and looked into her eyes. His anger was clearly visible. Cosmotine's eyes burned into Ash as he spoke in quiet tones, "I am Colony law. The Masters Twelve would tell you the same. I AM Colony law."

Ash defiantly looked back at Cosmotine with a deep searing look of utter hatred. She set her jaw and spoke through clenched teeth. "You serve the Colony, or you pay the consequences."

Cosmotine's smile widen until he uttered a guttural laugh. "Consequences? I think you misunderstand the situation ... rebel." Cosmotine took a step back and raised his hand to signal the guards standing behind Ash.

The guards ushered Ash across the room and into a small chamber no bigger than a closet. They pushed her inside and she fell back against the wall. A metal door with a wide swath of glass down the middle slid closed from top to bottom. Everyone in the room could look through the glass to see Ash standing in the small chamber.

Cosmotine, Topaz, and Ember moved towards the chamber door as Tephra was escorted by two guards to a spot just behind them. Tephra's heart sank and a pit formed in her stomach. She had a bad feeling about this. She didn't know much about Cosmotine, but she knew enough not to trust what might come next.

Ash placed her hands on the glass. Her eyes widened as her face turned pale. A sound of rushing water pierced the air and water began to fill the chamber around Ash's feet. It quickly rose to her ankles, knees, then waist. Cosmotine nodded to the guard, and the water stopped.

Ash pounded on the thick glass with her fists. "What are you doing? Get me out of here, now!"

Topaz raised his arm to signal the guards standing at the door of the primary conference chamber. The door slid open and a line of rebels were led into the room. Tephra recognized them as the people from Ash's party the night before. Gypsum was at the head of the line.

"We have caught your accomplices," said Cosmotine. "They have been brought here to see our new form of punishment for themselves."

Cosmotine smiled as he turned his head to survey the line of rebels standing behind him, lined up against the wall. Cosmotine turned back to face Ash. "Ash, you have betrayed the Colony. You deliberately defied the Supreme Principal and incited rebellious activity."

Ash curled her arms around herself. Her lips turned pale blue and she began to shiver. Cosmotine nodded to the guard standing next to the chamber. The rushing water began again. Water flooded the chamber up to Ash's shoulders and then just past her neck. Ash bent her head back to keep her nose above water in the small pocket of air at the top of the chamber.

"No!" cried Ash. "You can't do this! Killing is forbidden!"

"Yes, that's true, colonists must never be killed," replied Cosmotine. "But rebels ... that's different. Rebellion against the Supreme Principal is a rebellion against the Masters Twelve, which is a rebellion against the Colony. It will no longer be tolerated."

Tephra gasped. She tried to move forward towards the water-chamber door, but the guards held her in place. She looked over at Ember and then back to Ash. *Surely they won't kill her.* They couldn't, they just couldn't.

Cosmotine turned and looked at the rebels lined up against the wall. "You will watch your rebel leader be punished, and you will tell those who wish to rebel the fate they will face. Rehabilitation is no longer our only option."

Cosmotine spun towards the water chamber again, and yelled, "Shock her!"

An arc of electricity exploded from the top of the small chamber; the electricity ran through the seawater causing Ash to convulse. Her head went under water and her body bent wildly at her waist. The electricity stopped, and Ash floated in the middle of the chamber. She slowly moved her legs, found the chamber floor, and pushed her head up above the waterline to take a breath from the small air pocket.

"No!" yelled Tephra. Her body stiffened as she tried to pull her arms free. The guards grasp on her held firm. "Please ... let her go!"

"Quiet, new recruit." Cosmotine spoke without turning his head. He kept his gaze locked on Ash. "You will now tell me the details of your rebellious plot. I want names, plans, every detail you have!"

"No!" cried Ash. "No, no ...." Ash's voice grew hoarse. Clearly in pain, she tried to catch her breath, but no words were coming out.

"Shock her again!" commanded Cosmotine.

Electricity once again exploded from the top of the chamber and raced through Ash's body. Ash screamed and convulsed. Her body bent at the waist, and her legs curled up behind her. Ash floated slowly downward in the flooded chamber. She again placed her feet on the floor and used what little strength she had left to push her head back above the waterline. Gulping air and seawater simultaneously. Ash struggled to keep her mouth and nose above the water.

Tephra's eyes widened as a lump formed in her throat. She slowly shook her head. "No, no, let her go." Her knees buckled; the guards holding her arms were forced to support her weight.

"If you remain silent, rebel, I will dispose of you and move on to the next rebel standing against that wall. They will each get their turn in your place if you don't talk," said Cosmotine.

"Ok," whispered Ash, barely able to speak. "Send the others to Ten and I'll talk. Please do not torture anyone else, I'll talk," said Ash.

Cosmotine nodded to the guard next to the chamber, and the water drained through the floor . As the water left Ash slowly floated downward. Once the chamber was empty, she collapsed onto the floor.

Cosmotine motioned to Topaz, who leapt forward and opened the chamber door. He knelt down beside Ash and took detailed notes of the explanation she whispered to him as she lay on the floor.

When Topaz was satisfied he had received all he could from Ash, he stood and returned to Cosmotine's side. Cosmotine nodded to Topaz and looked down at Ash still sprawled on the chamber floor.

"That's good, Ash," said Cosmotine in a patronizing tone. "Aren't you happy to unburden yourself of this guilt? Now You can rest with a clear conscience." He looked over to the guard standing by the chamber door and nodded. The chamber door slid closed again and water once again flooded the small chamber.

"No, no, no!" cried Tephra. She leapt forward with all her strength, breaking loose of the guards hold on her. She darted to the chamber door and placed her hands flat against the glass. "Ash! Ash!" She pounded the glass.

The water rose. Ash slowly moved her legs underneath her. She seemed to have no strength left. The water engulfed her frame as the chamber filled to the top. Ash convulsed a final time and then went still. Her body floated peacefully in the center of the chamber. Her arms stretched down; her hair floated around her head. The room fell silent.

"You monster!" Tephra turned and spat at Cosmotine. Her captors had regained their grip on her arms. Her eyes burned into Cosmotine. She clenched her teeth and balled her hands into fists. A smile etched across Cosmotine's face as he turned and walked away.

Tephra turned her gaze to Ember and was surprised to see a look of shock on her face. Ember raised her hands to cover her mouth. Her eyes dipped down to the floor, but she didn't move. She remained fixed to her spot.

The guards holding Tephra dragged her past Ember. They held her in place next to the line of other rebels. As Tephra looked into Ember's eyes. She saw something there. Emotion? Ember had emotion? Before she could figure out what Ember was thinking, Ember dashed off after Cosmotine, catching up with him just before he exited the room.

"Supreme Principal, we shall send the rebels to Ten, but what about Tephra?"

Cosmotine stopped, cleared his throat and then turned to look directly at Ember. "Kill half the remaining rebels and send the other half to Ten to spread the news of our new punishment."

"Kill?"

"Do not defy me, Ember. This is a new era and I need to know that you are in support of the Colony. Defy my orders, and you will meet the same fate."

"I understand. What about Tephra? She could still be of use on One. Ash and her friends just brainwashed her. We can undo that."

"Send Tephra to Ten. Let's test her mettle. If she survives for a while, then we will bring her back—all the stronger for it. If she dies, then she was never worth recruiting in the first place." Cosmotine turned and left the room, his six bodyguards marching in two neat rows behind him.

Ember walked back to the line of rebels and looked towards the wall. She rubbed her hand down her face and just stared in silence.

Topaz interrupted her thoughts. "What does Cosmotine want us to do with these rebels?"

Ember turned and looked at Topaz. She paused for a moment

and then said, "Send them all to Ten, including the new recruit. I want them gone immediately! And don't mention this to Cosmotine, he has enough on his mind at the moment."

"As you command, Ember," said Topaz as he quickly turned and started barking commands at his guards. The guards moved the rebels into groups of four and five in preparation for their ride to Ten.

Ember glanced at Ash's lifeless form floating in the water chamber. He killed. She couldn't believe it. He killed her. This can't be real ... what could possibly be next?

TWENTY-SEVEN

ONE TO TEN

An hour later Flint emerged from the guard barracks on Seven with a fresh haircut and a new guard uniform. He was smiling from ear to ear now that he had the black guard uniform on. "Hey, Sarge, check this out!" Flint yelled to Granite as he approached him.

Granite was sitting on a bench with his head resting on his chest taking a nap. The sound of Flint's voice startled him awake.

"Oh geez, I thought you were a bad dream," said Granite.

Flint stopped in front of Granite and stood at attention, chest out, trying to look official. Granite gave out a sigh and slowly stood. He walked around the back of Flint and came around to meet him eye-to-eye—although Granite had to bend his neck backwards to look into Flint's eyes as the former field hand towered above him.

"Not bad, hayseed. At least you look the part." Granite cleared his through and drew in a large breath. "Cadet, as of now, you are mine. You don't eat, sleep, move, or talk without me telling you to do so, understand?"

"Yes sir."

"Sergeant!" yelled Granite.

"Yes, Sergeant!"

"Cadet," Granite's forehead scrunched together as his mouth formed into a frown, "I don't like you, I don't like any cadet, and I don't want to babysit you. If you make my life hard, you get stripped of your uniform and you get sent to Ten—not back to Seven with your fellow hayseeds. You'll go straight to the bottom." Granite pointed at the ground.

"Yes, sir." Flint didn't care what Granite thought or said. He was in the black uniform that gave him access to the bright, white elevator. Nothing else mattered.

"Sergeant!" yelled Granite, but with less bark.

"Yes, Sergeant!"

Granite took a step back and took a last hard look at Flint as if he couldn't believe Flint wasn't rattled.

"All right cadet, we've been ordered to escort some equals down from One. Let's go, follow me."

"Do we get to take the elevator?"

Granite stopped in his tracks and peered up at Flint. "No, we're gonna take the stairs all the way to One." He shook his head and turned back in the direction he was walking. Flint shrugged and fell in behind him.

The pair hustled across the busy central hub and strode to a smaller elevator shaft. The main supply hub had a large freight elevator that was used to transport shipments of supplies between levels. The freight elevator could hold a thousand crates of supplies, several hundred tractors, or thousands of people if need be. Surrounding the main freight elevator were six smaller elevator shafts used mainly to transport people. Each elevator was big enough to hold twenty people comfortably.

Granite and Flint reached the elevator door and Granite held his identification card up to a black box to the right of the elevator. A light flashed and then Granite stated "One," when a prompt appeared asking for the desired level. Granite took a step back and stared at the elevator door. A bright light came sweeping down the opaque elevator shaft, descending to meet the door where Granite and Flint were waiting. The elevator doors slid open. A guard with his new cadet stood inside the elevator and peered out at Granite.

"Hey, Granite, perfect timing," said the guard. "Join us. We are heading to One now."

"I figured, Basalt." Granite and Flint stepped onto the elevator. Four more guards joined them in the elevator before the doors shut and the platform began to ascend.

Flint was excited. This was it. The elevator. And for the first time, he would see One. The quick ascent made his knees buckle slightly as the platform raced upward.

"Oh man, this is great!," exclaimed Flint. The group of guards turned to look at him. He stared back.

"You all been in an elevator before?" asked Flint. No one responded. Granite rolled his eyes and shook his head in disbelief. "First time for me," continued Flint unfazed by the silence around him.

He waited for a response ... and waited. His smile faded and he looked down at his feet trying to get past the awkward silence. The rest of the ascent passed quietly.

The elevator jerked to a stop and the doors slid open. Outside was a pristine white room. The guards filed out of the elevator and made up two lines. They marched off in unison, heading down one of the many corridors leading away from the elevator lobby.

Flint looked around as he walked, trying to make sense of where they were heading. It was difficult to get a sense of direction because everything was stark white. The walls, ceiling, floors, all the same color white. The light overhead glowed from behind opaque panels. Doors appeared at irregular intervals on both sides as they marched. Some were single doors, other were double doors. There were no other people to be seen. The whole atmosphere was entirely different from Seven, where Flint had spent his entire life. Seven had people, activity, dirt. There was none of that here.

The men came to the end of a corridor and entered a set of

double doors. Inside there were a group of people being detained by guards.

"Good, you've arrived," said Captain Rotifer. "You men take this group of rebels to Ten, you men take the other group. You will take separate elevator banks and go directly to Ten. No stopping off at any other level. Use the priority code when accessing the elevator portal, understood?" said Rotifer.

"Yes, sir," said the guards in unison. The guards fanned out with each man taking hold of two rebel prisoners. Flint followed suit and grabbed the arm of a tall man and a short, slender woman.

Granite took the lead with his two prisoners, and lead the way out of the room.

"Follow me. That includes you Flint," ordered Granite.

Flint nodded his approval. Granite led his prisoners and the pack of guards back to the elevator lobby where they had just emerged. He worked the elevator controls, and a red light appeared over the elevator door. He turned and looked at Flint. "That red light indicates priority status. The elevator won't stop until we get to Ten."

Flint nodded his understanding, then looked down at the woman whose arm he was holding. She was short, slender, and had pretty features, he thought. Her face held a steady, stern look, almost solemn.

Once the eight prisoners and four guards entered the elevator, the doors closed, and the platform began its rapid descent. Flint looked over the faces of the other prisoners. They all looked clean but somber. He detected tear stained eyes in half of them. Most of them looked down at the floor.

Granite took out a small glass tablet from one of the many compartments on his utility belt. He scrolled through some pages with the flick of a finger. He pointed at the rebel farthest from him. "Give me your names." The rebels each took turns saying their names. Flint's prisoner was the last to speak. "Tephra," she said.

Flint liked the name. Tephra. Sounded exotic. He noticed that

Tephra didn't look down at the ground like the rest of the rebels. She fixed her gaze on the elevator door. Her eyes looked red and blood-shot. He didn't think any of the people on the elevator looked danger-ous. They looked more like a group of sad mourners.

The elevator came to a stop and the doors slid open. The guards escorted the prisoners out of the elevator and into a metal room. The walls, floor, and ceiling were all gray metal. There were lights shining from the ceiling every ten feet or so. The place felt cold, and the smell was dank and musty. Beads of water trickled down the metal walls as the group marched forward.

The guards took their charges to the far end of the room and through a metal archway. As they entered the primary reception chamber on Ten, the sound of machinery churning away washed over them. It was loud and pulsing. The ground shook slightly. There was a mix of moisture and mud clinging to the walls and the floor. At the center of the room was an oblong metal desk with half a dozen people seated behind it, each doing some sort of clerical work.

Flint stopped with each hand still wrapped around the arm of his captives. He crinkled his brow as he peered at the workers behind the desk. Each one was dressed in dark grey overalls, with a dark grey shirt underneath. Their clothes were smeared with dirt and mud. Some of them had goggles perched on their foreheads. This was nothing like Seven, where everyone wore different colors and styles of clothes, even to work. Heavy metal tools were strewn about the desk and on the floor. There were two metal doors behind the desk, each with smears of mud and dents in various places.

"Name," said one of the men behind the counter. He didn't look up when he said it, he just stared at a computer monitor perched on his desk.

"Sergeant Granite, escorting the following list of rebels to you." Granite handed his data pad to the man behind the counter.

The man grabbed the tablet, punched a couple of buttons on his computer and then handed the tablet back to Granite. The man behind the counter turned in his chair, raised his hand and motioned for someone to come forward. Behind him the metal door opened, and four more men in the same grey outfits emerged.

Flint glanced down at Tephra. She looked straight ahead without any fear in her face. He glanced at the other rebels. They all looked worried—some even scared. But not Tephra. She held her head up. Not high as if she were defiant, but straight and sure as if she were unfazed by her surroundings or what was to come. He wondered: *why her?* What made her seem so brave when the others seemed to shrink? Tephra glanced up at her large captor. He gave a nod and a smile. She didn't return the gesture. She just returned her intense gaze straight ahead.

The four men in grey overalls relieved the guards of their prisoners. Flint let go of the man's arm he was holding with his right hand, but he held firm to Tephra. Something about her made him want to hold on. Not let her go. Not yet.

She started to take a step forward to follow the others, then realized she was still being held. She glanced up again at Flint.

"You can let go," she said.

As if in a daze, he did as instructed and released Tephra's arm. She strode away from him to join the others being herded behind the heavy, metal doors. His eyes stayed locked on the back of Tephra's head until she was out of sight. The doors closed with a loud clang.

"What a crap hole, let's get out of here!" exclaimed Granite. He slapped Flint on the back, which made him flinch. He shook the fog from his head and turned to join the other guards as they scurried from the reception chamber back to the elevator. As they walked, Flint winced as he caught whiff of a sulfuric, putrid odor. Granite shook his head. He must have caught whiff of the same smell. "Oh man, this place smells awful!," exclaimed Granite.

The guards filtered onto the elevator, with Flint bringing up the rear. As he stepped onto the elevator, he turned around and took a long, final look at the dark grey walls oozing with beads of moisture.

He never saw anything like it on Seven. What would happen to the people they brought here? Would they survive? And what about Tephra?

TWENTY-EIGHT
ALLIANCE WAR

Seven Years Earlier — June 15, 2123 — Pacific Theatre, Alliance War

Cynthia wiped the sweat from her forehead with her shirt sleeve. The ship was hot and the pressure more so. She glanced at her monitor and then over to the assembled sailors in the weapons control room. This time it would be different.

She glanced back down at her monitor. *Where the hell is it?* "It's out there somewhere." She spoke without lifting her eyes from the monitor. Beeps and sounds emanated through the room, but no one spoke. They were all transfixed. Only a month ago, she was plucked from the ocean by this same destroyer. Most of her fellow sailors from the life boat were whisked away to receive medical treatment, but not her. Her position was too valuable. A few stitches to close the gash in her head and she was back in play. Ordered to lead one of the firing stations on the ship.

"Ma'am, we have an unidentified ship to port. Moving at forty knots," a sailor called out from the far side of the room.

"Got it." Cynthia punched several keys on her keyboard. She couldn't get a read. Was it friend or foe?

Cynthia glanced around the room and surveyed her subordinates. They were a good bunch. Young, well trained, and eager to please. But still, something felt off. She couldn't shake the thought of the young sailor laying on the ground. Dead crew members forever manning their battle stations as her former ship slipped below the waves. A watery grave for the unfortunate sailors that would never return home to their families.

Why was she here? She should have listened to her dad and gone to law school. She'd probably be home right now. Eating well and complaining about mundane things like crowded stores and bad traffic. It had all seemed so important until now. Facing another life or death scenario put her problems into sharp relief.

"Arm laser missiles and be prepared to fire on my command." Cynthia barked out the order and returned her focus to the monitor in front of her. She had to know whether to fire or not. It could all end so fast. Fire too quickly and she risked harming a friendly ship. Fire too slowly and she risked repeating her past mistake.

"We'd have an identification tag if it were friendly, right?" A petty officer to her left looked up.

Cynthia nodded. "Yeah, probably. But not always. You know how that goes with damaged ships and ... " Something caught her eye. She tilted her head and began punching buttons to change the orientation of the image in front of her. "Fire!" She yelled out and turned her head to look at her crew. They sat motionless—all seemingly holding their collective breaths. "Fire, now! Fire!"

The crew jumped to action. Each person began working their assigned stations. A series of laser missiles tore out of their tubes and raced into the sky. Large masses of pure, destructive energy ran up in an arc and then down towards their target.

Cynthia watched the trajectory of the laser missiles in her monitor. She glanced around and barked several more orders making sure the crew would be ready to fire again if needed. As the laser missiles neared their target, she held her breath. She hoped for the best. She bit her bottom lip and waited.

"We have impact on enemy ship. Confirmed hit and disabled." A voice rang out from the speakers mounted above with a report from the bridge. A confirmed kill for the crew.

A cheer went up throughout the room. They had done their duty and hit their mark. "Good job, team!" yelled Cynthia over the cheers. They had hit their mark as they had been trained to do. It felt good to be the victors—better than stumbling off a sinking ship.

Her shift passed without further engagement. Her replacement arrived and relieved her from her post. She felt good leaving the firing station. To finally have a win under her belt rather than a crippling loss. It didn't make the past go away, but it definitely softened the blow. She retired to the officer's mess and grabbed a plate of food.

"Excuse me, ma'am?" A young ensign stood next to Cynthia's table.

She looked up and shot the ensign a warm smile. "Hey, Jill. Take a seat." She pointed to an open chair. Jill slid into the chair and placed her tray on the table in front of her.

"Can I ask you something?" Jill leaned forward with big eyes.

"Permission granted," Cynthia let out a small laugh. She didn't know why the young ensign was being so formal. Perhaps she could help break the tension.

"How did you know?"

"Know what?"

"That the ship we fired on was an enemy ship?"

"I didn't know. Not for certain. But my instincts told me."

"You fired based on instinct?" Jill picked up her fork and slowly turned it in her hands.

"Yes I did, ensign, because instinct is all we got out here. You can think and think and think, but you won't ever decide that way. You got to trust your instincts. Most of the time it will lead you in the right direction." Cynthia picked up her cup and took a small sip. She placed the cup down and nodded. "Trust your gut, ensign. It will serve you well."

The young ensign nodded as she gazed down at the table seemingly pondering Cynthia's advice. Cynthia glanced at the ensign and smiled. That was her not so long ago. Untested, unsure, trying to find her footing. The meal passed quickly and the two parted to go their separate ways.

Cynthia lay in her bunk that night trying to get some sleep. Her mind was turning over the day's events. She had risen to the occasion this time, and it felt good. But she knew her life in the Navy was set to end. The war wouldn't last forever. *What next?* Thought Cynthia. *What challenge can I take on now?* She couldn't imagine there could be anything in her future as challenging as her time in the Alliance war. *An office job where I can make an impact sounds nice for a change.* She rolled onto her side and descended into sleep.

TWENTY-NINE

LOYALISTS LIVE

May 3, 2130 — The Colony — Level One

Ember caught up with Cosmotine in his large office near the edge of One. His office backed on to the edge of the Colony's glass dome. The large, thick glass panels rose thirty feet from the floor of the office to the ceiling above. A semicircular glass desk was placed in the middle of the glass wall. To the right of the desk was a large sitting area with a couch, several chairs, and a low table, all in stark white. To the left of the desk was a rectangular conference table with twelve seats.

Cosmotine sat at his desk looking at a large computer monitor. Ember could see a reflection of the monitor on the glass wall behind him. The monitor had names and faces on it. The rebels who were caught this day along with a few that had been sent to Ten several months before.

"Supreme principal," said Ember, "the rebel prisoners have been delivered to Ten as you ordered." Ember kept an eye on Cosmotine. She intentionally omitted anything about killing half the rebels since she didn't follow through on his order. She hoped he wouldn't notice the omission.

"Yes, yes, fine," mumbled Cosmotine. He kept his eyes on the monitor as he scrolled through each name and photo. Her failure to mention killing half the rebels seemed to escape his attention—at least for now.

Ember stood in front of the large desk and gazed at her mentor as he sat and thought. There were times when she wondered what this brilliant man was thinking. He seemed to think a lot. Always thinking. Always planning. Or was it scheming?

She noticed his wrinkles seemed deeper. The light from the monitor highlighted the deep grooves running up and across his forehead. She raised her hand and began rubbing her ear. A killing had occurred, and she was witness. The rules of the Colony were inviolate in her mind, but now a line had been crossed. *How could I not know of this new punishment?*

Her eyes darted down to the floor and then back up to his face. *Could he be trusted? What else does he know that I don't?*"

Cosmotine glanced up at his ward. "You are disturbed? Do not feel pity for the rebels, Ember. They mean to destroy the Colony."

"Yes, Supreme."

"We have worked together for a long time, Ember, have we not?"

"Yes, Supreme." She flashed a smile that quickly melted away.

"Yet, you have not returned to land since you arrived so many years ago." His lips curved into a warm inviting smile. "I have, Ember. I have recruited many colonists in my trips to land over the years. The world you remember—the wars and turmoil—has gotten worse."

She looked down feeling a shudder at the thought of her former life on land.

"But what if," continued Cosmotine, "we could make it different up there." He pointed upwards with his outstretched finger. "The value of the Colony spread throughout the world. What a wonderful thing that would be, don't you think?"

"Perhaps, Supreme ... but ... but it would be impossible. Trying to subdue the world would tear the Colony apart."

"Don't fret, Ember." He rose from his chair. "Your beloved Colony is safe in my hands." He walked around his desk and stood immediately behind Ember. She stood still, not moving, not turning to see him.

"Don't forget where your loyalty lies, Ember," he said in a low voice. "Together, we can accomplish great things. Loyalists live, dissenters die." He turned and walked out of his office, leaving Ember standing before his desk.

Ember slowly turned around and looked towards the empty doorway. She stood in the large office all alone. "I am loyal ... to the Colony," she spoke soft and firm. She strode from his office. She took in a deep breath and held her head a little higher. She didn't know what to do next, but biding her time was no longer an option.

THIRTY

NEW MEAT

Tephra trudged down a long corridor. She followed one of the men in grey overalls, but he said nothing. She glanced around as they passed various adjoining corridors. Each passageway seemed to curve off into the distance and then disappear from sight. There were few people around. An occasional miner walked by, avoiding eye contact as they went.

The other captives were guided away by grey-clothed miners as they passed by various junctures. Tephra continued straight. She noticed the dank smell and wrinkled her nose after catching a whiff of sulphur wafting in from a distant passage.

Soon, Tephra was the only captive being led by a single grey-shirted man. She fixed her gaze on the metal floor as she trudged along. The man stopped, causing Tephra to look up. She caught sight of a woman in the same grey outfit as the man who she had followed. The woman told Tephra to follow her. Tephra made no reply. She simply shuffled into place behind the older woman and continued her march deeper into Ten.

After walking to the end of the sweeping hallway, the woman took a sharp right. Tephra followed her through a doorway and glanced around the long, narrow room. It was filled with two long rows of bunk beds. They were made of metal and had thin mattresses. Some of the beds were occupied, most were empty. On the wall at the end of the beds was a metal bench with three metal toilets spread out evenly along the wall.

The woman led Tephra to her bunk and grunted, "Number three."

Tephra looked up and saw the number three etched into the top bunk in front of her. Her bunk was second from the wall.

Tephra looked at the woman, whose face was devoid of any emotion. "What's your name?" She asked in as kindly a voice as she could manage.

The woman looked confused at first, then looked down at her arm and then back up to Tephra "23," said the woman, as she pointed to a string of six digits tattooed on her arm; 23 was the last two digits. She brushed past Tephra and started for the door. Before exiting she stopped and turned. "Your jumpers are on the bed."

Tephra looked at the bed and saw a pile of grey clothes folded in front of her. She looked around for a place to change. "Hey," said Tephra calling out to 23 before she left the room. "Where's the bathroom?"

"You're standing in it." Twenty-three pointed to the metal toilets mounted on the wall. She gave a sly smile and then turned and left.

Tephra grabbed the grey clothes and looked around again. She looked down at her shoes, which were stained brown with mud and dirt, as were her ankles. As Tephra stood there surveying herself, a different woman entered the room. Her face was dirty, and her work boots were caked with mud. She kicked the boots off at the door and threw them into a bin with other dirty work boots. She turned opposite Tephra, went to a bottom bunk, and collapsed without saying a word or making a sound.

Tephra stared at the woman for a moment. She scurried over to the bunk and knelt down next to the woman. "Hey, are you here from One too?"

The woman didn't speak. She didn't move. She just kept her eyes shut, seemingly lost in sleep the moment her head hit the pillow.

"Can you tell me anything about this place?" Tephra nearly whispered the question. She reached out her hand to touch the sleeping woman's arm, but then held back. The woman looked dirty and exhausted. May be better not to try to wake her. Not that she could even if she tried.

Tephra stood and walked to the end of the long row of bunk beds towards the metal toilets mounted on the walls. To the right of the toilets was a doorway. She entered into the adjoining room. She looked left and saw a row of sinks. There was a horrible smell wafting in the air. Two sinks were broken and cracked, another two had dirty brown water pooled in them. To the right were the showers.

Tephra trudged to the showers, which consisted of a large open area with shower heads every eight feet. There were no doors or partitions on the showers. She placed her grey clothes on a mental bench by the showers and tentatively approach a shower head. As she did so, the water began automatically. At first, the water was rust colored and pooled on the floor before rolling down to a drain and falling through it. After a bit the water turned clear. She reached out her hand to touch the water. It was cold. She grabbed for a knob on the wall under the shower head and twisted it one way and then the other, it had no effect. The water ran the same cold temperature.

Tephra kicked off her dirty shoes and rinsed her feet and legs. She threw her white dress on the floor and pulled on her new dark grey overalls, shirt, and jacket. The new clothes hung on her body; none of the items fit well. She looked down and saw her baggy overalls caused her pant legs to pool at her ankles. She knelt down to roll up the cuffs.

As soon as she knelt down she was overcome with emotion. Her hands flew to her face as tears raced from her eyes. *Ash!* She was gone. Her only friend in this new world. Ash's lifeless form floating in the middle of the water chamber flashed across her mind. It was just like before; the lifeless sailors strewn about the ship. Her crew. She had let them down. Failed them. How had she let that happen again?

Ash was like her—so much alike. She had argued with her in Ash's room before they fled. She didn't mean it. She knew Ash meant well bringing her here to help fight for what was right. Maybe she could have done more. Tried to save her. Forced her to flee the little office before they were caught. *I knew that was dangerous.* She pounded the floor with her fist.

After several minutes passed by, she wiped her eyes with her baggy shirt sleeve and stood. She had to stay strong. She rubbed her temples. This place was rough. Now wasn't the time to fall apart. She glanced down and saw her white dress on the floor. She kicked it aside. Good riddance. She didn't want that dress to begin with, and she certainly didn't care what happened to it now.

She walked back towards her bunk when another woman approached her. This woman was older, heavy set, with a scowl on her face. She looked weathered and worn.

"Hey, you, follow me," said the woman.

"Who, me?" asked Tephra.

"Yeah, you."

Tephra began to follow. "What's your name?"

"We ain't got names here. Look at my arm, you see that number? That's my name. The last two numbers of the woman's arm read 75.

"Where are we going?"

"You'll see soon enough."

"But I have a right to know—"

The older woman stepped over to Tephra and scowled. Her rough-hewn features were streaked with deep wrinkles. Her eyes were hard. "You have no rights down here, softie. You do what you're told when you're told to do it. Understand?"

Tephra gazed into 75's eyes. Had the old woman been nice when she was young? If so, there were no remnants of that in her face now. Tephra set her jaw, but held her tongue. She slowly nodded her head.

"Good, glad we understand each other." 75 turned and marched for the door. "Now follow me." Tephra followed behind.

After following 75 for a while, they came up to a battered electric cart. She motioned for Tephra to get in. She took the steering wheel and Tephra took the passenger seat next to her.

"You start your shift now. I'll take you to the main entry point. I'm your shift lead. You can call me shift lead or you can call me 75. But try not to talk to me at all."

After several minutes, they reached a large metal elevator. They both exited the cart. 75 grabbed a helmet, a heavy drill, and gloves from the nearby tool closet. The tool closet was built into the rock, with a metal cage across the front. A man was standing at the cage opening. He appeared to be the one in charge of the tools and supplies.

"Here, put these on and carry this drill. Follow me."

Tephra threw the helmet on her head and pulled on the gloves. She took the drill in her hands. She began to teeter forward and then bent at the waist as the heavy drill pulled her to the ground. She tightened her grip around the drill and stiffened the muscles in her arms and legs. She leaned back with all her might. She managed to lift the drill up to her waist. She began to teeter over again and quickly leaned back a bit further, balancing the heavy drill on the top of her leg. She didn't dare move. The shift lead looked back at Tephra and stopped walking.

"No, no, not like that," said 75. "You take the strap over the shoulder and then turn on that switch to activate the power support." 75 grabbed the strap, roughly threw it over Tephra's head, and then flipped a red switch at the top of the drill. The drill whirred to life and the heft disappeared. Tephra nearly fell backwards. She threw out her foot and caught herself from falling. 75 turned and punched a button at the side of the elevator shaft while she shook her head. "Rookies!" she exclaimed.

The metal elevator arrived and the two stepped aboard. 75

punched a button inside the elevator and the metal, mesh doors slid shut. The elevator began its descent.

75 turned and eyed Tephra. "Here's your job. You go down this elevator shaft, you mine the ore, you work a twelve-hour shift. Then you return to your assigned barracks and you spend the next twelve hours pondering your bad choices that led you here. Then you repeat the process. Everyday. Probably for the rest of your life." Her face remained emotionless and calm. Her steely eyes burned into Tephra's face as she stood there.

"Why are you here?" asked Tephra. She wasn't particularly impressed with the older woman's gruff act. She'd seen it all before in the Navy. It hadn't impressed her then and it surely didn't impress her now.

75 smiled and gave out a short laugh. "I'm a Ten'er. That's why I got this tattoo. Ten'ers were either born here and get placed here after each probatum, or they are placed here from day one of being recruited. Either way, we are fixtures down here in the muck. We ain't here for 'rehabilitation' like you people." 75 paused and looked Tephra over a bit more and scoffed.

"Why don't you have names? Why use numbers?"

"Cause most Ten'ers don't last too long down here. No need for names when you'll probably be checking out soon. If the hard work don't kill ya, the dynamite will."

"Oh my God, that's awful!"

"Yeah, real terrible. But I'm a survivor. There's a few of us who are. But there are a whole lot more who gave their lives in the muck of the mines for the good of the Colony."

"Look, you might as well know now," explained 75, "we don't like you. Ten'ers take care of their own. We have to just to survive. But we don't like outsiders and that means we don't like you. Just do your work, don't make life hard on the Ten'ers in your crew, and try not to die. Follow those rules and maybe we'll hate you a bit less."

Tephra smirked. Fair enough. She hadn't exactly taken a liking to

75 as it was and she didn't much care if she was liked or disliked at this point.

Every several yards as the elevator descended, a rocky corridor would appear with makeshift lights attached to the ceiling. The light would flash into the elevator as they passed, and then disappear into darkness as the lift passed back into solid rock. After countless levels were passed, the elevator stopped and the two exited.

"Got new meat here fellas," yelled 75 to a group of grey-shirted miners. "Try not to work her to death in one day like you did the last one." 75 looked back at Tephra. "Just kidding. The last one didn't die in a day, she lasted two weeks!" 75 snorted and slapped her leg. She turned and strode away.

An old man with a rugged jaw shuffled over to Tephra. He carried a metal rod that he used as a cane to support his weight. He looked her over from head to toe and gave out a snort. "Softie," he mumbled. He waved his hand and motioned her to stand near the rocky wall. He pointed with his makeshift cane to a point on the wall and nodded his head.

She stumbled over the rocky floor and came to an abrupt stop next to the old man. Her eyes narrowed. She held a tight grip on her drill, afraid it would knock her over again. She shook her head having no idea what she was supposed to do. "Um … "

"He wants you to drill there," said a woman standing next to Tephra. "Just put the drill bit there and pull the trigger."

Tephra did as instructed. Her fingers gingerly cradled the trigger on the drill. She tensed, clenched her teeth, and squinted her eyes until they were nearly shut tight. She pulled the trigger and the drill jumped to life. The bit on the end pounded into the rock. Vibrations raced down the drill and flood into her hands and arms. She gave out a screech and released the trigger. The drill stopped.

The old man chuckled. Then his face hardened into a frown and he shook his head. "Again, keep going," he instructed.

Tephra opened her eyes and looked at the rock in front of her. It had barely been scratched by the hefty drill. She took a step back and shook her head. "I'm not doing this. I'm not going to stand here trying to work some dumb drill!"

A tall, younger man strode up behind her and grabbed her collar. She let out a yell. "Hey!"

The old man with the metal cane waddled up next to Tephra and put his wrinkled features close to hers. "Again, keep going." He took a step back. The man holding her collar gave her a shove. She stumbled forward. The tip of her drill hit the rock causing the strap around her shoulder to stop her forward momentum. She groaned and turned her head around. The young man was walking away. "Jerk!" She yelled to no avail. The sound of her voice didn't carry over the monotonous drilling all around.

She took a deep breath and shifted her stance, placing one foot behind her and one in front. She leaned into the drill and pulled the trigger again. This time she was more prepared for the shock of the tool as it came to life and bit into the rock wall. The drill droned away, pounding the rock in front of her. Small bits of debris flew out from the drill bit and pelted her face. She sneered, but kept going.

Her arms shook and her teeth rattled as she worked. She glanced to her right. A woman stood working just five feet away. She looked to be a bit older. Grey strips of hair mingled with black strands of hair that ran across her head and down her back. She had a rag wrapped around her hair at the base of her neck. Her face was covered in dirt and dust. Tephra tried to catch the woman's eye, get a sense of who she was, but the women never wavered. Her eyes stayed fixed on the spot where she drilled.

To Tephra's left a younger man worked. His intensity was the same. Complete focus on the drill bit in front of him. No time, or desire, to look around at his fellow miners. Tephra sighed and kept working. She leaned on her drill for support. Once the bit had advanced into the rock a chunk of ore fell to the ground. The old man with the metal cane walked up and kicked the ore to the side. A short guy in grey overalls hustled up and lifted the ore off the ground. He trudged back to the waiting ore cart and dropped his prize into it.

Tephra glanced back to see the cart. Her drill jerked and bucked upwards. She stumbled backwards and grabbed the drill with both hands. She closed her eyes and waited for her body to impact the ground behind her, but instead she stayed on her feet. She opened her eyes and glanced around. The drill's stabilizer had kept her standing. She let out her breath and smirked. Not too bad for a softie. She regained her footing and grabbed the drill with both hands. She stepped forward, punched the drill's trigger, and launched back into the rock. Digging out another groove to free the next chunk of ore. The pulsating rhythm of the drill lulled her into a sense of calm as the hours ticked by.

After several hours of working the drill a large whistle echoed throughout the mine shaft. The people working around Tephra stopped their tools and turned away from the wall they had been drilling into. Tephra released the trigger on her drill and looked to the woman on her right. "Quittin' time, let's go." The woman pointed with her head towards the elevator shaft.

Beads of sweat poured down Tephra's face. Her hair was matted and wet both from sweat, but also from the endless trickle of water seeping from the walls and ceiling of the mine. Her hands felt numb and the thunderous vibrations still reverberated throughout her body even though her drill was silent. Her muscles were sore from working the drill for the past several hours.

The miners formed two rows as they filed into the mine shaft elevator for the ride back up to their respective barracks. Tephra's eyes glassed over. She followed the person ahead of her without having any idea what she was doing or why. Her body ached, her mouth and throat were dry. A fine layer of dust covered her entire body. Her turn in the lift arrived and she filed in behind a group of miners. They rode in silence up to the barracks area. They trudged off the lift, hung their drills in the supply locker and marched towards their barracks.

"You, new meat, this way." 75 was standing at the end of a long corridor. She was waving her hand to indicate Tephra should follow.

She moved her feet in the right direction, but she felt like she had no control over her exhausted body. "Time to get you some grub. Follow me."

75 led Tephra down a long hallway and then through a doorway into the mess hall. She escorted her to the start of the food line and told her to grab a tray. Tephra complied without uttering a word. She shifted down the line. A string of workers waited to be served. When it was Tephra's turn she held up her tray. The man behind the counter plunked a plate down on it. The plate was filled with a large lump of dark gray mash. The food type was unidentifiable. Steam rose up from the large lump and felt warm on Tephra's face. The smell was unappetizing. At the end of the line, Tephra was handed a metal jug of water.

She turned with her dinner in hand and peered around the room. It was full of metal tables with metal benches bolted to the floor. She staggered over to a table across the room and sat down. Each table was rectangular and could seat eight to ten dirty miners.

"Rough day?" asked a woman seated across from Tephra. She hadn't noticed the woman when she sat down. She had barely released the food tray from her hand before she grabbed the metal jug of water and emptied the contents down her dry, dusty throat.

Tephra peered up at the person sitting across from her. "Seabreeze? I can't believe it."

Seabreeze smiled. "Hello, Cynthia."

"No, it's Tephra now."

"Oh, nice name. I like it. Tephra."

Tephra leaned forward. "This place is miserable."

A man sat down next to Tephra. He clanged his tray onto the table and grabbed for his fork. He began shoveling large forkfuls of the grey mash into his mouth.

"You get used to it after a while, I suppose," replied Seabreeze. She took a small lump of grey mash on her fork and held it out in front of her, surveying the contents of the bite.

"The heck you do!" The man spoke with his mouth full. Small bits of food flew out and splattered on the table in front of him.

Tephra took a small bite of the grey mash and crinkled her nose at the taste. "Yuck, what is this?"

"Left overs, what the other folks upstairs don't eat." The man pointed upwards with his fork. "They mix it all together, boil it, and add some salt." The man pounded his hand down on the table and laughed.

Tephra nodded her head and look sideways at the man. She thought he was unappetizing when the meal started, but he was getting worse by the minute.

"We used to have good food here, but that all changed a couple years ago. This mush has been our regular meal—three time a day."

Tephra turned her eyes back to Seabreeze. "What happened to you after you were escorted from the Hall of Equals?" asked Tephra.

"Hall of Equals!" The man sitting next to Tephra turned his head, speaking between large bites. "Good golly, got a couple of fancy ladies here, huh?" Tephra ignored the man and continued looking into Seabreeze's eyes.

"I was brought directly here, to Ten."

"Did you see the Masters?"

"No."

"Yeah, I thought so." Tephra let out a sigh. If the Masters truly were able to right the wrongs of Cosmotine, where were they?

"When do we get out of here?" asked Tephra.

The man next to her gave out a snort and dropped his fork onto the table. "Hey, nobody leaves Ten anymore ... not alive anyway." The man needled his elbow into Tephra's arm.

Tephra frowned and turned her head towards the man. "What do you mean? People move around the Colony, right?"

"Maybe, but it ain't good for business letting people out of Ten these days. The others may learn how we is treated down here now. How we live." The man's eyes went wide as he leaned closer to Tephra.

"What about the *probatum*? Being able to test onto another level?"

"Oh yes, the *probatum* works fine on every level, but it don't work here no more. Sure we all take the *probatum*, got to keep up appearances, but ain't no one been assigned another level since Cosmotine took over. Every Ten'er's *probatum* shows Ten every time, even the people who don't like it and aren't good at it. The only *probatum* we got is the drill and the dynamite. Live through another shift and you pass the test. Your reward is to come back and do another shift tomorrow. If you die, you fail. But then again, maybe that's a pass too—onto the ultimate level!" the man pounded his hand on the table again and gave out a hearty laugh.

Tephra looked back towards Seabreeze. "Things have changed, Tephra," said Seabreeze. "Things have changed."

THIRTY-ONE

ONE COLONY

A Century Earlier — July 24, 2030 — The Colony, Level Four

"Chuck, any word?"

Chuck glanced over his shoulder. Cathy stood behind him. She rubbed her hands together and bit her bottom lip. "No, Cathy, no word." Chuck put down his clip board and took Cathy's hand.

"Cathy, I think we have to face facts."

Cathy looked down at her feet. She didn't want to face any facts just yet. There was always hope. She glanced back up; her eyes filled with tears. "I ... I was just thinking that maybe they were delayed a bit longer than we expected."

Chuck nodded. "Yeah, maybe." He put his large hand on Cathy's shoulder and gave it a squeeze. "There's always hope, right Cathy?"

Cathy nodded. A single tear slid down her cheek. "Yes," she whispered.

"Hey, look at what I have here." Chuck grabbed his clipboard and scurried over to Cathy's side. "We've done a great job getting agriculture up and running. I mean we are really off to a great start here. Look at these production numbers, huh?"

Cathy nodded. "Yes, yes. You all are doing great." Cathy reached her hand to her left eye and wiped away the tears. She cleared her throat and shook her head.

"How's the energy generation coming along?" Asked Chuck.

"Fine, fine. We have everything on line now. Looks to be working well."

"Hey, that's great. See a little time down here in the Colony and we have worked out all the bugs."

"Chuck?"

"Yes, Cathy?"

"Do you think Leo will come? It's been nearly a month. I mean, he has to get here soon."

"Oh sure, Cathy. He'll come here soon. He'll come just as soon as he can."

"What do we do until then?"

Chuck paced away from Cathy. He stopped and turned around to face her. "We make you our new leader."

"What?" Cathy couldn't believe what she was hearing. Her? The new leader? That was absurd.

"Cathy, myself and the others on the counsel—all 12 of us—have been talking. We need someone with a level head, but also a positive attitude. That's you!" Chuck pointed a finger at Cathy. "You're a perfect choice. Besides your *probatum* identified you as a leader—our leader."

"Oh Chuck, please." She waved her hand to dismiss his statement. "Surely you're joking."

"No, I'm not. You will be our first leader. Congratulations."

Cathy rolled her eyes. She could feel heat filling her cheeks. "Well if that's what you really want."

"That's what the counsel wants Cathy. And that's where your *probatum* placed you. It's science."

"Ok, fine, but only temporarily—once Leo arrives then he has the job."

"Don't be silly Cathy. The job is yours for life. Believe me, Leo would agree with us if he were here."

"No, I'm serious. Once Leo arrives I'm stepping down and there's nothing you can do to stop me. You understand?"

"Sure, Cathy. I understand."

Cathy nodded. "Ok, good." She glanced around the engineering room and titled her head. "So now what?"

"Hmm?" Chuck had turned towards his desk to continue his work.

"What do I do now?"

"You go to work being our leader, Cathy. Build your team from the colonists on One. And be prepared to share your vision of the Colony with the counsel when we meet next week."

"Counsel of twelve, huh? Masters of your craft for each level." Cathy smiled. "Should be Masters Twelve."

"Yeah, that's not really my area of expertise, you know?"

Cathy turned and strode away from Chuck. *My vision?* She had some ideas kicking around in her head. Ideas she was never asked to share before now. This was her chance to make a mark on this new world. Order, peace, reason. The founding principles would be refined and then implemented. A home to all who journey here. A safe haven from the chaos of life on land. A new world civilization. But still, it would be better if she knew where Leon was. If she had his approval, his support, his counsel.

Cathy turned towards the doorway. She took several steps and then glanced towards the row of portholes revealing the dark, lifeless ocean outside. She twisted her lips and sighed.

"Leo, where are you?" She whispered.

THIRTY-TWO

WINDS OF CHANGE

May 4, 2130 — The Colony — Level Seven

"Darn it!" Misty dropped a broken pipe onto the ground and stood up straight. She craned her neck to look behind her. "Wheaty, Wheaty!" She waved her hand in the air trying to get his attention.

In the distance a man raised his head from the engine compartment of a tractor sitting across the field from Misty. He nodded his head and began walking towards her. Once he was close enough he replied, "What ya got?"

"Busted pipe again. Can you radio back to the warehouse for Acer to come out and fix this ... again?" Misty shook her head. The same pipe had been repaired the week before, but not to her liking. It having broke again reinforced her displeasure with the past repair all the more.

"Ah ... Acer isn't at the warehouse."

"What?"

"Yeah, he got recruited by the guards two days ago."

"Dang it, another one taken by the guards?" Misty slapped her hand on her leg. "What the heck are they doing taking so many people?"

Wheaty shrugged his shoulders. He stood silently next to Misty. She rubbed her chin and shook her head. "And all of my best people too." Misty dropped her hand and looked up at Wheaty standing next to her. He was at least a foot taller and his wide frame dwarfed Misty by comparison. "Well don't just stand there looking stupid," barked Misty. "Finish fixing that tractor."

Wheaty grinned, turned around and plodded back to the tractor. The days had gotten longer and harder since her field hands began to dwindle. Her sector was short-handed as it was before the changes occurred. Now it was nearly impossible to keep the place running efficiently.

Misty shuffled over to her farm truck and flung the door open. She jumped into the driver's seat and sped off towards the warehouse. The electric motor whirred along as a trail of dust rose up behind her. She reached the warehouse and stopped the truck with a sudden stomp on the brakes. Misty jumped out and grabbed a shovel from the truck bed. She turned to walk into the warehouse. As she approached, she saw an older man sitting in a rickety old chair outside the entrance. She stopped in front of him and plunged the shovel she was holding into the dirt at her feet.

"Hey, Cotton, is it just me or is there trouble brewing? We can't be expected to keep producing enough food without enough field hands. And we aren't the only ones you know. I hear tell other sectors are facing the same problem."

"What problem is that?" Cotton peered up at Misty and pushed his cap back a bit further on his forehead.

"A shortage of field hands! Are you even listening to me?"

Cotton waved his hand at her. "Yeah, yeah I'm listening."

"What do they need so many guards for?"

Cotton shrugged.

"And here's another thing, none of them took a *probatum* to be placed on Five as a guard. I know for sure Flint never had a *probatum* that placed him on Five; maybe he did now. But Acer couldn't even fix a pipe correctly, he sure as heck wouldn't be placed as a guard on Five." Misty reached up and scratched her head.

"Don't get yourself worked up, Misty. People come and go sometimes."

"Not like this you old fool. Not like this." Misty grabbed her shovel from the ground and started to walk into the warehouse. Cotton turned in his chair to face Misty as she passed.

"Well, what you know about *probatum*s anyway? Yours has pegged you a crop supervisor for years."

"Well I know enough that it must be taken; and it must place you on Five." Misty stopped mid-stride and turned her head to face Cotton. "I'm telling you something's not right. For the past year ... maybe two years, things have changed around here. Can't you see that?" Cotton turned back in his seat, placed his chin on his chest, and closed his eyes. "All I see is dirt," he mumbled.

Misty turned and strode into the warehouse. She placed her shovel in the storage locker and trudged over to the large office at the corner of the warehouse. She pushed open the door, which was already unlatched, and saw a group of field hands hunched over a table.

"Hey Misty, you care for a beer?"

"Might as well." She grabbed the nearest chair and pulled it back from the table. She sat down and gave out a sigh.

"Somethin' botherin' you, Misty?" The man to her right turned his head and clasped his large hand on Misty's shoulder.

"Yeah, but I'm not sure what to do about it."

"What's the problem?"

"We are losing field hands left and right. The guards seem to be coming around here every day plucking a new recruit—so they call them." The man across the table handed misty a glass mug with a dark liquid inside. She held the mug up to her face, but before she took a drink she continued, "What could they be doing with all them field hands?"

"I don't know, but it does seem odd."

Misty took a swig of beer and placed the mug on the table in front of her. "And none of 'em took a *probatum*, that much is clear."

"Really, you think these field hands are taken without a *probatum*?"

"I know so. There is no way all the hands we lost would've been placed on Five. No *probatum* among the lot of 'em."

"I heard the same thing is happening in other sectors. Field hands scooped up all over Seven. Making them new guards." The man next to Misty withdrew his hand from her shoulder and scratched his head.

"Something doesn't add up," replied Misty.

"You think it's the Commodore?"

"Who knows," replied Misty, "but I doubt it. There's something wrong up top."

"Up top? You mean like on One?"

"Yeah, on One." Misty took another swig of beer and placed the mug in front of her. "Something's wrong up there. And I'm going to figure out what it is."

THIRTY-THREE

THE TWO TEN'ERS

Tephra's entire body felt exhausted. She could swear even her hair hurt. A week had passed and the constant drilling never let up. When she wasn't working a drill, she would shovel the grey mush down her throat and trudge to her bunk. There was never enough food, or enough sleep. Morning came fast. Dust and dirt stained every crease in her hands and face.

"Rise and shine, softie." 75 stood at the foot of Tephra's bunk. She was hitting the metal bunk frame with a hammer, filling the entire barracks with noise.

"I'm up, I'm up!" cried Tephra. She rolled out of her top bunk and planted her feet on the ground. They hurt. Her hair was a wild mess, her eyes formed small slits.

"You're going to a new crew today, new meat. Get dressed and meet me by the elevator shaft in five." 75 swung her hammer and gave the bed frame a final knock before turning and walking out of the barracks.

Tephra rubbed both temples with her hands. *I wish 75 would drop dead.* She turned slowly towards the showers and shuffled from her spot next to the bunk.

"I heard you crying last night." A woman leaning against the bunk across from Tephra smirked. Her devilish grin evidencing her delight in Tephra's pain.

"It wasn't me!" Tephra shot the woman a deathly look. *Had she really heard? No, she couldn't have.*

"Yeah, right. I know my whimpers by now. But deny it if you must."

"Shut up."

"Easy, easy. I'm shutting." The woman held out her palms in self-defense.

Tephra trudged over to the doorway leading to the showers. She turned back towards the woman. "What's your name, anyway?"

"Me? What do you care?"

Tephra grimaced and shook her head. She didn't really care, so why fight it? The woman could drop dead for all she cared. She turned and shuffled to the showers. In the morning, the shower water was luke-warm at best. She ran her head under the flow and tried to open her eyes. Her legs throbbed with pain from all the work she was forced to endure.

She finished her shower and pulled on her clothes. She buried her head in her hands and sighed. *What the hell am I doing here? I don't know how much more of this I can take.* She thought of the world she had left behind. Had Brad's childish tantrums really been that bad? What she wouldn't give to be back there right now— clenching her teeth, but still comfortably seated at her desk. Her desire to escape, to try another challenge, now seemed foolish. *Why couldn't I just be happy with what I had?*

"There, there, don't cry again." The women from the bunk was strolling across the shower bay. Tephra looked up and scowled. She shook her head and ran out of the room. She sure as heck wasn't crying. What good would it do anyway? *I just need to get myself out of here.*

Tephra trudged out of the dorm and down the corridor to the elevator bank where 75 was waiting.

"About time! That was more like 10 than 5." 75 punched the elevator call button. She crossed her arms and tapped her foot while eyeing Tephra.

Tephra stood next to her not moving. Her arms hung by her side and her head sagged.

"New meat, grab your drill and gear! You know the routine. Let's go!"

Tephra jumped and turned towards the supply locker. *I know, I know.* She donned her gear, pulled gloves onto her hands, and started up her drill. She turned and followed 75 onto the elevator as the metal mesh door raised from bottom to top.

Once the elevator reached the mine shaft, the two stepped off. 75 lead Tephra down the shaft and arrived at a group of miners preparing to set off further down the tunnel.

"Hold up, got your newbie here." 75 called out. The group continued to walk away but two men stopped, turned and approached Tephra.

"Who's this now?" said one of the men.

"This here replaces the one you lost yesterday," replied 75. "Her name's Tephra. See if you can make her last a few weeks." She snorted and slapped Tephra's back.

Tephra rolled her eyes. *Lovely, same joke she always uses.* She was too tired to smile. She just stood there looking at the two men. 75 turned and trudged away.

"Heya," said one of the men. "Name's 93." He nodded his head and smiled. "This here is 11." He pointed at 11 with his thumb as 11 raised his hand and gave a small wave. Tephra remained silent, starring off into the distance.

"Hey, is she ok?" asked 11. "She's not ... coocoo ... is she?" 11 turned his finger in a circle next to his head.

Tephra shook her head to clear the fog. "What? No, no, I'm fine. Just tired." Tephra glanced at the two young men standing before her. They seemed different. Their faces weren't hard as nails like the rest of the people on Ten. They both had soft smiles on their faces, and their eyes seemed warm ... almost friendly.

"Oh yeah, drilling will do that to a person for sure." 93 nodded his head and turned an eye to 11. "Shall we get going then?" 11 nodded. They turned and walked down the mine shaft. Tephra looked down at the ground and followed behind.

93 turned his head back towards Tephra. He smiled. "We are Ten'ers. Born and raised." 11 turned his head and nodded. They both held back allowing Tephra to catch up. She walked in between the two as they continued down the shaft.

"You might have noticed that 75 is a bit grumpy at times," added 11.

"Grumpy? She's downright mean."

"Oh yeah, 75 is always like that. She's either mean, mad, or grumpy; her only three emotions. But we love her. She's like a mom to us."

"Yeah, you just don't take what she says real serious," added 93. "She calls us dumb morons all the time, but she also has helped us a ton with food and medicine and stuff."

The trio continued to walk down the mine shaft. The air was filled with fine dust, and the noise of the machinery was loud and relentless. It echoed against the rocks. The lights were bolted against the ceiling and they made strange shadows on the rock and the people working all around them as they walked.

When they reached the end of the shaft, 11 pointed to a spot in the rock where a small hole had been started. "You drill into that spot and keep drilling until you pull out a chunk of ore." Tephra followed his instructions and pulled the trigger on the drill, bringing it to life. The air was thick with dust around her. Her arms shook as the drill dug slowly deeper into the rock. She knew the routine by now. She leaned into the drill. The rhythmic whine of the equipment lulled her into a trance. She worked without thought.

After several hours of drilling, she was tapped on the shoulder. "Hey, stop for a minute, we have a quick meal break, here." She scrunched her forehead in disbelief. She never had a meal break before. She stopped her drill, threw the strap off her shoulder and placed her drill on a nearby rock. She had been working the drill for so long, that she still felt the vibrations running through her forearms even though the drill had been switched off.

11 shoved a metal cup into her hand and handed her what looked like a sandwich wrapped in tin foil. 11 had the same thing in his hand. He sauntered over to a rock and sat down. 93 joined him.

"Have a seat, Tephra," said 11 as he patted the large rock beside him. The mining corridor was damp, with water seeping from the walls and a trickle of water running underfoot. She edged to the rock and sat beside the two men. Both of them looked considerably younger than any of the other people working in the corridor.

"How long you two been down here?" asked Tephra, hoping to find out their age, as she took a drink of water from the metal cup.

"Forever," said 93.

"Yeah, we grew up in this mine shaft. We used to throw rocks down the abandoned shafts to see how far down the water was," added 11.

"Both my mom and dad lived here all their lives," added 93. "They're both dead now, but they worked right here. And I worked here with them once I was able to hold a drill."

At that moment an older man lumbered over to where they were sitting and sat down on a rock. He sighed as he sat. He looked up at the group and said "Hey, how you guys holding up today?"

"Holding up? You kidding me?" said 93. "I filled five carts myself this morning, I may set a new personal record." He held his head high and thumped his chest.

The older man shook his head and chuckled. "Stop making the rest of us look bad." The man looked over at Tephra. "When you get here?"

"First day on this crew," said Tephra.

"I'm Kevin. Hey I know you ... the transport ship, right?"

Tephra glanced at the older man again and realized he was the man that sat next to her on the transport ship. The one tussling with the men after she took her *probatum*.

"Oh yeah, I remember you," said Tephra. "Have you been down here the whole time?"

"Yeah, brought here straight away. I thought for sure I'd be an engineer, but they claimed I was a miner. Came here based on a promise of prosperity and efficiency." Kevin waved his hands in the air to mimic the grandiose nature of his statement. "Instead, I got worse than I had back on land." Kevin shook his head again.

"Other levels may have it easier, but they can't prove their worth like we do, ain't that right 93 ?" 11 slapped his knee.

"Sure! Why we do the single most important job in all the Colony—how else would it run were it not for our work?"

Kevin shook his head and looked down at his sandwich. "I'd do my part on any level, but this one."

"Hey, if you're so miserable how is it that your *probatum* placed you here?" 93 jammed his sandwich into his mouth. He took a large bite as his eyes remained fixed on Kevin.

"I don't know." Kevin took a swig of water and let out a low sigh. "I was placed here from the start, but I don't know how. I can't dig worth crap."

"Well, just do another *probatum*, you can do that you know," said 11.

"I know, I know." Kevin wiped sweat from his brow leaving behind a smudge of dirt on his forehead. "I've done it and it came up Ten." Kevin shrugged. He looked down at the sandwich in his hand.

"Why is your name still Kevin?" asked Tephra.

"It ain't," answered 11. "Look at his arm, it's 63."

"I'm Kevin, dang it! I'm not going by a dumb number."

"Say what you want, your name ain't Kevin no more." 11 nodded his head to accentuate his point. Tephra shrugged her shoulders and returned her attention to her sandwich. Eating mid-shift was a nice change of pace and she wasn't going to waste it. Besides, the sandwich was a thousand times better than the grey mush that had become her staple diet.

As everyone sat and ate in silence, the lights overhead suddenly turned from yellow to red. A siren began to sound. 11 and 93 jumped up onto their feet letting their food and drink fall to the ground

"It's a breach!" yelled 11.

"Run for it!" yelled 93. The two men began waving their arms, directing the crew to make for the exit. 11 grabbed Tephra by the wrist and pulled her to her feet. 93 grabbed both of Kevin's hands and pulled him up as well. They turned and bolted off, running down the corridor toward the elevator. Tephra instinctively ran after them, not knowing what was happening or why they were running. The miners that had been working around them began to run as well. Everyone sprinted back up the mine tunnel towards the elevator shaft.

Kevin gave out a cry as he lost his footing and his knee buckled. He slammed his head on the ground and rolled over onto his back. 93 jerked his head back and stopped mid-stride. Tephra nearly ran into the back of him. 93 and Tephra scurried back to Kevin; each grabbed a hand.

"Get up! Get up!" yelled 93. Kevin rolled back onto his stomach and tried to push himself up off the ground. He rose a few inches and gave out a howl.

"My leg, I think it's broken. I can't move it."

"Get up, dang it! There's no time, it's a breach!"

"Go! Just go on, I'll crawl back. I'll be fine."

93 looked down at Kevin. He looked back over his shoulder at the fleeing miners drawing ever smaller as they fled. He looked over at Tephra and back down at Kevin again.

"Just go, darn you! I'll be fine on my own. Go!" Kevin waved his hand. Tephra and 93 turned and took off in a dead run.

After taking a dozen strides, Tephra could hear a loud crash from behind her. The side of the tunnel where the group had sat just moments before began to cave in. Rock, dirt, and dust began to move in every direction. Behind it came a wall of water, pushing aside the heavy rock as if they were weightless. The water swirled and churned, gobbling up everything in its path. It carried the rock and other debris with it as it made a run down the tunnel heading towards the fleeing miners.

Tephra turned her head around and saw the wall of water. She turned her head back and ran forward with all her might. As she did so, the wall of water and rock had quickly turned into a slurry of thick mud, moving and thrashing in the tunnel. It caught up to Kevin and engulfed him in an instant. He gave out a yell but was consumed by the wall of liquid mud so quickly that his voice died out as he disappeared from view. 93 pushed his hand on Tephra's back.

Tephra's eyes widened as she ran. She had no idea they were in that much trouble. Tephra and 93 caught up to 11. The three sprinted past a large metal door that was closing quickly. The mud slurry approached as the door made its way into a large groove cut into the rock, sealing the miners off from the deadly waters on the other side.

Tephra kept running past the door and towards the elevator, 11 and 93 ran closely behind. The elevator was crammed with miners, trying desperately to leave. "Stand back, stand back," yelled a large man attending the elevator. "The seal door has closed; you are safe for now." The man's words had no effect on the surrounding miners; they continued to press towards the elevator door in a panic to escape.

Tephra stopped and tried to catch her breath. She looked back at the thick blast door that had shut behind her. She could hear rocks and other debris bumping up against the metal on the other side. She wondered if the door would hold.

"Come on, we'll never make it on the main elevator. Follow us." 11 waved his hand at Tephra to follow along. 93 and 11 ran up a smaller side corridor and then turned into another shaft. The pair wound around various corridors and shafts until they arrived at an area that was mostly dark, lit with a single dim bulb.

"Almost there," said 93. He flung open a door to reveal a small round room with a ladder in the middle of it. He grabbed the rungs of the ladder and started scaling upwards.

"You next," said 11 to Tephra. Tephra grabbed the ladder and followed upwards. 11 followed behind.

After climbing for several minutes, 93 came to another metal door and kicked it open with his foot. He jumped from the ladder to the opening and steadied himself. He looked back at Tephra, who had stopped climbing and was clinging to the ladder. He held out his hand.

"Just give a good push off the ladder, it's not that far," said 93 with his hand outstretched. Tephra paused. She wasn't sure she could make it. She shifted her weight to the side closer the door and gave a big push with her legs. She moved sideways through the air and barely missed the threshold of the door. She felt herself begin to fall and let out a scream—expecting to fall to her death. Her life flashed before her eyes. She waved her arms in every direction trying to find something to grab and then she stopped suddenly. Her chin hit her chest as her head fell forward. She groaned. Her body went limp.

93 had grabbed her overalls from the back of her neck, while 11 reached out to steady her legs.

"We've got you; we've got you," said 93. "Now give me your hand," he said in a calm voice.

Tephra reached her hand up and felt 93's hand reaching down. He pulled her up into the doorway and back several feet to make room for 11. 11 scurried up the ladder, made a quick leap, and landed on his feet just inside the doorway.

The two men grabbed each of Tephra's arms and helped her to her feet. Tephra was shaken but happy to be on solid ground once again.

93 turned and continued down the corridor. He turned a corner and came to a door with the number 93 crudely scrawled on it. He waved his hand and the door opened. The group entered a room with

metal walls. The lights flicked on from above, and a small bed was revealed pushed up against the wall in the corner of the room. There were several chairs scattered around the room and a small table in the middle. A doorway to the left led to a small bathroom. There were books piled on the table in the center of the room. A small closet was the only other doorway.

"My little home," said 93 to Tephra. "When mom and dad died, I wandered around a lot and eventually found this abandoned section of the mine. I brought 11 here too and we each staked out rooms for ourselves. We don't come here that much anymore, but it's nice to have it in an emergency, huh 11?"

11 nodded his approval. 93 opened a cabinet next to the bed that contained a small fridge. He took out some drink canisters and placed them on the table. "Here, have some of this," he said.

Tephra grabbed a chair and drug it over to the small table. She plopped down in her seat and placed her elbows on the table in front of her. She put her head in her hands and closed her eyes.

"What was that back there? What happened?" asked Tephra. She could feel her cheeks flash red with heat. A replay of everything that happened in the flooding mine shaft flashed across her mind. "We almost died!"

11 jumped in to explain. "It was a breach of the walls. We are so far under the seabed that it can be difficult to hold out the rock and the water. When the supports fail, the walls collapse and the tunnel floods. Happens fairly often. We lose a few people each time—just part of the job." 11 explained these gruesome details as if he hadn't a care in the world.

"Poor Kevin," said Tephra. "He couldn't even run. We tried to save him ... we just couldn't get him up." Tephra shook her head back and forth while still holding her forehead in her hands. "We should've done more."

"Yeah, well Kevin couldn't mine either," said 93. "If the water didn't kill him, 75 would have. Either way, he was not long for Ten.

There was nothing more we coulda done. Here, have a drink. It'll calm your nerves."

93 poured some liquid out of a bottle and into the metal cups he had placed on the table. He lifted his cup and said, "To Kevin, may you rest in peace as part of the Colony." He then took a large swig.

Tephra grabbed the cup in front of her and put it to her lips. She could smell the alcohol wafting up from the liquid inside. She threw her head back and emptied her cup. The liquid slid down her throat with a dull burn. She held the cup in her hand and turned it around with her finger tips. "This place is dangerous. I need to get out of here."

"Can be ... at times." 93 poured himself another shot and sat opposite Tephra. 11 pulled up a chair and sat beside him.

"Ain't really no worse than running from guards on Five or somethin' like that," said 11. 93 lashed his fist out and punched 11 on the arm. "Ouch, what's that for?"

Tephra glanced up. She eyed 11 for a minute. A thought danced in her head. *How does he know what it's like running from guards on Five?* "I need to get back to One. You know, back to where I started."

93 and 11 looked at each other.

"Yeah so?" 11 shifted in his chair and looked down at his empty cup.

"I'll bet there's a way to get there from here, huh?" Tephra kept her eyes glued on 11. He looked like the weaker link of the pair.

"Yeah, the elevator, which is monitored by the guards—like all the time." 93 let out a snort. "Good luck with that."

"Hmm, the elevator ...." Tephra glanced at 93. His eyes immediately turned away. He looked up at the ceiling. "But what if there was some other way? You know, like a passage."

"Other way?" 93 spoke while keeping his eyes turned upwards. "Don't know any other way."

"We don't go up top," said 11. "We ain't never been up top," he said to emphasize his point.

"Oh yeah, I'm sure you two don't go up top. I mean, it would take some smart maneuvering to get up there from here—without using the elevator that is." Tephra's eyes darted back and forth between the two Ten'ers. They both looked around the room avoiding eye contact with her. She was onto something. Surely one of them would break soon.

"Hey, you guys know anyone here who may have figured out how to get up top? I mean, like someone real resourceful, crafty, wily ... you know, smart?" A devilish grin rolled across Tephra's face. She didn't know how much more she had to lean on the two Ten'ers, but she guessed she was getting close. "You must know someone like that, right?" Tephra stood and walked behind her two new friends. She placed a hand on each of their shoulders and then leaned down to talk into their ears. "Anyone who knows how to get us here must know how to get us up there."

93 let out a sigh. "Ok, yes, we have been up top before. We know a few ways to get there, but none of them are easy. Worse yet, if they find out we went wandering around past Ten, we will be punished. You will be punished worst of all." 11 nodded his agreement.

"Yeah, well, I'm ready to risk it," Tephra patted the men on the back and turned towards the door. "Looks like a death sentence to stay here. Now let's get moving."

THIRTY-FOUR

GRANITE'S CHARGE

Flint and a group of guards rode the elevator back up to Five. They had taken captives from One to Ten several times over the past week. The assignment was always the same. Go to One, take hold of some white-clothed equals, herd them down to Ten, and then do it all again. Granite stepped off the elevator and walked to the guards' lounge—a large recreation area with chairs, couches, games, and a bar jutting out from the far wall.

"We're off shift, cadet," said Granite. "You can do whatever you want. I'm going to the bar." Granite walked away from Flint and trudged over to the bar. The bartender placed Granite's usual drink on the bar as he approached without saying a word. Flint had seen the same sequence play out every night for the past week. Granite plopped down on the bar stool and grabbed the drink with both hands. He leaned forward and slumped his head over the bar.

Flint glanced around the lounge and then strode over to stand slightly behind Granite. Granite turned his head to look at Flint with a stern look of disapproval. "What?" said Granite.

"Sarge, I have some questions."

Granite snapped his body around, stood in front of Flint and leaned in close to his face. "At the bar I sit by myself. I talk to no one and I want no one talking to me. Go entertain yourself and meet me at the elevator tomorrow. 0700 sharp."

Flint nodded his head and walked away as Granite lowered himself back into his seat and slumped his shoulders. Clearly, talking to Granite was a waste of time. He couldn't figure out why the old Sergeant had such a nasty disposition. His job looked easy. Heck, Flint had worked way harder down in the wheat fields on Seven. This guard stuff was a piece of cake so far. But for some reason, he just couldn't seem to connect with Granite. The grizzled old guard kept to himself, not letting anyone get close. Oh well, Flint didn't have time to figure Granite out. He had bigger questions he needed answered. Like when would the real guard work start? Hopefully, this wasn't all there was to it.

Flint strayed to the guard lounge and took a seat on a long black couch. He glanced around then sat back letting out a sigh. Being a guard wasn't what he thought it would be. *Why do we keep taking people down to Ten all the time? And why is Ten so terrible?* Flint shuddered remembering the sulfuric, putrid smells from Ten.

"Hey Flint." A guard walked over and sat opposite Flint in a black lounge chair.

Flint glanced up. "Oh, heya Acer. Didn't know you was here."

"Just arrived a couple days ago," said Acer.

"Oh ... ok. Didn't know you was up for a *probatum*."

"I wasn't."

"Oh no?"

"Naw, just got yanked from the fields. How 'bout you?"

"Same."

"Oh, yeah? No *probatum* placed you here? I thought you was gunnin' for this."

"Yeah, yeah, I was. But no *probatum*. Just brought here by that captain guy."

"Hmmm. Yeah same here." Acer sat back and rubbed his jaw. "How you likin' it?"

Flint sat up straight. "Ah ... I don't know. Not what I expected, I guess. We keep taking equals to Ten. That's about my whole job."

"Yeah, I've made a few of those trips too."

"Now, how can it be that so many people are being reassigned to Ten? I took the *probatum* every two months for a year and never got nothing more than placed back where I was."

Acer shrugged. "Don't know. Maybe they are different up there than us."

"Yeah ... maybe." Flint nodded. "Well Ten sure is different, wouldn't you say?"

"Oh yeah. That place is terrible. Smells bad too. I'm always happy to leave."

Flint nodded and sat back in his chair. His head swirled with thoughts. He looked down at the floor and rubbed the back of his neck.

"Hey, you want a drink?" asked Acer.

"Oh ... no, no."

"Suit yourself." Acer stood. "Seeya later." He gave a small wave and sauntered over to the bar.

Flint nodded his head and rose to his feet. He needed to find some answers. He certainly wasn't going to find any here. There was only one person he knew who might have some.

THIRTY-FIVE

BEYOND TEN

"Escaped!" yelled Cosmotine. "No one escapes Ten, find her!" Cosmotine exploded with anger at hearing a rebel escaping his well-crafted prison on Ten.

Ember recoiled at Cosmotine's anger, but she couldn't help but feel proud of Tephra. She knew that one was sharp.

"Sir, there was a blow out in the mining tunnel," explained Topaz. "They lost lives down there. She could be dead, but there are reports she was seen after the blast doors closed with two Ten'ers. Those two are missing as well."

"I don't care who she is with, find her, find the two Ten'ers, find them all. I want you to end this, now! And when you do find them, bring them to me. We will use the interrogation chamber and then send them to their watery graves."

Ember stood up. "Cosmotine, let me go with Topaz. Ten'ers can be difficult and I can communicate and get them to help better than Topaz."

Cosmotine waved his arm in consent. Topaz turned and scurried out of Cosmotine's office. Ember followed closely behind him.

"Get me the shift lead on communications now!" barked Topaz.

"Where are you going? Down to Ten?" asked Ember. She had to break into a jog to keep up with Topaz's long stride.

Topaz scoffed. "Yes, of course down to Ten. I will find some answers myself." The pair reached the elevator bank. They stepped onto the waiting lift as Topaz activated the priority code to Ten. They rode down the lift in silence. Ember could almost feel the thoughts churning through Topaz's brain. He looked to be disturbed. Something was outside of his control. That clearly bothered him; maybe even haunted him?

Topaz stepped off the elevator on Ten and trotted straight to the dirty metal desk. Topaz ordered the attendant to summon the shift lead working at the time the three disappeared. Shift lead 75 soon appeared from the side door.

"When was the last time you saw the three escapees?" asked Topaz when 75 entered the room, not waiting to exchange any pleasantries.

"Escapees?" asked 75 in a bewildered tone. "I'm not aware of no escapees." 75 walked over to the metal desk, heaved her drill on top of it, and slowly removed her gloves.

"Yes, the equal named Tephra and the two Ten'ers who have gone missing."

"Aw, they ain't gone nothin'. People disappear for a time down here. They always come back. Nowhere to go, now is there?"

"Is it possible the three of them were killed in the accident?"

"No, no, that didn't happen."

"How can you be so sure?"

"Well, because I saw 'em after the blast door was closed."

"What blast door?"

"When we have any emergency the large metal blast doors close to choke off any fire or keep out any water. When the water blow-out occurred, the alarm sounded, and the blast doors started to close. I distinctly remember seeing the three of them run through the blast door right before it closed."

"And you didn't stop them?"

75 took a step back and put her hand out in a defensive stance. "Stop them ... no ... I, I didn't know."

"Did you help them escape? Are you hiding the truth? Tell me now!"

Ember put a hand on Topaz's shoulder. She smiled warmly at 75. "I am sure you didn't realize they were escaping."

"Look, those two, 11 and 93, they're like sons to me. I practically raised 'em. Us Ten'ers, we stick close. Anytime there's trouble I look for those two—usually because they're the ones causing it. I was relieved to see them go through the door. It meant they were alive and well. I assumed they were just seeking safety."

"Where did they go?" Topaz slammed his hands on the metal desk.

"I have no idea. It's not unusual for those two to disappear for days, sometimes weeks, and then come back like nothing ever happened."

"What do you mean disappear? This is a locked floor, no one can come or go without me knowing about it."

"Oh really? Well, your majesty, I guess they know how to evade your little computers then. They probably just hide out in different parts of Ten. We have hundreds of miles of shafts we don't use no more. Been mining here for over a century, you know."

Topaz looked over 75's shoulder and stared off into the distance as thoughts raced through his mind. Ember bit her lip and then shook her head. *No, no way they found the tunnels.*

Topaz returned his gaze to 75. "It'd be impossible for them to use the elevator. We have trackers, computers, and monitors everywhere. Have you ever found another passage?" asked Topaz.

"Passage? What are you talking about, passage to where?"

Topaz rubbed his face and looked over at Ember. She froze, making her mind a blank slate, hoping he didn't see what she was thinking.

Topaz gave Ember a piercing gaze, then looked back at 75. "I'm not sure what I'm talking about. But have you ever found some mine shaft that led out of Ten?"

"No, no, nothing like that. Our mine goes out and down, not up. Look, I know you're frustrated, but I'm sure the three of them will show up. They're just taking a break and fooling around with that new girl probably."

75 grabbed her drill. "My shift has already started. My crew needs me, I have to go. Good luck on your search."

Topaz stood looking at the door close behind 75. Then he turned on Ember. "Do you know about a passage? You seemed to know something when I mentioned a passage?"

Ember shook her head. "No, no. I was just thinking about when I worked as an engineer on Four. Trying to think if there was any access or way around the cameras. But there isn't. I am as confused as you are."

Topaz and Ember returned to the elevator lobby on Ten. The doors parted and they stepped onto the lift. Ember called out for level One. Topaz remained silent.

"Aren't you returning to Five, Topaz—your office?"

"No." Topaz turned his head towards Ember as the elevator doors slid shut and the lift began to ascend. "Let's both go to One. To your office."

Ember swallowed hard. He must have known; or at least suspected she knew something. Something she was keeping to herself, at least for now.

The elevator reached One and Ember stepped off the lift, marching quickly towards her office. Topaz followed closely behind. She reached her office door, rushed to her computer and sat down. Topaz stood in front of her desk. He fixed his gaze on her and didn't move. She kept her eyes on her computer monitor as she said, "how can I help you?"

"Ember, you didn't look confused. You looked surprised. What do you know?"

The shafts. Wait, did she say that out loud? She gasped and suddenly stared at Topaz, as if she were peering into his soul.

Topaz shifted under her gaze. Finally, he barked, "What? What was it?"

Ember didn't seem affected by his bark. She looked out in the distance. *Yep, they had to have accessed the construction tunnels.*

As Ember thought, a guard burst through her door. "Commodore!" said the guard in an excited tone. "We have a cadet that's gone missing."

THIRTY-SIX

HINTS OF DESPERATION

Misty didn't usually fear any guard, but the two standing in her office were different. They seemed more aggressive than usual. *These two seem desperate, but why?*

"I already told you, I ain't got no more men for you." Misty shook her head to accentuate her point.

The two guards slowly advanced, causing Misty to take a few steps back into the corner of her office.

"You are hiding your best field hands and we want them now!" yelled one of the guards.

Misty put her hands up in front of her. "Now stay back, you hear. You've seen all my men. Shoot, you took the best of them already. I ain't got no more!"

One of the guards grabbed his baton from his utility belt. He raised it up above his head and took a quick step towards Misty. "You seem to be harvesting a lot of grain! You doing it all by yourself? You and that old geezer sitting outside?"

The guard brought the baton down and struck Misty on the head. She gave out a howl and slouched to the floor. A searing pain raced down her forehead. The top of her head began to throb. She reached up and covered her head with both hands. Peeking between her arms, she could see the guard raise his baton again; preparing for another strike.

Before the guard could strike, a large man in a black guard uniform grabbed him around the neck with his big meaty arm. The guard flew through the air as the man behind him flung him aside like a bushel of wheat. The guard struck the wall with such force that the baton flew from his hand. He landed on the floor, unconscious.

The other guard spun around to face his attacker. "No, no, what are you doing?" He took a step backwards and bumped up against the wall. The large assailant cocked his arm back and landed a solid fist square on the guard's face. His head bounced backwards off the wall and he fell to the ground in a crumpled heap.

Misty removed her hands from her head to get a better look; her eyes widened. "What ... who ... oh my goodness, Flint? You have good timing for once!"

Flint reached down and grabbed Misty's arm helping her over to the office chair where she sat.

"You ok, Misty?" asked Flint. He looked at the wound on her head as he gently patted her shoulder. He grabbed for a rag on the desk and pressed it against the cut.

"Yeah, yeah, I'm ok. A little sore here, but I'll survive." She took the rag from Flint's hand and gently dabbed at her wound.

"What the heck are you doing here, Flint?"

"I don't know. I wanted to see you, ask you something I guess."

Misty reached down to the bottom draw of her desk and took out a bottle of clear liquid. She unscrewed the top and took a quick swig. "We can't talk here, not now. Let's get to a safer place."

Misty struggled to her feet. Flint grabbed her arm and helped her stand and walk across the room. She kept hold of the bottle and smiled at Flint as they shuffled to the door. "I've never been happier to see you, dumb muscle."

Flint smiled back. "You need a lot more muscle around here it looks like." They exited the office and sat in the electric cart Flint had parked nearby. Flint turned the wheel away from the warehouse and sped off towards the dirt roads cutting across the fields. They drove across several crisscrossing dirt roads, turning in various directions until they reached a small shack hidden in the middle of the fields by the large almond trees.

Once inside the shack, Misty reached for the lights and they sat at either side of a small table. Misty plunked her glass bottle on the table and looked over at Flint.

"So what's your question?" asked Misty.

"How do I get to land?"

"You don't. Not now at least. Not while Cosmotine's alive. He's going to kill us all I fear." Misty took another swig from her bottle as Flint sat down. He felt defeated. He let his head drop into his hands and tried to think.

"What now?" Flint looked up at the ceiling. "What now?"

THIRTY-SEVEN

HOPE

A Century Earlier — July 24, 2030 — Colony Engineering Offices

"Leo, where are you?" David was walking through the office of Colony Engineering. The power was off, the halls were dark, all was vacant.

"I'm here." Leo popped his head out an office door.

David leapt backwards. He thrust his back up against the opposite wall of the hallway. "Oh geez, you scared me to death."

Only a month ago they were on the ship trying to make their escape. Leo gave in to David's plea and ordered the captain to stop. The chase was over. Mr. Hall had won. But he couldn't stop the others. The thousands that had already traveled through the crushing depths of the ocean to find a new life on the bottom of the sea.

"Sorry. I thought you heard me. I kept saying 'over here.'"

"Well, I didn't hear." David regained his composure and straightened his shirt. "It's time."

"Ok, ok. I just was trying to get the last of the data we had."

"I thought we already transferred all of that?"

"We did. But there was a bit more that I 'forgot' to mention."

David stepped closer to Leo and put his hands on Leo's arm. "Oh, Leo, no. You didn't keep secrets did you?"

Leo rolled his eyes and shook David's hands off his arm. "David, please. Just some private info, nothing important."

"Oh, private eh?"

"Yes, just some data that I had for myself ... for other projects."

"Oh ... I see." David bounced his eyebrows up and down and formed a wide grin. "Like pictures ... of ladies?"

"David, grow up!" Leo pushed past David and marched down the hall.

"Hey, I was just kiddin'." David ran to catch up with Leo. "They have a car waiting out front. We go from here to LAX and then on to Dallas—that's the first stop on our road show. They have it all mapped out for us. Oh, and they gave me your speech; they want you to stick to the script."

"Ok, alright, whatever." Leo pressed onwards without looking back. He reached the double glass doors to exit the building and stopped in his tracks. He glanced back towards the hallway they had just used to find the exit. "Hard to believe it's over, huh David?"

"What's over?"

"This!" Leo raised his arms. "All of this. Our life's work for the past decade just gone." He took several steps away from the door. "Just ... gone."

"Not gone, Leo. They're there. Our work was not a waste. Thousands of people starting a new life in the Colony as we speak."

"But we'll not see it!"

"Well we might. I mean, who knows. Maybe Mr. Hall will change his mind and—"

"No David. You know it's a lie. Mr. Hall is never going to change his mind."

David held his palms out. "Alright, alright."

He stepped closer to Leo and placed a hand on his shoulder. "You did it, Leo. You won. You've built the greatest habitat, the greatest civilization the world will ever know. History will never forget what you have accomplished. It doesn't matter if we see the Colony or not. It's there because of you."

Leo looked down at his shoes. Scuffed and worn. The shoes had walked a thousand miles inside these halls. He turned and pushed through the double doors. The Colony road-show was about to begin. He and David would travel the country, and then the world, extolling the virtues of their benefactor, John T. Hall. Maybe after it was done, they'd have a chance to work on something new. A new project, a new challenge, a new beginning for two aging scientists.

Leo glanced over to David. "There's always hope, right David? There's always hope."

THIRTY-EIGHT
THE ALMOND GROVE

May 8, 2130 — The Colony — Somewhere Below Seven

"You sure you guys know where the heck you're going?" Tephra stepped off the top of a ladder and turned to face the two Ten'ers. "We don't seem to be getting anywhere."

Tephra had followed 93 and 11 as they scooted through various corridors, tunnels, crawl spaces, and vertical shafts with metal ladders attached to one side. The circuitous path seemed to lead on forever with no true escape in sight. The two Ten'ers had used their mining hats, with lights pointed forward from the brim, to light the way.

"Well, if you didn't know, we were on Ten." 11 craned his neck back to look at Tephra. A swatch of light from his helmet crossed the wall and flooded Tephra's eyes as he looked back at her. "Ten! That's like a ways down you know. We have to climb up through Nine and Eight just to reach Seven." He pointed up with his index finger.

Tephra winced and held her hand up to shield her eyes. "Get that light out of my eyes ... geez."

11 spun his head back around, lighting the corridor ahead.

"Now Seven, that's a big place," added 93. "The biggest really. I think you'll like Seven." He came to the end of a corridor and swiveled his head first right and then left. "This way." He pointed to his left and walked down the corridor.

"Yeah I'm sure Seven is wonderful." Tephra rolled her eyes. She wondered if these two could ever understand what was at stake in the games Cosmotine was playing with the Colony. Still, there was no chance she could escape Ten without the help of these two.

"Where are we going to come out on Seven?" asked Tephra.

"Anywhere we want to." 93 put his finger to his temple. "But now that I think of it, we should probably head for the old shack in the almond grove. It's a good hideout."

"What do you mean anywhere?"

"Well, you see," 11 said, "there's access hatches throughout the Colony. We probably found most of them by now. We've been exploring this place for years."

"This one time we spent a week climbing up the access shafts we found and wound up all the way on One! Can you believe it? One!" 93 slapped his leg and snorted. "That was crazy. And then we found another path to a level above One. We had no idea that level existed."

"Yeah, that was scary. We almost got caught there. Only stayed a few minutes before we had to make a quick escape."

"Wait, you know how to get from here to One?" Tephra shook her head in disbelief. *How could these two be so resourceful?*

"Oh sure," 93 said. "We can get you anywhere in the Colony." He patted a ladder bolted to the side of the tunnel and then turned and continued walking up the corridor.

"Construction tunnels." 11 held his arms out above his head. "All around, nothing but construction tunnels." He lowered his arms and ran a finger across the metal side wall. "They was left over from when they built this place. Most of them have access points for water, electricity, that sort of thing. Some of them are just left-over construction areas. They was pretty much sealed off after the Colony was complete and no one uses them no more. They probably don't even know they exist."

"Hmmm." *Could be useful. These two have already made them useful ... for themselves anyway.* "Tell me more about the level above One, did you see much of it?"

"Heck no!" 11 shook his head, the light on his helmet swung back and forth in front of him. "We got outta there in a hurry. But we did see a room with markings on either side. A bunch of people sat around a long table. And then some guy walked in from a doorway at the far end. We thought for sure we'd get busted on that one."

"Yeah, that was too close," added 93.

"Did you see who was in the room?"

"Well," continued 11, "the people around the table were all wearing masks and then this tall guy dressed in all white, with black and grey hair, walked into the room."

"How long ago was this?"

"Not long, about a year or so I guess."

After what seemed like days, the trio reached the top of a ladder and opened a metal hatch. They climbed out of the shaft and emerged next to a small shack that was located in the middle of a grove of trees. Light streamed through the windows of the shack and illuminated the ground around them. 11 raised his head to the bottom of the shack's window and peeked inside.

"What do you see?" asked Tephra. 11 lowered his frame below the window and turned around. As he did so, a large man in a black guard uniform turned the corner and grabbed 11 by the neck.

"Who are you? What are you doing here?" asked the large man.

"No, no, don't hurt him." Tephra froze in place. *Crap, this is the worst that could happen.*

THIRTY-NINE

LOST AND FOUND

"Sir," said a voice from Topaz's radio, "we have an incident on Seven, two guards were assaulted and knocked unconscious by a man in a guard uniform. He had a cadet insignia on his left arm. Probably the missing Cadet."

Topaz clenched his teeth. "You think? Find him, Sergeant, find him now!" yelled Topaz. "And get me the missing cadet's assigned Sergeant. I want to see him immediately. I'm at the core complex on Seven, bring him to me."

Topaz turned to Ember. "So you were saying."

"It's noth—"

"Commodore Topaz, we have Sergeant Granite for you." Captain Rotifer stepped up and introduced Granite to Topaz. "Sir, Sergeant Granite." Granite sheepishly approached Topaz. Ember recognized the portly Sergeant from his missions collecting captives on One. She always thought he looked surly, but now she could see fear in his eyes.

"Sergeant Granite tell me about your cadet," said Topaz. "Any signs of discontent or trouble before he took off?"

Granite jerked his head back. Ember smirked. *He must have been expecting a tongue lashing, not a reasonable question.*

"No sir. Nothing that I saw. In fact," Granite paused and rubbed his cheek, "he seemed real eager, like happy to be wearing the black uniform."

"Hmmm. Well, that could be good or bad I suppose. Did he mention to you where he might go?"

"No, sir. He did talk about his supervisor at the warehouse a lot. Her name was Milky, Musty, something like that."

"Misty?" asked Captain Rotifer.

"Yeah, that was it, Misty." Granite's eyes lit up and he formed a smile.

Ember eyed the Sergeant. *What an oaf.* She caught a slight whiff of alcohol emanating from Granite's pores. She wrinkled her nose and looked over at Topaz.

"Misty's office is where the two guards were assaulted earlier this evening, sir." Captain Rotifer stuck out his chin as he spoke.

"Take me to Misty's office," said Topaz. "And take this drunkard to Ten." Topaz pointed at Granite and scowled.

Granite's face turned pale as the smile melted from his face. Topaz pushed past Granite and marched towards an electric cart with Rotifer marching behind him. The guards around Granite took hold of his arms and escorted him to the nearest elevator.

Ember stood still. When everyone was gone, she let out her breath. *I must find answers. What does Cosmotine know? Where can Tephra be?*

FORTY

DARKENING SKIES

"Easy, easy big guy." 93 put his palms out in front of him. He slowly raised his hands in the air as if he was under arrest. "We need your help."

The large man in the black guard uniform furrowed his brow, staring intently at them like he was trying to decide if they were trustworthy. He held a firm grip on 11's neck. "Hey, you guys are wearing clothes from Ten. I recognize them overalls."

"Yes." Tephra leapt up and held her palms out in front of her. "Yes, these two are Ten'ers, you're right."

"Tephra?" The guard pointed at Tephra with his chin. "You're Tephra, aren't you?"

"Yes. How do you know my name?"

"The elevator ride to Ten."

"You were the guard holding my arm! I remember you."

"Name's Flint. What are you doing here? Why are you with these two?" Flint released his grip from 11's neck. 11 scurried to 93's side and grabbed his arm.

"We need help, Flint. Can you help us?" Tephra titled her head sideways as she lowered her arms.

"I don't know. But we can't stand outside." Flint glanced around. "Come inside, we can talk there." He turned and scurried towards the door of the little shack. Tephra glanced at 93 and 11. They both shrugged. She stepped forward, following behind Flint. The two Ten'ers followed behind.

A woman stood inside peering over to Tephra. "Who are you?," asked the woman. Tephra made the introductions and asked if they could sit.

"Please sit. I'm Misty."

"If feels so good to sit down," said Tephra. "We've been climbing ladders and walking through tunnels for what feels like days."

"Couple hours, probably," added 93.

"Climbing and walking? From where?" Misty leaned against a short counter fixed to the wall of the shack. Her eyebrows arched upwards and she crossed her arms. Flint grabbed a chair and sat at the table with their new guests.

"Ten, of course." 11 grabbed his grey overalls with his thumb and held them out.

"No, you can't get here from Ten except by way of the elevators." Misty furrowed her brow. Tephra looked up at the older woman's face and smirked. *This ought to be good.*

"You can't, but we can." 11 bounced his eyebrows up and down as 93 grew a broad grin on his face. They both snickered.

"Are you sure?" asked Misty

"Could we get a drink, maybe some water?" Tephra hated to break into the conversation, but her mouth was dry, and she desperately needed some liquid relief.

"Where's my manners? Of course you can." Misty turned and grabbed some metal cups. She placed them on the table. She set two glass bottles of water next to them. "Help yourselves. I also got some stronger medicine." She held out her bottle of whiskey and raised her right brow.

The explorers grabbed for the water and filled their cups. They drained the contents and filled them again. After several cups of water, Tephra sat back and held up her empty cup to Misty.

"I'll take a hit." Tephra smiled.

Misty poured some whiskey into Tephra's cup and then poured herself a shot too.

"Cheers!" said Misty as she held her cup up in the air before downing the contents in a single gulp.

"Wow, now that's a whiskey drinker!" exclaimed 11.

93 sat forward in this chair planting his elbows on the table. "Bet you'd give 75 a run for her money."

"So tell me how you get from Ten to here without the elevators." Misty reached for an empty chair and sat at the corner of the table. Flint leaned forward in his chair to better take in the discussion.

"Well, we use the old, abandoned construction tunnels," said 93. "You'd think that others would use them too. But I guess they don't know about 'em. But they're easy to spot if you look and they're pretty easy to navigate once you get your bearings."

"Construction tunnels, huh? And you two figured out how to use them all by yourselves?" Misty popped her chin out.

"Yup," said 11. "Been exploring them things for years. Since we was kids really. Several large shaft lead to Ten. They're real easy to find down there if you just look around some."

"How far do they go?" asked Flint.

"Throughout the Colony. All the way to One." 11 pointed up with his finger.

"You know about these, Misty?" asked Flint.

"No, it's all news to me. But it does make some sense I suppose. The Colony was built in several stages, I know that much."

Tephra sighed and sat straight up. "I need to get back to One." She shook her head. The image of Ash floating in her watery grave burned in her mind. She still couldn't believe it was real. Was Ash really gone? Cosmotine's smug face flashed through her thoughts. Hate began to boil up. He had to be punished for what he did.

"Why's that?" Flint raised his head. "They'll just send you back down."

"The Colony is in trouble." Her eyes grew hard as she set her jaw. "Cosmotine killed Ash. He is changing the rules."

"Wait, killed?" Misty tilted her head. "No, you can't kill in the Colony. Not even the Masters Twelve can do that."

"He did it. I saw it with my own eyes."

"Oh no! We're in worse trouble than I thought. No, no, this can't be." Misty slowly shook her head as she gazed down at the table.

Flint crossed his arms as he sat upright in his chair. "The guards have taken on tons of new recruits. Thousands of them. No *probatum* passed or nothing. Just plucking people up, left and right."

"Yeah, they've taken nearly my whole work crew," Misty glanced up at Flint. "And them guards that attacked me, they were desperate. It was almost as if their lives depended on finding more recruits."

"Not to mention the dozens of people being escorted down to Ten from One," added Flint.

"Probably the new construction project and whatnot." 93 looked down at his empty cup and turned it in his hands. He slouched in his chair.

Tephra jerked her head to peer at 93. *Did he not know the importance of what he just said?* "What construction project?"

"The big silos, you know, on Ten," added 11.

Misty looked at Tephra with a look of utter disbelief. Tephra's eyes widened as she stared back at Misty. *Cosmotine! He's up to something big and no doubt terrible.* The construction Ash discovered in that small office on One, the Uranium symbol, could it be? She glanced around the room at the large man in the guard uniform, her two Ten'ers and the hardened field supervisor. Not a bad team: wisdom, muscle, resourcefulness. *This could work.* She rolled an idea around in her head. *Yes, this could work.* She cleared her throat and leaned forward, placing her hands on the table.

"We're in trouble," said Tephra. "There's no telling what Cosmotine is doing, but I think I might know what it is. And if I'm right, it'll mean the end of us all."

Misty shook her head in agreement, "we're in very big trouble."

FORTY-ONE
EDUCATING EMBER

Ember raced through the halls of One on her way to Cosmotine's office. *Things are getting out of hand. Tephra and the Ten'ers; a lost cadet and his former field supervisor. Never happened before.* Ember turned hard left and stopped short of Cosmotine's office. The hallway was empty. *Where's his guards?*

Ember slipped to the office door and peaked around the corner. Empty. She walked in and placed her hands on his desk.

"Ember."

Ember spun around and saw a young woman in white standing at the doorway. "Yes, what?"

"Supreme Principal Cosmotine asked me to find you."

"Here I am." Ember flung her arms out to her side. "Where is he?"

"In the primary conference chamber. He asks that you—"

Ember ran to the doorway and pushed the young woman aside.

"Do you need me to accompany you?" The woman rose up on her toes as she cupped her hands around her mouth. Ember waved her off with her hand as she jogged up the hallway without saying a word.

The door to the conference chamber slid open and Ember trotted through. She stopped short of the conference table and gasped. The room was full of people. Computer terminals had been erected along the wall. Monitors were arranged above each computer terminal and images of different parts of the Colony were broadcast on each screen. Cosmotine sat at the middle of the conference table. His guards stood against the wall behind him. He worked a keyboard and glanced around at the monitors above.

Ember cleared her throat and tried to regain her composure. She glided over to Cosmotine and stood at his side.

"Ember." Cosmotine spoke without looking up. "What have you to report?"

"I'm not here to report, I'm here for answers."

"Oh, I see." He turned his chair slowly to face Ember and held his arm out, pointing at the seat next to him. "Please, sit."

She gulped. She grabbed the back of the chair and turned it sideways. She sat and placed her hands in her lap. "What are you doing here? What are you doing with"—she looked up at Cosmotine and placed her hands on the arms of the chair—"the Colony?"

"Worried about your precious Colony are you?" He cracked a smirk and leaned back in his chair. "Well look for yourself." He waved his hand to his side presenting the row of monitors to Ember. "It's all right here. The whole plan laid out before you."

Ember looked from monitor to monitor. As she looked her mouth fell open; her hands came up to cover it. "It can't be!"

"Bold, yes?" Cosmotine cackled. "The future, my dear Ember, must be taken. By force if necessary. The old fools—the Masters Twelve—couldn't understand it at first. But I know it to be true."

"What does this all mean?"

"It means you and I will rule over a great civilization, Ember." Cosmotine leaned forward putting his hand on Ember's knee. "If, of course, you are willing to play your part."

Ember sat back and nodded slowly. *He means to ruin us all. He must be stopped before—* She shook the thought from her head and stiffened her resolve. She couldn't confront him now, not yet. She needed help, she needed Tephra. "Yes, Supreme. I am ready to play my part."

"Excellent news, Ember." He sat back and flashed a wide grin. "Come, let's make an announcement to the whole Colony. With the Masters Twelve at our side."

"Yes, Supreme." Ember stood, as did Cosmotine. She followed him out of the conference room. As the door slid closed, Ember turned to take a final look at the monitors inside. Her heart sank. She swallowed hard. Her precious Colony was in grave danger.

FORTY-TWO

PLAN FIVE

11 and 93 scurried up a long ladder. They were nearly at the top of the shaft. Tephra was climbing as quickly as she could, but she was well below them. At least Flint and Misty were with her. Those Ten'er boys were master climbers.

After the newly formed group finished their talk back at the shack, Misty guided them to a small pump house on the edge of the almond grove and unlocked the door. Inside were a heap of jumpsuits the field hands used when working in or around the pump house.

"Here, let's put these on. I'd imagine where we're going, we could use full jumpsuits. Plus, the pockets are nice and big to hold supplies," said Misty. Each of them picked up a jumpsuit and put it on. The suits had a slight musty smell. They had a warm lining on the inside and a slight water repellent feel on the outside. There were two large pockets on the chest of each jumpsuit, and then two more large pockets on the thighs. The group transfered their supplies into the large pockets, so they needn't carry anything by hand.

"Hey, not bad," said 93. "We found something like these in one of the tunnels around Three one time. They were great for carrying stuff while we climbed. We used them so much they finally wore out, holes everywhere." 11 smiled.

"Here, you will each need one of these," said Misty as she handed out hats with lights affixed to the front brim.

"93, 11, where is the closest access point to the tunnels?" asked Tephra. "We need to get to Five."

93 and 11 looked around for a minute, then looked at each other to confer without speaking.

"This way," said 93 while he motioned with his hand for everyone to follow. He set off across the adjoining field and they soon arrived at a patch of dirt next to the thick glass barrier of the Colony's outer wall. 93 took a few steps to the right, while 11 took similar sized steps to the left. After walking a few yards, 11 stopped.

"Here," said 11 rather nonchalantly. 93 turned around and ran over to 11 and the rest of the group gathered around.

11 reached down and cleared away a fair amount of dirt and debris. A round metal access hatch came into view as 11 worked. While 11 cleared the debris, 93 reached into his pocket and produced what looked like a wrench that had been welded together from various scraps of metal.

93 held the chunk of metal up and proclaimed to the others "Colony key." He chuckled.

Yeah that patched-up piece of scrap metal could not be the key to the Colony, if such a thing existed, thought Tephra.

Once 11 was done with his work, 93 reached down with the Colony key and placed it at the center of the metal hatch. He then grabbed the end of his makeshift wrench and turned hard while putting his weight behind it. The wrench slowly turned, as did the center of the hatch. After a quarter of a turn, a metallic click rang out and the hatch raised up from the ground.

"Welcome to the tunnels," said 11 with a smile. He gave 93 a pat on the back and then grabbed the half open hatch and lifted it the rest of the way open. The hatch creaked on its metal hinges and then came to rest fully upright.

"Ok, so we enter here and find the first vertical shaft upwards," said 93. "This tunnel will take us to any shaft we want really. We just have to wind around a bit depending on where you want to go."

The two Ten'ers jumped into the tunnel and motioned for the others to follow. Once everyone was in, 11 reached up, closed the metal hatch and turned a wheel on the underside to lock it back into place.

The tunnel the group stood in was around five and a half feet tall and five feet wide. "This way." 93 turned left and strode forward. He hunched down to miss hitting his head. Flint was nearly doubled over to fit his tall frame into the short tunnel. Tephra could nearly stand upright.

"How do you know where to go?" asked Tephra. "It's pitch black in here."

"Just trust us, we know," said 11. "Besides this outer tunnel curves around the entire base of the Colony. We get to a vertical shaft no matter which way we go."

"Always go to the left, I say," said 93.

"Don't listen to him." 11 shook his head and scoffed. "He's don't know these tunnels like me."

"Shut up 11. And try to keep up." 93 quickened his pace.

Tephra could feel the musty air fill her nose and lungs. She wrinkled her nose and held her hand in front of her mouth. *Enough to make a person gag.* After a while Tephra could see light up ahead. "What's that light from?"

93 looked up and then craned his head back to answer. "Vertical shaft. It rises up from that chamber. As he spoke the group emptied out into a large hexagon chamber. The roof rose up twice as high as the tunnel they had been in. Tunnels ran out in every direction with one vertical shaft straight up.

93 walked over to a metal ladder fixed to the side of the vertical shaft. "Here we are, now we can go up." He pointed up with his finger and then hopped onto the third rung of the ladder.

11 jumped onto the ladder behind him and the two scurried

upward. Tephra reached for the ladder rung and felt the cold metal on her hand. She winced. It felt wet and slimy. She reached her other hand out and placed her foot below. She started to climb. Misty climbed the ladder below her, and Flint made up the rear.

"Hey,Tephra, you sure you want to go to Five?" 93 hollered down, his voice echoed through the shaft. "We know plenty of places to lay low and hide out for a while if you want to. I mean Five is great and all, but that's where the guards are."

"We try to avoid that level." 11 peered down towards the others. "Too many guns and not enough us's."

"Yeah, we got a real nice set up next to Six." 93 held his hand out and touched the other side of the shaft while looking below trying to find sight of Tephra. "Has everything you need to relax. Food, drinks, we even snatched a few beds and the nice comfy blankets they use up on One. We could stay there for weeks!"

"No, my plan is simple," said Tephra. "We find Misty's field hands on Five and recruit them to go hunt down Cosmotine. I just hope we're not too late."

The two Ten'ers shrugged as if to say "so be it."

The group reached the top of the shaft and trudged down a labyrinth of tunnels. They reached another vertical shaft and began climbing again. After several hours of climbing and marching down tunnels, 93 and 11 stopped at the juncture of two tunnels. They turned to wait for the others to catch up.

As Tephra, Misty, and Flint neared, 93 pointed behind him with his thumb. "This is Five. It makes me nervous to be here, but I can show you the best way to enter the level without detection. You want to go to the lounge or the barracks?"

Tephra and Misty looked at each other and then both said, "Barracks."

Misty smiled. "Yeah, my field hands must be in the barracks, at least some of them."

93 nodded and then turned and began to head down one of the tunnels.

"Wait!" said Tephra. "What if they won't join us? Or enough of them won't join? Or we're too late?" She bit her bottom lip and tapped her foot. This was taking way too long. Cosmotine was on the loose and the clock was ticking. *We're running out of time.*

"That's a lotta 'ifs'." Misty placed a hand on her hip and cocked her head. "You can rest assured my boys will join. They don't want to be here on Five. I know it."

"Yeah, I think that's right, Misty." Flint nodded in agreement.

"Well, if you're right and they all join, then that is a lot of help." Tephra rubbed her cheek. "We don't need them all going to One. They would be more useful down on Seven to push back the guards. The ones you said were being aggressive. One doesn't have that many guards, right?"

"Well so I am told." Misty crossed her arms and looked up. "Heck, I have no idea, but the one thing I do know is that Seven is crawling with them."

"Let's split up." Tephra pointed at Misty. "You and Flint go with 11 to Five. Recruit as many field hands as you can. Misty can take them to Seven. Flint, you meet me up on One after you're done. We can capture Cosmotine."

"Ok, then what are you going to do?" asked Misty.

"I'll take 93 and go scout One for Cosmotine. See where he is and how many bodyguards he has."

"I don't know, Tephra." Flint shook his head. "That sounds awfully dangerous for you. I should go too."

"But I need you to help me round up our field hands, Flint." Misty protested.

11 and 93 looked at each other. "Um, excuse me, but me and 11 don't separate ... if you know what I mean."

"Yeah, we's a team, we stick together," said 11.

"No, this will work. I will be careful." Tephra patted Flint on the arm. "We're running out of time. Plus, Misty needs you more. If I get in trouble you'll be right behind me with your buddies, right?"

Flint nodded. "Ok, we'll have to round them up quickly."

"Ok, good, now get going." Tephra stepped back and glanced down the adjoining tunnel.

Misty and Flint turned and started off down the tunnel towards Five. Tephra turned her head, glancing at 93. "Well, which way to One?"

"Dang it, I told you me and 11 we don't—"

Tephra slid over to 93 and placed both her hands on his shoulders. She stood forward on her toes and leaned in to whisper in his ear. "It's ok. You can do this."

93 blushed. "Oh, alright. 11 go help them hayseeds and keep 'em safe."

"Alright, but I didn't get no kiss on the ear!" 11 turned and ran off towards Misty and Flint.

"It weren't a kiss!" 93 hollered down the tunnel after 11 as he disappeared from sight.

Tephra chuckled as she patted 93 on the arm. "Let's go."

FORTY-THREE

MASTERS CHAMBER

The vertical shaft leading from Five began to narrow near the top, as the two approached One. 93 exited the shaft and crawled into a small tunnel. The tunnel was barely three feet high and the same distance wide. He had to crawl on his hands and knees to make his way down the tunnel.

"Where are we now?" whispered Tephra.

93 stopped crawling, looked back at Tephra, and rolled his eyes. "Stop asking me that every five minutes! We're just under One. There are only two shafts that lead from here to the Masters level. We have to crawl for a while, so keep crawling ... and keep quiet!"

Tephra shrugged and continued to follow 93 down the long, low tunnel. Occasionally Tephra could hear footsteps above them as people moved about in the hallways of One. Eventually they arrived at a small junction, where a vertical shaft rose up.

"Here we are, the last ladder up." 93 grabbed hold of the ladder rungs and scurried up the shaft. Tephra followed close behind. They had been climbing for what felt like days, but this last climb was different. Tephra felt anxious, adrenaline coursed through her body, her breath quickened as she steadied herself for what lie ahead.

The pair climbed for several yards until 93 bumped up against a round metal cover. He paused, looked down at Tephra, and then back up at the cover. He took a big gulp. Before he moved any further he looked down at Tephra again.

"You sure you want to do this?"

"Yes ... open it. We've no choice."

93 nodded. He looked back up to the cover and pushed it open. Once the cover was out of its hold, he slid it to one side. Light peered into the shaft from the room above. The two climbed out of the shaft, and Tephra looked around the small room. It was dimly lit. Unlike One, this room was painted a light purple with ornate gold around the top. A round table sat at the center and there were doors on opposite sides of the room. The shaft they emerged from blended in with the round metal tiles that covered the floor so as to make the access point undetectable. 93 slid the cover back into place.

"Where to now?" asked Tephra in a whisper.

"I don't know for sure. This is the only level I don't know so good. Me and 11 only came here one time. It was full of guards in purple uniforms. We went through that door and nearly got caught." He pointed towards a door to the far right of the little room.

"Well, then let's go through this other door instead then."

93 nodded and they turned towards a door to their left. As they approached the door, it slid open automatically, which caused the pair to jump. They stopped in their tracks, looked at each other, and then approach the door.

They leaned their heads into the adjoining room and tried to look around, but the room was dark. It seemed big, but the size could not be determined in the darkness, so Tephra took a tentative step into the room. As soon as she did so, the lights came on and the room was instantly visible. It was a large room with walls that curved upwards. There were ornate carvings on the vertical supports spaced out every ten feet or so. Between the vertical supports was the thick glass walls of the Colony. They surrounded the room completely, except for the doorway where Tephra and 93 stood taking in the surroundings. The curved vertical supports met at a point at the top of the room. It was the top of the Colony.

The pair took another step and more lights came on from around a large oblong shaped table. The table was massive in size. It stretched the length of the room and was well over twenty feet wide at its widest point.

At the table sat six human figures on the left side, and another six on the right. Masks covered their faces and each one wore a purple robe that draped over their shoulders and disappeared under the table. They sat motionless. The room was completely silent and the light glowing down from the ceiling and up from the table made the room feel eerie with the ocean water pressing on the thick glass surrounding the room.

Tephra took a deep breath and stepped forward. 93 moved behind her and placed his hands on her arm. She frowned.

"Stop that!" She slapped at his hands and pointed to a spot next to her on the floor. "Get up here with me. Stop being a wimp."

93 shuffled forward and slumped his shoulders. Tephra gulped. She made her hands into fists trying to summon her courage. The hair on the nape of her neck stood up. *This feels all wrong.* Tephra took and step forward. 93 moved a half pace behind her.

Tephra reached the end of the table and fixed her gaze on the ornate masks worn by each Master. They were the same ones she saw in the orientation. "Masters?" Tephra called out with a waver in her voice. She cleared her throat and tried again. "Masters, I must speak with you."

The figures sat motionless. The room was quiet.

93 shrugged his shoulders and peered over at Tephra. "Sleeping?"

Tephra frowned. *Couldn't be sleeping. Not like this.* Tephra inched up one side of the table. She stood next to the closet Master, and touched the figure's shoulder. It felt bony, small.

"Master, I must speak with you," Tephra repeated. 93 stayed glued to his spot at the end of the table. Tephra peered over her shoulder at 93. He shook his head seemingly unsure of what to do next. His fearful gaze did nothing to help. She turned back to the Master and leaned slightly forward.

Tephra reached up to the Master's mask and pulled it up over the head. As she did so, a face appeared underneath.

Tephra shrieked and jumped back, "Oh gosh!" The face was half dried papery skin and half exposed bone and skull. The remaining hair on the top of the Master's head trailed back in dry wiry strands.

"He's dead!" She moved quickly to the next Master and removed the mask as well, a similar corpse appeared underneath. Tephra removed mask after mask and found bare skull after bare skull. Dead, all of them.

"They're dead, all dead!" Tephra scurried back to the end of the table, standing next to 93, taking in the ring of dead Masters she had revealed.

"Boy, I'd say," said 93. "That'd explain the lax security up here."

"93, stop about the guards, this is far more serious than lax security. Cosmotine has no limits. He killed the Masters to secure his power."

"Very good, new recruit, very good," said a voice from behind Tephra and 93. The two spun around and Tephra's eyes widened. Standing at the doorway was Supreme Principal Cosmotine.

"My brightest recruit with the wily Ten'er, what a pair you make." He had a devious smile on his face. As he entered the room, his cadre of bodyguards filed in behind him and spread out on either side. They stood motionless, awaiting orders from their master.

Ember entered the room behind the guards. She looked up and gasped. "Tephra!"

"I told you this place was trouble," whispered 93 to Tephra. She waved him off.

Tephra shifted in her stance and crossed her arms. "I've heard a lot about the great Colony before Cosmotine. The founding principles, the magnanimous leaders that came before. But now things are different. Why so much change? You don't believe in the Colony?"

Tephra took a step closer to Cosmotine. She wanted to observe his response from a closer vantage point. She had come this far, and no longer had the patience, nor the care, to be frightened of him. As Tephra moved closer, 93 took several half steps to keep pace just behind her.

"No, no, you're wrong," said Cosmotine. "I do believe in the power of the Colony. The only difference is that the other colonists see the Colony ending at these glass walls." He motioned with his hand towards the glass walls surrounding the conference room. "The Colony is so much more."

Ember took several steps forward. Her eyes moved towards Cosmotine and then back to Tephra. Her hands clutched her legs.

"What do you mean more?" asked Tephra. "You plan on expanding?"

93 grabbed Tephra's arm. She looked back at him. He seemed to be trying to tell her something. Tephra snapped her head back around when she heard Cosmotine laugh.

"No, there is no need to expand the walls of the Colony. You see, the Colony has the power to expand beyond our glass borders. We have the power to expand onto land. All of land. All living civilizations under the same principles, the same ideals, of the Colony. Peace, harmony, self-sustaining bliss."

Tephra furrowed her brow. "Sounds a lot like world domination. Is that what you're thinking? Taking over the world? Hasn't worked so well, historically speaking."

"History is a wonderful teacher. Provided we learn from the past."

"Hey, Tephra," 93 whispered into Tephra's ear.

Tephra looked to her side where 93 was clinging to her arm and said in a hushed tone, "not now."

"Yeah, but Tephra," said 93. Tephra held up her hand to stop him from speaking.

"So how are you any different from the past then?" Tephra asked Cosmotine.

Cosmotine took several steps closer to Tephra to further his explanation. They remained twenty feet apart, each standing firmly in their respective spots.

"These fools," he said motioning his head in the direction of the twelve corpses sitting in the chairs behind Tephra, "they were blind to the possibilities. We have no limits here at the bottom of the ocean. We can't be found, we can't be reached, we can't suffer retaliation." He smiled in satisfaction of his own words.

"We have access," he continued, "to an infinite supply of natural resources. In particular, uranium. And we have the time and man power to enrich our uranium."

"Nuclear weapons?"

"We cannot be harmed by nuclear fall-out. Mutual assured destruction, the one thing that has kept nations safe from all-out nuclear war does not apply here. We have the ultimate leverage. Die or join the Colony."

"Under your rule I take it?"

"Of course, who else would know how to rule under the tenants of the Colony?"

"Perhaps some people know better than you. The Colony is full of true believers."

"Perhaps," snapped Cosmotine, "but they do not have my vision, nor the fortitude to accomplish our goals. We can create a better world for everyone. Once we gain our advantage, my new guard army will travel to land with me leading them as the conquering hero. The entire world needs the Colony way—they want it. You can see that, can't you Tephra?"

"Your new guard army? No wonder so many field hands have been taken. They're no soldiers you know."

"They will be in due time."

"You cannot prevail, Cosmotine. Your plan is foolish."

Cosmotine circled past Tephra, moving in a wide arc. He reached the first Master at the table and carefully placed the mask over the corpse. Then he turned to face Tephra. "That's not a helpful view. Unfortunately, many within the Colony feel the same. Therefore, it was necessary to spur them along. Remove those who would stand in the way of our ultimate goal. The Colony cannot exist if we do not admit that the entire world would thrive under our system. We would be hypocrites for not bringing peace to the world when we have the ability to do so."

Tephra smirked. She couldn't believe the irony of Cosmotine's statement. "Through war? If you intend to bring peace, then why do so with nuclear weapons? Why not evangelize, sing the praises of the Colony, allow people to join voluntarily—not through threat of destruction?"

"Do you really believe that nonsense?" Cosmotine formed a sly smile. "The world refuses to see the appeal of peace. Some appreciate it, but most don't. There's too many prophets, too many politicians, too many pundits, too many profiteers. Surely, you can see that better than most—former Navy lieutenant. How'd the war work out for you? You know as well as I that the world needs our help, they just can't see it."

Cosmotine stepped away from the masked corpse. He clasped his hands together in front of him. "And you, Tephra, the one who somehow escaped Ten and found your way here—to the Master's level— you have a chance to join me in making a difference for the world." Cosmotine spread his arms as he sauntered forward. "You will be remembered throughout all time and human history as the co-creator of our new world vision. Be by my side and we can take over the world together."

Tephra turned to Ember. *Shouldn't she be by his side?* Ember locked eyes with Tephra and shook her head.

93 whispered into Tephra's ear, "I know a way out. I see the shaft entrance." Tephra reached down and grabbed 93's hand. She squeezed to indicate she understood.

"That is a generous offer, Cosmotine. Co-creator when I have done so little up to this point."

"You have opened my eyes, Tephra." Cosmotine lowered his hands and took several more steps towards Tephra. "More importantly you have shown your mettle. You see it was your *probatum* after all. The trip to Ten proved your worth. You are bold, no doubt. We need bold leaders now. We will accomplish great things together. Be my equal, join this partnership. Change your life and our world forever."

"Go!" said Tephra. 93 and Tephra turned on their heels and made for the shaft cover.

"Seize them!" yelled Cosmotine.

The guards sprang forward to pursue the two as they sprinted towards the hidden shaft cover. 93 dove for the cover with his Colony key in hand, he jammed it into the slight opening and pried the cover open. He threw his legs through the hole and grabbed the top ladder rung, spinning around to hold out a hand to help Tephra down the shaft.

As Tephra reached out for 93's hand the guards caught up with her. They grabbed her arms and pulled her back. 93's eyes widened. "NO!" He yelled and began to rise up out of the shaft to help Tephra.

"No, go, you need to tell the others," said Tephra. "Go now!" 93 hesitated slightly and then two of the guards rushed him. He paused. Tephra saw the guards getting closer and pleaded with him. At the last minute, with the guards nearly touching him, he grabbed the sides of the ladder, moved his feet to the outside of the rungs, and disappeared down the shaft.

The two guards approached the shaft and stopped. They seemed tentative to climb down into the darkness. Tephra smirked. *Not very brave soldiers. Figures.*

"Let him go," said Cosmotine. "We have our prize, and the entire Colony will know it as soon as we start our broadcast. Bring our new recruit over here to me. Tephra and I will sit and talk, on camera, for the Colony to see."

Cosmotine smiled as the guards guided Tephra over to a table with a camera perched on it. One of the guards brought over a chair and they forced Tephra to sit.

Ember stood still. Her hands were over her stomach. She stared at Tephra, but didn't move.

"Excellent." Cosmotine patted Tephra on the shoulder. "Now fix the Masters masks and we can get started."

FORTY-FOUR

MISTY'S MEN

"Here it is." 11 reached out and placed his hand on a round hatch embedded in the wall.

Misty and Flint came up behind 11 and looked at each other. "Let me go first." Flint shifted towards the door. "I can see who's around and clear the immediate area."

"Fine," said Misty, "but be sure to let us know as soon as we can come out. I want to see my field hands as quickly as I can." Flint nodded his approval.

11 grabbed the bar that sealed the door shut and began to raise it up and to the left. The bar was heavy and did not turn easily. Flint grabbed the end of the bar and flexed the muscles in his arm. The bar leapt upward knocking 11 to the ground.

"Dang, big guy, take it easy." 11 stood and rubbed a hand on his rear.

"Sorry, little guy." Flint smiled, ducked down, and stepped through the doorway.

The barracks was dimly lit. A few guards were milling about. Flint scurried to the nearest bunk and crouched down. He swiveled his head around surveying his surroundings. His bunk was only a couple of rows down. He unzipped the jumpsuit Misty gave him back on Seven. He took it off and shoved it under the nearest bunk. He tucked the tails of his guard shirt into his pants. He stood and peeked around the corner of the bunk. With any luck he might blend in. At least for now.

Flint slid his foot into the walkway between the bunks and shuffled forward. He stopped and looked around. A guard was folding his clothes several bunks away. The guard glanced up. Flint held his breath. The guard dipped his head as if to say 'hello' and went back to his task at hand. Flint exhaled. *Whew, passed the first test.* He scooted past the guard and continued up the walkway.

"Where are the field hands? There should be tons of 'em here." He mumbled to himself as he looked at each bunk he passed. Most were vacant, but a few had a guard sitting or lying down. None seemed to notice the rogue cadet striding past them.

The row of bunks stretched on for several yards and then gave way to a lounge area near the end of the room. Couches, tables, chairs, and a large monitor bolted to the wall. Several guards were sitting around a table playing cards.

One of the guards lifted his head as Flint approached. "Holy hayseed, if it ain't the cadet everyone is looking for!" said the guard. He jumped up, grabbed his baton and held it out in front of him. The other guards sitting around jumped up as well but they did not grab their weapons, they just stood looking at Flint.

The guard with his baton out took a shaky step towards Flint. The man was much smaller than the tall, muscular cadet.

"Alright cadet, we are taking you to see Topaz! You are a wanted man."

He took another tentative step closer. At the same time, Flint strode closer to the guard. The guard's eyes were even with Flint's chest. The guard titled his head back further and further until he was able to look into Flint's eyes. The guard gulped as he lowered his baton to his side. Flint looked down at him and smiled. "You gonna take me in, huh?" asked Flint. The other guards standing around the table didn't move.

"Put that stick down, darn you!" Misty raced up the walkway behind Flint and passed him by.

"Good gosh, Misty, what are you doing here?" said one the guards still standing at the table.

Misty came to an abrupt stop and nodded her head. "Wheaty! Acer! Hey guys!"

All the guards from the table gathered around Misty, except the one who drew his baton on Flint. They reached out to pat her shoulder and said their greetings.

"There's trouble in the Colony boys. We need your help or none of us will survive."

"Anything for you, Misty." Wheaty nodded and looked at the others. Everyone nodded in agreement.

"Yeah, but how?" asked Acer. "Not like we can just waltz out."

The guard standing opposite Flint hadn't moved. He stood still. Holding his baton at his side and keeping a wary eye on Flint. A trickle of sweat began to form on his brow.

"Don't worry about how we get outta here, I got that covered." Misty flashed a wide grin at her group of field hands and then glanced over to the guard with the baton. "Who's this?"

Wheaty glanced over to the guard. "That's Albite. Hey, Albite, can I see that baton for a sec?"

Albite moved his arm sideways and handed his baton to Wheaty without moving any other muscle. " Wheaty grabbed the baton, raised it up and hit Albite hard on the bicep.

"Ouch!" Albite grabbed his arm with his other hand. "That hurt, Wheaty."

"I ain't a guard anymore, Albite." Wheaty shook his head and formed a smile. "Man, that feels good. I can't stand these guard types."

"What we gonna do with him?" asked Acer. Acer came around back of Albite and stood at his side. Albite was boxed in with Flint in front, Wheaty to one side, and Acer to the other. Three strong field hands.

A devious smile stretched across Wheaty's face. "Let's run him through a chipper/shredder."

"Yeah, or the hay bailer." Acer smirked.

Flint placed his large hand on Albite's shoulder. "Or you can join us to help save the Colony. Your choice, buddy. What's it gonna be?"

Albite swallowed hard. He looked to his left and then to his right. "You guys aren't serious are you?" He formed a meek smile. "I mean, fine with me. Guarding isn't what it used to be. I am happy to help, but I have no idea what you all are up to."

"Neither do we, but when Misty says she needs help, we help." Wheaty rested the baton on his shoulder and glanced over to Misty.

"Ok, I'll help any way I can. Anything is better than taking equals to Ten every day." Albite exhaled and nodded his head.

Misty stepped next to Flint and waved her hand. "Alright crew, gather round. Here's the plan. We need to find as many of our field hands as we can. Have them meet back here." Misty turned to Albite. "Albite, if you think you can recruit any of your guard friends to help us, then bring them along. Otherwise, we need your help keeping the guards away."

Albite nodded. "Most of the former field hands are kept in this barracks and the next one over. There are a few guards here too, but not many. I'll start with them."

"Great," said Misty, "now we need to hurry, but don't make a ruckus. We have a way out at the back over here. Just meet back here in about twenty minutes."

As the group fanned out through the barracks, Flint put a hand on Misty's shoulder. "You stay here and keep everyone organized as they return," said Flint. Misty nodded without saying a word. She rubbed the back of her neck as she sat at the table. Flint turned and ran up the corridor outside. He found the next barracks down and peered into the doorway. Wheaty and Acer had already dashed inside and split up to round up their friends. They were talking to groups of field hands dressed as guards and passing along the message. Flint stayed at the doorway. He peered down the corridor. *Don't see anyone coming. Hope no one sounds the alarm.*

Flint let out his breath as groups of people, in twos and threes, began leaving the barracks. Flint pointed them in the right direction and patted some on the back as they went. "Let's go, but be quiet."

Albite came running up the corridor and stopped in front of Flint. "We had a few guards to subdue back there, but several others joined in. I'll look around here now." Flint nodded and patted Albite on the shoulder as he scurried into the barracks.

Each minute that ticked by felt like an eternity. Flint swiveled his head back and forth keeping an eye on the corridor outside. *We've gotten a lot already.* Flint had just turned back towards the barracks door when he heard a commotion at the back of the room.

"No! You're coming with me!" A voice called out. Flint could see Wheaty and Acer racing across the barracks. They were heading towards the back corner. Flint took off, dashing down the walkway between the bunks.

"Just calm down, Indium." Albite had his hands up. His palms were out as he took a step backwards.

"Calm down nothing, you're talking mutiny!" Indium held his baton above his head. He took a step towards Albite and then froze. Indium's eyes grew wide. He craned his head upwards as his mouth fell open. Flint rushed past Albite and placed his two large hands squarely on Indium's shoulders. Flint pushed the smaller man backwards and pinned him up against the wall. Indium's feet dangled above the ground and the baton fell from his hand. Wheaty and Acer raced up to Flint's side, but there was nothing for them to do. They stood back and crossed their arms.

"You should listen to my friend, he said to calm down." Flint bared his teeth. His eyes narrowed.

"Yeah, ok ... ok." Indium slid his head back until it hit the wall. His face had the look of complete terror.

"Good, good." Flint let Indium slide down the wall until he stood once more on the ground. "We have a job to do here and you're not going to get in our way. Understood?"

"I understand, I understand." Indium brought his hands up and clung to Flint's arms. A bead of sweat formed on his brow as he grimaced up at the big man holding his shoulders.

"Good, I'm glad we understand each other." Flint lifted the man off his feet again, strode over to an open locker that was bolted against the wall and threw the man inside. He slammed the door and waved his hand over a black square, locking it.

Flint turned towards Albite, Wheaty and Acer. "Go! Get back to recruiting." They nodded and took off. Flint shook his head and wiped his hands on his shirt. Ooh, *that guy was sweaty.* Flint strode back over to the barracks door and peered down the hallway. *Still clear. Hope we can gather the field hands without any more trouble.*

FLINT JOGGED BACK into the first barracks. He could see Misty standing in the middle of the lounge. Field hands in black guard uniforms crowded around her. Flint was shocked at the number of people assembled. Several hundred in all, he figured. He glanced to his right and saw several guards sitting on the floor. The field hands had them surrounded with batons out for good measure. *Looks like they handled their own trouble in here.*

Flint pushed through the crowd and found Misty in the center of the group, barking orders as usual.

"Fields hands!" yelled Misty. "We have a job to do. The Colony is in trouble. Your friends and family on Seven are in trouble. I've worked alongside most of you, lived alongside you too. I can tell you that something is wrong with the Colony. It is sick from above. Cosmotine has turned on all of us."

"We're done in the other barracks." Flint spoke as he stepped up next to Misty. "Acer and Wheaty are doing a final pass to find any stragglers. Albite went to the main bar to see who else he could find."

"Alright, good." Misty patted Flint's arm. "We need to get this group moving. It's gonna take some time to weave them back down to Seven in the tunnels."

"Where's 11?" asked Flint.

"He's back at the hatch waiting to usher the men through." Misty pointed to the back of the barracks.

"I need to go get Tephra." Flint rubbed his temple. "I don't want her to get into any trouble."

The television monitor above their heads flicked on. Flint looked up. There on the screen was Cosmotine and seated next to him was Tephra. Flint's heart sank. "Oh ... no."

"Colonists," said Cosmotine, "I bring you great news." Cosmotine smiled and wrapped his arm around Tephra. She leaned away and Cosmotine pulled her tighter.

"Tephra, our brightest new recruit, has joined me, and the Masters Twelve, to take the next step, the final step, in the fulfillment of the Colony. The outside world, the people of land, need our help. They too desire to live in peace and harmony as we have here in the Colony for so many decades."

Misty looked over to Flint with dread in her face. Flint looked back. As the pair turned their eyes back to the screen a voice called out from the back of the barracks, behind the hundreds of people standing along the length of the walkway. "Misty! Flint!" yelled 93 as he pushed his way through the crowd. Flint waved him over, but went back to looking at the screen.

"The Masters Twelve and I were tentative about this plan," continued Cosmotine, "but our newest and brightest recruit made a powerful argument to the contrary. She told us of the plight of the people on land, and their strong desire to share in our values and our mission. Together, we can make a difference. Fear not, your way of life will not be affected. You can and will continue in your important work. But the values that you believe in, and the hard work you do, will now make a difference not just here in our Colony, but in the entire world." Cosmotine flashed a large, charming smile as he spoke.

93 scurried to Flint's side. "Flint, they have Tephra."

Flint looked down at 93 and pointed to the monitor on the wall. "We know."

"No, they're dead, the Masters there behind them are dead!"

Misty turned her head and forced her way through the crowd to 93's side. "What did you say? Dead?"

"Yeah, I saw it myself, they're dead. The masks are covering skeletons, all dead!" 93 told Misty and Flint of Cosmotine's plans, the nuclear weapons, the world domination.

Cosmotine continued his speech, "I want to warn you, however, that there are those among us who would try to stop our plan. Who want to harm the Colony? They are attempting to take over and rule the Colony for their own benefit. These rebels must be stopped!" Cosmotine planted his fist on the table as he spoke.

"We have reports," continued Cosmotine, "of rebels from Seven making their way to different levels. We also have a rogue cadet named Flint who is helping these rebel forces." At this point a photo of both Flint and Misty appeared on the screen. "If you see either of these two colonists, contact a guard station immediately."

"Rebellion will not be tolerated. Those colonists hearing this broadcast who wish to rebel, be forewarned. You will not prevail."

Cosmotine paused in his remarks, sat up and smiled broadly. "But rest assured now that we have Tephra by my side, the Colony will finally achieve its ultimate goal. The world will be our Colony."

The monitor blinked off. The barracks room remained silent. No one talked, no one moved. *This is it*, thought Flint. Sides must be taken. The rebellion was here.

Misty took hold of Flint's arm as she stepped onto a chair and then hopped onto a table. "Listen up!" Misty clapped her hands together. "You heard Cosmotine ... that crazy idiot has lost his marbles. It's time to choose. Either you're with us or you're against us. The Masters Twelve are dead. Cosmotine has no limits. He will destroy our way of life. He will destroy our Colony. You can accept that, or you can join us to do something about it!"

Misty jumped down and started to push her way through the crowd heading to the doorway into the construction tunnel from which they emerged into Five a little over an hour ago.

"I will fight," yelled Misty as she walked. "I might die," Misty turned to face the crowd again, "but I will die knowing I did everything I could to save our Colony, and to save every last one of you." Misty turned and continued her march towards the tunnel hatch.

"What are you all waiting for!" yelled Flint. "We can't let Misty go it alone. Let's fight!"

With that a yell erupted in the room as hundreds of men and women raised their hands and yelled "Let's fight!" in support of Misty.

"Grab as many weapons as you can carry!" yelled Misty as she stood just inside the tunnel door. "We have to move out now!"

The room full of people grabbed their batons and supplies. A few carried side arms and the occasional rifle. They filed out the hatch following the procession led by 11.

93's eyes grew wide as he looked around at the mass of people leaving the barracks.

Flint smiled and said to him, "everyone loves Misty."

"Yeah I can see that. But I need to help lead the way. Misty doesn't know where she is going."

"No, she's got 11," replied Flint. "You need to lead me to One. We're going to get Tephra back."

FORTY-FIVE
LOYALTIES REALIGNED

As soon as the camera's red light went out, Cosmotine released his grasp on Tephra. "Excellent work, Tephra," he said as she was pulled out of her chair and restrained by two guards. "You're a natural on screen."

"Drop dead! You will fall!" Heat welled up in her cheeks, a fiery anger burned in her chest. She clenched her fists as two guards held firmly onto her arms.

"Yes, yes of course I will. You know, I just made you a star. You could still join me in my vision. The whole Colony now knows it was your idea after all."

Just then, Ember ran back into the chamber. She had left before the broadcast. "Supreme," said Ember, "we have a problem."

"Ember! Not now!"

"My apologies, Supreme Principal, but you must come at once."

"Guards, take this prisoner to the holding cells."

Ember turned and walked quickly for the door. Cosmotine scowled a final time at Tephra. "Think over my offer. It's not too late to make a name for yourself." He then turned and marched out of the

Masters chamber. Tephra sneered at the back of his head as he left. She wanted to strangle him with her own hands. She pulled her arms one way and then the other, but the guards' grasp on her held firm. They escorted her out of the room.

EMBER STEPPED into the small elevator that led from the Master level to One. Cosmotine joined her along with two of his guards.

"What's the emergency, Ember?" He asked with a noticeable irritation in his voice.

"It's Five," said Ember. "Hundreds of guards have gone missing. No sign of using the elevator, they just disappeared."

"The Ten'ers," muttered Cosmotine. "With the help of the rebels, no doubt!" He had a look of fury in his eyes. "Get me Topaz, immediately!"

"He's on his way to your office now," said Ember. "Supreme Principal, perhaps another broadcast to clarify your thoughts would be prudent."

"Prudent? Prudence got us here in the first place, Ember!" He peered over to Ember. "You've lost your focus. You're quickly losing your usefulness."

The elevator doors opened and he stormed out with his guards following behind. Ember paused. She watched her mentor march down the hall. She stepped off the lift and looked down while letting out a breath. She had lost her standing with the Supreme Principal and it hurt, even though she didn't believe in him anymore. She needed order. She needed to stop him. She couldn't believe she was going to do this. Go against the Colony. No, not the Colony. Cosmotine. This was for the Colony. She could do this.

She glanced up and strode away from the elevator, quickening her pace as she went. She needed to see someone who would likely be at the guard station on One. On her way to the guard station, Ember stopped at her office to grab her old engineering records. She had done some research into the construction tunnels, and she had obtained an old blueprint of the structure during construction. All was stored on a small data pod. She sat in her chair and turned towards the back wall to retrieve the device.

"So here you are," said Topaz as he entered Ember's office. Ember turned around with a fright having been startled by the sound of Topaz' voice. "Cosmotine gave me orders to find the missing guards, but I realized you weren't with him. It's not like you to miss out on the drama."

"Is that what you think this is?" asked Ember. "Drama?"

"No, I think it's either mutiny or revolution. Mutiny if we win, revolution if we lose."

"You've never been one to ponder losing, Commodore."

"No, no, I don't like to lose. Don't even like considering losing. But I can see when the time may be ripe to join a winning team." Topaz walked closer to Ember's desk and leaned forward with both arms planted on the desktop.

"That sounds like mutiny."

"All in how you look at it. You know something I don't, Ember. What's going on?"

"The Masters are dead, Topaz." Ember could feel heat welling in her cheeks. "You knew this for some time and kept it from me."

"Please, don't be dramatic. Have you seen a Master lately? You think they'd just sit in their conference chamber forever if they were alive? Any fool could see that without me telling them."

"We see what we want to see, I suppose."

"Yeah, we do."

"What else do you know that I don't?" asked Ember.

Topaz paused and shrugged.

"Topaz, you might as well tell me. I am going to find out, and it would be better coming from you."

"You haven't told me what you know."

Ember continued to stare, a more piercing stare this time. She didn't even blink.

"Nuclear weapons," said Topaz finally.

Ember smirked. She crossed her arms and drew in a deep breath. "I know about that plan. Another secret of yours. How long has this been in the works?"

"Cosmotine has been mining and enriching uranium on Ten for several years. Ever wonder why so many equals were sent down? Or why no one ever leaves Ten? We needed more miners."

"No, they were sent down for violating Colony protocol."

"Yes, of course, and how convenient that each one had a violation. And all the violations seemed to be against the Supreme Principal."

Ember looked down and realized what she had done; that she had assisted Cosmotine with his dirty work without realizing it. Or without wanting to realize it.

"Yes, you see it now," said Topaz. "And you were a helpful accomplice. In any event, the nuclear weapons are nearly ready and Cosmotine plans to use them to conquer land. The planet will be our Colony."

"We will be destroyed!" Ember jumped to her feet. "We cannot conquer land, we cannot start war, we will destroy the world and ourselves in the process ... that's chaos!" Ember recoiled. Her worst nightmare, the chaos of total war, rushed into her brain, flooding her thoughts. "No, that's chaos," she repeated.

"I need to oversee my guards on Seven," said Topaz. "Do what you will with this information. If the tide begins to turn and you need me, you know how to find me." Topaz turned and left Ember standing alone in her office.

After watching him leave, Ember looked up and marched out into the hallway. She trotted to the guard station. Once inside, she approached the sergeant on duty.

"I need to speak with the prisoner," said Ember.

The Sergeant looked up nonchalantly and then snapped to attention upon realizing it was Ember was standing before him.

"Yes, of course," said the Sergeant. He reached down, pushed a concealed button and the door to Ember's right slid open. Ember strode down a corridor and then stopped abruptly just outside a small interrogation room. She paused. She glanced left and then right. No one was around. She steadied herself and then waved her hand across the black square next to the doorway, causing the door to slide open.

FORTY-SIX

NEW ALLY

Tephra plodded along with her arms held firmly by her captors. She rode the elevator down to One and then marched through a series of corridors. Thoughts of Cosmotine's smug face flashed across her mind. The fool, he'd kill them all for his own ends. The guards guided her through a door marked "guard station." A chubby sergeant seated behind a desk reached over and pushed a concealed button. The door to the right slid open and she was ushered through. Down the hallway they went until arriving at a small interrogation room. She was pushed through the door before it slid shut.

She was alone. She began to pace back and forth. She bit her lip and stepped over to the door. She tried to open it, but the door didn't budge. She felt around the edges of the door. *There must be a space, an opening here somewhere.* Her fingers glided along the edges where the door disappeared into the adjoining wall. It was flat and smooth.

Tephra wrinkled her brow and turned around. She leaned her back against the door and crossed her arms. Getting caught wasn't part of the plan. Hopefully, 93 was able to escape—tell the others. She had no idea who might have seen the broadcast. She had to get free. She had to stop Cosmotine before he hurt anyone else. The lunatic had already killed so many—the Masters, Ash, who knows how many others. This paradise under the sea had become a nightmare of her own choosing. *No, I'm not going to settle for that; not without a fight. I've gone through too much to lay down now.*

As Tephra stood there thinking, she noticed a grate at the base of the wall. It was round, two feet wide or so. She cocked her head. *Hmmm, wonder if that leads to a tunnel.* She crossed the small room and knelt down by the grate. A cool whoosh of air danced around the grate. She could feel the flow as soon as she placed her palm up to it. That air must be coming from somewhere. She curled a finger around the middle slat of the grate and pulled. Nothing happened. She scrunched her lips and looked around the grate's circumference. She didn't see any screws. She reached both hands onto the slats and tensed her arm muscles. She was just about to pull, when the door behind her slid open.

Tephra jumped up and spun around. Ember appeared at the doorway. She stepped in and the door slid shut. Tephra's heart sank. Not her again.

"Tephra, I need to speak with you." Ember stood with her back straight. She held her chin high but didn't move from her spot inside the door.

"Oh ... do you?" Tephra crossed her arms and shifted her stance. She was not exactly in a position to refuse a request from Ember.

"Not here, we need to go somewhere else. Follow me, quickly." Ember turned and opened the door. She hurried down the hallway. Tephra jumped across the room and followed. Ember darted down the hallway, glancing over her shoulder ever few seconds. She walked with a speed Tephra hadn't seen her use before.

Ember guided Tephra through a maze of hallways and rooms until they arrived at a small room rear the end of One. Ember opened the door and ushered Tephra inside. She placed her hand on Tephra's back and gently pushed her in. Tephra frowned and looked behind her. The door slid shut. She could see a small bead of sweat on Ember's upper lip. Ember wrung her hands and walked over to round table in the middle of the room. "Please, sit," said Ember.

Tephra sat as requested. "What are you doing?"

"The Colony's in danger of being destroyed. Cosmotine has gone too far. He must be stopped."

Tephra sat back upon hearing these words. Ember blinked at Tephra and buried her hands in her face for a moment. Giving a big sigh, she sat forward.

"You, of all people, should know how to do that." Tephra pointed her finger at Ember. "And I'm not sure I believe you anyway."

At that moment, a round vent at the bottom of the wall behind Ember started to shake. Tephra titled her head and stood up from her chair. "No, stop, let me push," said a voice behind the vent. The vent moved slightly and then flew out from the wall, clanged across the floor and came to a stop at Ember's feet. 93's head peered out of the vent as he looked around.

"Oops, this one's occupied," said 93. He started to retreat back into the vent when Tephra called out, "No wait, 93, it's me, Tephra!"

93 put his head back out of the vent opening and crawled through slowly raising to his feet. He smiled big at Tephra and waved but did not move from where he stood. He looked over to Ember and said "Hi, ma'am!" flashing a shy smile.

As 93 spoke, a large, bulky figure emerged from the vent opening, crawling on his knees and then unfolding his frame to stand at full height.

"Flint!" cried Tephra. She ran over to Flint and gave him and 93 a hug.

Ember stood and took a step back. She glanced up at Flint, looking a bit scared. "So, this is the cadet they've been looking for?"

Flint smiled and hugged Tephra back. "Feels good to stand up," said Flint. "Feels even better to find you. I didn't think this Ten'er could find his way out of a wet paper bag."

93 jumped back at hearing the insult and replied, "Hey, I got you here didn't I?"

"Where are the others?"

"Misty and 11 are taking the guards we recruited down to Seven," said 93. "They're gonna stop Cosmotine in his tracks."

"Don't be so sure about that." Ember stiffened. "Topaz has sent two thousand guards to Seven to stop the incursion. Your friends are in danger."

"Who's this?" asked 93.

"This is Ember, Cosmotine's chief lieutenant," replied Tephra.

Flint bolted forward and grabbed Ember's arms. 93 jumped in front of Tephra and spread his arms out wide. "Oh no you don't!" yelled 93. Tephra put her hands in front of her face and gave out a yelp. She wasn't anticipating the sudden action.

Flint restrained Ember's arms behind her. "Looks like we got our first prisoner," said Flint.

"Guys, guys, please, it's ok." Tephra pushed 93's arms down and walked past him. 93 relaxed his pose as Tephra walked opposite Ember. "Though come to think of it, I kinda like you better this way." Tephra smirked and crossed her arms.

Ember grimaced. She shifted her body and looked like she was going to try to free her arms, but Flint's size and strength made that impossible.

"Please, tell him to let go," said Ember. "I came to you on my own free will—not orders from Cosmotine."

Tephra tilted her head. "Hmmm, well you did seem a bit harried. Flint, let her go, but keep an eye on her."

Flint nodded and released his grip. Ember took a step forward and exhaled. She reached up and rubbed her right shoulder. "Geez, that hurt." She scowled over her shoulder at Flint.

"Tough," replied Flint.

Ember straightened her dress and looked over into Tephra's eyes. Tephra noticed that Ember's eyes seemed to be welling with tears.

"Tephra, I will not let the Colony fall," said Ember. "I spent my life working to build an orderly world. The Colony is order. War is chaos. I can help you and your friends, but it won't be easy. There are many dangers."

"We understand the dangers, Ember, but there is no other way. Cosmotine is obviously dead set on his plan."

"Yes, I know. He killed the Masters; next he will kill us all."

"How can you help us?"

"I'll give you a head start to get back down to Seven." Ember cleared her throat and reached out her hand. She handed Tephra a small data pod. "These are my codes, they will give you full executive clearance on the elevators. I also put some useful information about the construction tunnels on here."

"What about Cosmotine?"

"I'll take care of Cosmotine. I can keep him busy for quite some time, but I'll need your help to take him prisoner. After you're done on Seven, come back here to One and meet me in the Hall of Equals. From there we can capture Cosmotine together."

Tephra nodded. She looked up at Flint and he nodded back. "Alright, let's get going," said Tephra. At that, 93 bent down and started to crawl back into the open vent.

"No, 93, not that way!" said Tephra. "We have the codes; we can use the elevator like normal people."

"Oh," exclaimed 93 as he stood back up, "old habits die hard I guess." He looked at Ember and gave an awkward hand wave along with an embarrassed smile. Tephra and Flint ran out of the room. 93 stood still continuing to look at Ember.

"93," said Tephra sticking her head back into the room, "let's go, now!"

93 looked to the door, looked back at Ember with a blank look, and then took off in a run leaving Ember standing alone.

FORTY-SEVEN

PLOWSHARES INTO SWORDS

Misty knew 11 was up ahead guiding the rebel troops through a maze of tunnels and vertical shafts. The group moved as quickly as they could, but the space was tight, and it took time to traverse the many ladders and causeways.

After several hours, the rebel troops emerged on Seven. They gathered in a large field near the edge of the Colony. 11 had guided them to a secluded spot, well clear of the main elevator complex where the guards would surely be amassing their own men for the impending fight.

The rebel guards were tired and drained from the long climb down from Five. Misty emerged from the construction tunnel, pushed her way through the people milling about outside, and found 11.

"Hey, 11," said Misty. "We need to get to my warehouse, I hid some useful things there, underground."

"That's not too far from here, but it'll be guarded don't you think? I mean they know you'd want to go back there."

"Maybe, but we have to try. You think you could take a raiding party through the tunnels and come out close to the warehouse?," Misty asked.

"You kiddin' me? I could get this whole lot on the roof of the warehouse if you want."

"No, just underneath will do," said Misty smiling at 11's confident bravado. Misty drew out a rough sketch of her warehouse using a stick in the dirt. She explained where to find the hidden cache.

"It's up to you to figure out how to get it back here, but whatever you do, make it quick."

11 nodded his approval. He turned and walked up to a group of men and women standing together. He pointed, explained the operation, and the group of a dozen rebel guards followed 11 back through the hatch into the construction tunnels.

Misty turned to look at her former field hands. They looked out of place. Most were wearing black uniforms that did not fit well. None look particularly like military men and women. Could these hayseeds be whipped up into a fighting force?

As thoughts churned through Misty's mind, she heard someone calling her name from a distance. "Misty, Misty!" The voice was getting closer.

"Misty, thank God we found you," said Tephra. Misty could hardly believe her eyes. Tephra was standing before her. Misty wasn't sure Flint and 93 could rescue Tephra. And she certainly didn't expect them here so soon.

"Tephra, you're alive!" Misty gave her a hug.

Flint came up and stood next to the pair. "93! You did it!" said Misty as she ran over and gave 93 a hug. He didn't hug her back; keeping his arms straight by his side while Misty grabbed him around the middle and squeezed.

"Misty, Misty, enough, that kinda hurts there," said 93.

Misty released her grip and smiled at him. "I'm just glad your safe, 93."

93 smiled. "Hey, where's 11?"

"He's fine," explained Misty. "He's just running a group of our people over to the warehouse to pick up a few things I hid underground."

"Misty," said Tephra, "we have to group up and get ready to fight."

"I know, Tephra." Misty gazed at the people gathered around. "They're not guards—no soldiers in the bunch—and they've never fought in any battle before, but they have heart."

"Hey, they're tougher than they look," Flint interjected. "Remember we are field hands, your field hands, we work all day—physical work. There's no guard who can compare to that."

"He's right, Misty," replied Tephra, "Besides they're all we've got. They came because they believe in you. That's strength enough."

Misty looked down as her eyes filled with tears. "They're good men and woman, the lot of them." Misty smiled and her eyes softened as a tear dripped down the edge of her right eye.

"I talked to Ember," explained Tephra, "she's on our side ... I think. We need to come up with a plan to keep the guards off their toes, and buy as much time as possible."

"What good will that do us?" asked Flint.

"It will give Ember time to act and us time to maybe get reinforcements," said Tephra. "We may not beat the remaining guards in numbers, but if we hold out, we may not have to."

"Fine," said Misty, "but you need to lead them, Tephra."

"Me? You are the field supervisor; you are their leader."

"This is no field hand work. This is war. We need a bold leader. There's no one else that fits that description here, Tephra. You're it."

"She's right," added Flint, "We know nothing of war, but we have big hearts, big hands, and a big work ethic. You say it and we'll do it."

Tephra paused. Her eyes darted back and forth between Misty and Flint. She frowned.

Misty could see the doubt in Tephra's face. "You've become our leader, Tephra," said Misty as she gently took hold of Tephra's hand. "How many other equals escaped from Ten? None. How many other equals discovered the truth of the Masters Twelve? None. How many other equals confronted Cosmotine face-to-face and survived to not only tell about it, but to do something about it? None."

Tephra looked down as Misty's words swirled around her. "We are not asking you to be our leader out of charity, Tephra," continued Misty. "You've earned this position. We're just stating the obvious. You are a bold leader. We will follow you."

Tephra titled her head upwards towards the sky and let out a sigh. She lowered her head and fixed her gaze squarely on Misty's eyes. Misty held her breath. She knew Tephra was their only hope now. She just had to accept.

FORTY-EIGHT

RISING EMBER

After Ember left the small room where she had led Tephra, she scurried down the maze of corridors to reach Cosmotine's make-shift office—the primary conference chamber. As she approached the conference room door, she paused. Doubt started to creep in. Ember had served Cosmotine for so many years that the thought of betraying him, going against his wishes, was foreign and scary. Ember looked down at her feet. Was she really ready to do this?

Ember had spent her life trying to please one man. Helping him was helping the Colony, so she thought. His way was the way of the Colony. Peace, tranquility, and order came through the Supreme Principal. Everything Ember believed in, and everything she worked hard to achieve, had no greater purpose than helping, and more importantly pleasing, Cosmotine. Yet now Ember had learned that pleasing one man, instead of being true to her own convictions, was leading to chaos. She had been blind to the reality all around her. She could have seen it sooner, done something sooner. So much time had passed. Was it too late? She hoped not. She couldn't go back in time, but she could take action now. The Colony, her Colony, needed her now. The time to stand up for something greater than herself, greater than Cosmotine, had come.

Ember looked up again and stiffened her resolve. She approached the door and it slid open. As she entered, she could see a rush of activity happening all around the room. Cosmotine sat at the center of the large conference table while various guards rushed around providing him with updates, relaying his orders to various people throughout the Colony, and watching monitors showing activity on Seven.

Ember walked to the middle of the conference table opposite Cosmotine and squared her shoulders. "Supreme Principal, we need to talk."

Cosmotine looked up from his data pad and shot Ember an angry look. "No, Ember, we don't." Cosmotine returned his focus to the work beneath him. Dozens of data pads spread around him on the table held diagrams of maps and handwritten notes.

Ember turned and walked briskly over to a panel in the wall. It was the power supply to the large conference room. Being an engineer, Ember knew how to shut down power to the room by swinging open the panel and disengaging the main circuit breaker. The conference room went dark except for the red glow of emergency exit lighting running along the baseboards.

Everyone inside the room stopped immediately in their tracks, not knowing the cause of the power outage. "Everyone evacuate the room now," Ember yelled. The doors slid open and the room full of guards and assistants trotted to the light-filled corridors outside the open doorways.

"Ember!" shouted Cosmotine. "You're interfering with Colony business!"

Once everyone was outside the room, Ember reengaged the power, closed the doors using the control panel nearest her, and locked them. She then walked back over to the conference table opposite Cosmotine, pulled out a chair and sat confidently down.

Cosmotine made a fist and brought it down hard on the table

with a loud bang. "There is nothing for us to talk about; you need to leave!"

"I disagree. We need to discuss the future of the Colony."

"The Colony has no future unless we secure it for ourselves. Can't you see that?"

"The Colony has everything it needs to survive—with or without you."

Cosmotine rose to his feet pointing a finger at Ember. "Are you questioning MY leadership? I made you what you are, you fool. I picked you up from the dirt on Seven, dusted you off, and gave you everything you have now."

"You used me. You used me to further your own ends without ever revealing your final plan."

Cosmotine turned in a huff and walked towards the think glass window framing the outside of the conference room. After taking a few steps he turned to face Ember again. "You would've never understood. Just like the others, your vision is too narrow. Your ends are too meager. Your resolve is too weak."

"I am weak no more. You killed the Masters Twelve and hid their deaths for your own ends."

"Those fools killed themselves. They were antiquated and refused to see reason."

At that moment one of the conference room doors slid open and in walked Topaz.

Ember startled and jumped from her chair. *I thought the door was locked.* She looked over to see Topaz enter and then turned her gaze back to Cosmotine. Topaz was just another pawn in Cosmotine's game. And a fickle one at that as far as Ember was concerned.

"Our forces are assembled and awaiting orders," said Topaz.

"Excellent!" exclaimed Cosmotine. "You see, Ember, at least our Commodore understands the importance of supporting my plan. Why can't you?"

"Perhaps I don't understand it. Or perhaps I don't understand you."

"That's right," said Cosmotine with a slight smile, "You don't understand me." Cosmotine walked slowly around the end of the conference table and then turned to approach Ember on her side of the table. Topaz walked over to join them but stood several paces away from Ember.

"Let me explain myself to you." He held out his hand to Ember. She looked down but refused to grab it. "Follow me."

They sauntered to the far side of the room where an array of monitors was temporarily assembled to monitor the happenings on Seven. To the left of the monitors was the water chamber Cosmotine had used to torture and kill Ash, along with other rebels.

Cosmotine pointed at the monitors. "We have over two thousand armed guards standing ready to take the rebel group. Look over here," he pointed at the monitor to the far left. "These are the rebels. They have nothing to fight with."

Cosmotine turned and smiled at Ember. "Isn't that quaint. Maybe they'll fight with shovels."

"Sir, they also have a few firearms," said Topaz as he strode over to the monitors.

"A few firearms, really?" said Cosmotine with some amusement. "We have far more guards than they have rebels."

"What if the guards turn?" asked Ember. "Change allegiances?"

"You really don't see the big picture do you, Ember," said Cosmotine. He turned to look Ember in the eye. A steely gaze descended on his face. His mouth straightened. Cosmotine brushed past Ember and approached a bank of monitors on the edge of the conference table. He pushed a few buttons and the screens flickered to life.

One of the screens showed a large section of the glass wall on Seven with what appeared to be tape affixed in a large square. The square looked to be fifty feet high and just as wide.

"What's the square taped to the glass on Seven?" asked Topaz.

"Explosive charges," answered Cosmotine with a devious smile. "Enough to blow that section of wall out. The flooding will be fast and will cause other portions of the Colony wall to fail as well. The glass will be gone, but the metal superstructure will remain to support the upper levels."

"You're insane!" cried Ember.

"Sir, you'll kill our own guards," said Topaz.

"If the guards turn to the other side, or somehow lose the upcoming battle, they deserve to be destroyed. Of course, I would prefer to have my guards remain intact, but I will not lose—under any circumstance." Cosmotine erupted in a low, gargled laugh.

Ember saw the devastation in Topaz's eyes. She looked at him, pleading to join her side. But the coward just looked between the two, weighing his options. Figures. He only cares about being on the winning side.

FORTY-NINE

THE ADMIRAL

"You're asking a lot, Misty. I don't know these people like you do. They're your field hands, they know you as the boss. I don't think I can do it."

Misty slowly nodded her head. She glanced over her shoulder and surveyed the field hands spread out behind her. She looked back at Tephra. "They know me to be their crop supervisor—some of them, not all of them. And they know you to be an outsider. But if they only knew who you are, what you've done. They will follow you Tephra. Trust me, I know."

Tephra could tell, Misty wasn't going to take no for an answer. She eyed the field hands milling about. They didn't look like a fighting force. No discipline, no formation, no training. But what choice did they have? Everyone here—the colonists of Seven—was born and raised in a peaceful world. They hadn't known military life, training, skirmishes, war. It was as foreign to them as was the life of surface dwellers. At least she knew. She had training, military life, hardships. More so than any of these people. The last thing she wanted was to replay the past where her choices would decide who would live and who would die. But in the coming war, someone had to make those choices. If not her, then who?

"Misty, I think you're crazy for even asking me to do this. But if you and Flint are sure you want me to lead, then fine. I'll do it." Tephra set her jaw and nodded her head. "I have no idea why you want me to do this, but I'll lead!"

Misty and Flint flashed big smiles. "We are sure, Tephra," said Misty. "We couldn't be more sure."

Tephra looked around and found an old barrel sitting sideways in the field. She lifted it upright and climbed on top.

"Everyone gather round!," yelled Tephra. The rebel guards shuffled towards Tephra. She looked around and was surprised by the number of people she saw from that vantage point. She looked down and took in a long, steady breath. *I can do this.* She shifted her head up and slowly turned as she spoke.

"My name is Tephra. I was an equal on One, for a time at least. I saw Cosmotine kill my friend, Ash. He sent me to Ten, but I escaped. Now, we have learned that the Masters are dead and Cosmotine has a plan to take over the world ... destroy us all."

The people around her stared with little emotion in their faces. Tephra gulped and stiffened her resolve. "Look, you don't know me and I don't know you, but if we are going to save the Colony, restore it to what is once was, what is should be, then we will have to stand up and fight!"

The people glanced at each other with mouths agape. Tephra glanced down at Misty and shook her head. Misty grabbed Flint's arm and quickly hoisted her leg onto the barrel where Tephra was standing. Flint pushed Misty onto the barrel and placed his hand on her back to steady her stance.

"Hey now!" shouted Misty. "Cosmotine is sending a guard army down here to wipe us out. All of us. Why? Because we mean to stop him! And we can stop him, but it's gonna take work. And it's gonna take a fight!" Misty threw her fist in the air.

"We have to act quickly," added Tephra. "Misty has asked me to be your leader. I have led people into battle before. I don't know how we're going to do it just yet, but I do know one thing. This is your home, these are your friends and family. If you want to save them, if you want to save YOUR Colony, then now is the time to fight for what you believe in!" Tephra glanced around at the faces of the men and women standing around her. They looked back at her with wide eyes.

"You heard our new Admiral!" yelled Misty. "Are you gonna fight for our Colony or not?"

The assembled mass erupted in cheers and applause. They threw their fists in the air and chanted back to their new leader, "fight, fight, fight!"

Tephra glanced at Misty. She had a large smile on her face. Misty wrapped her arm around Tephra's shoulder and held her other hand in the air, making a fist. Tephra looked back out into the crowd.

"You are no longer guards, and for now you are not field hands either," exclaimed Tephra.

"And you sure as heck ain't rebels," added Misty.

"You are defenders!" Tephra threw her fist in the air. "And you will defend the Colony and win back the home you love!" The crowd erupted into cheers again. Misty and Tephra leapt down from the barrel. Flint patted Tephra on the shoulder.

"Well done, Admiral," said Flint.

Tephra turned to Misty. "Misty, if I'm the leader, then you're my second-in-command."

"Fine," replied Misty. "What do you want me to do?"

"I need you to separate the defenders into units of twenty-five so we can dispatch them in different directions."

"Ok, I'll get that done right now."

"And appoint a sergeant for each unit. Someone smart and wily enough to lead the group; hopefully without anyone being harmed." Misty nodded her head in approval.

"Flint," continued Tephra, "I need you to use the elevator credentials from Ember to go to Ten and round up all the equals and maybe a few Ten'ers who want to join our cause."

Flint nodded his head. He grabbed 93 by the arm—his trusted Ten'er—and then looked around to see who was nearby; pointing to half a dozen defenders and instructed them to follow. They sped off to begin their journey down to Ten.

No sooner had Flint and his team left, then a large tractor appeared in the distance. It was driving rapidly over the open field and heading in their direction. Its electric motor emanated a high-pitched whine as it tore across the field.

"Admiral," said one of the defenders as he ran up to Tephra. "There's a tractor approaching from the East, should we take up some sort of defensive positions?"

Tephra looked up, saw the tractor, and yelled, "Spread out, be prepared to fight if this is an attack!"

Misty ran over to Tephra. "I don't think that's trouble, I think it's ...." A man driving the tractor could be heard yelling something, but he was too far away to make out the words. After a momentary pause, Misty continued, "11!"

11 came driving up to Misty and stopped the tractor hard in front of her. Behind the tractor was a long hay trailer piled with supplies. Two more tractors pulled up behind, driven by the defenders who had accompanied 11 on his mission to recover the cache of supplies Misty had squirreled away in the warehouse.

"Good golly, Misty, there was a load of stuff in that basement," said 11 with disbelief.

"Is this all of it?" asked Misty.

"Yup," replied 11, "we hooked up these trailers, piled it all on, and tore outta there. Course the place was empty, not a guard in sight, but still. They could be anywhere."

At that moment, 11 looked up and saw Tephra, not realizing she had been standing next to Misty the whole time. "Tephra! You made it back!" 11 reached out and patted her on the shoulder.

Tephra smiled, appreciating the awkward gesture on 11's part. "I'm glad you're safe, 11."

Misty walked over to the supplies on the trailers and motioned to each unit sergeant to gather around her. She handed out clothes, rations of food and drink, and various farm tools—mainly shovels and picks. "Get your people out of those awful black uniforms and into these clothes," said Misty. She handed out boxes of clothes stored away in all sizes. Most were overalls and shirts, a few pants. And all new work boots for the entire group. Misty had hidden away hundreds and hundreds of pairs of clothes.

"Misty," said Tephra, "where'd you get all these clothes?"

"I set aside a few extras each time a new load of clothes was passed around," replied Misty with a knowing smile. "It adds up after so many years. Never know when they might come in handy."

"You're full of surprises, Misty," said Tephra as she patted Misty on the back.

"I like to be ready ... for anything," replied Misty.

Tephra glanced at the people crowded around her. Most of them, even the former guards, were armed mainly with batons. A few had a service pistol strapped to their belt, but these numbered less than a couple dozen. Tephra rubbed her chin and frowned.

"Something wrong?" asked Misty.

"Yeah, we have no guns." Tephra pointed to the assembled crowd. "We either have to shovel the guard army to death or hit them with batons. Either is a poor choice against rifles. Surely, the guards will be armed."

Misty nodded. "Yeah, we have few firearms on Seven. Really no need for 'em."

As Tephra and Misty contemplated their problem, Wheaty walked up next to them with a shovel in one hand and a new pair of boots in the other. "Same old boots we got before," grumbled Wheaty.

"Stop complaining, Wheaty," retorted Misty. "We got bigger problems to consider right now—we got no guns."

"Hmmm ... oh, right." Wheaty plunged the shovel into the ground and sat in the dirt to put on his new pair of boots. "Too bad we ain't got the key to them old rifles we stocked away when them new ones arrived." Wheaty worked the laces of his boots as he tightened them around his foot.

"Wait, what?" asked Misty.

Wheaty didn't respond, he just kept looking at his feet and trying to tighten the laces.

"Wheaty!" Misty thumped him on the head.

"Ouch! What was that for?" Wheaty reached a hand to the top of his head.

"What are you talkin' about? Old guns?"

"Huh? Oh yeah, well a couple weeks ago they gave us new guns, when we were guards. They made 'em for us in that new construction area on Ten. I was part of the group that replaced the new ones for the old ones. We took the old ones to a warehouse near the ship dock on the other side of Seven and locked them up. I think they were going to ship them out somewhere. May already be gone for all I know."

"We need to get those guns!" Tephra's eyes grew wide. "We need Flint's help."

Misty nodded her head and looked around the field. She pointed out an electric cart at the edge of a dirt road. "Come on, let's catch Flint before he goes to Ten."

Tephra nodded in agreement. "11, Wheaty, Acer, follow us."

FIFTY

FLINT'S LUCK

"No, I can't reach. You need to go higher." Tephra spoke softly. She peered down at Flint.

"All right, just a sec." Flint grunted and flexed the muscles in his shoulders and biceps. His hands were wrapped around Tephra's feet. He pushed upwards while extending his stance onto his toes. Tephra shot straight up. She grabbed the bottom of a window sill and pulled herself halfway through. Her feet dangled outside the window, as her head and torso disappeared inside the building. Tephra pulled herself through and stuck her head back out of the window.

"I'll scout around in here. You go with the Ten'ers to see if there's a way for our defenders to carry these guns out."

Flint glanced up at Tephra and gave a thumbs up.

"Flint ... pssst ... Flint." 11 spoke in a hushed holler. He was waving Flint over to a hole in the ground. Flint turned to jog over to 11.

Inside the window, Tephra perched on a narrow beam. Her stomach was tight, and her eyes were taking far too long to adjust to the dimly lit warehouse. She had no idea how she was going to get from the rafters to the floor, but she had to find a way. The cavernous warehouse spread out for yards in either direction. It was mostly empty, but Tephra could see a stack of crates near the center of the building. She had just enough room to crawl along the narrow beam that ran below the window line. She moved several inches at a time. Her nails bit into the wood rafters as she crouched low to ensure her balance didn't falter.

Tephra reached the end of the building and found a series of horizontal supports leading from the rafters to the floor. She reached out her foot and gingerly searched around for the beam below. She couldn't find it. She shifted her weight clear of the beam she was straddling. Her body tightened as she hoped to find the beam below before her arms gave out and she fell to the concrete floor. Her arms ached and her foot swung wildly back and forth trying to find the next beam.

Tephra could feel her arms about to give out, she dropped another inch down, and her foot connected with the thick beam. She gave out a sigh and quickly planted both feet on the beam. She lowered herself down and crouched onto her knees, nearly hugging the thick beam with both arms. Beads of sweat formed on her forehead. Her breath quickened. She took several deep breaths trying to shore up her strength, and courage, to find the next beam down.

Tephra inched slowly downward, beam by beam. Her foot finally met the concrete floor. She turned and slumped onto the ground. Her stomach ached from being clenched the entire time. Her palms were filled with sweat. But she made it. After several minutes of rest, she stood and caught her bearings. *Where's the door?*

Tephra glanced around. The warehouse had small slivers of light emanating from the windows near the roofline. There were no lights on. Tephra meant to keep it that way. She didn't know if turning on the lights would notify anyone, but she didn't want to find out. Her eyes moved around the walls of the building. She took a few steps, then froze. "There it is." She fixed her gaze on a single door at the middle of the warehouse. *That should be the right one. Our defenders can get in there.*

Tephra scurried across the warehouse floor and stood opposite the door. She reached out her hand and then hesitated. *What if the door sets off an alarm? It doesn't matter. We need a way in ... and maybe a way to get these guns out.* She reached for the doorknob. Just before grabbing it the doorknob began to move. She froze. First right and then left, the knob seemed to move on its own. Her eyes widened as she took a step back. The door swung open as light flooded in around it.

"Gotcha!"

"Knock it off, 11." 93 brushed 11's hand from his shoulder.

"Guys, focus, we need to find a way into the warehouse so we can get the guns out." Flint walked behind the pair of Ten'ers. His shoulders were hunched over as he tried to keep his head from knocking against the top of the tunnel.

"Alright, alright." 11 waved his hand in the air as if to dismiss Flint's scolding. "You know most of the tunnels don't empty into a warehouse."

"What? Now you tell me this?" Flint shook his head. "Then why the heck are we down here?"

"Tephra ordered us to find a way in, right?" 93 craned his neck around as he spoke.

"Well, yeah."

"To us, that means go into a tunnel." 93 looked in front of him again. "There's always a way in somehow."

11 nodded his head. "Yeah, I remember this one time when we was—"

"Shhhh!" 93 stopped and threw his hand up in the air, palm out.

Flint crowded close to 93 and tilted his head sideways. "You hear something?"

93 nodded his head and looked at the top of the tunnel. "Footsteps." He took a few more steps forward and then stopped and tilted his ear up. "Yup, more footsteps."

"What's that mean?" asked Flint.

"We must be below the warehouse. Must be closer than I thought." 93 scratched his head.

"Dang tunnel must run right under it." 11 walked a few steps down the tunnel. The light on his hat swept along the top as 11 looked up. "You think we can get in from here?"

"Not without a blow torch," replied 93.

Flint pushed past the two Ten'ers. He ran his hand along the smooth metal surface making up the top of the tunnel. The metal felt cold to the touch. After several feet, he felt a hand on his back.

"Screws here." 11 tapped Flint's back with his finger. Flint spun around. He hadn't realized 11 was so close behind him.

"How'd I miss that?" asked Flint.

"Ya ain't got tunnel eyes like me." 11 smiled, clearly pleased with his own performance.

"Oh yeah? Well how do you propose we remove those screws? With your tunnel eyes?"

11 gasped. "Good gosh, no."

93 scooted up to Flint's side. "Colony key anyone?" He held his home-made metal tool in his hand and wiggled it back and forth.

Flint's eyes lit up. "Oh yeah, now you're talking. Get them screws out and let's see if we can get in here."

"Where are the crates?"

"Over here."

Two guards strode through the door and made for the stack of crates near the center of the building. Tephra held her breath. She squeezed her back up against the wall, her arms pressed against the wall beside her. The door concealed her form from view—at least for now.

The guards walked with their backs towards Tephra. She scrambled towards the corner of the warehouse. A single crate, used for hauling apples, sat in the corner. Tephra jumped inside and crouched low. She caught her breath for several moments and then raised her head above the edge of the crate to peer out at the guards.

"What are we supposed to do with all these crates?"

"Move 'em onto the ship."

"Geez, that's too much work for just two of us."

"We aren't moving them, knucklehead. They're supposed to be sending some field hands to do the work. We just need to supervise."

"Oh good, I thought we were in for a lot of work." The guard placed his rifle on the nearest crate and leaned against it. "So when do the workers get here?"

"Soon."

Tephra lowered herself back down into the empty apple crate. *They're expecting field hands.* She looked down at her loose-fitting overalls and large, clunky work boots. *And we look like field hands.* She had an idea, but she needed to get out of the warehouse first. She creeped out of the crate and kneeled low against the wall. She shimmied along the cold metal wall keeping her eyes locked on the guards. After several feet she felt a slight gap in the wall. She glanced up. *Another door ... perfect.* There was a stack of crates in front of the door, blocking it from the guards' view. She unlatched the deadbolt and slowly turned the knob. She opened the door just enough to allow her slender frame to slip through.

"YOU'RE TURNING it the wrong way, it's righty tighty, lefty loosey." 11 shook his head.

"I know, I know!" 93 stopped working his tool and glared at 11. "Just let me work here, ok?"

"Fine, fine." 11 held up his hands as if to surrender.

Flint stood back from the two Ten'ers. They were making slow work of undoing the screws. Flint turned and glanced up the tunnel. He moved forward and looked up as he went. *Wonder if there could be a hatch here somewhere?* He put his hand on the tunnel wall as he walked. He could hear 93 muttering behind him.

Flint quickened his pace into a jog. After several yards he stopped. Above his head was a tell-tale round hatch. By this point, he had followed 11 and 93 through so many tunnels he knew what the round metal piece was the moment he spotted it. He glanced back at the two Ten'ers, but they were too far away to holler at. Besides, they were bickering over how to remove the screws still. He reached up and pushed the hatch upward. It didn't budge. He squared his stance and placed both hands firmly on the metal circle. He pushed upwards with his entire body. The hatch gave way and lifted out of its hold.

With the hatch open, Flint was finally able to stand fully upright. His head poked out the hatch opening. He grabbed the edges of the opening, and lifted himself through. He glanced around and could see the back of the warehouse to his right. A concrete path led from there to the ship port entrance on his left.

Flint hopped out of the hatch, placed the cover back into place, and crouched close to the ground. He didn't see anyone around. He scurried over to the back of the warehouse. He looked left and then right. Near the far corner was a single doorway. He moved to the door and placed his large palm on the doorknob. He slowly turned the knob until he heard a click. "The door's unlocked?"

Flint opened the door as little as he could to allow his broad shoulders to enter the building. He cradled the door closed and stayed low in a crouch. A stack of crates was in front of him. To his left was a single crate on the ground. He slid over to the single crate and grabbed the edges to peer inside. It was empty.

"Misty, Misty!" Tephra ran across the open field trying to get Misty's attention. Misty spun around and glanced up.

"Tephra! What's wrong."

"I have an idea. Gather up the others and follow me. You think you can get your hands on a tractor with a trailer?"

"Yeah, I'm sure we can. They got 'em all over here. Why?"

"Just get a tractor set up as quickly as you can."

Misty nodded and ran off to gather up Acer and the other defenders in their raiding party. Tephra paced back and forth. Her hand was on her chin as she tapped her lips with a finger. "We may need a diversion though."

***

"Where is she?" Flint mumbled to himself as he glanced around the warehouse. He saw two guards by the crates stacked in the middle of the building. But he saw no sign of Tephra. Was she captured, or just hiding somewhere?

Flint crawled out from behind the wooden crate. He moved along the wall and tried to stay as low as possible. He maneuvered to the opposite side of the large pile of wooden crates in the center of the warehouse and scurried to hide behind them. He crept along the crates, getting closer to the guards.

"You know what's weird?" One of the guards was sitting on a crate. He ran his palms down his thighs as she spoke. "We never used the old rifles. Why get new ones?"

The other guard shrugged. He was leaning his back against a crate and looking down at his feet. "I don't ask questions like that ... and neither should you. At least not now." He shifted his weight and turned to the side to face his fellow guard. "Of course, now it looks like we may be using those rifles after all."

"You mean the rebels?"

"Yeah, few hundred from what I understand."

"Ah come on, that can't be real. A war? In the Colony?" the guard shook his head and smirked. "What are they going to fight us with anyway? Shovels?"

MISTY BARELY SLOWED the tractor enough for Tephra to reach up and grab hold of the roll bar. Tephra hoisted herself up on the step of the tractor as Misty mashed the throttle down. The tractor jerked forward.

"Go to the side door," said Tephra. "We can get in there and then open the large roll-up door next to it."

Misty nodded and turned the steering wheel. The tractor tilted to the left as it turned right. Tephra glanced back over her shoulder and saw the rest of her defenders perched on the trailer behind. They each had tools in their hands—mostly shovels. *I hope we can replace those with rifles soon.*

Misty raced around the corner of the warehouse and followed the wall down to a small door with a roll-up door next to it. She swung the tractor out and then aimed for the roll-up door as if she meant to drive right through it. At the last minute, she stood on the brakes and the tractor came to a sudden stop.

Tephra jumped down and waved to the defenders to follow. She ran up to the doorway and placed her hand on the knob. She pressed on the door and peeked inside. "Flint?" She could see his large form hunched behind the rifle crates. He had changed into field hand clothes back at the base along with the rest of the defenders. His right suspender hung low around his large bicep. The two guards were on the other side. "What's he up to?" This wasn't the diversion Tephra had planned, but maybe it would work just fine.

Tephra waved her defenders in and motioned towards the roll-up door. "Get that thing up as fast as you can. You two follow me." Tephra pointed at two defenders. She turned and ran across the warehouse towards the rifle crates with the two defenders in tow.

As she closed in on Flint's position, she saw him stand and turn to face the guards. He didn't seem to notice Tephra racing towards him.

"We're taking these rifles," said Flint in a low stern voice. He patted a crate with his large palm. The two guards jumped to their feet and turned to face Flint.

"Holy crap, you scared the heck out of us." The guard threw his hand up to his chest. "Dang near gave me a heart attack."

"Don't ever do that again!" The other guard yelled.

Tephra pulled up next to Flint. "Sorry, guys. He's just here to help out." Tephra patted Flint on the arm as he looked down at her with a confused look. "You were expecting us right?"

"Yeah, yeah," said one of the guards. "Alright, you need to take these crates to the ship dock."

"Wait a second ... wait just a second," the other guard squinted as he glared at Flint. "I remember you—you're that missing cadet! They showed us your pictures when we were—"

Flint planted his right fist in the guards face, causing the guard to reel backwards. He fell hard to the ground and groaned. Flint glared at the other guard who was still standing next to him.

The guard still standing took a step backwards. "I don't remember you at all." The guard put his hands up in front of him with his palms out. He grimaced. "Memories not real good, you know."

"Geez, Flint you knocked that guy out cold," said Tephra.

"I know, but luckily this guy has a bad memory." Flint chuckled.

Tephra rolled her eyes. "Well get them out of here while we load the trailer." Tephra glanced up and saw Misty pulling the tractor through the roll up door. She circled the crates and parked close by. Flint grabbed the guard who was still standing while two defenders grabbed the guard laying on the ground. They took the pair to a small closet at the side of the warehouse, threw them in, and barricaded the door using the empty apple crates nearby.

The defenders started piling crates of rifles onto the trailer. They worked in teams, handing crates from one to the other until they arrived on the trailer.

"Come on guys, keep it moving. We've got to get out of here as quickly as we can!" Misty barked at the defenders while they worked.

Flint returned to the group. He jumped in and started throwing crates onto the trailer.

"We got to go, Misty!" Tephra looked around nervously. She dashed to the roll-up door and peered outside. Looking left and then right, she didn't see anything in sight. *All clear for now at least.* Tephra glanced behind her to check on their progress. The trailer was half full and there were still a few dozen crates on the ground. A loud whirring noise filtered in behind her. *What's that noise?* Tephra glanced back outside and tilted her ear towards the front of the warehouse. She turned to get a better look. A large electric truck full of guards in black uniforms rounded the building. They were followed by several tractors pulling trailers with field hands perched on each trailer. The entire convoy was barreling towards her.

Tephra jumped back and punched the door close button. "We got company!" she yelled over her shoulder. She reached for the small door and slammed it shut with one hand and then rotated the lock with the other. She turned and ran towards Flint and Misty.

Misty ran over and met Tephra midway back. "What is it?"

"Guards and field hands. Tons of them." Tephra kept running until she was back with the group. "We aren't getting out that way."

The men stopped working. They looked up at Tephra with blank faces.

"Now what?" asked Flint.

Tephra walked around the crates. Her mind raced. She rubbed her chin. *There's got to be another way. We won't make it out any of the doors now.*

Tephra stood still. She could hear the guards banging on the roll-up door from outside. Misty and Flint ran over to her. "Driving out on the tractor isn't going to work," said Tephra

"We have to do something!" pleaded Misty.

"Let's just drive right through them," suggested Flint.

"No, there's got to be a more secure way than— The ground under Tephra's feet began to shift. First right and then left. She leapt backwards as a square section of the floor gave way and fell downwards.

11 stuck his head up through the square hole in the floor. "Heya!"

"11!" Tephra ran up and patted him on the head.

93 stuck his head up through the hole too. "We found a way in just like you told us to."

"No, you just found a way out!" Tephra waved her arms and signaled the men to start dropping the crates into the square hole in the floor. The men jumped into action, moving crates as fast as they could.

"11, 93 —take these crates as far down the tunnel as you can." Tephra said. "And then come back and get more. We need to move as many as possible."

The men worked as fast as they could. The guards outside had started ramming the door. After three heavy thuds, the door buckled in the middle, but still held firm.

"They're almost through, get the last of the boxes and let's go!" Tephra yelled as she pushed on a defender's back trying to hurry him towards the hole. The defenders threw down the last of the crates and then jumped through the hole. 93 placed the square piece back into position while 11 tightened the screws around the outside.

"Everybody, go that way." Tephra pointed back down the tunnel. Her eyes were wide and beads of sweat ran down her face. "We'll take as many crates as we can back to base and then come back through the tunnel system for the rest." Tephra paused. She tilted her head sideways. She could hear a herd of footsteps from above. They scurried one way and then the other. Everyone in the tunnel froze.

Tephra put a finger in front of her mouth. "Be quiet, but get going." She nodded forward with her head.

"Flint," whispered Tephra.

"Yeah?"

"I need you to go back to your original mission. Get as many people from Ten as you can."

"On it, Admiral." Flint smiled and shot Tephra a wink.

FIFTY-ONE

THE SCOUTING MISSION

Tephra pointed to a spot on the ground. Her defenders dropped the crates and tore off the lids.

"Rifles!" yelled Tephra. "Everyone grab one and then get back to your units." The defenders crowded around the crates. Tephra pushed her way out of the crowd.

"So what now?" asked Misty stepping up to Tephra's side.

"We need to get our troops into position."

"Ok, where?"

"Not sure. Probably on either side of the road for now. It would be good to know what the guards are up to. You think we can scout up this road and find out?" Tephra pointed up the wide dirt road.

"Yeah, that leads to the main elevator complex at the middle of Seven." Misty nodded her head. "Probably where the guard army is assembling."

"Let's take a walk. I need to see the guards for myself." Tephra glanced around to locate 11. He was standing near the crates helping to hand out rifles. She waved him over. He and Misty joined Tephra along with a half dozen defenders. Each member of the group carried a recently-captured rifle, except Tephra.

"I don't need a gun," explained Tephra at the outset of their sojourn, "just binoculars if you have them."

"Yes, I do," said Misty as she handed a pair of large binoculars to Tephra.

"Wait here a sec. I need to confer with the unit leaders." Tephra trotted over to a group of her sergeants standing together. They greeted her with a quick salute. Several other sergeants scurried into the circle to hear what the Admiral had to say.

"I want half on one side of the road and half on the other. Got it?" The assembled sergeants nodded in unison. "And try to dig some trenches, if you can. Something about three feet deep so our troops can hunker down out of sight. We'll be back soon." Tephra turned and dashed back to her little scouting group. "Let's get going."

The scouting party crossed the road and dashed towards a set of rolling hills at the edge of a wheat field. While most of Seven was flat, several areas had man-made rolling hills for citrus orchards. They skipped around the leafy citrus trees undulating up and down the rolling hills. After cresting half a dozen hills, the scouting party came to the last small crest of a hill and hid just behind the top. The land beyond was flat and bare for about a mile and then paved after that. The edge of the central elevator complex.

Tephra put the binoculars up to her eyes and scanned the horizon. "They have the guards split up into divisions it looks like. There must be a couple thousand at least."

"Do you see any vehicles?" asked Misty.

"No, just their little carts they zoom around in." She lowered the binoculars and looked at Misty. "What type of vehicles did you mean?"

"I don't know. Maybe armored vehicles, who knows what Cosmotine has up his sleeve."

Tephra put the binoculars up to her eyes again and scanned around a bit longer this time. "I don't see anything like that. Odd that the guards are sitting around. Are they waiting for orders or something?"

Misty reached for the binoculars and Tephra handed them to her. Misty took a long look around sweeping back and forth across the horizon several times. "That is odd. They don't seem to be in any hurry."

Tephra lowered herself below the crest of the hill and looked up at Misty. "Why would they wait?"

Misty sat down next to Tephra. "If I had the larger army," responded Misty, "I wouldn't waste any time sitting around."

"Perhaps Topaz is not with them to order them forward."

"Well, they have other commanders. There was a very unpleasant captain that would come to the warehouse to recruit field hands. He seemed like the type that could command guards. It doesn't take the Commodore to order guards into battle. Any of us could do that."

"Right ...." Tephra scratched her forehead. "But it would take the Commodore to order the guards NOT to advance."

"You think Topaz doesn't want a fight?"

"He may not want a fight just yet. Maybe he's stalling. Or maybe Ember is on our side and helping us in ways we don't know."

Tephra rose up and looked at the guard army again through her binoculars. "Well, it seems most likely that the guards will come down this main road when they do move out. I think splitting our defenders is the right move. Half on one side of the road, half on the other."

"I dunno, Tephra, that could be risky. What if you're wrong and they come another way?"

"Well, that's a risk we may have to—"

"Where's 11?" Misty stood up.

"What ... um ... 11?" asked Tephra.

"11 isn't here," responded Misty. "Hey, you guys seen where 11 went?" The defenders shook their heads no.

Misty and Tephra took a few steps back down the hill, out of sight of the enemy, and called out, "11! 11!"

Before they could call out again, a voice came from behind them. "What?" Misty spun around and saw 11 standing a few feet behind her.

"11, geez you scared me. Where'd you get off to?" asked Misty.

"Just a bit of scoutin.' Saw some boxes."

FIFTY-TWO

EMBER'S STAND

"I won't let you destroy the Colony!" yelled Ember. Topaz jumped at her yell.

"You and what army?" asked Cosmotine.

Just then the conference room door slid open and Captain Rotifer walked in. "We are prepared with the explosive charges, Supreme Principal."

"Excellent, Captain."

"Captain Rotifer, what are you doing here?" asked Topaz.

Rotifer puffed up his chest and smirked at Topaz. "Special assignment, sir."

"Commodore Topaz, your men are not advancing, why is that?" asked Cosmotine.

"Uh." Topaz shuffled his feet a bit and then stood to attention. "I was waiting for the right moment to strike, sir."

"Captain Rotifer," commanded Cosmotine, "order the assembled guards to advance and attack the rebels. You are now in charge, Commodore Rotifer."

"Yes, sir, as you command," Rotifer replied heartily. A wide smile crossed his face as he spun around and marched out of the room.

Ember glanced at Topaz. His eyes moved to the floor as his mouth fell open. He placed his hand over his mouth. His eyes were wide, he looked like he had just been punched in the gut. Ember enjoyed the look on his face. Served the coward right.

Topaz shook his head and looked up at Cosmotine. His face hardened. "You know, Cosmotine, you are now alone in a room with one enemy," Topaz said pointing at Ember, "and one who was on the fence," pointing at himself, "so that might not have been the best move."

"There's nothing either of you can do to stop my plan. I will need new leaders in our new world, there will be room enough for you both once we have succeeded in taking over land."

Ember walked deliberately in front of Cosmotine and held up her hand. "NO! Your plan will fail. Your plan has already failed." Topaz walked up next to Ember and faced Cosmotine as well. Cosmotine took a defensive step backwards.

"You may have miscalculated this one, Cosmotine," said Topaz. The two walked towards Cosmotine as the older man continued to back up until he had reached the corner of the room and his two confronters stood before him.

"Please, you must see reason," pleaded Cosmotine. "There is a better world that we can share. There is plenty of power for us all."

"I don't want your power," replied Ember, "I want peace and order. That's what the Colony stands for, not chaos!"

At that moment, the conference room door slid open and a dozen guards barged into the room. Ember craned her neck around to see the guards enter. Cosmotine pushed a button on the wall and then lunged forward and grabbed Ember's arm. He twisted her wrist and gave a hard push, causing her to fall backwards. She landed inside the open water chamber. Cosmotine punched the button on the wall again and the chamber door slid closed, from top to bottom.

Ember jumped back onto her feet, just as Topaz turned and ran hard towards the nearest exit door. *Coward!* The guards rushed over to help Cosmotine, but he waved them off. They assembled behind him.

Ember placed her hands against the thick glass that ran down the center of the chamber door. She had seen this chamber used several times on Cosmotine's enemies, but she had not seen it from the inside. There was little chance Cosmotine would let her escape now. She had to stall for as much time as she could. The more she was able to distract Cosmotine, the more time the rebels would have a chance to turn the tide of the war in their favor.

"Looks like we trapped the canary," said Cosmotine as he looked through the glass to see Ember inside the chamber.

"Maybe you have," replied Ember. "But to what end?" *How can I stall him? What would Topaz do?* "Are you sure you have thought of everything, Cosmotine? Tephra is smart, and her army is growing."

"Tephra may be smart, but I am smarter. I have thought of every contingency possible."

"I don't like to lose, Cosmotine, and neither do you. I'm not sure your plan can prevail. And no one can think of everything. Are you sure you will be on the winning side?"

"Yes, of course I will. I meticulously created my plan, and kept it from those who might not agree." Cosmotine flashed a devilish smile.

"You were smart to do that. I would have objected. But when I see that your plan could be successful ... might even be inevitable, it makes me think."

"Think of what?"

"Think of how I can help you solidify your plan."

"You no longer have any use to me, Ember."

"Don't I? Over the past several years no one was more instrumental in helping you locate and neutralize those pesky equals who sought to stand in your way."

"Yes, true." Cosmotine placed a hand to his chin as he listened to Ember.

"Who else do you trust? Topaz? He is a coward."

"Hmmm, true."

"What do you need of me, Cosmotine?"

Cosmotine turned and paced a few feet away from the chamber. He stopped and turned back to face Ember. His hand was still on his chin. He glanced upwards.

Ember's eyes darted to the guards standing by the wall. Their eyes were fixed ahead of them. She could not make eye contact with anyone. She looked back at Cosmotine as he lowered his head and fixed his gaze on her.

"What I need of you, Ember—" Cosmotine strode back to the chamber. He stood in front of the glass and metal door. He furrowed his brow, his eyes burned into Ember's eyes. She stood her ground and stared back.

"Kill Tephra." He grinned.

Ember flinched. She didn't mean to; she just couldn't help it. The thought of killing anyone, but especially Tephra, caused her head to fall. She glanced down at the floor as her hand came to her stomach. Not kill. Not Tephra.

Cosmotine let out a low chuckle. "I didn't think so."

Ember looked back up to his face. "Wait, I can ... I will ... do it." Ember tried to sound convincing, but the waiver in her voice betrayed her ruse.

"Ember, my dear, you could have found a position in my new world, but instead you have found a new place at the bottom of the ocean."

Ember shook her head. Her face hardened. She clenched her teeth and balled both hands into fists. She pounded on the glass wall between them. "You are a fool Cosmotine. You will never win. The Colony won't allow it—I can promise you that."

"Impossible! I AM the Colony. My plan IS inevitable."

"I don't have to convince you of anything because the rebels will destroy you!" Spit flew from Ember's lips as she yelled. "The Colony will stop you! And when they do, you will be convinced enough."

Cosmotine's eyes grew red with anger. He reached over and hit a button hard with his fist. Water filled the chamber up to Ember's waist. Then a bolt of electricity jumped from the top of the chamber and raced down through Ember's body. She shrieked with pain as her knees buckled momentarily plunging her head below the water line. She stood back up, steadying herself with a hand on the glass door in front of her.

"It is you who cannot win, Ember. You will never beat me."

"I have won. I've finally stood up for what I believe in," replied Ember as she breathed heavily, having a difficult time speaking between breaths. "You have already lost. You only think you are still in charge. But the colonists are rising up. Their belief in the Colony is stronger than you could ever be. Your time is running short, Supreme."

"Liar!" Cosmotine scowled again and punched a button causing the water to rise quickly in the chamber. The water filled up to Ember's shoulders, then neck, then to the top of her head. Ember swam to the top of the chamber, lifting her mouth and nose above the water line so she could grab a final, big breath before the water completely filled the chamber. With only inches of air left at the top, he stopped the water.

He stood looking at Ember as she struggled to push her nose into the tiny air pocket at the top of the chamber. "You are all the same," said Cosmotine through gritted teeth. "You are weak, and you thereby sentence yourselves to certain death." He reached down and finished filling the chamber with water. There was no more air in the chamber; only clear, cold, salty seawater.

FIFTY-THREE

THE FORBIDDEN WAR

Tephra glanced at 11. "What do you mean by boxes?"

"Well I found—"

"Admiral," a defender said, "there is some activity with the guards."

Tephra looked through her binoculars. "Something has changed, the guard army is beginning to move out." Tephra lowered her binoculars and looked at the rest of the group. "We have to get back and warn the others." The entire group turned and began jogging back to the defender's camp.

As Tephra reached the defenders position, she glanced to her right and noticed half the defenders were still digging. They didn't have time to finish their trenches. *What the heck is going on here?* Others were spread out in a flat open field. No hills or trees to provide natural cover. A few defenders looked to be kneeling in shallow trenches, but their heads and torsos were exposed.

"Those defenders don't understand what they need to do. They are exposed," said Tephra. "They didn't dig deep enough. We need a better position for them."

"Funny that they don't just use the irrigation tunnels to hide," said 11 as he looked over at the topography of the field. "They're just in front of the tunnel access hatches." 11 shook his head as if the defenders were being intentionally foolish.

"Yeah, he's right," responded Misty "I know about irrigation tunnels."

"Can we get the men inside?" asked Tephra. "And can they easily exit? I don't want anyone trapped in a tunnel."

"No problem," said 11, "all you need do is spread 'em out. There's an access hatch every thirty feet or so. Or we can always go down to the main chamber, all the irrigation tunnels empty into a large chamber. There's twenty or so of them chambers around the Colony. They connect through bigger pipes."

Tephra smiled. "Alright. Why don't you take command of all units in the open field? Take them to the irrigation tunnels and position them across as many access hatches as it takes to get everyone inside, and out if necessary. Got that, Captain 11?"

"Oh. my name's just 11 I don't go by no captain or nothing. Now, there was this guy on Ten, a new recruit, and he used to call himself colonel all the time, but I never knew what that meant or why he did it; just liked the sound of it I suppose. And then—"

"11." Tephra placed her hands on 11's shoulders. "We need you to lead these men. You can't do that unless you have a military title. You're captain now. Get it? More importantly, get your butt over there and get those defenders hidden in the irrigation tunnels and tell them the guards have moved out and are planning something ... NOW!"

11 jumped and ran over to the men in the field. Misty turned to Tephra, "I am going to go with him since I can help locate the hatches." Tephra nodded her approval.

Tephra turned left. The defenders from her scouting mission followed her. They ran across a field of wheat that had grown to waist height. The wheat rustled in the breeze, shimmering back and forth. She could barely see the defenders crouched low in the middle of the field. She wrinkled her forehead as she approached the defenders.

Did they only dig down a foot? They don't look too protected from gun fire.

She stopped next to a long line of crouching defenders. There was no time to dig. They'd have to make do with lying low in the wheat field. She glanced to her right and saw a large warehouse resting at the far edge of the field. She scolded herself for not having the troops take up position in the warehouse. *Well, a good fallback position anyway.*

She turned and walked down the line of crouching defenders. She could see they were ill prepared. Some of them held their rifles out in front, trained on the open road as they should be. Others seemed to have the rifles resting at their sides, or placed across their arms sideways. She came up to an unprepared defender and kicked his boot. "Hey! The rifle goes in your hands not next to you." The young man grabbed the rifle in both hands and held it out in front. "There, that's better. Aim for the road—that's where they'll be ... probably."

She continued plodded down the line of defenders. She needed to talk, say something. "OK, troops! The guard army is approaching as we speak. They will move down the main road. That's where we found them formed up as a single army on our scouting mission. So aim for the road."

She glanced up and down her line as the defenders finished moving their firearms into position. "Remember, stay hidden until I give you the command to attack! No one moves until I say so!" She stopped in the middle of her line and crouched low in the wheat.

After waiting for what seemed like ages, a group of guards appeared marching down the middle of the road. Tephra strained to see through the wheat. She raised her head just slightly over the wheat to glance over the field. She frowned. *Why so few?* This wasn't the size of the guard army, it was only a few dozen of them. Tephra felt a pit form in her stomach. Something wasn't right about this.

The defenders to each side of Tephra began to move. She

reached over and placed her hand on a young woman's back. She could feel her body trembling from fear, or adrenaline, or both.

"Steady, defenders, steady." Tephra spoke in a hushed yell.

The guards continued their march down the road. They were nearly perpendicular to the hidden defenders in the field. Tephra raced through her options. She looked at the guards and then glanced over her shoulder to the warehouse at the edge of the field. They could fire now, or they could retreat. If they stayed hidden, and didn't reveal their position, the entire line of defenders could probably make it inside the warehouse without having to fire a shot—or having a shot fired at them. Something wasn't right about this small group of guards. Was it a trap?

"Pop ... pop, pop, pop." Rifle fire erupted to Tephra's left. As she turned her head, more rifle fire erupted to her right. Nearly her whole line stood and started firing at the guards on the road. They hadn't given Tephra a chance to finish her thoughts. They had decided for her.

The guards began a quick retreat. The rounds fired by the defenders flew high and wide of their mark. A single guard was struck in the arm. The guards returned fire. As soon as the guards' guns erupted, the defenders hit the deck, flinging themselves back down in the tall wheat. It was too late. Their position was revealed. And they had barely wounded a single guard.

"Dang it! What a waste!" Tephra spat the words out. She couldn't believe her defenders got ahead of her. The heat of battle was impossible to control. She had learned that lesson before, now here it was for her to learn again.

"Everyone up! Up, up up!" She ran down the line yelling out instructions. "We are moving out! Head to the warehouse, now! Everyone, head to the warehouse now!"

A defender trudged up to her and set the butt of his rifle on the ground. "Why so fast? We beat them guards. They ran in an instant. We won this thing!"

"You idiot!" Yelled Tephra. "You haven't won anything yet. That was just a ruse. They sent a few dozen guards down the road to flush us out and you all took the bait!"

"The bait? What bait?"

"There's over two thousand guards around here somewhere. They aren't on the road and now they know where we are. You can bet your life the guards will be coming, but not that way." She pointed to the road as she scowled at the defender standing in front of her. "You all need to get to the warehouse before the real guard army shows up."

Tephra ran up and down the line prodding her troops to move out. The defenders moved slow and steady. Many seemed almost reluctant to follow her orders, although they plodded a few steps just to show they were trying.

"Smoke! Fire!" A young man and woman ran up the Tephra. "Admiral," said the young woman, "over that hill ... all the smoke."

Tephra glanced to the low sloping hill at the edge of the wheat field. A long line of smoke bellowed up from one side of the field to the other. Flames chewed through the wheat as the fire raced across the field towards the defenders. Behind the flames, a thousand guards in their black uniforms could be seen marching in long, deep rows.

The defenders, seeing the fire, broke out into a run. As they ran, bullets began to fly through the smoke, coming from the rifles of the guard army.

"Move! Move! Move!" shouted Tephra as she ran among her troops ensuring every defender alighted from the field and galloped towards the warehouse.

As the last of the defenders moved out, Tephra turned and pumped her arms as she sprinted through the field. A defender running just in front and to the left of her arched his back and fell to his knees. Dark, red blood seeped into the back of his shirt. He buckled forward and plunged face first into the ground. A woman stopped and knelt down beside the fallen defender. Tephra rushed up and grabbed the woman by the arms.

"No time, you must keep moving."

"But admiral, he's been shot!"

"I know, you'll be next if you don't move out. Move!" The women leapt to her feet and dashed forward.

Tephra took two strides forward when a woman to her right spun around and fell to the ground on her back. Her eyes were open, but they remained still, lifeless. Blood pooled around the back of her head. A man stopped and dropped his rifle. He cradled his fallen comrade around the shoulders. "No! Sister, No!" The man cried out. He lowered his head touching foreheads to his fallen sister.

"You must keep moving!" Tephra grabbed the man's collar in her hand and jerked his head upwards. "Not now! Keep moving!"

The man regained his footing and darted away. Tephra glanced down at the fallen woman. She sighed and then sprinted off in full retreat.

Tephra ran up to those who stopped to help the wounded and grabbed them by the arm. "Keep going! You must get up!" She pleaded with them to move. As she helped one young man off the ground, she turned towards the advancing guards. They were moving quickly. Her heart pounded in her chest. She shoved him on the back trying to get him moving faster.

The smoke began to waft towards the defenders, thick black ash filling the air, and the lungs, of the defenders running for their lives. The bullets continued to trace a path through the smoke. Some of the bullets raced harmlessly by whistling through the air as they flew, while others found their mark.

After running for what felt like hours, the defenders finally reached the warehouse on the edge of the field. It was well outside the wheat field, surrounded by dirt and then a concrete pad at its base. The defenders filed in and took up positions throughout the building. Tephra was the last person to make it inside. The defenders spread out on the first and second levels, their weapons pointing out of the windows and doors of the warehouse, awaiting their attackers.

Tephra glanced around at her harried defenders. They were breathing hard, each one wet with sweat and fear combined. She figured that over the course of the last several minutes she had lost nearly a third of her defenders to the relentless hail of bullets. It was her worst nightmare. She was their leader, she decided to take a stand in the field, she was responsible for so many dead. Her mind swirled with regret. *Not again*, she thought. *Not again.* Tephra glanced down and felt a gag reflex, she just wanted to puke. She took a deep breath and glanced up at her defenders.

Tephra shook the thoughts from her head and strengthened her resolve. Now was not the time to dwell on what was done. She needed to think. If they had been trained soldiers, it would have been different. Perhaps that was her mistake, they weren't trained solders. They weren't trained anything. They could hold out for a while longer in the warehouse, but they were not going to survive the onslaught for long. They were outnumbered, out trained, and for the time being, outfoxed.

As TEPHRA's defenders sprinted across the burning wheat field, Misty and 11 could see the fire and devastation befalling them. They looked at each other and knew what the other was thinking. If half the guard army was over in the wheat field, the other half would be falling on them any moment.

11 yelled for all defenders to return to the access hatches. Misty followed suit. The men around her stood still. They glared at the destruction, some of them held their mouths agape. Others shook their heads slowly as if what they saw couldn't be real. A defender standing in front of Misty grabbed her arm. He peered into the old crop supervisor's eyes. "How could this happen?"

"Snap out of it!" Misty shook loose of his grip and grabbed the man's collar. "Get down the hatch now, or you'll be next!" She shoved the man aside and ran in front of the group. "Don't just stand there gawkin', get your rears down into the tunnels ... now!" The defenders spun around and crowded around the hatch. Misty ran down the line to the next group of defenders and yelled at them as well. 11 took off in the opposite direction to do the same. The defenders grudgingly turned and made their retreat.

As the last of the defenders were slipping into the tunnel, the other half of the guard army appeared behind their line. Several stragglers among the defenders were standing above the hatches. The guards open fire, hitting several defenders and killing them instantly. The last of the defenders jumped down the access hatches and sealed them shut. The defenders were so focused on escaping, they did not return fire.

Inside the irrigation tunnels, 11 pushed past the defenders huddled below and led them forward toward the large chamber where the irrigation tunnels met.

Misty hustled up next to 11 and asked, "What's the plan, Captain?"

"These tunnels exit into bigger tunnels and access points near the center of Seven. We have to head to the heart of the enemy, so we have room to maneuver and regroup. The other tunnels are too narrow."

"What? You mean we are going toward the guards, not away from them?" said a defender.

"Listen to your Captain. We can do this," Misty said firmly.

THE GUARDS who stormed across the burning wheat field took up positions outside the warehouse. A few of the defenders opened fire, but their bullets fell far short of the guards. They were too far away. Tephra looked out the nearest window with her binoculars and could see the bullets hitting the dirt well before the guards.

"Hold your fire!" commanded Tephra. Some of the defenders stopped firing, several did not hear her. "Hold your fire! Hold your fire!" Tephra yelled as she walked down the line of defenders. Eventually everyone complied.

"They are out of range. There's no reason to waste ammunition shooting at the dirt."

"Admiral," said one of them, "what's your plan now? They have us trapped here."

"We wait. They won't approach yet; they know they will get mowed down before they make it inside." Tephra only half believed what she was saying. She saw the men and women run at the first sign of fire, but it was in a panic not a controlled retreat. These were no soldiers. Even though many had been former guards, they were field hands at heart. If the guards rushed the warehouse, the defenders would likely be overwhelmed.

Tephra knew she could not face the guards on their own terms. Fighting soldier to soldier only worked if both sides in fact had soldiers. She had no soldiers, she had field hands—plain and simple. She needed a new plan. There had to be another way to fight.

Tephra walked quickly through the warehouse, trying to get ideas. The warehouse was large, over a hundred yards long. The floor was cement and the walls were made of steel beams with corrugated steel sheeting between the beams. The roof was slanted on either side to form a neat crest down the middle. During harvest season the large open area would be filled with crops. There was a beat-up tractor against one wall along with various farm equipment and a few empty barrels. A series of metal boxes lined the floor. Each box held various equipment that was used by the tractor to plow the field or harvest grain. The metal storage containers were ten feet long, six feet wide, and four to five feet high—varying from box to box.

Tephra noticed a room at the back of the warehouse. *Perhaps there's something helpful in there.* She trotted across the warehouse and peered inside the room. It looked to be a workshop. Metal working tools lined a metal bench. Large drilling and sawing machines were bolted to the floor. Tephra looked over to the nearest defender and called him over.

"What's your name?" asked Tephra.

"Wheaty," replied the defender.

"You know what all these tools are in this room?"

"Of course," replied Wheaty with enthusiasm, "that's the metal shop. Every warehouse has one, we have to fix our own equipment you know."

"You know how to use it?"

Wheaty rolled his eyes. "Yes, yes, I've been working in the shop since I was a small child, learned it from my father. That was my main job before being recruited by the guards."

"How about that tractor over there, does it work?"

"I'm sure it does. Every self-respecting field hand keeps their tractors working." He called over to a couple of his friends. "Hey, Yarrow, Spruce, go see if that tractor starts." Wheaty pointed towards the tractor and the two field hands took off running.

"Wish there were a few more tractors," said Tephra.

"There are," responded Wheaty, "they're all parked out back. Probably a half dozen more at least." Wheaty called over to a group of defenders, "Go check how many tractors out back. Pull them into the warehouse here near the metal shop." He glanced back at Tephra. "What do you want with the tractors anyway?" We can't ride 'em outta here, we'd get shot in an instant."

"Just pull together every tractor you have and get those hay trailers over here too. I have an idea."

She was wrong when she thought these people weren't trained in anything. They were trained in something. *These people may not be great with a rifle*, thought Tephra, *so let's give them tools they know how to use.*

FIFTY-FOUR

EQUALS AND TEN'ERS

Flint and 93 clung low to the ground. "I thought you said the elevator would be in front of us?" asked Flint with his teeth clenched. He shot 93 an angry look.

"Yeah, well it is," replied 93. "We just need to get through the back entrance."

"All I see is a wall."

"Just keep down, and keep quiet. I'll get us in there." 93 moved from being prone on the ground into a crouched position. He glanced around and scurried over to the tall wall in front of them. They were at the back of the main elevator complex. Flint and his team had followed 93 through the tunnels and emerged at this spot. So far, they had been able to crawl on their bellies through the thick brush on the back side of the complex. But they reached a dead end.

Flint scoffed. *He said this would be easy. Should'a known his idea of easy is never easy!* Flint looked behind him at his fellow defenders. They slowly creeped up next to him on their bellies.

"Psst! Psst!" Flint glanced up and saw 93 waving him over. Flint pushed himself off the ground and into a crouch. He scurried over to 93's side. The low brush that had concealed him before stopped a few feet short of the elevator complex wall. He was exposed. If anyone happened to walk around the corner, they'd be spotted for sure.

"Found the door," said 93. "Get our troops over here."

Flint turned and motioned for the rest of the team to assemble around him. As the troops approached, 93 turned and opened a small door, only four feet high. They crawled into the small space on their hands and knees. Flint glanced around. It appeared to be a maintenance area. It was short, but wide, spanning the full width of the complex. 93 crawled to the other side and opened the same size door cut into the opposite wall. He popped his head out and waited a moment. Flint crawled up behind him.

"See anything?" asked Flint.

"A few guards leaving on the other side." 93 was looking out across the main elevator complex. He looked back at Flint. "As soon as the path is clear … ." He turned to look out again. "Wait for it … ok now!" 93 flung the door open and scurried over to an open elevator. Flint sprinted behind along with the rest of their troops. The flew onto the elevator and Flint punched in the access code he had gotten from Ember. The door slid closed and the lift began its descent to Ten.

"Whew, made it." Flint let out a breath and flopped his back against the elevator.

"See, easy," said 93. Flint rolled his eyes and shook his head.

The ride was short. Flint and 93 stepped off the elevator on Ten with their small group of defenders. Flint had made the trip from the elevator to the main desk dozens of times before, but he had no idea what lay behind the reception area. He took a step forward and 93 stepped up next to him.

"Flint, we may have a little problem here."

"What's that?"

"It's easy to get into Ten, but it's not so easy to get out. They don't exactly have an open mind here."

"So what do you propose?"

"The usual, I guess."

"Tunnels?"

"Yeah."

"We don't have that much time, and we still have the elevator codes. They worked to get us down here, they'll work to get us back up."

Flint patted 93 on the shoulder. "We'll leave a couple defenders at reception. I'm sure they can convince the Ten'ers to let us out. And if they don't, then their guns will." They marched to the main desk. Several people sat and stood behind the desk, largely uninterested in the arrival of their latest guests. They were preoccupied with various tasks and clerical work.

"We need to see every equal you have here," said Flint.

The man behind the desk in dark gray work clothes looked up, showing Flint his expressionless face. "Why?"

"Because we are the defenders and we have come to liberate them so they can fight alongside us in our—"

The man behind the counter held up his hand. "I don't need to know that," replied the man, "just a simple reason—visiting?"

Flint felt slightly embarrassed. He thought the man was trying to defy him or question his motives for asking to speak to the equals.

"Yeah, visiting," replied Flint.

The man in grey let the group enter Ten. Before disappearing through the door, Flint turned and asked the man in grey, "which way?"

"Second corridor on the right," said the man.

"You two stay here." Flint pointed at two defenders. "Make sure they are 'willing' to open the doors when we return." The men nodded and stood on either side of the doorway. Flint entered Ten as the doors quickly slammed shut behind him.

The hallway the group walked down was dimly lit. The walls were wet with water occasionally dripping from the ceiling as they strode down the main corridor. Flint quickly realized that the man in grey had been fooling him. There were multiple corridors heading in multiple directions.

"Ok, 93, this is your home," said Flint. "Lead the way."

93 scratched his head and looked up at Flint. "You're kiddin' right?"

"No. I'm not kidding. This is why I brought you along to help us navigate this maze."

"But Flint, I ain't never been here before. This is where the outsiders come through. We Ten'ers don't come here. We never come here. Well maybe some of us does, but not me, not ever!"

Flint rolled his eyes and looked around. Various corridors spanned out around him, some of which were straight while others curved out of sight. There was no one around. The halls were empty.

"Where's all the people?" asked Flint to no one in particular.

"Workin' probably," replied 93. "This is mining time right now. Everyone would be down in the mines."

"How do we get to the mines then?" asked Flint. 93 shrugged his shoulders not having a ready answer. "Well, my guess is every corridor leads to the mine eventually since that's where everyone is expected to work. Let' go this way and see what we can find." Flint pointed in the direction of the nearest corridor and the group followed along behind him.

The group, led by Flint, plodded down the long corridor. Every few hundred feet a doorway would appear and reveal a small room lined with bunk beds. The rooms were empty. No one even sleeping, just clothes and bedding strewn about in haphazard style. The party pressed on, walking deeper into the core of Ten.

After walking for some time, the corridor stopped, and the group entered a larger room. The walls were dirt and mud, with large timbers placed every ten feet to hold back the earth. The ceiling was a crisscross of wooden and steel beams. At the center of the room was a metal elevator shaft, exposed on all sides, but wrapped with strong steel mesh.

"Hey, the elevator!" said 93.

"You know where that leads?"

"Of course! It goes down into the mine."

"You know how to work it?"

"Oh sure." 93 jogged over to the control panel. He flung open the metal door and pushed a few of the grey buttons inside. The sound of electrical motors whirring to life filling the air as several cables began to spin rapidly up and down the elevator shaft. After several minutes, a metal elevator ascended before them and came to a stop. 93 lifted open the metal elevator gate and stood to one side to allow the others to board the elevator. Once inside, 93 pushed a few more buttons and the metal lift began its long descent into the mine shaft.

"How long is this gonna take?" asked Flint.

"I dunno, probably a while," said 93. "I ain't never been up this high on Ten."

"So the guys who have been throughout the entire Colony, haven't been to the top of Ten?" asked Flint, a bit skeptical at the idea.

"Well yeah, why bother? There's great food on Seven, delicious drinks on Five, comfortable blankets on One, and a great place to hide and relax on Six. The top part of Ten ain't gonna be anything better than that."

Flint shrugged. It made sense. If you want to escape Ten, no need to check out through reception.

The elevator shook and scrapped against metal as it descended into the mine. After several long minutes the lift slowed and then stopped. 93 flung the metal gate open and the group exited the elevator.

Flint could hear the sound of drills and other mining equipment coming from down the shaft where they stood. The shaft was dimly lit by a string of light bulbs hastily attached to the ceiling of the tunnel. 93 looked around for a moment to get his bearings and then waved for the group to follow him.

"You know where the equals will be?" asked Flint.

"They're spread out for sure. Some miners are given equals to train ... and abuse."

"Any idea where we can start to look? We really need to find Seabreeze first, that's the woman Tephra mentioned."

"I don't know no Seabreeze." 93 frowned and shook his head. "But I know where the miners are and I know they have some equals with each team of miners, so we can start there."

The group followed 93 as he trotted through various tunnels and down a few smaller shafts. Now that he was in his element, he began to move faster as he expertly navigated the depths of the mine shafts.

Flint was relieved when they came upon a large cavern filled with miners. He was about to approach them, but 93 stuck out his hand to stop him. Confused, Flint looked out and heard a big woman say, "What the heck have you got there, 51?"

A tall, slender woman stood up and handed a gem to her. "Looks like we hit another gem pocket" said 51. "Not uranium ore."

"Geez, worthless. Put the darn things in the cart and send them off to One. Those idiots can string them around their heads for all I care."

Flint spun around to ask 93 what they were waiting for, but he wasn't there. He had crept up into the cavern and moved behind the woman barking orders. He put a hand on the big woman's shoulder. "Freeze right there!" said 93.

The woman spun around in surprise, but quickly turned to relieved excitement as she saw 93 standing in front of her. She reached out, grabbed 93 around the middle and lifted him off the ground with a huge bear hug.

"What the heck are you doing here? I thought for sure those guards would have arrested you by now." She put 93 down and looked at him with grave concern. "93, those guards came down here asking about you. No, it was the head one, the Commodore. I'm worried for you"

93 gave a laugh. "You don't have to worry about me, I can escape

from any guard. But we have a bigger problem now. There's a war 'bout to start up on Seven!"

"War! What the heck are you talking about, you must be mistaken. There's no war in the Colony."

"I know, but now there's war."

Flint stepped up next to 93 in an attempt to help explain. "There's trouble up top. The Supreme Principal has killed the Masters Twelve, he plans to use the uranium ore to create nuclear weapons. There're many people on Seven who want to stop him, but he has amassed his guards as an army to fight us."

"No wonder the quota doubled!"

"The uranium quota doubled?" asked Flint.

"Yes, over the past week we have been slaving away round the clock, to pull as much uranium outta this place as possible. We stopped mining all other mineral deposits. Some of them minerals we stopped mining are needed for this Colony too."

"My friend Tephra," said Flint, "and me too, along with 93, we formed a band of folks called the defenders."

"Tephra? That softie you escaped with?" 75 glanced at 93 ; giving him a wink and a slug on the arm.

"Yeah, well she ain't no softie after all," exclaimed 93. "She's an actual leader. She took Cosmotine on—right to his face. I saw it myself. And then she was captured by him and we helped her escape." He nodded his head to confirm his statement in earnest.

75 scrunched her brow and rubbed her chin as if weighing whether to believe the statements she just heard.

"We want to stop Cosmotine," added Flint, "but we need help to fight his guard army. We need your help and the help of everyone sent down here from One, Ma'am."

"Ma'am. I ain't no Ma'am." 75 swung her head towards Flint and placed both hands on her hips. "Where is the Supreme Principal? I'll punch him in the mouth myself, that sea snake, I'd like to ... " 75 growled. Flint stepped back. Man, she had a tough growl.

"Leave that to us," said Flint. "Right now, we need help, as much of it as we can find."

75 looked over to her large crew and yelled, "Shut it down! Shut it down!" Everyone stopped their drills and turned off their equipment. They gathered around 75. Once they had assembled around her, she let Flint talk.

"Is there anyone here that was an equal?" asked Flint. The people looked at each other tentatively.

Flint furrowed his brow. "Listen, I am not here to harm you. Cosmotine has killed the Masters Twelve and plans to take over the world using nuclear weapons. The uranium you are mining now is for that purpose."

Half of the assembled crowd gasped at what Flint had said, the other half merely looked back with blank stares.

A tall, slender woman standing near the back of the crowd pushed her way forward and came to stand opposite Flint.

"I am Seabreeze, I was part of a small band who opposed Cosmotine's changes. I always knew we were in trouble, and I suspected the Masters Twelve had been captured, imprisoned, or worse. Are you sure they're dead?"

"Yes, our leader, Tephra, has seen it with her own eyes. She has also heard Cosmotine describe his plan to her. We heard from Ember ourselves when she helped us rescue Tephra from One."

"Ember?! She's Cosmotine's lackey, she would never betray him. It must be a trap!"

"Well she helped us rescue Tephra, trap or not," replied Flint dryly. Flint had little time to discuss the possible scenarios with Seabreeze. He needed recruits, and he needed them now.

"Look a guard army has been amassed on Seven. Our band of defenders need help. We have a few hundred people, but the guards have a couple thousand, and probably more in reserve. We need as many able-bodied people as possible."

Seabreeze nodded in agreement. "I can round up the equals. We have quite a few here now. I have located most of them and I know where they work."

75 spoke up, "And me and 93 here can round up the miners. They don't know why this is important, but they'll follow us if we tell 'em to. We can probably gather a couple thousand."

"We have to work fast," said Flint. "The battle could start any minute; we need people up top now! Let's split up and get moving. I'll go with Seabreeze to help her; 93 you go with 75 and gather your friends. We can meet at the main elevator on Ten, where we came in."

With that the teams split. The equals in the crew followed Flint and Seabreeze, while the miners made off with 75 and 93. There was no time to waste. Battle was brewing. Flint knew his defenders didn't stand a chance without reinforcements.

FIFTY-FIVE

THE GAME OF WAR

11 trotted through the winding irrigation tunnel, leadings his defenders into a main chamber where the tunnels met. Each of the eight tunnels emptied out three feet above the chamber floor, and it was was much larger than the tunnels from which they emerged. The chamber had a hatch at the very top, but it was sealed shut. The middle of the chamber floor held a large grate, ten feet in diameter with a vertical shaft plunged down into the depths. The entire chamber was dark and damp. Trickles of water flowed in from each of the tunnels and ran across the chamber floor to the grate in the center of the room. 11 had a light mounted to his head, and another flashlight in his hand. Misty also held a flashlight, as did several dozen of the defenders.

11 climbed halfway up a ladder mounted to the side of the chamber and motioned for the guards funneling out of the tunnel to gather around him.

"Over here," said 11, "everyone gather here."

11 jumped down and Misty stood next to him. "Where to now, 11?"

"Well," said 11, "I ain't no fighter as you know. I'm more of a hider." 11 rubbed his head. "93 and me used to play this game using these same tunnels. We'd show ourselves to some guards just long enough for them to run after us, then we'd hide. Once they lost us, we'd find them again, they'd chase us, but they could never find us. We never did get caught. We figured even if we did, the worse they'd do is send us back down to Ten, which was home to us." 11 smiled at the memory of the past prank. "Wish this was a game now. Not a real life and death situation."

"Maybe it is a game," replied Misty. "Or at least like a game."

11 furrowed his brow. "Whadda ya mean?"

"We can't fight the guards head on, but if we harass them, keep them off balance, maybe we can survive until reinforcements arrive."

11 smiled. "Well now we're talkin'!" 11 clapped his hands and rubbed them together. "Heck, I know all 'bout that. If I knew this whole captain thing was just a game, I would've asked to be one long before now."

Misty smiled at 11's enthusiasm; excited that she had finally found the right way to motivate him.

"Ok, listen up my fellow de-fen-ders!" yelled 11. "Here is how the game is played." 11 divided the remaining defenders up into groups of five. He used the grime and mud clinging to the side of the tunnels to draw a map of the adjoining tunnels. He gave each team of five specific instructions on how to get to a their designated access point. Once there, they would emerge from the tunnel, fire quickly, and then escape back down the access hatch. All teams were to meet back in the main chamber after they were done.

"Now, I will be running the tunnels to be sure no one gets lost and everyone is going in the right direction. The goal is to harass and escape quickly. Don't get shot, don't get caught, and don't ever show up in the same place twice. Be sure you close the access hatches completely. They are hard to spot once they are closed, and nearly impossible to open from the outside without the right tools."

After answering a few questions 11 ordered the five-person teams to move into position. 11 took the lead for one set of teams, Misty had lead for another set. "Y'all count to ten and then go, don't wait for anyone else, we will all go when we go. Don't stop until you complete your assigned mission and meet back here."

The teams began climbing into different tunnels leading off of the main chamber. They used three tunnels, avoiding the one they had recently used to escaped into. The tunnels they chose allowed them to span out to take up positions on the flank and rear of the guard army that had previously attacked them. Since that attack, the guards had camped outside the previously used access tunnels expecting the rebels to traverse the same path.

Misty trotted down a tunnel, a dozen teams followed behind her. She reached her intended hatch and stopped. She pointed upward with her flashlight and five defenders formed around her in a tight circle. She reached up to loosen the hatch. "Ready? On the count of three. One, two, THREE!"

The team leapt up through the hatch. Misty pointed to her left. They were facing the flank of the guard army. The defenders around her pointed their rifles and shot in quick succession. The guards jumped and scattered, clearly disoriented by the surprise attack. Before any guard could get off a shot, the team jumped back down the hatch. Misty reached up and sealed it tight.

"Good work, team. Head back to the main chamber, I'll take the next team forward." Misty pointed to the remaining teams standing behind her. She turned and scurried up the tunnel making sure to pass several hatches so as not to reveal themselves too closely to the first point of attack.

The next team repeated the same sequence of events. They appeared, shot, and disappeared just as fast. Misty led the teams further down the tunnel. Several times when she emerged from a hatch, Misty could see another set of defenders firing on the rear of the guard army. The pace quickened as teams of defenders started revealing themselves all around the guards nearly simultaneously.

The guard army began rushing around in confusion. Even when

they managed to reach what they thought was the point of attack, there was no one to be seen.

Misty smiled as the defenders popped up and came back down. The plan seemed to be working. She turned into another tunnel and felt someone barrel into her.

"Dang it, now, you have to watch ... " said Misty as she pulled herself up and looked down at 11 laying on the ground. "Oh, 11, I didn't know it was you." Misty held her hand down to help 11 up to his feet. 11 jumped up without assistance.

"No time, I've got two missing teams to find. The teams started to get confused. It's hard to see down here," said 11 as he pushed past Misty. "Make sure you lead all the people back to the chamber," he yelled as he ran off.

Misty nodded in agreement even though 11 couldn't see her. She peered around and was soon joined by a five-person team running up the tunnel.

"Other way, people," said Misty. "We need to get to the main chamber quickly." Misty pointed with her flashlight and the defenders turned and ran in the prescribed direction. Misty jogged off after them.

Her five-person teams continued to pop up and then run back down. A few times she had to redirect them when they tried to go up a hatch where another team had already been.

She turned her head when she heard 11 running back to her yelling, "Dang, dang, dang."

"Two teams went up the same hatch," said 11.

"That's bound to happen, 11, this is war."

"No, no, it's worse," said 11, "the access hatch stayed open, the guards are coming down."

"Oh no!"

"Get your troops out of the tunnel. I got to go back and direct the rest of 'em back to the chamber."

Tephra saw the guards drop their rifles and pick up shovels from a supply cart. They began to dig a long trench along the edge of the warehouse grounds. This was a lucky break. The guards had kept their rifles trained on the warehouse for hours. The defenders inside the warehouse had been hard at work. Now was their chance.

"Now," Tephra shouted. The wide roll-up doors on either end of the warehouse were ripped open and six tractors emerged, three tractors from each end. Each tractor had been modified with metal sheets welded into place around the driver. The driver would normally be visible, but the metal pieces rose up four feet on all sides to shield the seated driver behind.

Behind each tractor was a long hay trailer. Each trailer had a row of metal boxes lined up neatly down the middle. Each box had a series of small square holes cut out from which the rifles could fire.

The tractors made a sweeping turn as they exited the warehouse on either side. They fanned out, spacing themselves fifteen feet apart. Every tractor headed directly for the guards at full speed. The tractors' electric motors strained under the weight as they tore across the warehouse grounds and sped towards the field.

The guards scrambled out of their shallow trenches and raced to grab the nearest rifle. Before any of them could get a shot off, the tractors were on top of them. They drove straight and fast, splitting the guard's ranks as the black-suited guards dove out of the way.

Defenders hiding in the metal boxes on each trailer began throwing shards of metal, and scrap pieces of farm tools at the guards. Other defenders opened fire with their rifles. The metal boxes were only four feet high, but completely covered the defenders crouching down inside. Bullets and shrapnel were hurled at the surprised guards as the tractors passed by. Once they were on the other side of the guards' line, the tractors turned. The group to the North turned and headed toward the group to the South. As the tractors raced towards each other, the bullets and farm parts continued to fly from the trailers being pulled behind. The defenders had hit their marks. Guards lay wounded and dying along the tractors' paths.

Tephra held the steering wheel of her tractor with a firm grip. She hadn't let up on the accelerator since they started their mad dash out of the warehouse. So far, her plan was working. The first phase, to drive through the guard army, worked like a charm. The next phase could be a bit more difficult. The tractors were to meet on the other side and drive down the rear of the guard army causing as much damage as possible.

She peeked above her metal shield to take stock of the enemy. She could see a guard sergeant shouting orders to his troops. The guards around him formed into a tight circle of thirty to forty troops. They pointed their rifles outward. Other guard troops followed suit, making circle after circle.

Tephra heard a loud bang. She glanced over her shoulder and caught sight of trailing smoke wafting from the motor compartment of the tractor behind her. The electric motor wailed in pain, giving off a high-pitched screech. The weight of the tractor plus the trailer must have been too much. The tractor began to slow. The driver turned the wheels hard right trying to get some distance between the tractor and the guards before his momentum ran out. Tephra prayed the men would make it out.

She had an idea. She mashed her brakes and her tractor shifted forward from the sudden stop. She yanked the wheel full left and stood on the accelerator. The tractor jumped forward as she turned around. She wanted to place her own tractor between the guards and the disabled tractor to give her defenders more time to abandon ship safely. Tephra knew they were sitting ducks in the stalled tractor and would soon be overrun by guards if they stayed put.

The defenders on the disabled tractor leapt out of their metal boxes and scurried over the side of the trailer. They sprinted across the burned-out wheat field heading for the rolling hills where the guards had started their attack earlier in the day.

Having seen an opening, the guards opened fire on the tractors. The bullets ricochet off the metal sheets, but they found their mark in the tractors' soft rubber tires. As each tractor's tires were hit with multiple rounds, they began to deflate, slowing their run across the field. The tractors hitched and bucked; each driver tried to keep them moving. Tephra turned her wheel left and then right in a futile attempt to keep her tractor on course. Nothing worked. The tires went flat and could no longer move over the soft dirt of the wheat field. Within a few minutes all of the tractors ground to a halt.

"Move out! Everyone off the trailer! Let's go!" Tephra stuck her head out of her metal shield and barked orders to the defenders on the trailer. She grabbed the rifle she had jammed behind her seat and started firing rounds at the guards to provide some cover for her retreating troops. The defenders leapt from their boxes and jumped onto the ground. They chased after the other defenders who had already sprinted off towards the rolling hills.

Tephra jumped out of her make-shift metal box and dashed off to catch up to her troops. The defenders from the other tractor were flying across the field too. As luck would have it, the tractors formed a barrier between the guards and the retreating defenders. Tephra found Wheaty in the flood of troops. "If we can make it back to the citrus orchard, we have a chance to hide and return fire!" As they ran, gun fire erupted from behind. The guards were reformed, reorganized, and advancing.

The defenders finally reached the first hill and sprinted up into the grove. Tephra stopped at the base of the hill. She looked back checking to make sure all her troops made it safely into the grove. As the men and women ran by, Wheaty stopped next to Tephra. He glanced at her and opened his mouth as if to say something, but instead his face went blank. He slowly looked down. He glanced back up to her and his eyes rolled up into his head. His knees buckled. He fell to the ground and then flopped face-first into the dirt. Blood began pouring out from under his shirt; the gunshot wound to his back clearly visible.

Tephra knelt down besides him. "Wheaty? Wheaty? Please no!" She placed her hand on his back wanting to help him, but she knew he was already gone. Likely dead before he hit the ground. Tephra waved to two passing defenders wanting them to grab Wheaty's arms and drag him up the hill to safety. They looked at Wheaty crumpled on the ground and instead took hold of Tephra's arms. One man on each side.

"He's dead, Admiral, we need to get you to safety," one of the men said. They guided her up the hill and into the grove. As they went, Tephra looked back over her shoulder. Wheaty's body lay motionless on the ground.

———

MISTY SAW the defenders pouring out in all directions as they reached the main chamber. The chamber began to fill up and people milled about, not sure what to do next. She worried they would be overrun by the guards if they were not prepared to resist the next wave of attacks.

"Listen up!" yelled Misty. "Stand at the far end over here and prepare your rifles. The guards are going to come through the same passage you did, so be prepared to open fire as soon as all our defenders are out of that tunnel."

Misty grabbed people by the arms and pushed them into position. They clumsily complied not sure what was happening. She grabbed one man's rifle that was strapped to his back and shoved it into his hands. "Hold this dang thing and get ready to fire it! But wait until our defenders come through first," Misty commanded.

A couple more defenders straggled out of the tunnel and then no one else emerged. "11? Darn it, 11. Come on."

All the men stared at the tunnel. No one appeared. The men looked at Misty. Misty swallowed. "Ready your guns; the guards are coming."

Hearing footsteps, Misty said, "Ready, aim." Some of the defenders lifted their rifles; the rest were too stunned, then 11 stepped through the tunnel. "I think I got all the men o—"

Gunshots erupted from deeper in the tunnel. Bullets flew

through the air, piercing the space around them, ricocheting off the metal walls of the tunnel. Instinctively, the entire group of defenders knelt down, as did Misty.

Misty was the first to stand. But when she did what she saw forced her back on her knees. 11 was laying prone on the floor. She ordered two defenders to grab 11 and bring him to the back of the chamber. Misty helped too. "The rest of you aim your weapons and fire the moment you see someone come through that tunnel."

Misty and the defenders carrying 11 scrambled into the back of the chamber. Misty could see multiple blood stains at 11's shoulder and lower back. She laid him down gently. Misty took off her jacket, balled it up, and used it as a pillow under 11's head. 11's eyes were open, and he was still breathing, albeit with shallow breaths. Misty placed her ear to 11's chest; she could hear him breathing—and his heart beating.

"No, no, no, no," whispered Misty. "Hang in there 11. You're gonna be fine, just stay with me," Misty cajoled as she squeezed 11's hand.

Gunshots went off. Misty raised her head. *They are here, the guards must be here.* Misty prayed her troops were up to the task. A defender came and reported to her, "They can't get through if we can keep the pressure on. The opening is too small."

Misty placed 11's hand gently on the ground and then stood and spun around. "Keep up the pressure then, we can't let them get through!" *We can't let this fight go to waste,* she thought to herself knowing she had no medical help for 11. *We have to survive just a little longer.*

OUT IN THE ROLLING HILLS, Tephra and her men hunkered down behind the hill. They readied their rifles and found spaces to perch behind trees. Tephra knew they couldn't hold out here forever. They could fall back, going deeper into the citrus grove, but that would probably only delay the inevitable. Eventually, the grove would end, and the defenders would be backed up against the central elevator complex, and fresh reinforcements besides.

"Use your heads, guys," ordered Tephra from her position crouched behind the hill. "Fire as soon as they appear over the top, but no one be a hero. Fall back quickly once they overwhelm our position here. Head for the next hill, use the trees as cover if you can."

Tephra glanced up to the top of the hill. They were coming. The guards would crest the small slope any minute. The fight wasn't over just yet, but the end was near.

FIFTY-SIX

AWAKENING

As the guards advanced across the burned-out field, they reached the bottom of the first hill behind where the defenders hid. The guards stopped. They didn't move. Tephra paused wondering why they were waiting. She stuck her head up over the hill to see what was happening. The line of guards, standing just a few yards below her, were looking up towards the sky. All of them.

Tephra sat back down, turned and looked up to the sky as well. She could see a huge cloud of dirt and dust rise from the opposite hill. The same dust cloud was rising from the main road, and from the field across the main road where the other half of the defenders had started their fight.

"What the heck is this?" asked Tephra,

Tephra tensed, getting ready for battle. She lifted her hand and pointed at the dust cloud. Her troops hunkered down below her turned around and stared at the approaching cloud. What now?

A few seconds later, a long line of people emerged from the hills opposite the defenders. The line stretched from the hills across the main road and continued across the adjoining empty field. There were tens of thousands of people. They were dressed in clothes of the colonists on Seven, of miners on Ten, of equals on One, and even of black guard uniforms on Five. There were others mixed in as well, making up all the other levels. They marched along, nearly shoulder to shoulder. Tephra slowly let out the breath she didn't even know she was holding. As they emerged from the hills and came closer to Tephra, she could see the people in the first four to five rows carried rifles and other assorted firearms. The people behind carried anything they could get ahold of: shovels, rakes, hoes, machetes, metal bars. Anything that could be used as a weapon.

This mass of people was three times as long as the guard's line and stretched back to a depth Tephra couldn't see. The people just kept coming, pouring out of the grove, up from the road, around the hills. There was no end in sight.

The Guard army fell back in retreat. They walked slowly backward, not bothering to fire a shot. The opposing force was so overwhelming, there was no reason to fire. No good could come of it.

More and more people advanced over the hills. Those in back were men and women mixed together. All of them had a defiant look on their faces. They clearly meant business.

Tephra smiled when she saw Flint run through the grove and up the short hill. She was fixed in her spot even as colonists poured around her in slow pursuit of the guard army retreating through the burned-out wheat field behind. She couldn't believe her eyes. All these people, from every corner of the Colony, coming together.

Flint ran up to Tephra "I found you!" He held out his hand and helped Tephra onto her feet. 93 came running up behind him.

Tephra leapt up and wrapped her arms around Flint. "You did it! You brought us help!" Flint returned the hug.

"Most of 'em brought themselves," said 93. "We just pointed them in the right direction."

Tephra let go of Flint and wrapped an arm around 93's shoulder. "You did great, Ten'er. You did great!"

"We have to go accept a surrender, I think Admiral," said Flint.

Tephra looked up and sure enough the guards were putting down their weapons. There were just too many colonists.

The defenders, with their ranks swelled to nearly the entire population of the Colony stopped halfway across the field and stood their ground. Over half of the guards laid down their rifles and walked over to the defenders' line. They asked to give up and join the defenders. They wanted nothing more to do with the guards or their ridiculous war.

Tephra and Flint marched past the defenders, traversed the open field, and came face-to-face with a sergeant. "You surrender?" asked Tephra.

The sergeant paused. His choice was made for him as the guards standing behind him all laid down their weapons.

"Take them to the warehouse," ordered Tephra. "They can be kept prisoner there for now." Tephra left a contingent behind to guard the warehouse while the remaining defenders began their trek across the fields to round up the rest of the guard army lingering in the open field where Misty and 11 started their fight.

As they marched across the barren field, Tephra looked around at the tens of thousands of people following behind them. "Where'd they all come from, Flint?" asked Tephra.

"They came to defend the Colony," said Flint without looking over at Tephra. "We gathered up the equals on Ten, and then the others on Ten wanted to help too. Once we arrived on Seven, people began pouring out wanting to join us. They came from everywhere, tens of thousands of them."

Tephra marveled at the thought as she looked out behind her. A sea of colonists following them across the open field. "That's not all," said Flint. "We were also joined at the central elevator complex by people who came down from Three and Four. And guard reinforcements from Five fell in too—most of them were former field hands anyway. They used the freight elevator to come from every level. We are not alone, Tephra. People still believe in the Colony."

As the defenders approached the remaining guard army huddled around the access hatches, the guards began to look up in amazement. The same sequence unfolded with over half the guard army units lowering their weapons and joining with the defenders. The remaining guards were taken prisoner.

But unlike in the hills where they found Tephra, there were no defenders in sight. No 11, no Misty, and no anyone else.

"They have guards pursuing the defenders below ground," said Flint after speaking to one of the defecting guards who joined their ranks.

"Shoot, that means they may have Misty and 11 cornered down there," replied Tephra with sudden concern in her voice. "We have to get down there and see if they're still alive!"

93 jumped up when he heard 11's name. "I'll go get 'em!" shouted 93. He pointed at a few of the defenders standing by and motioned for them to follow.

"93, wait up!" shouted Flint as he jumped in behind 93's group of defenders making their way down the tunnel. Tephra followed behind.

Tephra ran up and grabbed Flint's arm once she caught up to him in the tunnel. "No, you need to come with me," said Tephra. "Cosmotine!"

FIFTY-SEVEN

PURSUIT OF QUARRY

Flint jumped up the nearest ladder and climbed out of the tunnel with Tephra behind him. Flint grabbed two rifles in his large hands and flung one onto each shoulder using the shoulder straps. He motioned with his head for them to take an electric cart that was parked nearby. The pair jumped on board and took off for the nearest elevator. Tephra knew they had to act quickly, and she hoped their recently turned ally, Ember, would be on One to help.

As the two entered the elevator, they remained silent. Thoughts churned through Tephra's mind. Cosmotine had been cornered. His guards were done. But what if he didn't know? Would he surrender if he didn't know he was trapped? Would he do something terrible if he did know? He was still dangerous. Until he was captured and subdued, anything was possible when it came to Cosmotine.

The elevator stopped at One and the doors slid open. They stepped off the lift and stopped. Tephra looked one way and then the other. She didn't know which way to go.

"I'm not that familiar with One," said Tephra, "but let's go this way. We have to be fairly close."

The pair took off running down the hallway to the left. The

hallway curved with various doorways marking either side of the hall as they went by. The hallway came to an end and exited out into the main corridor. Tephra recognized the corridor as the same one that previously led her to the Hall of Equals.

Once in the main corridor, the two turned right and ran towards the Hall, where Ember said they would meet. As they approach the large double doors that marked the entrance to the Hall, a side door swung open and a man sprinted out, nearly knocking them over. Flint grabbed the man's shoulders to stop him.

"What the heck are you doing ... " exclaimed Tephra. "Topaz?! Where are you going?"

"I'm trying to find ... help. I'm so happy I found you." He looked nervous and fearful.

"Where's Ember?" asked Tephra.

"I don't know for sure when I last saw her, she was with Cosmotine."

"Working with him or against him?" asked Tephra.

"No, no, not with him. We were confronting him ... together. But we were ambushed by a new Commodore, Rotifer. I must get out of One. I will be captured and probably killed."

"What happened to Ember?" asked Tephra.

"I told you. I don't know what happened to her. When I left the conference chamber, she was standing next to Cosmotine. I'm not sure she made it out of there. She's probably still there."

"You ran?" asked Flint in an accusatory tone. "You didn't try to save her?"

"There was no time. It all happened so fast."

"Do you think she's with Cosmotine now?" asked Tephra. "Is she alive?

"She may be, but ... she was thrown into the water chamber, she was trapped."

"Oh no!" Tephra raised a hand to her chest.

"I don't know what happened after that," replied Topaz.

"You are going to take us to see Cosmotine." Flint tightened his grip on Topaz's shoulder.

"No, no, no, he's guarded; I can't, I won't."

"You can and you will," said Flint. He turned Topaz around and pushed him towards the door he had just used to enter the main corridor. "I have two rifles and plenty of bullets. I can use them on you or on Cosmotine, your choice."

"Fine, fine. I'll take you back to the conference chamber. I don't know if he's still there, but that's where I last saw him."

FIFTY-EIGHT

SPARK OF LIFE

"Get ready for the onslaught people," said Misty. Her heart was pounding. She stood in front of her troops and planted her feet. "This is it. Our final hoorah. Let's go out with a bang and take as many of those guards with us as we can." Misty raised her rifle, tucking the butt of the gun into the crook of her shoulder.

Gunfire erupted further down the tunnel. Misty put her hand up to signal the defenders to hold their fire. There was no sight of guards and no bullets flying into the chamber. What could it be? That's *odd*.

The gunfire stopped. Heavy footsteps could be heard approaching the chamber from the tunnel occupied by the guards. Whoever was coming made no attempt to hide their approach. It sounded like dozens of people marching through the tunnel. As the footsteps drew near, Misty raised her rifle and motioned with her head for the defenders around her to do the same.

"As soon as you see the first guard, start shooting and don't stop until you're out of bullets."

The footsteps grew louder, nearer. Misty froze and held her breath. Suddenly a head popped out of the tunnel. Misty's finger began to squeeze the trigger of her rifle as a small bead of sweat trickled down her forehead.

"Y'all still alive?" asked 93. He jumped out of the tunnel and landed in the chamber, just ten feet in front of Misty.

"93! You almost got your head shot off," yelled Misty as she lowered her rifle. "Where did the guards go? They were right up that tunnel."

"We got 'em all rounded up!" said 93 with a large smile.

"What the heck are you talking about?"

"Me and my defenders just cornered the guards in the tunnel. The rest of the guard army surrendered up top. They're done. The colonists, tons of them, came to our rescue. They helped us stop the guards."

Misty smiled looked around at her defenders and yelled "you hear that you morons, we won!" Misty grabbed 93 and gave him a big hug around the middle.

"Where's 11?" asked 93.

"Oh no, 11, I forgot, oh how could I forget." She grabbed 93's hand and guided him to the back of the chamber where 11 was laying on the floor. "We were expecting a fight. We didn't think we'd survive. He's back here. Hurry, he needs help."

Misty looked at two defenders. "You two, go get help, get medical help, hurry. Everyone, we need help for 11 now! Go, now!"

Misty and 93 quickened their pace. 11 lay with his head propped up. His shirt was stained with blood. His eyelids were closed.

"11! 11!" 93 put one hand to his stomach while reaching out to touch 11's arm with his other hand. "Can you hear me?"

Misty took a step away from 11, not wanting to intrude. But 93 motioned her to stay. She stood by 93's side, then leaned against the wall. Seeing 11 like this, well, it just took everything out of her.

11 slowly opened his eyes and gave a half smile. "Hey, 93, you dead too? Join me in heaven did ya?"

"No, 11 you're still alive." 93 placed his hands gently on 11's cheeks. He peered into his eyes. "We have more tunnels to explore, 11. You can't go yet."

Misty knelt beside 11. She placed her hand on his forehead. So many boys she had raised into men through her work in the fields. She stroked 11's hair. None had died—none had died like this. Her throat grew tight. 11 is tough as nails, tougher than anyone she had ever met, ever worked with. She glanced up at 93. His face was flush. He kept his eyes locked on 11.

"Ok, then." 11's voice was weak, and his breathing was shallow. "Did we lose?"

"No, 11, we won. We won!" 93's voice cracked as he spoke. A single tear dropped from his left eye and rolled down his cheek.

"Well dang. I didn't think that'd happen," said 11 between halting breaths as a smile worked its way across his lips. "We was losing here, 93, but we tried hard ... real hard."

"I know you did, 11. You did great." 93 patted 11's shoulder.

"I'm tired. I feel like sleep now," said 11.

"No 11 stay with me," said 93 in a much louder voice this time. "Stay with me!" 93 grabbed 11's hand and squeezed it gently. 11 laid his head back and closed his eyes. 93 leaned down, put his other arm under 11's neck and gave him a kiss on the forehead.

"I ain't kissing' you back," said 11 as he opened one eyelid and flashed a little smile.

93 smiled. "You dummy. You stay with me!"

Misty laughed. 11 looked up at her. "Hey, Misty, we did it." Misty flashed a warm smile and nodded. She couldn't talk, she couldn't utter a word. If she had, she would have burst into tears. She knew as much. So instead, she stayed silent.

93 put his other arm around 11's hips and slowly lifted him up. "Make way now," shouted 93, "we gotta get 11 outta here."

FIFTY-NINE

THE ULTIMATE PLAN

Topaz led Flint and Tephra around several sweeping hallways as he shuffled back to Cosmotine's make-shift command center in the primary conference chamber. As they approached, Topaz came to a stop several yards from the conference chamber door.

"He's in there," said Topaz pointing towards the door.

Flint looked over at Tephra and then back at Topaz. "So why are you stopping here?"

"You wanted me to take you to Cosmotine, I've done that."

"Really?" said Tephra. "You afraid of your old boss?"

"I don't know how many guards he has in there with him. If you two think you can take on a unit of guards, then be my guest."

Tephra grabbed the extra rifle strapped to Flint's back. "Coward!" she said as she marched forward in a huff. "Go ahead and hide here Topaz, we'll take care of this."

Flint jumped forward and walked just behind Tephra. Rifle at the ready.

As they approach the conference chamber door, it slid open. The pair walked inside the large room and saw no one inside. There were monitors and communications equipment spread out across the conference table. Data pads and other items were strewn about. Data pods littered the floor, looking as though the people in the room made a quick exit.

"Did Topaz trick us?" asked Flint. "Cosmotine's not here."

"No, this is his command center for sure, I've been in this room before and I know.... " Tephra stopped in her tracks looking at the water chamber where Ash had been killed. Tephra inched over to the chamber door. Her mouth fell open as she placed her palm against the cold glass.

Inside the small chamber a body floated. The figure was clothed in white. The body slowly turned, revealing Ember's face. Tephra gasped. "No," she whispered.

Ember's face was lifeless. Her lips were blue. Her eyes were wide open; they sat perfectly still. Her hair floated peacefully around her head.

"He killed her," Tephra whispered. "He KILLED her!" she yelled. Her teeth clenched. Anger rose up her back, she felt her body burn with hatred for Cosmotine and all that he had done. How could he be so cruel?

Tephra turned and looked up at Flint. He had been staring at the small chamber as well, but he said nothing. The sight froze him where he stood.

"We must stop him!" yelled Tephra.

Soft footsteps began to approach, they were coming from the doorway near the center of the conference chamber. Tephra and Flint looked towards the door and saw Cosmotine emerge from the narrow hallway.

"Cosmotine!" yelled Tephra from across the room. Tephra and Flint slowly moved away from the water chamber and towards Cosmotine.

"Such a waste," said Cosmotine. "She was my apprentice from such an early age, you know," he continued in mock sympathy. "But in the end she, like the Masters Twelve, could never understand our greater purpose. Such a shame really."

"You are a dead man!" yelled Tephra. "You have no guards to help you now. You're all alone."

Cosmotine's eyes widened for a moment, and he looked unsure. Then he slowly smiled. "Wrong. I have reinforcements after all," he said waving his hand behind them.

Tephra and Flint looked over their shoulders to see Topaz standing there with his handgun. Tephra rolled her eyes and looked forward again.

"Geez, this guy," sighed Tephra. "Never any help when you need it."

"Yes, I can agree with you," said Cosmotine. "Perhaps we're not so different after all."

As Cosmotine talked he walked over to the conference table. He placed his hand on a control panel and pushed several buttons. A red warning appeared on the various monitors mounted on the wall, well in sight of Tephra and Flint.

"You know what that warning is?" asked Cosmotine. "It's the beginning of the timing sequence to ignite explosive charges I had mounted to the wall on Seven. You see, I saw your rebels being defiant. And my guards would have stopped them too, but the other colonists suddenly woke up from their haze. No matter though, the wall will fall and then all will be crushed and drowned under the weight of the ocean. You can't win. No matter what you do you cannot beat me."

Tephra looked at Flint. Her heart sped up. She tightened her grip of her rifle. Should she shoot now and risk being shot by Topaz, or wait for Topaz to slink away like a coward?

Commodore Rotifer stepped into the conference chamber from the door behind Cosmotine, opposite from where Topaz stood with his gun.

"Sir, we have lost all troops on Seven, they have laid down their weapons, we must activate—" Rotifer stopped in his tracks and reached for his own service pistol. He unholster his gun and held it out in front of him. He pointed the barrel at Tephra and Flint.

"Commodore Rotifer, thank you for joining us," said Cosmotine. "You have failed in your duties to subdue the rebellion." Rotifer backed up, unsure. Cosmotine reached across the table, picked up a handgun sitting in its holster at the far edge, took the pistol out and pointed it at Tephra and Flint. "Commodore, despite your grand failure, I will win as I've already started the blast sequence. You can join me in my escape submarine. Go ahead, get it started up for me."

Rotifer let out the breath he had been holding, smiled, and nodded his head in recognition. He took a few cautious steps towards the doorway leading to the escape sub. He kept his service pistol trained on the defenders across the room. As he neared the doorway, he lowered his gun, turned his back on the room and began to walk through the doorway. As he did so, Cosmotine raised his handgun and fired three quick shots into Rotifer's back. Tephra jumped at the sound of the gunfire, not expecting it. Rotifer slumped to the floor. He was dead before he hit the ground.

"Another sacrifice in the war for the Colony," said Cosmotine with a smile. He turned his gun and fired several shots towards Tephra and Flint. They instinctively ducked down to the floor while Topaz flung himself to the ground in a prone position. Their defensive actions gave Cosmotine enough time to charge towards the doorway leading to his escape submarine, closing the door and locking it behind him.

"Are you ok?" asked Flint to Tephra.

She nodded. "Yes, I'm fine. Are you?"

"Yes."

"Me too, I'm fine," said Topaz. "If anyone cares."

"Shut up!" yelled Tephra as she ran over to the control panel on the conference table. The red warning screen had been replaced by a count-down that started at 60 seconds but had counted down to 35.

"How do we stop this thing?" yelled Tephra.

"I dunno," replied Flint

Both of them began pressing buttons on every control panel they could see. The countdown continued: "34, 33, 32, 31." The numbers rushing by nearly too quickly to count.

Topaz walked over to the control with a confident air about him. "Here, let me enter my credentials, I can shut it down in no time." Topaz punched several buttons in quick succession. The countdown stopped at 25. The two defenders breathed a sigh of relief.

Suddenly a box popped onto the screen that read "Access Denied." The countdown resumed, "24, 23, 22, 21."

"Brilliant, Topaz, such a hero," sneered Tephra.

Topaz panicked. "I don't understand, that should have worked!"

"Flint try the code Ember gave us."

Flint pulled the keyboard closer to himself and typed in the alpha-numeric code that had once been Ember's authorization credentials. The countdown stopped again at 17.

Suddenly the box popped up again that read "Access Denied." The countdown resumed, "16, 15, 14, 13."

"No, no no, this can't happen!" yelled Tephra. "Try harder, shoot the damn thing!"

Flint and Topaz both began shooting at the control panels. The countdown continued, "Ten, nine, eight, seven, six … ."

"Crap!" Yelled Tephra.

"Three, two, one … detonate." The computer screen kept flashing the word detonate. The trio looked at the monitor that showed a steady feed of the large square of explosives on the glass wall. Nothing happened. They held their breath. Nothing happened. They looked at each other. Nothing happened.

"Did we stop it?" asked Tephra. Both Flint and Topaz shrugged their shoulders in unison.

SIXTY
COPPER FIGURINES

93 placed 11 on a gurney that had been brought up from the medical unit. Several medics were working on him. They had stabilized him for transport to the hospital near the main elevator complex. The gurney was strapped down to the medical cart, and the medics hopped up front preparing to drive off.

Misty stood near the medics. She was about to ask what she could do to help when she saw 93 pull something shiny from 11's pocket. He had no sooner extracted the object, then the cart sped away heading to the medical unit.

93 held up the shiny object to inspect it. "What the heck is this?" asked 93.

Misty shrugged. She took the object from 93's hand and turned it around. "Looks to be wire. Copper wire." The wire was rolled up into a thick ball giving off a dull sheen.

"Oh yeah, he likes to collect copper wire. Makes little figurines out of it." 93 glanced at the wire in Misty's hand. "But where'd 11 get that much copper wire from, Misty?"

"I have no idea. That boy is a real pack rat."

Misty turned as she heard her name. Tephra was yelling something, looking all wild. As she got closer, she could make out one word she was saying, "Explosives."

"No time to explain. Are there any engineers around?" Tephra said all in one breath.

<hr>

THE ENGINEERS STEPPED AWAY from the large square taped to the glass wall. The lead engineer trotted over to Tephra, who was standing nearby. Flint stood by her side.

"It's been disabled already," said the engineer.

"Disabled?" asked Tephra.

"Who the heck disabled it?" asked Misty.

"Maybe it was never hooked up to begin with," suggested Tephra.

"No, it was definitely there at one time," said the engineer. "The main terminals still have some wire attached. But the rest is just gone. Cut out and removed it looks like."

"Hey, 93," called Misty. "You got that wire on you from 11's pocket?"

"Yeah, right here." 93 jogged over and held it up for the engineer to look at. The engineer took the wire from him and inspected it.

"Yeah, that's the stuff," said the engineer. "Looks like the right length too. And you see these cut marks? They match the cuts made to the wire that is still attached at the control box and on the first explosive charge. Did you take this off the charge box young man?"

"Me? Oh no, I'm not the wire guy," replied 93. "I like shiny rocks."

Misty rolled her eyes and then turned to the engineer. "It was 11, a different Ten'er, he had this in his pocket. Maybe he made off with it. Probably had no idea he was defusing a bomb."

"We can get the rest of these charges down within the hour," reported the engineer. "Our team will get it done immediately." He handed the bundled copper wire to Misty.

"Good," replied Tephra. "Please be careful. Let me know when the job is done." The engineer nodded in agreement and then turned back to his crew and began giving orders.

As Tephra, Misty, and Flint turned to leave the glass wall, a defender sprinted up to them. "Admiral, we have disarmed all of the guards and we are ready to transfer them to Ten."

Tephra responded, "No, I want Flint to lead them. They won't do us any good on Ten."

"You mean be the commodore?" asked Flint.

"Yes, or whatever you want to call yourself."

"Admiral?"

"If you must." Tephra rolled her eyes at the thought of such a lofty title.

"I don't want to lead them, Admiral. I will do whatever you ask me to do for now, but I want to go to land. You know, when you go back to land."

Tephra looked down quickly when Flint mentioned land. She moved the toe of her boot around in the dirt and thought of the best way to answer him.

"Flint, the thing is ... I'm not going back to land."

"You? Not going back to land? But I thought after all this ... after all you went through, you'd want to go back."

"I did want out of here at first. But I found a bigger purpose here in the Colony, Flint. I found a bigger part of me."

"I see." Flint sighed and kicked a rock. "So, you're not going back to land then?"

"No, Flint. I'm staying here. This is my home now."

Flint looked out into the distance.

"Admiral," said a defender as he pulled up in an electric cart. He jumped out and stood beside Tephra. "Doctor asked to see you."

"Must be about 11," said Tephra. "Misty, 93, its time, let's go!" Tephra turned and touched Flint on his forearm. "You can come too, it's probably about 11."

"Yeah," said Flint, "yeah, I'll come with ya."

Flint hoped into the driver's seat of the electric cart. The other three jumped in as well and Flint took off for the hospital unit. Once there, they scurried inside to 11's room.

11 was in bed, with numerous IV's running into both arms. His eyes were closed, and he was breathing slowly. A man in a white overcoat entered the room.

"We were able to remove the bullet fragments," said the doctor to the assembled group. "He was given a blood transfusion, lost a lot of blood after being shot, but he is stable now. Should be on the road to recovery."

"Is his breathing like that normal?" asked 93.

"Yes, why?" asked the doctor looking a bit perplexed by the question.

"He sounds quiet," replied 93. "11 always snores, so something is wrong."

The doctor smiled and grabbed 93's shoulder. "He's fine, I'm sure he'll be back to snoring soon, don't worry." The doctor turned and left the room.

11 slowly opened his eyes. "Where is this now?" he asked.

"You're in the hospital unit," replied Tephra. "You came through surgery; everything is looking pretty good."

11 tried to sit up, but instead he grabbed at the incision in his abdomen and laid back down. "Oooohhhh. It ain't feeling pretty good."

Misty held up the balled-up coil of copper wire. "This yours?" asked Misty.

"Hey, where'd you get that? That's my figure making wire. I was gonna make a nice figurine for Tephra."

"You can have it back," said Misty. "Go ahead and make that figure. We'd love to see it."

"Yeah, you saved the entire Colony because of that figure making wire, 11," interrupted 93. "You're a hero! You're just not smart enough to realize it."

Il smiled. "I do love to collect copper wire." He turned the wire in his hand as he looked it over. "Especially when it's coming out of a charge box into a series of explosives. Now that's real nice figure making wire, I think."

PROLOGUE

Misty stood in the middle of a group of twelve people. The newly elected Masters Twelve were announcing their selection of the new Supreme Principal. The Masters stood on a large stage in the Hall of Equals. Their faces were broadcast on screens throughout the Colony. From One to Ten, every colonist was able to watch the Masters at work.

After the war, the Colony regrouped. The colonists held a mass gathering on Seven where they chose a new group of Masters Twelve. They abolished the rule of the mask. Each Master would bear their own face to each other and the public. They would also make their regular offices on the level that they served, gathering in the Masters chamber only when required.

Misty was one of the newly appointed Masters Twelve for Seven. She demurred at the idea of being a Master, but finally gave in when she was cajoled by all of her former field hands. There could be no better choice for Seven, no better guardian.

Flint was offered the second post as Master for Seven. He declined. No amount of cajoling would change his mind.

"I am no Master," explained Flint. "I have no desire to make decisions for the colony. I am a field hand. It's where I belong."

Seabreeze was selected as the Master for One. The Masters Twelve convened after being appointed and selected their new Supreme Principal.

"I am so very proud to announce," said Misty, "our new Supreme Principal, Tephra!" A large applause erupted throughout the Hall of Equals. But it was no match to the applause that erupted on Seven. Tephra, defender of the Colony, had been appointed by unanimous vote.

Tephra was shocked since she had been a colonist for such a short period of time. After the ceremony she rushed up to Misty with a grave look on her face. The other Masters gathered around her.

"Master, surely you'd want someone who has lived the life of the Colony longer than I have to be your Supreme Principal," pleaded Tephra. "What do I know about running the Colony? What do I have to offer?"

"You have nothing, but your instincts, Tephra. And that's all you need. You were an outsider, but you're not that anymore. You saved the Colony and you taught us something in the process."

"What could I have possibly taught you?" asked Tephra.

"You taught us to stand up for what we believe in, Tephra. This Colony started with a grand idea, but we had lost our way. We became complacent. We were content with being told what to do, rather than helping to set our own course, and fighting for that goal."

Seabreeze took a step closer to Tephra, "People matter, Tephra. You have the instincts, the skills, and the judgment to be our leader. You will be a great Supreme Principal."

"Yeah, and besides," said 93, "you always got us smart folks to ask questions on what to do and what not to do, so there you go!" 93 was standing behind the Masters, leaning over Misty's shoulder as he talked.

Tephra smiled. She was happy to see that 93 was there. He had been offered the position of Master of Ten. He turned it down. So did

11. Instead, it was given to 75, who was beside herself in excitement about the recognition.

93, however, was appointed as a special advisor to the Masters Twelve. He and 11 were supposed to keep their eye on things and report if anything was amiss. To 11 and 93 it just sounded like a good excuse to run around the Colony. Or in other words, business as usual.

"So tell us, Tephra," said Seabreeze, "what's your vision for our future?"

Tephra glanced down as she rubbed her chin. She looked up and smiled. "I want the Colony to return to its roots. Peace, order, science. The things that made the Colony great to begin with and allowed this place to survive and thrive for a century."

"Sounds good, but what does it actually mean?" asked Misty.

"It means being true to ourselves, Misty. And being fair. And transparent. No more secrets. We need to operate in a way where everyone knows what is happening. Maybe even let the colonists grade us on how well we do. We're all in this thing together after all."

"Well said." Seabreeze crossed her arms and titled her head. "But can it really be done?"

"There's always hope," replied Tephra. "There's always hope."

Supreme Principal Tephra shut down the nuclear weapons program; learning that none of the missiles had yet to be armed. The uranium enrichment program was halted, except for the stock piles needed to fuel the Colony's nuclear energy generators. She also gave Ember a proper burial at sea. The Colony built a statue in honor of Ember, Ash, and all those who lost their lives in the Colonial civil war.

Ten was restored to its former purpose of providing minerals to the Colony. Ten'ers were given freedom to come and go from Ten when not working to enjoy the rest of the Colony.

Topaz was sent to Ten for "rehabilitation." He was the one person occupying Ten who was not allowed to leave. He spent his days mining and cleaning the barracks. 75 worked him hard but let him rest at least one day a week if he behaved himself. She still didn't forgive him for the interrogation she underwent when he was "Mr. Fancy Pants," as she puts it. But she thinks he may come around after he cleans the latrine a few hundred more times.

Cosmotine had escaped, his whereabouts were unknown. Tephra thought long and hard about whether to pursue him and bring him back to the Colony to answer for his crimes. It seemed pointless now. How would they find him? How would they capture him? Was it worth the emotional toll on the Colony, or was it better to let the colonists heal?

"Flint, you want to see stars, right?" asked Tephra. She had been Supreme Principal for a little over a year.

"Yes, I still do," replied Flint. "That was the whole reason I became a guard in the first place." Flint grabbed a bottle of liquid from his fridge and placed it on the small table. Tephra had come to his apartment to speak with him. She travelled throughout the Colony on a regular basis to meet with colonists and check on them. She travelled from One to Ten and back again, always on the move. Different groups from around the Colony were invited to dine in the Hall of Equals each week.

This day, Tephra was returning from meeting a group of field hands in another sector on Seven and she had an idea to stop by Flint's apartment and see if he was home. Flint placed two small tumblers on the table in front of them and poured some of the liquid into each glass. They raised their glasses and said "Cheers.'

"I have been thinking about an assignment that I need your help with," explained Tephra.

"Oh, really?" asked Flint. "What have you got in mind?"

"Justice."

Flint smiled slightly. "Cosmotine?" Flint knew immediately what Tephra was thinking.

"Yes, in part. But there's more. Something far more important than Cosmotine."

"What's more important that catching Cosmotine?"

"We need new recruits, Flint. The Masters Twelve have come up with some big plans for our Colony. We want to share the news about the Colony on land and let those who wish to join come here. To do that, we need a representative. Someone who knows the Colony better than anyone. Someone who can explain the virtues and the purpose of our grand experiment." Tephra smiled as she finished talking, hoping that Flint would get the hint that she wanted to send him to land.

Flint grew more interested as Tephra spoke. He slowly leaned forward, earnestly listening to her words. When she was finished, he sat back, took a swig from his glass, and stood up straight.

"I'm your man!" said Flint. "You want me to go to land, don't you? I get to see stars!" Flint was smiling from ear to ear, hardly able to contain his excitement.

"That's what I'm saying Flint. I want you to be our representative on land. And as a side benefit, you'll see all the stars you could ever imagine."

Flint pumped his fist in the air. "Oh yeah!"

"But before you go, Flint, you need some training. Land isn't like being here in the Colony. There's things you need to know, and learn, to be able to successfully interact with the surface dwellers."

"Alright, I'll learn whatever I have to. You lead the way. I don't think it'll be that hard though. I mean I'll just walk right up to the first person I see and say 'hey, surface dweller, you want paradise or what?'"

"First lesson," said Tephra as she stifled a laugh. "Surface dwellers don't call themselves surface dwellers."

"Oh," said Flint, "well I guess I have a couple things to learn then." Flint sat back down and finished his drink.

"We'll get you fixed up," said Tephra as she patted Flint on the arm. "You'll see."

ACKNOWLEDGMENTS

I'd like to thank my spouse for giving me the inspiration (along with a hearty shove) to write this book and keep with it during the tough parts. And much thanks goes to my editor, Katie Chambers at Beacon Point. Her insight and guidance was truly invaluable. Also, Dr. Jessica Moyer for her keen editor's eye.

Also, a big thanks to those who read the manuscript when it was in its roughest state. This list includes my sister, Dr. Lesley Davidson-Boyd, Pete Rogers, and my child-hood friend, Scott Stradling. You each gave me invaluable insight into the story I was trying to tell.

ABOUT THE AUTHOR

K. C. Weston is an emerging author of dystopian/sci-fi novels. This is K. C.'s first book in the genre. Originally from Colorado, K. C. lived on a horse ranch as a child and moved to the far more temperate climate of San Diego, California, as an adult. K. C. is an avid sailor, which sounds cliche for an author, but is actually true in this particular case. No really, K. C. is certified by the American Sailing Association. Well, now that just sounds like bragging, doesn't it? Never mind, let's just say K. C. likes whatever you like and has been doing the exact same thing for years. What a wonderful coincidence that you both have so much in common. Except comedy, of course. K. C. hates anything remotely funny or silly.